The Distance

by Alexa Land

Book Eleven in the

Firsts and Forever Series

Books by Alexa Land Include:

Feral (prequel to Tinder)

The Tinder Chronicles (Tinder, Hunted and Destined)

And the Firsts and Forever Series:

Way Off Plan

All In

In Pieces

Gathering Storm

Salvation

Skye Blue

Against the Wall

Belonging

Coming Home

All I Believe

Hitman's Holiday (short story)

The Distance

Dedicated to

Stacey

With So Much Love

Thank You to
My Beta Readers
I appreciate you so much!

Thanks also to
My Firsts & Forever Group on Facebook
for the enthusiasm and encouragement

And Special Thanks to
Anita F.
and Jessica T.
for naming the love of Jessie's life!

Contents

Chapter One

I checked myself out from every angle in the frothy wedding gown, and decided white was definitely not my color.

"You look adorable, Jessie," Nana told me. My employer's real name was Stana Dombruso, but most people used her nickname, because she felt like a grandmother to us all. At the moment, the petite eighty-year-old was also wearing a great, big, fluffy wedding dress and preening in the mirrors that surrounded us.

"I look like Barbie's flat-chested sister Skipper," I told her, sliding my red baseball cap back on my head. "Also, this dress is failing the comfort test big-time. It's super itchy, weighs a ton, and I keep feeling like my nipples are about to fall out." I grabbed the top of the strapless, heavily beaded bodice with both hands and hoisted it toward my chin.

"So, that dress is out," Nana said. "This one is, too. I look like a float in the Rose Parade." She wasn't wrong. Her white-on-white dress was festooned with three-dimensional fabric flowers and definitely parade-worthy.

From behind us, a booming voice with a thick Spanish accent exclaimed, "You are a vision, Nana!" Mr. Mario, her friend and hairdresser, came into the room and fluffed his big, ruffled skirt. He then started carefully smoothing his collar-length salt-and-pepper hair in the three-sixty mirrors. The wedding dress he wore was more cream than white, and looked pretty good with his faux tan.

"I've decided I hate this dress," Nana said, tugging on the puff sleeves and making them stand out like a linebacker's shoulders. "I like Jessie's better, but he has a list of grievances."

"I don't understand mine." I scooped up an armload of the skirt's many layers, which revealed my turquoise sneakers. "When I was a kid, I had a little net for when I needed to clean my fish tank, and it was made out of this same, exact stuff. Why would anyone want to get married in a huge goldfish net?"

"That shit's called tulle, and it's supposed to be all elegant-like," Nana told me. "But now that you said that, all I see is a big fish net. I still like the beading, though."

I hoisted my skirt higher and scratched my thighs with my short fingernails. That tulle stuff was miserable. "I need someone to explain to me why any woman would want to be completely uncomfortable on what's supposed to be one of the happiest days of her life," I said.

"It's a small price to pay for looking this good," Mr. Mario said, admiring his reflection in the cream silk number. He occasionally moonlighted as a drag queen, so he was probably used to the horrors of women's formalwear.

A rustle of fabric announced the arrival of five of Nana's little girlfriends, who stuffed themselves into the mirrored room with us. They were all over seventy-five, under five-foot-two, and each wore an enormous wedding dress. "I like this one, Stana," her friend Miriam said, spinning as much as she could in her lacy frock. The little room was wall-to-wall brides at that point.

"Nah, forget all that lace, it's too fussy," Gladys said, waving her hand dismissively. "What you want is simple and elegant, like this." She flung her arms out to the sides, and in the process knocked Miriam's wig off.

"Damn it, Gladys, watch your paws," Miriam huffed. When she bent over to retrieve her wig, she bumped into Mr. Mario, who went over like a felled tree and took Nana and most of her friends with him. When his hairy legs flew into the air, the skirt dropped back to reveal tiger-striped socks, five-inch gold heels, and skimpy, leopard-print briefs. I managed to remain upright until a little old lady named Sylvia grabbed my skirt to try to hoist herself up, and then I fell right on top of her.

"You okay, Syl?" I asked, trying to locate the floor in that sea of fluffy dresses so I could push myself up.

Someone's hand found my ass in the cloud of tulle and gave it a squeeze as Sylvia exclaimed, "Oh, I'm fine! This is more action than I've seen in a decade!"

She gave me a gummy smile, and I called, "Everyone, watch where you step! Sylvia's teeth flew out again."

Just then, the mirrored door swung open, and Sylvia and I and two more ladies spilled out into the hallway. I looked up at Nana's grandson Dante, who wore an impeccable black suit and an amused expression. He raised an eyebrow at me and said, "Really?"

"Just help me up," I told him. He pulled me to my feet, and then he and I began picking up little old ladies and lining them up in the hallway.

When everyone was upright, Nana said, "I need a side-by-side comparison. Let's go out into the showroom so I can see all these dresses in a row."

The shop's two employees were being remarkably accommodating and grinned when our procession filtered into the main part of the bridal boutique. They were even modeling wedding dresses for Nana, because she wanted to see them on people and not on a hanger. I carried my skirt bunched up in my arms to keep from tripping over it, and lined up between Mr. Mario and Gladys as Nana put on her big, round glasses and assessed us carefully.

Finally she declared, pointing around the room, "I like the beading on Jessie's dress, the sleeves on Miriam's, the skirt on Muriel's, the bodice on Mr. Mario's, and not a damn thing on the dress I'm wearing." She turned to one of the salespeople and asked, "You got anything like that?"

The younger of the two shop workers, a slim blonde with lots of makeup and flat-ironed hair, tapped her chin with a manicured fingertip as she thought about that for a moment, then said, "Possibly. Let me go look in the back."

"I love my dress," Muriel said. "I feel like Cinderella." She was wearing a pink gown with a skirt big enough to smuggle the carriage into the ball.

"But you look like the evil stepmother," Gladys shot back.

"I'm telling you, Nana," Mr. Mario said, still completely working that cream-colored number, "have something custom-made, just for you. That way you can get exactly what your heart desires."

"But what if I don't like the dress when it's finished? I think it's better to see something ready-made and know exactly what I'm getting."

"But you are not a ready-made kind of woman, Nana," he told her. "You're a one-of-a-kind creation all the way!"

She said, "You know, the first time I got married, I was barely out of my teens. I wore a frumpy, off-white dress with long sleeves and a high collar, which had been handed down in my family. It looked like a nun's habit. I figure anything's gonna be a step up from that, and there are so many pretty dresses here to choose from. Oh, like that!"

Her brown eyes lit up at the giant monstrosity the salesperson brought from the back. The thing was completely over the top. It had little puff sleeves, so much beading on the bodice that I was surprised the salesperson could lift it, and a full skirt with probably twenty rows of ruffles. The top third of the dress was white, but the ruffles morphed from pink to red in an ombre effect, with the darkest color at the bottom. It was enough to make even a Disney princess reconsider her lifestyle choices.

"The only sample we have of this particular gown is both tall and plus-size, though it could of course be ordered in petite if you like it," the blonde woman told her, holding up the sparkly garment by its hanger and draping the enormous skirt over her arm to fan it out. I knew Nana wouldn't want to wait, but she was barely five feet tall and probably eighty pounds soaking wet. If she tried to put that dress on, we'd have to send in a Saint Bernard with a barrel of brandy to find her.

"I can model it for you, Nana," Mr. Mario offered. "I'm the tallest one here." He was maybe five-ten, and that (plus the heels) made him a lighthouse in the sea of little old ladies.

"I want to compare it to the bodice of the dress you're wearing, though," she told him, "so I don't want you to change. Besides, it's not quite accurate that you're the tallest one here." She turned to her grandson Dante, who had to be six-four, and beamed at him.

He'd been leaning against the wall with his arms crossed over his chest, and stood up quickly as he exclaimed, "Oh no. Not going to happen. We weren't even supposed to stop here, we were on our way to the wine shop! I'm only along to offer opinions on champagne for the reception, not to model wedding dresses!"

"Oh come on, be a sport! You're the only person it'll fit," Nana cajoled. "That'll be the last dress I look at today, I swear. After that we'll go straight to the wine shop, no more dilly dallying. But until I see it on a person, how do I know if it's my dream dress?"

He said, "It's not. You and your posse already tried on fifty dresses, and you didn't like any of them."

"But what if it is? What if this is the one and I miss out on it just because you're stubborn?"

"Have Jessie try it on," Dante said, gesturing at me. "For some reason, he's perfectly willing to go along with this craziness. Why, I'll never know."

"This is fun," I told him. "Besides today, when would I ever get to try on a wedding dress? You have to open yourself up to new experiences in life."

"This is one life experience I'll gladly do without," he said.

"You know your grandmother, Dante. Do you think there's any way on earth she's going to leave here without seeing that dress on someone? If you play along, we can be out of here in fifteen minutes. Otherwise, I anticipate two or three more hours as we try on every frock in the place."

He sighed dramatically, then turned to Nana. "I'll only do this under two conditions: no one takes pictures, and no matter if you love the dress or hate it, it's the last one today. After I model it for you, everyone gets dressed, we get back in the limo, and we proceed to the wine shop. Agreed?"

"Scout's honor," Nana said, flashing him the hang-loose symbol by making a fist and extending her pinky and thumb. "Now hurry up and change. I'm growing old over here!"

Dante's shoulders slumped in defeat, and the blonde salesperson told him cheerfully, "I left a tulle petticoat in the first dressing room on the right. Be sure to put that on underneath, so Nana can get the full effect."

He muttered under his breath, snatched the dress, and stomped off to the dressing room. As soon as he was out of earshot, Nana chuckled delightedly and fished her phone out of her bra as she said, "He didn't say anything about video." She told the salespeople, "There's a hundred bucks in it for both of you if you sneak in the back and hide his suit when he comes out here. I love my grandson, but the boy needs to lighten up. He's been so damn serious lately!"

The older of the two salespeople, an elegant-looking woman with short, silver hair, grinned and said, "I'm on it." She picked up the skirt of the silk wedding dress she was modeling and slipped through a doorway to my right.

Nana poked at her phone a bit, then handed it to me and said, "Here, Jessie, you know what to do." I quickly dialed Dante's husband Charlie and his brother Vincent, put them on a video conference call, and hit record.

Dante emerged a couple minutes later, scowling as he crossed his muscular arms over his chest. Funnily enough, the fluffy gown fit him pretty well, though he was so tall that it barely skimmed his ankles instead of reaching the floor. Nana doubled over in a fit of laughter, the Rose Parade gown billowing up around her, and Dante knit his brows and asked me, "What happened to no photos?"

"I'm not taking pictures, I'm on a video chat with Charlie and Vinnie. Give 'em a wave," I said, twirling my free hand like a beauty pageant contestant.

"Go ahead, Dante, spin for us," Nana managed. He sighed dramatically and did as she asked.

When we got a look at the back of the dress, I started laughing, too. A huge, pink bow adorned his backside, and as I panned the camera down, I said, "Look Charlie, your husband's ass is gift-wrapped all nice and pretty for you." On screen, Vincent was laughing so hard that he had to take off his glasses to wipe the tears from his eyes, and Charlie was beaming delightedly.

Dante fought back a smile and tried to glare at me. "I don't know when or how, but there will be payback for that video call."

"I didn't have time to get Gianni and Mikey on the line," I told him. "You popped into that gown faster than a squirrel going after a bag of circus peanuts! But the good news is, I'm recording this, so I can email it to the rest of your brothers."

"Oh shit," Nana exclaimed. "I suddenly realized what you remind me of with that white top and the red bottom. You look like a giant tampon, Dante!" On screen, Vincent howled with laughter and disappeared from sight as he fell to the floor.

Dante rolled his eyes and tried to make a dignified retreat, but his skirt got stuck on something in the doorway and he was pulled up short. Two of Nana's girlfriends rushed forward, freed the skirt, and pushed on his ass to stuff him and that big dress through the door. Just as he vanished from sight, the salesperson returned with his suit in a white shopping bag, and Muriel hid it under her full skirt. Meanwhile, I said goodbye to Vincent and Charlie and handed the phone back to Nana.

"You know," Nana said, "I got no problem with anybody of any gender wearing whatever the hell they want. So when I say Dante looked ridiculous, it's not because he's a man in a dress, but because wedding dresses in general and that one in particular are so totally over the top! I thought I wanted a big, sparkly gown because I never got to wear one the first time around, but now that I think about it, maybe not. Don't even get me started on the symbolism of wearing white! What kind of bullshit is that? And what am I trying to do in a huge, flouncy dress, make people think I'm a princess? Please. That's a major downgrade when you're already the queen. Plus, every one of these gowns failed the comfort test big-time. I'm not saying I'm gonna marry my honey in a track suit, but damn, I'm sweating like a snowman in hell in this thing, and that ain't pretty!"

Dante reappeared (bunching up the skirt so he could fit through the doorway) and said, "Very funny. Where's my suit? I'm not going to leave here in this."

"Oh, did you misplace it?" Nana asked, trying (and failing) to look innocent. "I'll buy that gown for you so you have something to wear home."

Dante reached behind him and unzipped the dress, then stepped out of it, leaving him in a pair of fairly modest black boxer briefs and black socks. "Thanks, but no thanks. I'll just go home like this if you pranksters insist on playing hide-and-seek with my clothes."

Nana's little girlfriends flocked to him and hung off his big biceps. "For the love of God, nobody give him that suit," Gladys exclaimed.

But I took pity on him and asked Muriel to give him the shopping bag. As she handed it over, I said, "He's a married man, ladies. He's also gay."

"None of that makes him any less of a babe," Sylvia said with a wide, gummy smile.

"I almost forgot, we have to find Syl's teeth," I called to the group. That distracted the women long enough for Dante to escape.

Eventually, the dentures were found, we all changed back into our regular clothes, and Nana pulled a thick wad of cash from her black handbag, which she handed to the older salesperson. "You're a peach," Nana told her. "I know we pretty much took over the joint since we got here, so consider this a tip for bein' such good sports. Divvy it up between you and the little blonde."

"This was the most fun I've had at work in thirty years," the woman told her with a big smile, accepting the money and handing it to her coworker. "Come back any time you like, and we'll see if we can find you something to suit your taste."

Once outside, I held the door to Nana's stretch limo and rubbed a water spot off the roof with my thumb as she and her friends climbed in back. A few months earlier, Nana and I had painted a rainbow over the top of the car and a big stripe down each side to liven it up a bit. But after everyone told us the stripes looked like two big cocks, a friend of mine who owned a body shop gave it a new paint job. He'd done a much better job than we had, so now the entire limo was covered end to end in a sparkling rainbow, each color blending perfectly into the next. Nana was a huge advocate of gay rights, and the rainbowmobile was her none-too-subtle way of showing her support.

The senior contingent decided to postpone the trip to the wine shop in favor of heading to Mr. Mario's salon, so they could primp for a party Nana was throwing that night. So basically, Dante had come along for no reason. He sat up front and chatted with me as we rolled slowly through typical Saturday-in-San-Francisco traffic and up and down the steep hills.

We stopped at the salon first, and then I headed to the Marina District, where Dante co-owned a restaurant with his husband and lived above it in a spacious loft. "I've been meaning to ask you," I said, glancing at him as I pulled up to a stoplight, "how are things going now that you're back in charge of the family business?"

The Dombrusos had once been major figures in the world of organized crime. Even though they'd gone legit in recent years, apparently it wasn't the kind of thing you could ever completely walk away from. There were still rival families and old grudges to contend with, and lately there had also been dissention from within the Dombruso clan. Dante's cousin Jerry had been running the family's business interests ever since Dante stepped down a few years ago. But when another cousin, a sweet guy named Nico, fell in love with someone from a rival family, Jerry had been outraged and had taken out a hit on both Nico and his boyfriend Luca.

Fortunately, it had been called off before anyone got hurt, but after that, Dante resumed control of the family.

"It's fine," Dante said, pushing his black hair from his eyes as he watched the traffic. "Everything's under control."

Of course he'd say that. Dante was the type of man who'd carry the weight of the world on his shoulders and never once complain. But a bit of strain had appeared around his eyes since he'd been back in charge, and he was definitely quieter, more stoic, and seemed like he always had a lot on his mind. He'd actually started to remind me of his brother Vincent, who'd always been serious like that.

"Have you heard from Jerry?"

"Not a word." He'd offered his cousin a position within the family (like the old adage said, keep your friends close and your enemies closer), but Jerry had resigned after a few weeks and disappeared. It seemed like Dante and Vincent (who'd stepped up as second in command) were holding their breath, waiting for the other shoe to drop. No one was dumb enough to believe Jerry had just decided to bow out gracefully and relinquish control without a fight. He wasn't that type of man. He'd simply known he was outgunned when Dante and the rest of the family confronted him, and he'd pretended to play along. It was anyone's guess when and how he'd lash out at them, but everyone was certain it would happen.

Dante's brother-in-law Trevor was just exiting the restaurant with his dad TJ when we pulled up a few minutes later. Even though they looked a lot alike with their slender build, dark hair and blue eyes, it was hard to believe they were father and son, since TJ could easily pass for twenty-five. They waited for us as I parked.

I tried to hurry around the car so I could open Dante's door for him, but he opened it himself before I got there and said, "You know you don't have to do that for me."

"Sure I do. I'm the chauffeur." I didn't wear a uniform anymore, because my job was pretty casual and had expanded way beyond driving the limo, but that was still what I'd been hired to do.

"You're more than that, Jessie," he said. "You're a member of my family, who also happens to drive my grandmother around. Thank God for that, because it's scary as shit when she gets behind the wheel."

His words stirred up a lot of emotions in me, since I really wished I was a part of the Dombruso clan. But I pushed them down and distracted myself by wiping water spots off the limo with the cuff of my blue hoodie. Meanwhile, Trevor called, "Damn, you changed out of your pretty frock, Dante. Charlie will be disappointed! I hear you were a vision in satin and ruffles."

Dante grinned at that and said hello to Trevor and TJ before asking, "Is my husband inside?" When Trevor nodded, Dante hurried into the restaurant.

TJ said, "I'd better go, I need to get back to work. Nice to see you, Jessie. Trevor, I'll talk to you soon."

"You sure you won't change your mind and come to the party tonight, Dad?" Trevor asked.

His father shook his head. "Big crowds aren't really my thing. Have fun, though."

TJ said goodbye and took off, and I joined Trevor in the alcove in front of the restaurant's polished wood door. My friend sighed as he watched his dad disappear into the stream of pedestrians on the sidewalk, and I asked, "Everything okay?"

"Yeah, I just worry about him. He tends to isolate himself. I knew that party would be out of his comfort zone, but I'd hoped he would come anyway and maybe meet a few people."

"I'm glad you'll be there, though. I thought you might be working." He was a chef's apprentice at Dante's restaurant.

He turned to me and said, "I took the night off. I just came in to sample a tasting menu the chef's putting together." I studied my friend as he was speaking. We were both in our twenties, and like me, Trevor looked a lot younger than he was, especially in the baggy sweatshirt and jeans he was wearing. People tended to underestimate both of us based on our appearance, but in Trevor's case, they were wrong to do that. Not only was he building a brilliant career, he was also happily married to a great guy named Vincent and was an amazing dad to their adopted son Josh. In other words, I might look like a shorter, blonder version of him, but Trevor was light years ahead of me in every aspect of his life. When he turned to me, his brows knit with concern and he asked, "Are you alright, Jessie? You seem a little sad."

I hadn't thought it showed, and I quickly pulled up a smile. "I'm fine."

"It's okay to admit it if you're not, you know," Trevor said.

After a moment, I confessed, "I've just been having so much fun today, and it's kind of bittersweet. I used to have a lot of days like this, but they're getting to be few and far between. It's a bummer to watch myself growing obsolete at the best job I've ever had."

"How are you becoming obsolete?"

"Well, you know. Nana doesn't need me like she used to. Her fiancé Ollie bought a convertible last month, so he drives her around, except when it's a group outing and she needs the limo. Plus, let's face it, eighty percent of my job description was partner-in-crime, but now Nana has a new wingman for all the schemes and adventures she dreams up."

"I didn't think about that," Trevor said.

"Don't get me wrong, I'm absolutely thrilled that Nana found Ollie. They're perfect for each other, and she deserves a happily ever after, especially after her jerk of a husband dumped her for a woman half his age. I mean, come on! Who does that?"

"A total asshole, that's who."

"Exactly. Nana deserves all the happiness in the world after the shit she's been through. This job was one in a million though, so I can't help but be a little depressed now that it's starting to wind down."

"I get it, but you're a part of this family, Jessie. Even if your job's changing, that's never going to. You know that, right?"

I really wanted to believe him, and it was great that both he and Dante had said it, but I couldn't help but think they were just being nice. I said, "I feel like a jerk for turning Nana's happiness into a negative."

"That's not even sort of what you're doing! You're just sad about your job, which is understandable."

I decided to make my escape before I got all emotional. "I'd better run, I have to get to the house because Nana's expecting a delivery."

"See you tonight," he called as I returned to the limo.

*****

I parked in Nana's driveway about thirty seconds before a whole fleet of delivery vans pulled up. The next day was Valentine's Day, and also the wedding anniversary of two guys who Nana considered a part of her family, so she'd decided to throw a huge bash. She loved parties and looked for any reason to celebrate, so the holiday and Skye and Dare's anniversary were the perfect excuses to go all out, as far as she was concerned.

Once I signed for the delivery, a small army from the party store began unloading a truly staggering number of balloons. A young woman with cropped, bleached hair stopped right in front of me and looked up at the house. She was holding a billowing cloud of red, white, and pink heart-shaped balloons by their curling-ribbon tethers, and murmured, "Holy shit."

Nana's home always made one hell of a first impression. I'd learned when she first hired me that it was called a Queen Anne Victorian, and it was enormous, gorgeous and close to a hundred years old. To me, the house with all its elaborate period details always looked like something out of a movie, grand and whimsical at the same time. The latter was partly due to the fact that we'd painted its façade top-to-bottom in an iridescent rainbow, under the guidance of one of Nana's artist friends, a talented guy named Christopher Robin. The house and limo were a matched set.

"It's like gay Disneyland," the woman murmured. She looked at me and asked, "Do you live here?" When I nodded, she said, "Lucky," before heading into the house with the rest of the balloon parade.

No doubt about it. Nana had taken me in a little over a year ago, just weeks after I was hired as her driver, because my building had become overrun with a massive, truly disgusting ant invasion. Even after the problem was eradicated, I stayed at Nana's house and let the lease run out on my apartment.

I loved living there. I got to pretend I was part of a family again, something I'd sorely missed after my real family disowned me when I came out, and the Dombrusos played along. But I felt like I was taking advantage of Nana's hospitality, especially since I wasn't on call twenty-four/seven anymore.

I was startled from my thoughts when a deep voice behind me asked, "Where do you want this dick?" I grinned and cued up a snappy comeback, but when I turned around, my mouth fell open and I forgot what I was going to say. One of the delivery guys was holding a nine-foot pink cock, and there were several more lined up right behind him, each carried by a delivery person with a poker face. The shaft was artfully crafted out of a spiral column of smaller balloons, topped with a large, slightly pointed balloon for the head, and flanked at the base by two even bigger round balloons. The cocks were actually quite well-done, if not at all what I'd been expecting.

"Is this the Aphrodite's Temple balloon package?" Nana and I had placed the order with the web browser on my phone at the last minute, and we hadn't really been paying much attention. So only then did I realize the description of 'impressive, pink Grecian columns' had been tongue-in-cheek.

"Yeah. It's usually ordered for bachelorette parties. Do you want us to take it away?"

"Oh hell no." I stepped aside so the dick parade could filter past me. I thought it was hilarious and knew Nana would get a kick out of it.

An enormous balloon arch followed. It was also part of the Aphrodite package, so it consisted of red and white hearts interspersed with pink dick-shaped balloons, which jutted out at every angle. I had the delivery people frame the front porch with the arch, and waved and flashed a smile at the asshole neighbor across the street when he got out of his Mercedes and glared at the house.

Once the downstairs and the grand ballroom on the third floor were decorated and the last delivery person filtered out, I shut the door and chuckled as I took in the scene before me. It was festive, no doubt about it. The curved banister leading to the second floor landing was lined with dozens of balloon hearts and foot-long dicks, and I'd had the party company place a dozen of the giant peens randomly around the spacious foyer. They looked like a big, pink, dick forest.

Someone knocked as I was admiring the décor, so I threw my arm around the nearest towering peen and struck a pose. When I swung the door open, River Flynn-Hernandez, who was both the caterer for the party and a friend of the family, raised an eyebrow at me and said, in an accent that was an interesting mix of California surfer and Louisiana drawl, "Nothin' that happens at Nana's house surprises me anymore." I could understand that. Anyone who visited regularly knew to expect the unexpected.

He placed several canvas grocery bags just inside the door. I followed him out to his van in the driveway and asked, "Where's Cole?" River and his boyfriend worked together and were usually inseparable.

We both picked up crates of produce, and as we carried them to the house he told me, "Cole's not coming. It's okay, though. I just got off the phone with Trevor, and he said he'd come early and help me cook."

"Is Cole okay? He didn't catch that flu that's going around, did he?"

"He's fine." River just left it at that and took a right turn into the big, sunny kitchen.

As I helped him unpack the boxes onto the long, granite-topped kitchen island, I said, "Your brother's here." I pointed to the backyard with a bunch of carrots.

"I know, I saw Skye's truck." River's long, sun-streaked brown hair was pulled back in a messy ponytail, and he tucked an escaped tendril behind his ear as he said, "I'll go out and say hi in a minute, some of this stuff needs to be refrigerated."

When everything was unpacked and the refrigerator was loaded, he said he needed to run back out to his van for something, and I told him I'd be in the backyard. I paused to check my reflection in the gleaming chrome of a giant espresso machine Ollie had bought the week before. I'd been growing out my blond hair, and pulled off my baseball cap and tried to finger comb it a bit before giving up and putting the cap back on. I then pulled down the zipper on my hoodie, but what the hell did I think I was doing? I was built like a sixth grader, so it wasn't like I was going to impress anyone with my manly pecs. The fact that I was wearing a t-shirt that said 'You suck. I like that in a man' really wasn't going to impress anyone, either. I pulled the zipper up again before grabbing three bottles of water from the fridge and heading outside.

Funnily enough, the peen theme continued out in the yard. Two long rows of Italian cypress trees lining a wide, paved path had been trimmed into tidy columns, and each was flanked by a pair of round shrubs. That horticultural gem had been dubbed Cockhenge at some point, and while Nana swore she hadn't had them trimmed to look like cocks on purpose, she'd ended up liking it and had left them that way.

At the end of the long pathway, Cockhenge culminated in a recently-added stone and concrete platform. A huge metal sculpture of two male faces in silhouette was under way on top of that base. The face on the right was tilted back and the other face hovered above it, held up by a thin column of metal whose curve suggested the front outline of a neck. The silhouettes were almost but not quite meeting in a kiss, and the lips of the face on the right were parted slightly, as if in anticipation. Even though the sculpture wasn't even halfway done, it was already gorgeous.

The artist, a cute guy named Skye with shaggy, blue hair and a quick smile, was prying a piece of metal off the face on the left when I stepped into the yard. He did that a lot. He was a total perfectionist when it came to his artwork, and if he didn't love something after he welded it in place, he went after it with a crowbar and tried again.

Skye had been working on the sculpture since early December. He was at Nana's house three or four days a week, usually accompanied by his husband Dare. They were such a cute couple, so obviously in love and completely devoted to each other.

Dare was a dancer, and had been choreographing a routine with a friend while his husband welded. When I came outside, he took a break and picked up a towel to wipe the sweat from his face and short, brown hair. He taught classes to earn a living, and was also working on an original ballet production with the all-gay-male dance troupe he'd been assembling.

That day, and at least a couple times a week, the couple was joined by a dancer named Haley, who was helping with the choreography. Skye and Dare usually worked out of a warehouse in Oakland, but Nana's house was pretty centrally located in the city, so it was a good place to meet up. Nana encouraged that, of course. She loved having lots of people around.

Haley was a tall African-American guy with a muscular body, who wore his hair in short dreadlocks. He was undeniably sexy. I was trying to stop crushing on him though, because he clearly thought of me like a kid brother. At twenty-four, I was only three years younger than him, but I got it. I was short, skinny, and looked like I was in my teens. No wonder I wasn't even a blip on his radar.

They all stopped what they were doing and said hello when I joined them, and thanked me as I handed out the water bottles. I was also greeted by Skye and Dare's dog. The black and white boxer nuzzled my hand until I scratched his ears, then went back to sniffing the landscaping.

Even though it was a sunny day, there was a bit of a breeze, and the dancers pulled on sweatshirts over their tank tops before taking a seat on a couple patio chairs beside the sculpture. "Aren't you guys freezing out here?" I asked as I sat down on a corner of the stone and concrete base. "You can move into the ballroom upstairs if you want to."

Dare said, "It's really only cold if we stop moving, which we never do for long."

"Plus, you want to stay close to your hubby," Haley said with a teasing grin.

"Plus that," Dare admitted. Skye sat on his husband's lap and kissed him on the tip of his nose.

"It's a good thing I like you two," Haley told them as they smiled at each other. "Otherwise, I'd pretty much be going into a sugar coma over here. Speaking of which, I'm having serious doubts about this Valentine's party tonight. The entire holiday is just this big, glaring reminder for us single people that we're alone. If it wasn't also a celebration of your wedding anniversary, I'd give it a skip and spend the rest of the weekend on my couch with a frozen pizza, a bottle of tequila, and reruns of the Golden Girls, in a show of solidarity with my single brothers and sisters everywhere." Man, could I relate. I almost volunteered to be his date for the party, but I didn't want him to feel like he had to say yes, just because I put him on the spot in front of our friends.

River stepped out the back door just then, and as he came toward us down the path, Skye called, "Hey, bro! Where's Cole?" I glanced from one to the other. They were half-brothers, and looked nothing alike. Skye was fair-skinned with blue eyes, while River's darker coloring reflected his father's Latino heritage. They'd even grown up in different parts of the country, which meant only River spoke with a drawl. They were really close though, and I envied them. I missed my brothers and sister every day.

River sighed as he dropped onto the patio chair beside Dare's and said, "I don't want you to make a big deal out of it, which I totally know you're going to, because you're like that."

"Make a big deal of what?" Skye asked.

River looked at the ground as he said, "Cole and I have been havin' some problems. He's sleepin' on his friend Miranda's couch these days."

Skye exclaimed, "Oh my God! Are you two breaking up? I've never even seen you bicker!"

"Okay," River said, drawing a circle in the air around his brother, "this is you making a big deal of it. And just because we never bickered in front of you doesn't mean everythin' was rosy. Cole's a very private person. He barely even showed me what he was feeling, so he sure as hell wasn't going to share our problems with you or the rest of our friends and family."

"But how could he just move out?" Skye asked.

"He's been really unhappy," River said. "I knew something was bothering him, it was obvious for weeks. But instead of fixing it, I fucked it all up. I tried to get him to talk about it, but he wouldn't. That was so frustrating. After a while, without even realizing what I was doing, I started picking fights with him about meaningless shit, like never replacing the empty toilet paper roll or forgetting to pay a bill, which was totally asinine of me. Eventually, it dawned on me why I was doing that shit. I was pissed off at him because he wouldn't fucking talk to me, and that anger kept leaking out in these stupid little ways. As if a roll of toilet paper is ever reason enough to snap at someone."

"I get why you were annoyed, though," Skye told him.

River scrubbed his hands over his face, then leaned back in the chair as he said, "When I realized I'd been acting like a douche, I went to see Cole and tried to apologize, but it didn't seem to make a difference. Meanwhile, I still don't know what the fuck is going on with him or why he started withdrawing from me in the first place, because he still won't fucking talk to me."

Haley asked, "So, does this mean you two have broken up?"

River shrugged and told him, "I don't know. Things are just up in the air at this point. I have no idea what's going to happen."

His brother said, "I'm so sorry you're going through this. Is there anything I can do?"

"Just help run interference for me at this party. A lot of people we know are going to be here to celebrate your anniversary, and I really don't want to have to tell each of them what I just told you. Cole would fucking hate it if everyone knew his personal business. So just, I don't know, tell people he's home with a cold or something. I realize I'm asking you to lie to our friends and that's totally shitty, but if I have to tell fifty people my problems, I'm gonna fucking lose it."

Skye said, "Alright, the official story is that your boyfriend's home with a cold. That's all anyone needs to know."

I chimed in, "When you get ready to cook, I'll help you. I'll just have to pick Nana up when she's done at the salon, but that won't take long and then I can do whatever you need me to. I don't want you to stress about this event when you already have so much on your mind."

"Thanks, Jessie. I appreciate it," he said.

"We'll all help you cook," Skye said. "I'll just have to get cleaned up first." He was wearing denim overalls and a blue thermal shirt with the sleeves pushed back, and was definitely on the grubby side after a day of wrangling pieces of rusted metal.

"Great. Trevor's also going to help out, so we've got the catering gig covered. Now everyone stop staring at me, please," River said, shifting uncomfortably. "Talk amongst yourselves. Here's a topic: Jessie racing his teensy car tonight. Is that really happening?"

I raised an eyebrow at Skye and said, "Way to keep a lid on that."

"I just told my brother, but don't worry, we all made sure it didn't get back to Nana." Dare and Haley knew too, since I'd let it slip while I was talking to the three of them.

"I don't think Nana would disapprove of you going back to street racing," River said. "I don't think she disapproves of much at all."

I said, "No, but she might want to join in and I wouldn't want her to get hurt. Nana's the kind of person who'll try anything once. *Anything*."

Haley looked skeptical. "There's no way she'd want to race. She has to be, what, eighty years old?"

"Yeah, but that makes no difference. All of life is one huge bucket list to Nana," Skye told him. "It's kind of great, actually, but that list probably shouldn't include drag racing."

While Haley mulled that over, I turned to River and said, "That 'teensy car' is going to shred the competition tonight."

"You're not going to the party?" Haley asked.

"I won't be gone long. I'm just going to slip out, destroy my competitor, and come right back."

"Dude, it's like, a thirty-year-old Honda Civic. How's that going to outrace anything?" River asked.

"She *was* a thirty-year-old Civic," I told him. "Now Sharona's a race car. Every single system in that car has been replaced, rebuilt, and upgraded. She can't lose."

"You sound pretty confident," Haley said.

"She's ready. I am, too. I've been away from racing for over a year and I'm dying to get back to it."

Skye winced at that. "Unfortunate choice of words, Jess, since your last race ended in a crash."

Haley asked, "What happened?"

"Another driver happened. My tire blew just as I was coming off the line, which would have been alright. I wasn't going that fast yet, so I could have held it together. But this asshole named Trigger clipped my fender right in the middle of that and my car rolled. I was thrown clear, so I was basically okay except for a limp that took two months to go away, but my car was totaled. I loved that car," I said, shaking my head. "I spent over three years and a small fortune perfecting her and had just gotten her to the top of her game."

"Not to trivialize the rest of that, but Trigger? Really?" River asked.

"Most people don't use their real name on the street circuit," I told him, "since it's not exactly legal."

"So, what's your racing name?"

"Rocket." I pointed a finger at him and said, "Don't laugh."

River grinned at me. "As in the Marvel Comics raccoon?"

"Maybe."

Skye said, "I'm curious about street racing. Can Dare and I come along?"

His brother shot him a look. "Is the part you're curious about the twisted metal after they wreck and the sculptures you could make out of it? Because aside from that, I can't imagine that it would be very interesting to you." When River realized what he'd said, he turned to me with wide eyes. "Not that you're gonna crash this time. I'm sure it's going to be fine. I didn't mean to, like, get all morbid or anything."

I just shrugged. "Crashes happen. That's something every racer accepts. And now that you mention it, I wish I'd known Skye back when I wrecked. It would have been awesome if Gloria had gotten to live on in a sculpture, instead of just rusting away in some junkyard."

"Why are your cars always girls?" Dare asked.

"I dunno, they just are. And you're welcome to watch me race sometime, but tonight's probably not a good idea. Nana would notice if the guests of honor snuck out. Besides, all I'm doing is going head-to-head against Trigger in a grudge match, assuming the cops don't show up and end it before it even begins. The whole thing will be over in a few seconds, and for that you have to drive an hour each way to the middle of nowhere," I pointed out.

"Is it going to be hard to get behind the wheel after crashing last time?" River asked. "If it was me, I think I'd be nervous, but you don't seem to be."

"I was rattled right after it happened, but I've gotten over it and I'm looking forward to racing again. For the past couple months, it's just been me and a stopwatch while I fine-tuned Sharona, but it's so different when you're up against another driver."

Haley took a sip of water, then said, "Don't take this the wrong way, but you don't look like a street racer."

"Sure I do. They aren't these big, tough, alpha dudes like in the movies. Mostly, they're seventeen- to twenty-four-year-olds who spend all their time under the hoods of cars, not in the gym bulking up."

Dare asked, "How'd you start racing, anyway?"

"I began when I was seven with go-kart racing. It sounds hokey, but believe it or not, a lot of pro racers start out that way. When I got older and found I had a knack for fixing up engines, it just dovetailed with my love of racing. It's been a big part of my life since I was a kid, apart from this last year when I needed to start from scratch with a new car."

"Do you think you'll ever try to race professionally, like Formula One or something?" River asked.

I stood up and stretched my arms over my head. "Nah. This is enough for me." I turned to River and changed the subject by saying, "I think I'll go in and start washing all that produce you brought, unless you want me to start somewhere else with prepping the food for the party."

"That's as good a place to start as any," he said, and our little group headed into the house.

Chapter Two

A quarter mile. One thousand, three hundred and twenty feet. That was the distance I needed to cover, as fast as I possibly could.

I whispered to my car, "You can do it, Sharona. I believe in you."

My last race more than a year ago had ended violently and dramatically with my car rolling half a dozen times. The asshole who'd caused the wreck was just a few feet away, behind the wheel of a twin turbo Mustang Mach 1. Five hundred dollars was on the line, but I didn't give a damn about the money. This was a grudge match, plain and simple. We were finishing what we started all those months ago.

I revved my engine and took a couple deep breaths. My heart was pounding and I fidgeted a bit, tugging at my seatbelt and adjusting the ball cap I wore backwards to hold my blond hair out of my eyes. Then I glanced at the car to my right.

The black Mustang's V-8 engine was deep and throaty compared to my Civic's. It had originally been built in the seventies, not my favorite era for Mustangs. But then, what a car started out as didn't matter nearly as much as what it had been transformed into. My competitor had turned his car into a brutish lion. I'd turned mine into a cheetah.

I caught the other driver's eye and stared him down. I knew him only as Trigger. He held my gaze unflinchingly, a muscle working in his jaw as he ground his teeth. I scowled at him before turning my attention back to the quarter-mile of asphalt ahead of me.

We were in a part of the South Bay forgotten by development, on an empty road at the foot of some scrubby hills. A heavy-set guy named Julio stepped out onto the road, a little less than halfway down the course. Only in movies and video games were races started by hot women in skimpy outfits. Julio was holding his phone and waiting for each spotter to check in. Half a dozen guys were watching for the police all around the raceway.

Any moment now. I adjusted my grip on the gearshift as adrenaline shot through me. God I'd missed this. When I revved my engine again, the purr was so sweet.

Julio signaled the start of the race by shining a flashlight at us, then booked it off the road. My heart leapt as I threw the Civic into gear and slammed the gas pedal to the floor. Sharona's tires and the Mustang's squealed as a cloud of smoke billowed behind us. Both cars found traction in the same instant and lunged forward. The Stang fishtailed coming off the line. I did too, but I regained control quickly.

Trigger swerved toward me sharply as our odometers shot past a hundred. He narrowly missed sideswiping my car, and I drew in my breath and eased off the gas as I jogged to the left, away from him. In the next instant, I regained my focus and floored it, but it was already too late. The other driver had pulled ahead. A couple seconds after that, it was all over.

I crossed the finish line right behind the Stang and cut the engine before launching myself from my car. Trigger got out too and glared at me as I ran at him. I didn't care that he had a good four or five inches and fifty pounds of muscle on me, I was furious. "You did that on purpose," I yelled. "You knew I'd flinch if you came at me, after wrecking me the last time! What's the matter, too afraid of losing to run a clean race?"

"I *did* run a clean race," he growled. "It's not my fault if you can't keep your shit together when you're behind the wheel! And newsflash, I didn't wreck you last time! You lost control when your tire blew, and *you* swerved into *me*! Quit blaming me for your own fucking mistake!"

"The race had just started when I had that blowout! I wasn't going that fast, and no fucking way would I have spun out of control if you hadn't tagged my bumper!"

He pushed his dark hair back from his eyes and exclaimed, "Are you high? It was a miracle you didn't kill both of us!"

I tried to get in his face, which would have been easier if I wasn't so much shorter than he was, and told him, "I know what happened. Lunging at me was a dick move! You have no business racing, since apparently you can only win by intimidation, and on top of that, you're barely holding it together every time you get behind the wheel!"

Trigger yelled, "You don't know shit! And why don't you accept some fucking responsibility? The wreck last year wasn't my fault, and I didn't purposely come at you this time either! If you're that skittish, maybe you shouldn't be racing!"

My friend Zachary, who'd snuck out of the party with me, had reached us by then. He pulled me back as the four dozen guys who'd watched the race clustered around us, and said, "Come on, Jessie, let's just go."

I turned and walked away from the crowd, taking a deep breath and shaking out my hands. Adrenaline still flooded my system and was making me jittery. Zachary went with me, and my friend Kenji jogged to catch up with us. Since the last time I'd seen him, he'd bleached and colored his spiky hair a silvery white and looked a bit like a comic book character. "Dude, I thought you were going to punch that guy," Kenji exclaimed.

"I don't normally go around punching people," I said, still trying to calm down, "but I almost made an exception back there. He really pissed me off."

"He's a dick. It's like he thinks he's too good for the rest of us," Kenji said. "He never talks to anyone. He just shows up every week, wins a couple races and leaves with the money."

"He wins?"

"Yeah, pretty much every race."

I'd randomly started climbing one of the low hills beside the track, wanting to put some distance between myself and Trigger. As I replayed the race over and over in my mind, a bit of doubt began to creep in. After a while, I stopped walking and turned to my friends. "Kenji, you know what goes on out there. Am I totally off base here? He came at me, right? That's what it felt like to me, but what did it look like from your perspective?"

He hesitated, chewing his lower lip before saying, "Honestly? I don't know, Jessie. I mean, yeah, the Mustang totally swerved at your Civic, but he was fishtailing the whole time. One thing you're right about for sure is that he's barely in control of all that horsepower every time he races. He's got a beast under that hood. It'd be tough for any of us to control it."

I thought about that for a while, then asked, "What do you think, Zachary? What did you see?"

"To me, it looked like he was swerving all over the place. Did he come at you intentionally to try to rattle you? I have no clue. Only he could tell you that."

I looked at the makeshift track below us as I mulled that over. It was bathed in an oddly yellow glow from the row of streetlights along the asphalt. Trigger's Mustang was gone, and two other cars were getting in position to race. Kenji's older brother had pulled Sharona off to the side, out of harm's way. Her iridescent purple-to-green paint job shone even in that weird lighting. I took off my baseball cap and ran my fingers through my hair to push it back from my face, then put the cap on the right way around. Finally, I said, "I guess I really don't know if he spooked me on purpose today, but that wreck a year ago was definitely his fault."

"I always thought so, too," Kenji told me. "Trigger's probably the most aggressive driver out there right now. I've seen him bump other drivers plenty of times when he's racing, and I'm pretty sure he does it just to intimidate them. It's always at the start of the race, so it usually doesn't do much damage, besides pissing off the other racer. You're the only one who crashed as a result of it, since he tagged your fender just as your tire blew out."

"So how the hell could he say the crash was my fault? I could have been killed! For that I don't get so much as a 'sorry'?"

"Apologizing would mean admitting it was his fault," Kenji said. "But according to him, he never does anything wrong."

I sighed, and after a moment I changed the subject by saying, "Check it out, they're getting ready to go again. I think I recognize the orange Camry, that's Rio's car, right?" Kenji nodded and I asked, "So who's in the red Acura?" The two cars were lined up at the end of the track, and Julio was in position with his phone, waiting for another all-clear.

"This eighteen-year-old named Six. He's been showing up pretty regularly for the last couple months."

"Why does he call himself Six?"

"No clue."

"He any good?" I asked.

Kenji grinned at that. "You're about to find out."

Julio gave the signal and ran off the track as tires squealed and a cloud of smoke billowed from behind the racers. Both cars shot forward, but then the Acura took off like it had a jet engine. "Holy shit," I muttered. Just a few seconds later, it finished a car length ahead of the Camry. "What the hell does he have under the hood?"

"About forty grand, that's what. Everyone's saying he's a trust fund kid, and that he wins by outspending his competition," Kenji said. "But they're just jealous. The kid's got balls, and he's got skill. He might also have access to some serious coin, but that doesn't change the fact that he's a hell of a racer."

Kenji's phone buzzed, and when he pulled it out of his pocket, I glanced at the time on the screen and said, "Shit, we have to go. I didn't mean to ditch my employer's party this long."

As we all started back down the dusty hillside, Kenji fired off a text to his girlfriend, then said as he returned the phone to his pocket, "So, are we going to start seeing you back here on a regular basis, Jess? I've missed you."

"Yeah, I'm going to try to come every weekend now that I have a car again. It was just kind of depressing to be here when I knew I couldn't race."

"I can imagine."

"Do you want to come back to the city with Zachary and me?" I asked. "The party's probably just getting warmed up."

"You mean the party hosted by the eighty-year-old grannie you work for? No thanks, I'm good."

"He obviously hasn't met Nana," Zachary said with a little grin.

"You're right, he hasn't." We reached the group of racers, and I went up to the eighteen-year-old with the Acura and stuck my hand out. "Hey, I'm Rocket. That was a hell of a race."

The kid shook my hand and looked me over with a guarded expression. He was tall and lean with chiseled cheekbones and dark blond hair that dipped over ice blue eyes, and he wore a slick leather jacket that wasn't doing anything to dispel his trust fund kid reputation. "Six. I saw you race once a couple years ago, I'm glad you're back at it. Maybe we'll have the chance to go head-to-head sometime." He had a refined English accent, so as soon as he spoke, he seemed less trust fund and more heir to the throne.

"That'd be awesome. Oh, I assume you know Spike," I said, introducing Kenji by his racing name, "and this is my friend Zachary."

Six said hello to Kenji, and his eyes lit up as he turned to my companion. "What, just Zachary? No perfectly embarrassing nickname like Zippy or Z-force or Zoomer?"

My friend smiled shyly as a blush crept into his pale cheeks. He tried to hide it by tipping his head forward and almost disappearing behind a curtain of hair. It reached his chin, and was currently dyed black with a red streak along the right side of his face. "Um, no. I don't race, so there's no need for a nickname. You guys are rocking yours, though."

"Why thank you," Six said playfully.

Zachary glanced up from under his hair and asked, "Why are you called Six?"

"That's a fairly involved story, which I'd be happy to share with you sometime," he said, his smile unmistakably flirtatious. Zachary colored even more.

We chatted for a couple more minutes, and after we said our goodbyes and were back in my Civic, I grinned at my friend. "You totally got hit on back there. He was cute, too!"

"He was beautiful. But come on, eighteen? I'm five years older than him."

"That's not so bad."

"Sure it is. What would we possibly have in common? Besides the age gap, he looks and sounds like he spends his time yachting, or jetting off to the south of France on a whim. Nothing about me would hold the interest of a guy like that."

I said, "Not only are you making a lot of assumptions, but you're a sweet, kind, amazing person, and he'd be lucky to know you."

Zachary fidgeted with the zipper on his black jacket and said, "That's nice of you, Jess, but come on. It'd be like 'The Prince Dates the Pauper', only worse, because in this case the pauper is an ex-prostitute. I'm sure that'd sit well with his highness and his family."

"You're rejecting yourself before he has a chance to."

"I know." Zachary looked out the passenger window, and after a while he turned back to me and grinned a little. "He looked like he could be Benedict Cumberbatch's blond younger brother, didn't he? He even had the accent! I about died when he started talking."

"You like that guy! Should we go back? Maybe we can invite him to the party."

My friend's expression grew serious. "No, just keep going. It doesn't matter that I thought he was cute. He's too young, too rich, and too perfect. He's not only out of my age range, he's totally out of my league."

I frowned at that, but did as he asked and got on the freeway. After a while I said, "Thanks for coming with me tonight. It was nice to have a friend there. I wasn't sure if I'd still know anyone after a year away from racing."

"It was interesting, thanks for letting me tag along. I'm sorry your race didn't go better. I totally thought you had it, right up until those last couple seconds."

"Yeah, me too." I changed lanes, then glanced at him and asked, "Do you want me to take you back to the party, or home? You didn't look like you were having a very good time before I whisked you away on this field trip."

"The party, I guess. Chance will be expecting me to come back."

"Yeah, I saw you all arrived together. How's it been living with your friend and his family?"

He said, "I don't belong there. Chance and Finn are newlyweds, and on top of that, they've only been the legal guardians of Chance's kid brother Colt and his boyfriend Elijah for a few months. They're in the process of coming together as a family, and I feel like I'm intruding."

"I'm sure they don't think you are. Chance is your best friend, and he cares about you."

"But I still feel like I am. I need to move out, but that would be a lot easier if I had a job, and if this city wasn't so insanely expensive." As he was speaking, his slender hands kept fidgeting with the zipper on his jacket. I noticed he'd chosen to wear head-to-toe black to a Valentine's Day party.

"No luck finding work, huh?"

He shook his head. "The only jobs I'm qualified for pay minimum wage, and I can't live on that. If I went back to prostitution, I could support myself. But that can't happen right now. Never mind that Finn's a cop, and that Chance started a whole new life and quit the business. I'm living with two high school kids. What kind of example would I be setting for them if I went out and turned tricks every night?" Zachary sighed and added, "I wish I'd never given up my studio apartment in the Lower Haight. I didn't realize what a good deal I'd been getting. I've looked at similar apartments since then, and they're all three times more than I was paying."

"Why'd you give it up?"

He laughed humorlessly and said, "Ironically, because I was running from Chance, and now I live with him. He used to live right across the hall."

"Why would you run from your best friend?"

He was quiet for a long moment before saying softly, "Because I was in love with him, and when he got involved with Finn it shattered me."

"Oh God. It must hurt so bad to see him with his new husband every day!"

"It's not like it was when they first got together. I've made a lot of progress. Every day is a lesson in letting go." He fell silent and turned his head to look out the window again as my heart broke for him.

When we reached Nana's house and got out of the car, I went around and grabbed him in a hug. I wasn't exactly a big guy, but he felt tiny and fragile in my arms. He hesitated for a moment before sinking into the embrace. I told him, "I had no idea you've been going through so much. You usually don't say anything."

"You're right, I don't. But you're easy to talk to, Jessie. I kind of feel like you're the same as me in some ways, like maybe you're hurting inside too, but never want anyone to know it. So, I don't know. I guess I thought you'd understand."

"I totally get it, and I want you to know I'm here for you, day or night. Seriously, any time you need a friend, pick up the phone or come on over."

He let go of me and stepped back, his hair hiding his eyes again as he looked at the pavement. "I appreciate that, Jessie. I don't exactly have a lot of friends, so that's…well, it's kind of huge."

"Come on," I said, taking his hand. "Let's go fill our bellies and enjoy the party. The caterer made way too much food, and I happen to know the mini pizzas are excellent because I helped make them." Zachary gave me a little smile and let me tow him into the house.

Inside was total mayhem, of course. It was well past midnight, but there was absolutely no indication that the party was winding down. Dombrusos, drag queens, little old ladies, gay guys in their twenties, artists, musicians, families, and a whole lot of people who didn't fit into any particular category were laughing, dancing, drinking, and generally making merry.

As we waded into the chaos, Nana's fiancé Ollie hurried over to us, bow and arrows in hand. He was wearing pink long underwear with little wings on his back, a bulky cloth diaper, and red high-top sneakers. Ollie drew back his bow and shot me with an arrow. The heart-shaped foam tip bounced off my chest. He flashed a huge smile, yelled, "Direct hit," and disappeared back into the crowd. His Chihuahua fetched the arrow, and then he and Nana's big, furry mutt followed Ollie. Both the dogs were wearing pink sweaters with red hearts.

Zachary chuckled and leaned close to be heard over the music and noise. "It was worth coming back just for that."

We filled a couple plates at the lavish buffet, which was still overflowing several hours into the party, then wound our way through the kitchen and stepped out into the much quieter backyard. Several guests had had the same idea. We joined Skye and Dare and a group of their friends, who sat around a glowing fire pit to the right of Cockhenge. Chance and his husband were a part of their group. So was River, who pulled a couple more chairs over for us. He'd donned a façade of rehearsed cheerfulness, which would have been convincing if I didn't know better.

Skye's best friend Christian was sharing a lounge chair with his husband Shea, and he called to me from across the fire pit, "So how'd it go, Speed Racer?"

I shot Skye a look, and he said, "Okay, I might have told a couple more people, but it didn't get back to Nana. I promise."

I turned back to Christian and said, "It sucked. The other racer is a douche and I thought he was going to slam into me, possibly on purpose. Basically, he played chicken with me and I lost."

"That does suck, but hey, at least you made it back in one piece," Haley said. He was holding a huge, half-empty margarita glass and looked like he was feeling no pain.

"Yeah, but I'm also pissed. I hate that guy, and I never hate anybody!"

"I think you just really need him to apologize for making you crash last year," Zachary said.

"I do, but he never will. It's like my friend Kenji said, that'd be the same as this guy admitting he was wrong, and he's not about to do that. Instead, I'll settle for another rematch. Next time, maybe I can race him on a divided track or something so he can't pull his usual bullshit."

"Maybe you should let this go," Dare suggested before taking a drink from the bright blue cocktail he was sharing with his husband.

"I can't. I need one more shot. I *had him* tonight, right up until I thought he was going to slam into me and send my car rolling again."

We chatted with our little group for another half hour or so, until we were joined by Chance's kid brother Colt and his boyfriend Elijah, who both looked exhausted. Chance, Finn, and Zachary decided to head home with the boys, and I got up and walked them out. I gave Zachary a hug and said, "Talk to you soon, okay?"

"For sure. Thanks for everything tonight, I had a good time." He offered me a little smile.

I'd followed them to the porch and stayed out there even after my friends took off. I just wasn't in the mood for a big, noisy party that night. I would have retreated to my room, but that wasn't an option since it wouldn't be much quieter in there.

After a while, I decided to go for a drive. I felt better as soon as I got behind the wheel and turned the key. The sound of the engine was as soothing as listening to music. To me, at least. I headed for the coast, and as I drove, I replayed the race over and over in my mind, especially the way the big Mustang serpentined as Trigger tried to keep his car in check. I'd been watching him out of the corner of my eye the entire race, and it had felt intentional when he swerved toward me, a sharp break from the steady pattern his car had been following.

Maybe I wouldn't have flinched and eased off the gas if he hadn't wrecked my car last time. Racers swerved or even bumped the other car occasionally, it was usually no big deal. But this was different, given our history. Trigger knew what he'd done to me a year ago, so he had to know lunging at me would make me flash back to the accident. That felt so underhanded. It was like punching someone in the face, and later pretending to throw a punch at them. Of course the person who'd been hit was going to flinch.

The more I thought about it, the angrier I became. On impulse, I headed south to a neighborhood called Bernal Heights, out past the Mission District. I'd heard Trigger worked in a garage out there, someplace called Vic's, or Nick's, something like that. I didn't expect him to be working at that hour, but I went anyway, just to check it out. Once I found the shop, I could show up Monday morning and demand a rematch. Getting an apology for almost killing me a year ago would also be nice, but I wasn't going to hold my breath.

Bernal Heights was built around a huge, grassy open space dominated by a pair of fairly nondescript hills. It was called, to no one's surprise, Bernal Heights Park. It always seemed odd to me that the people who built out almost every square inch of San Francisco took a look at that pair of hillocks and decided, "Nah." The neighborhood around the park was nearly as jam-packed as the rest of the city, but those two undeveloped hills stood as an example of what the area would have looked like if San Francisco had never happened.

I circled around the park to Cortland Avenue, where a lot of the neighborhood's businesses were clustered, but didn't spot a garage as I drove the length of it. Eventually, I pulled over and consulted my phone. A place called Kit's sounded right, and when I found it, I stopped in the quiet street and checked it out.

The garage was good-sized, probably big enough to hold six or seven cars, but it wasn't much to look at. It sat by itself on a weedy lot at the very edge of the neighborhood, close to the freeway. Most of the paint had worn away, exposing rough-looking wood siding. The pair of graffiti-covered metal doors that made up the front of the shop didn't look any better, and a sign above them was so faded that it was almost illegible. Apparently Kit wasn't big on the concept of curb appeal.

A light was on under the metal doors, and when I'd driven up, I'd caught a glimpse of movement through a glass door on the right side of the shop. Really? Someone was working at this hour on a Saturday night? Well, that or somebody was robbing the place, but what self-respecting crook would choose to knock over a complete crap pile?

I backed the car up to get a better look at what was happening inside and spotted Trigger through the glass door. Well good, I wouldn't have to wait until Monday. I parked and went up to the door. Surprisingly, it swung open when I pushed on it, jingling some old-fashioned chimes to announce my arrival.

Trigger was dressed in a tight, black tank top and worn-out jeans, and was washing his hands in an industrial sink when I came

56

in. The shop's interior was spotless and well-maintained, in sharp contrast to the outside. His Mustang and two black, late sixties Impalas were lined up on the far side of the concrete floor. The Stang's hood was up, and an empty paper coffee cup and a greasy shop rag decorated its fender.

To say he was surprised to see me was a major understatement. Trigger's brown eyes went wide and he blurted, "What the fuck are you doing here?"

"I want an apology. I also want a rematch, but first we have to find a track with a concrete barrier down the center to keep you from coming at me again."

He raised an eyebrow. "If you think I'm capable of purposely trying to wreck your car, why would you come here? I mean, according to you, I'm guilty of attempted murder. I also must have the reflexes of a cobra, since I managed to hit your careening car in the split second that your tire blew out. Yet here you are, strolling into the lair of someone who'd have to be a complete sociopath, given your accusations."

"I don't think you meant to hurt me. You're a dick, not a psycho. You probably just wanted to knock my car out of commission. But that's still incredibly dangerous and a really shitty thing to do to someone, so would it kill you to say you're sorry? Just once? Would those words make you shrivel up and die, right here on the concrete?"

His voice rose as he exclaimed, "Why would I apologize when *you* hit *me*?"

"Oh yeah. I swerved right, hit you, and then my car went flying off to the left, where it rolled half a dozen times. Because physics works like that!"

"Sure it does, when we're talking about your little Fisher Price car ricocheting off a solid metal object!" He stormed over to his Mustang, picked up the paper coffee cup and said, "Here's a demonstration so you can understand this once and for all. This cup will stand in for your toy car, since they weigh about the same. My Mustang will be playing herself in this reenactment. I'm driving along, minding my own business, but then your tire explodes and oh, look!" He threw the cup at the Ford's fender, and it bounced off and rolled across the floor. "See that? That's exactly what happened! Cause and effect. You hit me, you bounced off, and the stupid embankment on the side of the road acted like a ramp, so you went airborne and then you rolled. I'm sure that sucked, I'm sure it was scary as shit, but what it wasn't was *my fucking fault.*"

"Thank you for that brilliant reenactment, and your point would have been made spectacularly, except for the fact that I was actually driving something made by Mazda and not by fucking *Dixie.*"

"Whatever. My car weighed twice as much as yours, so the result was the same."

"Except that here's what actually happened," I said, marching over to the coffee cup. "You hit me, and my car did this." I stomped on the cup and flattened it. "And yet, somehow, saying you're sorry is just asking way the hell too much from you!"

Trigger's voice rose again. "Fine. I'm sorry you hit me. I am, actually. It sucks that you got hurt, and that you wrecked your shitty toy car. But *you* were what caused all of that!"

"Asshole!"

"Fucking *stop blaming me!*"

"No, because you're to blame!"

Trigger threw his hands in the air and yelled, "You refuse to see this from anything but your own misguided perspective!"

"So do you!"

"Get the fuck out of my shop. I'm so sick of you and your kind!"

"My kind!" I narrowed my eyes at him. "Don't tell me you're also a homophobe, as if just being a regular asshole wasn't enough!"

"You're gay?"

"Duh!"

"Well, how was I supposed to know that? It's not like you're wearing a sign around your neck."

I said flatly, "No, just three beaded necklaces."

He waved his hand dismissively and said, "That doesn't mean anything." Okay, he had a point there.

I asked, "So, if you didn't mean gay people when you said 'my kind', what label were you trying to stick to me?"

"Spoiled brats who fix up their cars on mommy and daddy's dime. Was your Civic a high school graduation present?"

I stared at him and said, "Dude, I'm twenty-four."

"Oh, come on! There's no way we're the same age."

"Are you ever right about anything? I mean anything *at all*?"

"It's impossible that you're twenty-four. You barely look old enough to shave!"

I rolled my eyes and pulled my driver's license from my wallet, then went up to him and held it in front of his face. "Satisfied?"

Trigger grinned and said, "That's the worst fake ID I've ever seen."

"Based on what?"

"You called yourself Jessie James, and spelled Jessie with an i-e."

"Granted, I've regretted that last name, and I'll probably change it again, but the ID's not fake."

"What do you mean, change it again?"

"I legally changed my name a few years ago, because the one my parents gave me completely sucked."

"What could possibly be worse than Jessie-with-an-i-e James?"

"None of your damn business," I said as I shoved the license back in my wallet and returned it to my pocket. "Neither is this, but James was my middle name. That's why I used it. It wasn't because I have a great love of bank-robbing outlaws."

He chuckled and said, "Wow, you're kind of insane."

"And you're an asshole. Which is worse?"

"Oh, okay. I'm an asshole because I won't buy in to your delusions and tell you what you want to hear."

"No, you're an asshole because *you're an asshole*."

Trigger knit his dark brows. "That's enough name-calling for one night. Go home, Jessie James."

"Sure," I said, my stubbornness flaring, "just as soon as you apologize for ramming my car and making me crash last year and for running a dirty race tonight!"

His voice rose again, and so did the color in his cheeks. "It's not unusual for cars to swerve at those speeds when they're in the straight-away, and sometimes they bump into each other! If you can't understand those basic facts, you have no business racing!"

"Oh no. Do *not* try to explain racing to me! I've been doing this most of my life! That's how I know the difference between an unintentional drift and the crap you pull when you're on the track!"

"You don't know shit, and I told you to get out."

"Not until you fucking apologize!" He grabbed my upper arm and started to tow me to the side door, and I yelled, "Let go of me!"

He went right on pulling me across the shop. "No matter what I say, you just won't listen. You think you know everything! You think you know me, but you don't have a fucking clue!"

"I said *let go of me*!" I tried to yank my arm from his grasp and hip-checked him fairly hard in the process. That threw him off balance, and he fell over and pulled me down with him. Trigger rolled over so he was straddling me, and I swore at him and almost slapped him as I flailed around and tried to free myself.

He caught my wrists and pinned them to the floor on either side of my head as he exclaimed, "Just calm down!" When I finally stopped struggling, we stared at each other for a long moment as I caught my breath and my heart raced.

Without warning, lust shot through me like a jolt from a defibrillator. When Trigger let go of my wrists, I grabbed the front of his shirt and pulled him to me. In the next instant, we were kissing wildly. I rolled over so I was on top of him and devoured his mouth, and he ran his hands down my back and grabbed my ass. I had absolutely no explanation for what was happening. None at all. I went with it anyway.

After a couple minutes of kissing passionately and pawing at each other, I tumbled off him and shucked off my jeans and briefs, then dumped my wallet onto the floor and rifled through its contents until I found a condom and a packet of lube. While I did that, Trigger pushed down his jeans and pulled off his shirt, revealing a thick, hard cock, a smooth, muscular chest and a sexy tattoo on his ribs. My lust ratcheted up another couple notches at the sight of him, which I hadn't thought was possible, since it was already through the roof.

I handed him a condom, and as he put it on with shaking hands, I tore open the lube with my teeth and quickly worked some into me before wiping my hands on a clean shop rag. The concrete floor was cold when I leaned back on it. I didn't care.

I parted my legs for him and rubbed my throbbing cock, and he knelt between my thighs and asked, "You sure about this?" Hell no, not even a little, but I was absolutely going to do it anyway.

When I nodded, Trigger lined up his cock with my hole. I pushed back as he pressed against me, opening myself for him. When his length slipped inside me, I let out the breath I'd been holding. He picked up my legs and pushed them to my chest, almost folding me in half as he began to thrust into me.

I tried not to overthink what was happening, which soon became really easy. It was so wild and primal that it forced out all concerns, all questions, until I was distilled down to nothing but pure sensation. Nothing mattered except the way his thick cock stretched me, and the feeling of his rough hands on the back of my thighs, and the waves of pleasure radiating through me as he pounded my prostate. My cock twitched and leaked precum as I moaned incoherently and drove myself onto him, trying to take him as deep as I possibly could.

He muttered, "Oh fuck," as he drove himself into me again and again. With each thrust, he almost pulled his cock from my body before driving it in me to the root. The sound of his body colliding with mine filled the quiet garage. He let go of my legs and fell forward, his face inches above mine. As he met my gaze I grabbed ahold of him, clawing his back, frantic with need.

All too soon, my orgasm detonated. I yelled incoherently as I arched up off the concrete floor, shooting all over myself, and a moment later he cried out and grabbed me as he came too, pulling me against him. I came harder than ever before, my head spinning, and wrapped my arms and legs around him, clinging to him, as if that would somehow keep me from flying apart.

We were both shaking by the time our orgasms finally ebbed. My heart pounded in my ears, and it took a few moments to catch my breath. He eased his cock from me and stood up shakily, and I immediately reached for my briefs and began to get dressed. He threw the condom in a metal waste barrel before pulling up his jeans and zipping them. Neither of us said a word.

The moment I was dressed, I headed for the door. I paused for only a moment to glance at him over my shoulder when I reached the exit. Trigger was turned partly away from me, his shaggy, dark brown hair covering his face. He had two more tattoos on his back, a small blackbird just above his waistband on the right, and a slightly larger blackbird in flight on his left shoulder blade. But what stood out more was the web of red welts on his back from where I'd clawed at him with my short fingernails. Shit, had I really done that? Guilt and confusion vied for the top spot as my emotions churned and I bolted from the garage.

When I got behind the wheel, I shoved the keys in the ignition and took off like a shot. I only drove a few blocks though before pulling to the curb in a quiet residential neighborhood and taking a deep breath. I leaned against the headrest and closed my eyes as I tried to get myself together.

What the hell had just happened? Since when did I fuck people I hated? God, Trigger of all people. Okay, yes, he was sexy as hell, but he was also a total asshole. That was an irrefutable fact. So how did we go from fighting to fucking in the blink of an eye?

And why the hell did it have to be the best sex of my entire life?

Ugh. I sat up a bit and looked down at myself. I was absolutely disgusting. My red t-shirt was soaked with semen and sticking to my chest. When I flipped down the visor and looked in the mirror, I realized two things: my baseball cap was gone, and I had cum in my hair. Awesome.

Oh man, and my house was packed with people. I was sure Nana's party was still going on. That was going to be the most embarrassing walk of shame ever.

I pulled a handful of fast food napkins from my car's center console, tried to wipe the cum from my hair, and dabbed at my shirt. Not surprisingly, it didn't help at all. I thought for a moment before pulling my phone from my pocket.

I sent Zachary a quick text that said: *Hey, you still awake?*

He replied just a moment later with: *Yeah, what's up?*

Is it okay if I come by? I need to borrow your shower and some clothes. Long story.

He wrote back right away. *Sure, no problem. Everyone's asleep, so go around to the back door. It's quieter than coming in the front.*

Thanks. I'm only a few minutes away, see you soon, I texted before tossing my phone aside, grabbing my hoodie from the backseat, and putting it on to hide my gross t-shirt.

Fifteen minutes later, I pulled up in front of a fairly plain, rectangular building beside the bay. It had been a small warehouse, then a restaurant, and was now home to Chance and Finn, two teen boys, and for the time being, Zachary. The front was little more than corrugated metal siding, but they'd been working on fixing it up in the few months they'd owned it. The tall, sliding door had been painted dark red, and river rock delineated a tidy front yard. A few shrubs and small trees softened the industrial exterior, including a pair of cypresses in big red pots, which flanked the front door. All of that was a big improvement, given how it had looked when they'd first bought it.

I followed a gravel path around the left side of the building and crossed a concrete patio to the back door. Lit rows of bulbs around the patio swayed in the breeze coming off the water and cast long shadows. The back of the building was glass, and it was dark inside, except for the soft glow of a single table lamp. Zachary was curled up and reading in that little pool of light.

I tapped on the glass door with a fingertip, and he jumped up and let me in. "Hey," he whispered. "You okay?"

"Yeah. I, um, had an unexpected encounter tonight and things got messy."

"Define messy."

"I came all over myself while Trigger was fucking me."

Zachary looked startled, but then a smile spread across his face. "Are you serious?"

"Oddly enough, I am."

"How did that happen?"

"Hell if I know. I'll tell you the whole story, but can I clean up first?"

"Yeah, of course. I put some clothes in the shower room for you, and there are clean towels on the hooks along the back wall. I also found a blanket and pillows for you in case you want to sleep on the couch tonight. It's pretty late."

"Thanks. Where's the shower room?"

"It's where the men's room used to be when this place was a restaurant. Since they didn't actually need ten toilets, Chance and Finn made the ladies' room unisex, then gutted the men's room and put in two shower stalls."

"Why two?"

Zachary shrugged. "I dunno. I guess they figured it would speed everyone along in the morning or something."

The converted bathroom almost felt like a locker room, except for the dimmer switch on the lights, the attractive golden-brown tile on the floor and walls, and the spacious, private shower stalls framed by walls of etched glass. Still, the wooden bench in the center of the room and the half-dozen hooks with towels along the back wall had a definite gym vibe.

I showered quickly and washed my hair, then put on grey sweats and a long-sleeved black t-shirt before joining Zachary on the couch. After I told him the story of what had happened, I asked, "How the hell is it possible to have the best sex of your life with someone you can't actually stand? And what possessed me to do that in the first place? Or him, for that matter. I'm not exactly his favorite person."

"Since there's actually a name for it, I guess it's not that uncommon," he said, tucking his bare feet under him.

"Oh God, there is, isn't there? I've always thought the whole concept of a hate fuck was gross, but I guess that's what I just did. I have to say though, it sure didn't feel like hate while it was happening."

Zachary asked, "What did you say to him afterwards? How did you leave it?"

"I'm not proud of this, or any of it, but I just got dressed and left without saying anything. The moment we finished, it became painfully awkward. We'd been yelling at each other right before it happened, so it wasn't like we were suddenly going to make polite conversation."

"Who initiated it, you or him?"

I had to think about that before saying, "I guess I did. He had me pinned to the floor, and all of a sudden I got really turned on. When he let go of me, I grabbed him and kissed him."

He said, "Sounds hot."

"It was, but now I don't know what to make of it."

"Don't overthink it. You were attracted to each other, you fucked, and that's that. It might be a bit awkward next time you see him at the races, but there's no reason to feel bad about this."

"You're right. It just threw me off." I glanced at him and asked, "Do you think less of me because I did this?"

"Of course not." He grinned a little and added, "You know, now that I think about it, I hated a lot of my customers, going all the way back to the trick who claimed my virginity. All of that probably counts as hate sex, so I'm clearly in no position to judge."

"Oh God," I murmured, then quickly added, "I don't mean to sound shocked. I just didn't know you lost your virginity to a client." My heart broke for him a million times over.

He nodded and admitted quietly, "It's fucked up, I know. So's the fact that I've never had sex with anyone who wasn't paying me."

"Never?"

Zachary shook his head. "I tried. I clumsily propositioned Chance once when he was single, but he thought I was kidding. Thank God. Like this living arrangement isn't awkward enough."

I whispered, "I wish things had been different for you, Zachary."

He tried to brush it off, and said, "Could have been worse." My friend picked up a red-and-brown-striped throw pillow and fidgeted with it. After a moment, he added, "You know, I don't usually open up about any of this shit, but you're easy to talk to. Thanks for listening, Jessie, and for not giving me a lot of unsolicited advice or trying to fix me."

"It'd be nuts for me to try to fix anyone when I can't even fix myself," I told him as I slid close and leaned against him.

Zachary put his head on my shoulder and asked, "Why do you need fixing? It seems like you have it all together."

If only that were true.

Chapter Three

Nana and Ollie (and their dogs) had gone out for Valentine's
Day brunch, so the big house was oddly quiet when I got home the
next morning. Two of her grandsons had been staying there when I
first moved in, but they'd both found love over the last year and
went off to live with their partners. Only I remained.

Most of the decorations were still in place from the night
before, but the peen forest in the foyer had apparently been heavily
logged. Only six stragglers were left behind, and they were
clustered around the front door, as if they were eager to go join
their friends. I assumed some of the guests had taken the other two
dozen balloon phalluses home, and grinned at the thought of cars
driving all over the city with giant dongs sticking out the windows.

The house smelled a bit like a funeral parlor, since Ollie had
had dozens of bouquets of flowers delivered to Nana for the
holiday. Roses, lilies, and things I didn't have a name for covered
almost every surface in the living room and kitchen. I had to move
three flower arrangements aside just to get to the huge chrome
espresso machine.

I needed caffeine desperately, so I sighed in frustration as I
spun dials and poked at the complicated device. After living in
Italy, Ollie claimed he couldn't function without espresso and
bought the professional-grade appliance, replacing the standard
coffee maker. He'd shown me how to use it more than once, but
somehow the nuances escaped me. The two-inch-thick all-in-

Italian instruction manual clearly wasn't going to shed any light on the situation, either.

My need for caffeine grew more critical with each passing minute, but the only thing I managed to brew was a headache. Chance and Finn had invited me to stay for breakfast after I spent the night on their couch, but I'd decided to head home instead of intruding on their family time. They'd been trying to make heart-shaped pancakes while Colt and Elijah, the teenagers in the household, chuckled and called their guardians corny. The boys were clearly enjoying every minute of it, though. It was all very cute, and very sweet, and in just those few minutes, I totally understood why Zachary felt like a third wheel, despite the Chinns' efforts to include him (that was the celebrity couple name Zachary and I had come up with for Chance and Finn, which the newlyweds found endlessly amusing).

I took off my hoodie and tossed it on top of the refrigerator since the counters were florist central, then tried to make sense of the staggering number of knobs and dials. As the water warmed somewhere inside the machine with a low rumbling sound, I actually managed to grind and dispense some coffee beans, which I caught in a little metal cup with a handle. Progress!

From there, I moved on to frothing the milk with a steam spigot that protruded from the right side of the contraption. It went remarkably well, and I felt pretty good about myself as the milk foamed up and tripled in volume. But I forgot to turn off the spigot before pulling the pitcher away, so it blasted the frothy milk all over the front of me. Well, crap. It wasn't all that hot, thank God, but Zachary had gone above and beyond in the friend department and had washed my clothes for me, and now my red t-shirt was once again ready for the laundry.

I jumped a bit as someone knocked on the door just as a thin column of steam shot up from the top of the machine. Shit, that wasn't right. I quickly turned some knobs, but all that did was produce a second steam column and a sharp hissing sound.

Whoever was outside knocked again. Damn it! I gave a couple knobs a final spin and ran to the front door. When I flung it open, Trigger was standing there holding my wallet and baseball cap, and his mouth fell open as he stared at me in abject horror.

"What?" I demanded, before realizing I was surrounded by giant balloon penises.

That wasn't what he was staring at, though. "Did you seriously not change your clothes from last night?"

"Dude, who are you, the hygiene police? Not that it's any of your business, but—" I'd been about to tell him they'd been laundered, but when I looked down at myself and noticed the huge splatter of white foam all across the front of me, I exclaimed, "Jesus! No! That's not what it looks like!" My words were partially drowned out as the hissing sound in the kitchen suddenly went up several octaves and a few decibels.

"What is that?" he yelled over the noise.

"The espresso machine. Shit!" I turned and ran back to the kitchen. Steam was shooting out of the appliance from half a dozen locations, and it had begun to shimmy and rattle, jerkily walking itself across the counter like a reanimated corpse. I dodged the steam as I quickly twisted every knob, but nothing changed.

Trigger appeared beside me and tossed my hat and wallet on top of the refrigerator. He then flipped a tiny, silver switch, pulled the sleeve of his sweatshirt over his hand for protection, and slid open a panel at the top of the machine. A mushroom cloud of steam billowed out, and the hissing and rattling stopped instantly. He turned to me and exclaimed, "What did you think you were doing here? You were running this machine way too hot, it could have exploded and killed someone!"

"Well, good news," I snapped, instantly annoyed, "I was the only 'someone' here, and I know you wouldn't have lost any sleep mourning my untimely demise!" I pushed my hair out of my eyes, and when my fingers came away with foam on them, I sighed and stripped off my t-shirt, balled it up and used a dry section to wipe my face and hair.

"You're a total and complete disaster," he told me. "If you can't even figure out a coffee maker, why doesn't your car explode every time you turn the key in the ignition? Or do you pay someone to work on your Matchbox car for you?"

"No, I don't pay anybody! And this thing is hardly a *coffee maker*, it's an Italian Rube Goldberg device! I defy anyone to actually produce a cup of espresso with this thing without first dedicating twenty years of their life to studying its unfathomable complexities!"

Trigger shot me a look, then turned to the machine. He flipped the little switch again, closed the panel, and spent about a minute doing various things before handing me a cup of espresso and grinning smugly. He'd drawn a precise Chevy logo on the top with foam. "I hate you," I said.

"I know."

I added a splash of cold milk and slammed down the espresso (which, damn him, was absolutely perfect), and as I put the little white cup in the sink, I said, "You worked at Starbucks, right?"

"Hell no. I worked at an independently owned coffee bar in North Beach when I was in high school." He turned back to the machine and wiped it down with a dish cloth. "You should really treat this better. It's the Ferrari of espresso makers, but I suppose a spoiled rich kid like you takes things like this for granted."

"I'm hardly a spoiled rich kid."

"No, of course not. You just live in a multimillion-dollar mansion in one of San Francisco's most expensive neighborhoods and have a five thousand dollar espresso machine."

"Jesus, was that thing really five thousand dollars?"

"More, probably. That's what it would cost wholesale." He tossed the rag into the sink and started to leave the kitchen as he said, "I brought your wallet back. It was under my shirt on the floor of the garage. I didn't use your credit cards or anything, but since you think I'm Satan's spawn and probably don't believe me, feel free to cancel them."

"Thanks for bringing it and my lucky hat back."

He glanced at me over his shoulder as he headed into the foyer. "Wow, you actually said thank you. I didn't know you had it in you."

"Bite me."

"Ah, there's the Jessie-with-an-i-e James I know and hate."

"You didn't hate me all that much last night, on the floor of your shop," I said, despite myself.

He stopped walking and turned to look at me, narrowing his dark eyes. "I made sure to turn on the fan in my garage this morning. I can only assume there was a serious carbon monoxide problem in there, because I must have been completely high to do that with you."

"Fuck you, Richard."

"Why are you calling me Richard?"

"Oh you're right, you're really more of a Dick."

Trigger rolled his eyes and headed for the door again. "If you want people to believe your fake ID, maybe stop acting like a child, Richie Rich."

"Dude, I'm the chauffeur. Do I really look like I belong in a place like this?"

He paused again and turned back to me. "Do you drive the limo that's parked in the driveway?" When I nodded, he said, "While you drive it, are you dressed like a big, pink Care Bear with a rainbow on your belly?"

"Funny! Do you have a problem with gay pride?" He frowned at me and I said, "Don't tell me, let me guess. You're probably so deep in the closet you can see Narnia. Am I right?"

"I what?"

"Okay, technically it was a wardrobe, but that's a type of closet so it's still funny."

"What the actual hell are you talking about?"

"Narnia."

"You're a total lunatic."

"And you're a closet case."

"Whatever you think I am doesn't change the fact that you drive around in a sparkly rainbow car and live in Rainbow Brite's dream home."

"So Nana's enthusiastic about gay rights. The world would be a much better place if more people were even half as loving and supportive as she is!"

"Nana?"

"My employer."

"Ah, so you work for and live with your wealthy grandmother. But you're not rich," he said with a smirk.

My voice rose as I asked, "Why do I bother trying to explain anything to you? You don't listen, you think you know everything, and you always have to be right!"

"Right back at you, every word of that!"

"Why the hell did you have sex with me last night when you obviously can't stand me?"

He put his hands on his hips and exclaimed, "Again, right back at you!"

"I have absolutely no idea!"

"Me neither!"

Trigger turned and stormed to the front door, which was kind of funny because he had to push several towering balloon dicks out of the way to reach it. He then swung the door open with such force that all the dicks skittered backwards in the updraft. For a moment he just stood there, holding the door open, glued to the spot. Then he slammed it shut and ran back to me.

I grabbed him in an embrace as he pulled me off my feet and crushed his lips to mine. He cupped my ass with both hands, and when I pushed my tongue in his mouth, he tasted so sweet. I stopped kissing him just long enough to strip off his t-shirt and sweatshirt and nipped his bare shoulder before kissing him again.

Trigger carried me to the curving staircase, his lips never leaving mine, and I wrapped my legs around him and rocked my hips to rub my swelling cock against his through our jeans. He sat me on the fifth step up and fumbled with my zipper before freeing my cock and going down on me. As he sucked me almost frantically, I moaned and arched my back, bracing my elbows on the stairs. But after a moment I regained enough of my senses to say, "Not here. I don't know when my employer's coming back."

"Where?" he asked, breathing hard as he looked up at me from between my legs.

"My room." I stumbled to my feet and pulled up my pants, then grabbed his shirts and his hand and ran up the stairs with him.

When I flung open my bedroom door, I blurted, "Holy crap!" The small room was completely filled wall-to-wall with what looked like all the missing nine-foot-tall dick balloons. The only open space was a two-foot square just inside the door, so I could open it.

"What the ever-loving fuck?" Trigger exclaimed.

"Dante, probably," I said, mostly to myself. "He owed me one after I called his brother and husband while he was wearing that giant tampon dress."

"What?"

"Nothing, never mind." I shut the door and towed him down the hall to what had been Dante's room, pushed Trigger inside, and locked the door behind us. I then threw his clothes on the floor and kissed him passionately.

He quickly maneuvered me to the bed and when I sat down on it, he fell to his knees in front of me. Once my cock was back between his full lips, his eyes slid shut and he actually murmured, "Mmmmm." Trigger stroked my shaft as he sucked me, and when I ran my fingers into his thick, dark hair, he looked up at me. When our eyes locked, my cock twitched and my breath caught.

No way was I going to last long, given how great that blowjob felt, and in just a few minutes I mumbled, "Oh God, I'm about to cum." I expected him to pull off me, but instead he redoubled his efforts, grabbing my ass as he took most of my length. I moaned as

I came in his warm, wet mouth, and he swallowed without hesitation.

I fell back afterwards, trying to catch my breath, but before I hit the mattress, Trigger was on his feet. A very obvious erection strained the fabric of his jeans, so it made zero sense to me when he pulled on his t-shirt and sweatshirt and headed for the exit. "Hang on," I called as he unlocked the door and slipped through it. Of course he didn't listen. Nothing new there.

I jumped off the bed and pulled up my briefs and jeans as I followed him. "What about you? Don't you want me to return the favor?" I called.

"I have to go," he mumbled. Seriously? He was actually turning down a blowjob? A team of scientists should be studying him, because he had to be the only male of the species to ever do that.

He left the house in a hurry, and I went downstairs and watched him through the living room windows, standing back a bit so he didn't see me. He was driving one of the cars I'd seen at his garage, a black '67 Impala. It was the same model used in the TV show Supernatural. I wondered if that was what he was going for.

Trigger opened the car door, stood there for a few moments, then slammed it and headed back toward the house. I waited for the knock, but a couple seconds later, I saw him retreating to the Chevy again. He did that four more times over the next minute. Conflicted much? I considered going out and getting him, but I was every bit as conflicted as he was, so I stood my ground.

Finally, he got in the car, started the engine, and took off like a shot, apparently looking to put some distance between us as fast as he could after finally making up his mind.

I sighed and dropped onto the sofa. I couldn't believe that had happened again. I also couldn't wait until the next time. The second half of that made me want to whack my forehead against the wall. I was wildly attracted to someone I couldn't stand. What was I supposed to do with that?

I was still contemplating my conundrum when Nana, Ollie and their dogs got home sometime later. Nana's huge, hairy, brown mutt was named Tom Selleck, for reasons that made sense only to Nana. He ran over and tried to climb on me as soon as he spotted me on the couch, while I flailed around and tried to fend off his advances. He'd always been way too interested in me, in every inappropriate sense of the word. But then, Diego Rivera, Ollie's little Chihuahua (who was dressed in a pink sweater with a red heart) yipped and left the room. Tommy immediately forgot about me and ran after the Chihuahua. It suddenly occurred to me that I was, through no fault of my own, in a gay love triangle with two dogs. That was so messed up.

"Hey there, Sweet Pea," Nana said, sticking her head in the living room. She was dressed in a tasteful pink Chanel suit, which she'd paired with red sunglasses with heart-shaped frames. "I didn't see you at first. Ollie and I bought a bunch of stuff to make a nice Valentine's Day dinner at home, since all the restaurants are so crowded today. Do you want to join us? We're about to start cooking, since my homemade marinara is best when it simmers for a few hours."

Nana meant well, but wow did that make me feel pathetic. My best Valentine's Day offer was to be a third wheel to my eighty-year-old employer and her honey. I got up and said, "Thanks, but I'm just about to go out, right after I run upstairs and change."

"Okay, Jessie, have fun! We'll save you some dessert," she called before heading to the kitchen.

I'd forgotten all about the wall-to-wall balloon dicks until I opened my bedroom door again, and spent the next few minutes untangling the giant junk Jenga and lining them up in the hallway. Dante (presumably) had really made an effort to fit as many dicks as he possibly could into my little room. The last one was tucked under the covers in my bed. I left that one there because it made me chuckle, then got dressed in a fitted pink button-down shirt and one of my best pairs of jeans. I figured I might as well sell the idea that I actually had somewhere to go by dressing nicely.

I grabbed my leather jacket and jogged downstairs, where I found Nana and Ollie in an embrace. She was giggling while he dotted kisses on her cheek. Oh yeah, definitely a third wheel. "Happy Valentine's Day, you two," I said. "See you later." They called goodbye as I headed to the front door.

When I got behind the wheel, I didn't start the engine right away. Instead, I rolled back my sleeves, pulled out my phone and found Zachary's name in my friends list. I texted him and asked if he wanted to hang out, but he wrote back: *Wish I could. I let the*

Chinns talk me into going to Six Flags in Vallejo with them. They wanted to do something special for the boys on Valentine's Day. We're about to get on a huge, puke-inducing roller coaster. Pray for me.

I grinned at that and thought for a moment, then messaged River, but he was on his way to go surfing at Fort Point. I scrolled through my contacts list, looking for single friends that wouldn't be with their boyfriend/girlfriend/spouse that day. Haley came to mind, but I didn't have his number and didn't know him well enough to ask to hang out anyway.

There were several more single guys in my contacts, but the problem was, I'd slept with them. Many of my friends started out as love interests. After I smothered each one in turn and we broke up, we usually remained friends. But there was something beyond awkward about sending a, 'hey, wanna hang out?' message to an ex on Valentine's Day. It just reeked of desperation, in addition to announcing loud and clear, 'why yes, I am still single and completely alone today'.

I chastised myself for always needing to be with other people in the first place. Why couldn't I just go to a movie or a restaurant by myself? What was so hard about that? Although, okay, doing either of those things alone on that particular holiday would make me look like an enormous loser. If I couldn't make myself go places on my own the rest of the year, I sure as hell couldn't do it on Valentine's Day.

After a while, I realized what I really needed to do was stop thinking about myself and turn my attention to other people. I drove across town to one of my favorite bakeries (ignoring all the happy couples on the sidewalks, the people carrying flowers or balloons for loved ones, and every other reminder of just how single I was). When I got to the bakery, I bought every cookie they had. I had them divide them up into ten little boxes of half a dozen each, and the rest went into three great, big, pink boxes. "Sorry to wipe you out on Valentine's Day," I told the woman behind the counter as she neatly arranged rows of heart-shaped sugar cookies in one of the containers.

She flashed me a smile and said, "Honey, don't you worry. We already have dozens more coming out of the oven in back. The shelves will start filling up again in just a few minutes."

Once my car was loaded with cookies, I stopped off at a drugstore and bought a pack of the type of Valentines kids took to school. They were Star Wars themed and painfully corny, which made me happy, and sported slogans like 'Yoda Best' and 'You R2 cool, Valentine' and 'I Chews You to be my Valentine' (that one featured Chewbacca, of course). My favorite had a picture of Princess Leia on it and said 'You're my only hope, Valentine.' I stuck one of the Leia cards to Sharona's dashboard.

I spent the next couple hours driving all over San Francisco, delivering cookies and Valentines to my friends. I saved a box for Nana and Ollie, which I'd deliver when I went home that night. Until then, those two needed a little privacy.

Next up were the three big boxes. The first went to a soup kitchen and community center for the homeless, where my friend Christopher Robin volunteered. I took box number two to the LGBT community center where I'd met Nana, and where I used to attend a weekly support group. For the final delivery, I drove to SOMA. The busy South of Market district included an eclectic blend of high tech companies, museums, shops, and the city's huge convention center, and was also home to my friend Christian's nonprofit.

The Zane Center offered free art and music lessons to the community, with an extensive program for children. I volunteered there one day a week. I had nothing to teach since the center obviously didn't include classes on rebuilding engines, so I mostly just helped out in the office.

I paused for a moment when I walked up to the building and admired the bright, colorful mural that adorned the entire façade. It made me happy every time I saw it. Christian had painted a whimsical playground and had included kid versions of everyone who'd helped get the center off the ground, including his husband Shea, his best friend Skye, Nana, and even me. A seven-year-old towheaded Jessie was off to one side, pushing a red toy car across the blacktop. Christian had totally nailed it.

The center was hosting a Valentine's Day open house, and it was crowded. For some reason, I'd thought it wouldn't be very busy so I hadn't signed up to work it, but I realized as soon as I walked in the door that I should have. Also, several of my closest friends were volunteering, and I could have just handed them their cookies in person instead of going to each of their apartments.

I paused at the wide front counter, put down the bakery box and took off my jacket. The reception area was sleek and industrial. It was also sunny, thanks to several large skylights in the three-story ceiling. Overhead, a graceful kinetic sculpture of a couple dozen mixed-metal wings spun slowly on the air currents. Skye had really outdone himself on the giant mobile.

Heather, one of the volunteers who worked at the reception desk, smiled and said, "Hi Jessie, glad you could make it. Want me to stash your coat behind the counter?"

I thanked her and handed over my jacket, then gave her a heart-shaped cookie before carrying the box to the long buffet table in the community room. The vibrant space was adorned with framed artwork made by students and furnished with colorful couches, tables and chairs. At the moment it also held a couple hundred people, mostly families.

Christian came up to me and said, "Aw thanks, Jessie, that was nice of you," and after I put down the cookies, he gave me a hug.

"I should have planned ahead and ordered more. I don't know why I thought the open house wouldn't be crowded."

"I'm surprised at the turnout myself. I thought a lot of people would have plans on Valentine's Day."

I took a good look at Christian as he was talking. He'd had a brain tumor and believed he was going to die when he founded the nonprofit, and the Zane Center was meant to be his legacy. Since then, he'd survived experimental drug treatments, brain surgery to remove the tumor, endless rounds of chemotherapy, and had come out on the other side with only a few lingering effects. His fine motor skills weren't completely back to one hundred percent, but he worked hard in physical therapy and had regained much of what he'd lost.

He'd regained something else as well, and I wondered if he realized it. When he'd thought he only had a few months to live, Christian had lost his spark. He went from being colorful and outrageous to sort of closing in on himself, and his outward appearance had reflected that. But that spark was back and shining like a beacon. One of the most obvious changes was the fact that he was growing his light brown hair into a wild, tousled mane, after losing it during chemo. Even more significantly, the light was back in his big, green eyes. He'd ringed them with guyliner and was dressed like a rock star with lots of silver jewelry, which also told me the old Christian was back and better than ever.

I felt a little prickle of tears at the back of my eyes, and crushed him in another hug. When I finally let go of him, he grinned and said, "What was that for?"

"I'm just happy to see you, Christian." There was a lot more to that than he realized and he probably thought I was nuts, but that was fine with me. "Now tell me what I can do to help. It looks like you're short a few volunteers."

"Dare could use a break, it'd be great if you took over the Valentine table for a little while. It's set up against the back wall," he said, pointing to his right. "Shea and I are about to run out and buy some more snacks, we planned for a crowd a third this size."

"On it," I told him and started to make my way across the room. My friends' alternative rock band was playing, and when I waved at them, Dev, the lead singer, gave me a salute. I greeted several more friends on my way to the craft table. All of them were helping out, and I felt like a shmuck for not having volunteered in the first place.

Dare was covered in a fair amount of glitter and seemed happy to see me. After we exchanged hellos, he rubbed his nose, transferring even more purple glitter to it, and said, "It's pretty self-explanatory. The kids can make cards for whoever they want, most are choosing to make them for their mom or dad. Since the paint and glue needs time to dry, they can hang them up over there if they want to." He gestured to his right, where three long, red ribbons had been fastened to the wall. Each was lined with clothespins and held dozens of colorful kid creations. The card station had clearly been popular.

After Dare left for his break, I took a seat behind the long folding table and tidied up the supplies a bit. There were watercolor paints and markers and dozens of little pots of glitter, which explained the sparkly tabletop. I gathered up the cardstock and patterned paper into neat piles and outfitted each of the four work stations with a few basic supplies, then sat back and waited.

The four yellow chairs lined up in front of the table were empty, but I wanted to be ready in case a second wave of kids descended.

After a while, I noticed a pair of big, brown eyes watching me. A little girl was peeking out from behind a concrete pillar, and when I waved at her, she waved back hesitantly. She seemed really curious about the art supplies and kept getting up on her tip-toes to take a look at what was in front of me, but seemed too shy to actually approach the table. I had an idea for putting her at ease and picked up a pair of safety scissors and a sheet of pink paper. I then stuck my tongue out in a pantomime of concentration, waved the paper and scissors around a lot and made a few wild cuts. The little girl cracked a smile.

I got up, carried my cut-out blob over to her, and knelt in front of her as I said, "I tried to make a heart, but it looks like a marshmallow." That made her smile again. "Do you think you could help me? Maybe if you draw a heart for me, I can cut it out and then it won't look so squishy."

The girl followed me back to the table, then hesitated again. She was wearing a pink knit dress over a pair of flowered jeans, and she twisted the hem of her skirt between her chubby little fingers for a few moments as she took a look at the art supplies. She was a pretty serious kid, which struck me as kind of unusual for a five- or six-year-old. But what did I know? It wasn't like I spent much time around children.

When she finally sat down, she picked up a crayon and knit her brows in concentration as she carefully drew a heart on a piece of red paper. When she handed it to me, I said, "Thanks for helping me. I want to make a card for someone special. Is there someone you'd like to make a card for?"

"My daddy," she said.

I took a look at the paper in my hand and said, "Wow, that's a perfect heart, thank you. I'm going to cut it out and put glitter on it, and then glue it to this purple paper. What color do you want to use for your card?"

I fanned out the stack of cardstock, and she pushed her long, dark brown hair out of her eyes and thought about it for a few moments before selecting a light blue piece. "Great choice! Blue's my favorite color," I told her.

"It's my daddy's favorite, too."

"Is your daddy here?"

She nodded. "I don't want him to see the card until it's done, so will you help me hide it if he comes over here? I told him not to because I wanted to make him a present, but sometimes grown-ups don't listen."

"For sure. Should we have a secret code if you see him coming, so I'll know it's time to hide the card? Maybe you can say pink puffy poodle, and then I'll throw myself on top of the table so he won't see what you're working on."

That earned me another smile. "You're silly," she said.

"Thank you." Her smile got a little bigger.

We both worked on our cards for the next few minutes. I carefully cut out the heart she'd drawn, and filled it in with a glue stick before sprinkling it with red glitter. Meanwhile, she folded the paper in half and concentrated on drawing a picture with markers. After I glued the heart to the front of a purple card, I wrote a message inside it and fanned it a bit to speed the drying process while idly scanning the crowd.

A tall, dark-haired figure halfway across the room caught my attention. His back was to me, and I admired the view. Tight, black jeans accentuated a perfect ass, and the black t-shirt he wore showed off big biceps, broad shoulders, and a narrow waist. Damn.

When he turned around and I realized it was Trigger, I was startled, but then I took the opportunity to study him as he looked around the room. He really was a handsome guy, with strong, even features, flawless olive skin, and lips so full and sensual they gave me a million bad ideas. In fact, when he wasn't saying anything, he was damn near perfect.

If I'd had the word 'perfect' written on a piece of paper, I would have crumpled it up and tossed it over my shoulder after what happened next. A tall woman with short, dark hair joined him, and I knew in an instant she wasn't just a friend. There was way too much of a connection between them, something in the way they interacted that gave the impression they just belonged together. His expression when he looked at her was tender, loving. She rested her hand on Trigger's shoulder and whispered something in his ear, and he tipped his head back and laughed while I considered throwing up in my mouth.

Ugh, I felt dirty. I absolutely hated cheaters. I wanted to go over there and punch him for using me to cheat on his girlfriend, but no way was I going to make a scene at Christian's event. Next time I saw Trigger though, it was going to get ugly.

I finally tore my attention away from the happy couple, who were taking turns whispering to each other and laughing, and pushed down my anger so I could focus on the little girl sitting in front of me. She was studying her drawing with a grave expression. She'd drawn an adorable picture of herself holding hands with her dad in a field of flowers. "It needs something," she said.

"Glitter?" I gathered several little plastic containers and lined them up in front of her.

"I don't want to make a mess," she said.

"Why not? Making a mess is fun. See?" I scooped a bit of glitter from the tabletop and tossed it in the air. Okay, so maybe teaching a kid to make a mess wasn't exactly on page one in the Responsible Adult Handbook, but there was something in her big, dark eyes that just made me want to see her smile. I had a feeling she didn't do nearly enough of that.

The glitter toss earned me a little grin. "It's in your hair now," she told me.

"Does it look pretty?" The grin turned into a smile and she nodded. "Well, good. As long as it looks pretty, then I'm glad it's there. Do you want some in your hair, too?"

She seemed to thoroughly weigh the pros and cons of that suggestion, and finally said, "I better not." Aw. It kind of bummed me out that she'd turn down glitter.

The girl picked up a red pen and drew a few hearts on the card, then said, "I think it's done. Do you have a en'lope?"

"I do. What color?" I fanned out the envelopes and held them in front of her, and she picked a blue one.

"I almost forgot to write inside." She picked up the red pen again and drew some squiggly lines inside the card as she recited, "Happy Val-times Day Daddy, Love, Izzy."

"That's a pretty name," I said. "My name's Jessie."

"My real name's Isabella, but everybody calls me Izzy."

She put the card in the envelope, drew another squiggly line on the front of it and slid off the chair. "Thank you, Jessie. I liked making cards with you."

"Remember when I said I was making mine for someone special?" She nodded and I handed her the card. "Happy Valentine's Day, Izzy. I made it for you." The big smile she gave me was the best thing ever. "There's a secret message inside, you can have your daddy read it for you. Do you see him? It's pretty crowded in here." She looked over her shoulder, then turned back to me and nodded again. "If you come to the Zane Center to take classes, maybe I'll see you again. I volunteer here."

"Daddy thinks I should learn to play a insta-ment. I told him I don't want to, but we came here today anyway. I'm happy we did, because you're nice. Plus, there's cookies." I smiled at her before she turned and dashed into the crowd. When she ran up to Trigger and handed him the blue envelope, my jaw dropped.

Oh my God, what a sleazeball! He was the worst kind of cheater, one with not only a girlfriend (or wife!) but also a kid. And I was a total moron. Even if I hadn't known he had a family, I *had* known he was a jerk, but I'd slept with him anyway. Who knew he'd stoop that low, though?

Izzy opened the card I'd made and held it up to show him the inside. I'd written, 'Will you be my Valentine? Check the box' and I'd drawn two squares next to 'Yes' and 'Ewww no, boys are extra super gross and have tons of cooties'. I'd also drawn a funny picture of a bug-eyed cootie.

When Izzy turned and ran back to me, Trigger looked to see who'd been helping his daughter at the card table. His eyes went wide when he saw me, and I scowled at him for a moment as I walked around to the front of the table. The little girl finally reached me, grabbed a pen and drew a big X in one of the boxes. She then held the card up to show me what she'd marked and yelled, "Yes!" I threw my hands in the air, jumped up and down, and whooped and cheered wildly. She laughed delightedly and ran back to her father.

Someone chuckled behind me and a familiar voice asked, "Yes what?"

I turned to Skye, who was balancing a plate of snacks on a red plastic cup, and said, "I just got picked to be the Valentine of the cutest girl in this place. You should be super jealous."

"Oh, I am."

Dare joined us and handed me a cup of punch as he said, "Thanks for watching the table. Was it busy?"

"No, just one little cutie." I glanced over my shoulder as Izzy and her parents disappeared into the crowd. I felt bad for that sweet child. She deserved so much better than an adulterous father.

*****

I stayed for the duration of the open house, helped clean up afterwards, and lingered as long as I could with the last of the stragglers. Skye and Dare took off for their reservation at a romantic restaurant, and Christian and his husband Shea invited me to their house for dinner, but it was still Valentine's Day (ugh, would it never end?) and I knew they'd rather be alone, so I told them I had someplace to be.

Since that wasn't even remotely true, after I left the art center I just ended up driving around for a while. For no real reason, I crossed the Golden Gate Bridge and circled the edge of the bay. I pulled over at a parking lot with a phenomenal view, sat on Sharona's hood and zipped up my jacket against the breeze.

The scene was straight out of a postcard, between the bridge to my right and San Francisco's iconic skyline sparkling in the distance against the purple early evening sky. Of course, the spot was hardly a secret, and plenty of other people were enjoying the view as well. I tried to ignore the fact that everyone else was on a date. Next Valentine's Day, I was definitely hiding in my room.

Despite myself, my thoughts drifted to Trigger and were accompanied by a sharp stab of disappointment. But why? I should be mad that he had a girlfriend, not disappointed. I had no business sitting around moping over him.

It still hurt, though.

*****

When I got home later that night, I put Nana and Ollie's box of cookies on the kitchen counter, beside the note they'd left me. I'd purposely stayed out late to give them some privacy, but the message said they'd decided to head to a pet-friendly B and B after dinner and would be back in the morning. Had I known, I would have skipped driving around aimlessly for hours and the lonely fast food dinner I'd eaten in my car.

The note also said there was dessert in the fridge, which perked me up a bit. I decided to change before indulging in something sweet and a whole lot of Netflix, so I went upstairs and consulted my flannel pajama collection. The pair I chose were green with a repeating pattern of skateboarding Santa Clauses, because they in no way reminded me it was Valentine's Day. Since I was going for maximum comfort, I also put on a pair of thick wool socks. I then scooped most of my hair into a messy ponytail, which rose from the top of my head like a whale spout, and because no one was around to judge me, I tucked my three-foot-tall stuffed polar bear under my arm. Before returning to the kitchen, I pulled the last balloon peen out from under the covers and added it to the row of stiffy sentinels in the hallway, so I could fall into bed when I came back upstairs.

Since I was planning to cocoon in front of the television and binge watch Supernatural until I passed out, I decided to gather plenty of supplies. I got a bag of popcorn going in the microwave, then checked to see what was for dessert. Even though living with Nana had taught me to expect the unexpected, I still jumped a bit when I opened the refrigerator.

What at first glance looked like a row of ejaculating penises proved to be bananas topped with one large strawberry each, dipped in either white or milk chocolate. They'd been assembled on wooden skewers, neatly arranged in a block of florist's foam to hold them upright, and apparently they'd each been topped with a dollop of whipped cream at some point. But as the cream deflated, it had trickled down the sides in a pretty unfortunate way.

I gathered a light and dark fruit peen, a bottle of water, and a couple cans of soda, to minimize the number of times I'd have to get off the couch. By the time I added the bag of popcorn, my hands were pretty full, so I scooped up the bear in a headlock under my arm. Then, just because, I also found a box of red licorice in the cupboard and added it to my bounty.

There was just one TV in the house, in the family room on the ground floor. It was accessible by a long hallway that extended off the foyer, past the curved staircase. I'd just started to head that way when someone knocked on the front door, and I muttered, "Really?"

Using my index fingers, I managed to get the door unlocked and turned the knob, then used my foot to push the door open. I'd expected it to be one of Nana's friends, since she knew half of San Francisco. What I most definitely had not been expecting was Trigger.

He was dressed in the same t-shirt and jeans he'd been wearing at the art center, plus a black leather motorcycle jacket, and he was fidgeting nervously with a bouquet of daisies. I was so dumbfounded that all I could do was stare at him. My appearance pretty thoroughly threw him off, too. His mouth actually fell open as he took it all in, his gaze lingering on the chocolate cocks as he knit his brows and tried to work out what he was looking at.

Trigger was the first to regain the power of speech, and mumbled self-consciously as he held up the flowers, "I, um, brought you these. Looks like your hands are full, though. What exactly are you doing?"

I stared at those pretty, white daisies for a long moment, and a lump formed in my throat. I turned and almost ran to the kitchen, and he followed me and said, "Shit, was this wrong? I debated the idea of giving flowers to a guy for a long time, but finally decided, why not? I guess I fucked up, though. Sorry. I didn't mean to offend you or anything."

Every surface in the kitchen was still covered with bouquets, and I had to push some aside with my elbow before I could put down the food and drinks. I perched the bear on a barstool, took a deep breath and got my emotions in check before saying, "All my life, I wished someone would give me flowers. But, God, not like this."

"Not like what?"

I'd been so mad at him, but now I just felt heartbroken as I turned to him and said, "Take those home and give them to your girlfriend, Trigger."

"I don't have a girlfriend."

"She was your wife? That's even worse."

He knit his brows and asked, "What are you talking about?"

"Do you think I'm blind? I saw you at the art center! And don't even try pulling that 'she's just a friend' bullshit! The connection between the two of you was off the charts."

"Please tell me you're not talking about the tall brunette with short hair," he said.

"Of course that's who I'm talking about!"

"Oh, gross!"

"What is?"

"Dude, that was my twin sister, not my *wife*! I don't know what the hell you think you saw between us, but just no!" He tossed the daisies in the sink and said, "You always assume the worst of me. Apparently you even think I'm capable of using you to cheat on someone! Why the hell would you sleep with me if you think so little of me?" I actually didn't have an answer for that, and when I didn't say anything, he turned and headed for the door.

"Why did you come here tonight?" I asked as I trailed after him.

He didn't break his stride as he said, "To say thank you for being so nice to Izzy. She talked about you all evening. I was also going to ask you out on a date instead of just taking you to bed, but why the fuck would you go out with me when you think I'm a total lowlife?"

I followed him out the front door, but stopped on the porch and called, "Trigger, wait."

He was halfway across the yard when he turned to look at me and said, "What if you're wrong? What if every single thing you've ever assumed about me isn't true? What if I didn't hit your car on purpose that day you wrecked, and what if I run a clean race every time I get behind the wheel? What if everything you think you know about me is all based on your own misperceptions?"

Trigger didn't wait for an answer. He got behind the wheel of his Impala, the big engine roared to life, and he pulled away from the curb. I stood on the porch and kept staring after him, long after he'd gone.

When I finally went back inside, I carefully arranged the daisies in a vase and cleaned up after myself around the kitchen. I then picked up the bear and the flowers and took them with me to my room. After the stuffed animal was returned to his chair beside the desk, I put the flowers on my nightstand and curled up on my side, hugging a pillow to my chest.

As I stared at those pristine white flowers, I replayed what I'd seen that day in its new context and realized he could be telling the truth. There was love and an undeniable bond between him and that woman, but there hadn't actually been anything romantic about it, not even a little. It was definitely the kind of connection twins might have. I'd jumped to conclusions, and yes, I'd assumed the worst of him.

What if I was wrong about everything else, too?

Chapter Four

I ended up sleeping in the next morning, since it had been almost daybreak before I managed to fall asleep. I kept replaying everything I thought I knew about Trigger over and over throughout the night, including every race I'd ever seen him run, and especially the one where I crashed. I'd been so sure I knew what happened, but the more I scrutinized it, the blurrier everything became.

When I finally went downstairs, Nana was on the warpath. "What's wrong?" I asked when I found her pacing and muttering to herself in the living room.

"I've had it with that asshole neighbor across the street," she said. "First he stole the gay pride flag from the front of my house, and now this!"

"What did he do?"

"He took that pretty balloon arch off my porch!"

"Are you sure it was him?"

"Well, who else would do it? When Ollie dropped me off this morning and I noticed it was gone, I looked across the street, and there was Humpington in his driveway with a smug grin on his face."

"I think his name's Huntington."

"Details," Nana said. "I went over there and asked him point blank if he'd taken the balloons, and he told me I should be glad he didn't report my penis decorations for public indecency. Then he told me to show some class! Can you believe the nerve of that steaming turd of a monkey humper? Tellin' me to show some class!"

"So, he didn't admit to taking them."

"No, but I'm sure he did, and as soon as he leaves, I'm gonna go over there and get some evidence! You'll help me, right, Jessie?"

"Of course. Let's try not to get arrested for breaking and entering, though. They might not let you out in time for your June wedding."

"Don't worry, we won't get caught."

I asked her, "Do we need backup? Should we call Dante? And where's Ollie?"

"Dante is a stick in the mud, he'll just try to stop us. My sweetie will be back soon though, so he can help. He's at an appointment at Christopher Robin's art gallery to work out some details for that upcoming new artists showcase, the one with his painter friend Ignacio Mondelvano. They're including a couple of Skye's sculptures too. Since his pieces are huge, they rented a warehouse for the show."

"Sounds like they're going all out."

"You don't know the half of it. Christopher Robin had the brilliant idea to turn the whole thing into a fundraiser and make use of that large space. He started a scholarship program for LGBT youth in the arts, so he thought it'd be fun to host a cross between a masquerade ball and a costume party so he can sell tickets and raise money. There's one part of the show he needs your help with, though."

"Sure, anything," I said.

"Your friend Chance is a stubborn one. He's a brilliant photographer, and this could be his big break since it's going to draw a lot of media attention. But because his husband and Christopher Robin's are cousins, he refuses to let Christopher show his pictures in his gallery. Chance keeps calling it nepotism and says Christopher wouldn't be interested in his photos if he wasn't family. Could you talk to him? Maybe he'll listen to you and agree to be a part of this show."

"I'll see what I can do."

Nana grinned and patted my arm. "I knew I could count on you."

We talked about the masquerade ball for a few more minutes, until Ollie got home and agreed to act as lookout. "We just gotta get in his backyard and check Humpington's trash can," Nana said. "I bet you anything my property is in there!"

Ollie (and the two dogs) lined up in Nana's front yard to watch for Huntington's return, and she and I circled around to the alley behind her neighbor's house. His back gate was locked, of course. I told Nana I'd hop the fence and check the trash, but she wasn't really the type of person to just wait on the sidelines. She slipped her stockinged feet out of her low-heeled pumps and said, "I'm going in. Give me a boost."

I knew better than to try to talk her out of it, so I laced my fingers together and she stepped into them and tried to pull herself up. That wasn't entirely successful, so she ended up climbing onto my shoulders, and then hoisted herself up and over the top of the seven-foot-tall iron fence. The fact that she was doing all of that in a Chanel suit actually proved to be her saving grace, because when she toppled over the other side of the fence, her skirt caught on one of the metal pickets and kept her from hitting the ground.

It also meant she was hanging there like a piñata, and I quickly scrambled over the fence so I could help her down. "Well, shit! I'm caught like a fish on a hook," Nana exclaimed. Just a moment after I got underneath her, the skirt tore completely in half, but I managed to catch her before she hit the ground. "Next time, we're bringing a ladder," she said as I put her down.

The skirt was still hanging on the top of the fence, and when I realized she was wearing a skimpy red thong under her pantyhose, I blushed and quickly looked away. She noticed my reaction and said, "Don't worry, everything's covered that's supposed to be." Um, yes and no. She hurried over to the garbage can, and when she raised the lid, Nana yelled, "Aha!" She reached in and pulled out a big handful of the deflated balloon arch. "Damn, look at all those limp dicks." She held up a shriveled penis balloon by the tip and shook her head. "They were all so perky, too! And now it looks like a hundred old guys went skinny dipping in January." Nana shuddered and dropped the balloons back into the can.

My phone beeped, and I checked the text message and told her, "Ollie says Huntington is pulling into his driveway. We have to go."

"I have half a mind to march up to Humpington and kick him in his dingle berries," Nana huffed. "Who does he think he is, stealing my personal property from the front of my house?"

"You have the evidence, so you could report it to the police," I said. "For now though, since we're actually trespassing, we need to go. Otherwise he'll be the one pressing charges."

Getting over the fence was even more graceless than it had been the first time. I gave Nana a boost onto the lid of the trash can, then hurried over the fence and tried to help her down. She used the same technique and tried to fling herself over the metal pickets, which produced the same result. Her jacket caught and tore, and Nana cursed like a sailor. "I really liked that suit," she huffed. "I'm adding that to Humpington's shit list." Nana unbuttoned the jacket and basically fell out of it into my arms. She'd been wearing a red satin bustier under the jacket, and I put her down quickly as my cheeks ignited.

While she put her shoes on, I climbed back up and freed the skirt and jacket from the fence. But when I tried to hand them to her, she said, "Those are no good to me now. My tailor won't be able to salvage them, not the way they tore through the fabric." She took off down the alley, working that thong, bustier and pantyhose, and I hurried after her.

The outfit covered as much as most bathing suits, but she still turned the head of every neighbor she encountered as we emerged from the alley and circled around to the street. Huntington was still out front, engaged in some sort of heated debate with Ollie, who apparently had been stalling for time. Both men stopped and stared when Nana came into view, and Ollie called, "Hubba hubba! You're a vision, hot stuff!"

The neighbor had a much different reaction, and turned red as he exclaimed, "Have you no shame, woman?"

"I must've left my shame in my other thong," Nana told Huntington, holding her head high. "And don't you be filing this away in your spank bank, you old pervert! You're not man enough for a woman like me!" The neighbor turned red and sputtered indignantly, and Nana added, "By the way, I know what you did, and you fucked with the wrong broad. Payback's a bitch, Humpington!"

"I'm sure I have no idea what you're talking about," he said.

"Oh, I think you do." She linked arms with Ollie and they marched up to her house as the dogs and I led the way. When Nana reached the top stair, she looked back over her shoulder at the neighbor and slapped her rear a couple times before going inside.

Nana said, "If Humpington got his shorts in a bunch over a couple harmless little dicks in a balloon display, just wait. He's about to have cocks up the ass!"

Nana, Ollie and I spent the next hour making plans and calling in reinforcements, and Cockstock was born.

*****

"Are you seriously getting paid for this?" Zachary asked as he dropped into the lounge chair beside mine and I handed him a big, pink, dick-shaped water bottle. It was the following Saturday afternoon, and I'd spent the better part of the week at Cockstock. I'd been appointed supervisor, since Nana and Ollie were busy planning the wedding and helping Christopher Robin put together his masquerade ball/new artists show.

"Basically. I've always been salaried, with the understanding that I help out where needed. This week, I'm needed in Peen Paradise."

"Where exactly did you find that shirt?"

I was wearing a yellow t-shirt that said, 'Got Cock?' but he was probably referring to the Hawaiian shirt I wore over it, which was bright red with a repeating pattern of smiling, cartoon cocks wearing leis and dancing the hula. "At a shop in the Castro. Almost everything they carry is penis-themed. Mr. Mario and I cleaned out half their inventory."

Zachary took a sip of the cocktail in the water bottle and said, "This is good. What is it?"

"Peen-a Colada." I grinned at him when he shot me a look and said, "Once the dick theme was established, Nana ran with it."

"I can see that." The front yard was designed to drive Nana's homophobic, dick-hating neighbor completely batty. Every balloon penis pillar from Valentine's Day graced the yard (they were holding up fairly well, though a couple looked like they could use a shot of Viagra). Strands of colorful penis lights hung from the palm trees, and dozens of rainbow-colored dildos were lined up all along the top of the waist-high wrought iron fence which fronted the lawn. The *piece de resistance* though was the 'fucking bronco'. Nana had found a mechanical bull shaped like a great, big penis at a party rental shop, and had it placed front and center in the yard.

To make sure nobody tampered with the display (or dicksplay, as we'd taken to calling it), she'd also hired every out-of-work go-go boy in the city to dance in the yard in ten-man shifts around the clock, both to add to the festivities and to keep an eye on things. Nana had told them they could wear whatever they wanted, but the vast majority had opted for the go-go boy uniform of sexy briefs in various styles and colors. They all seemed enthusiastic about the gig, not just because Nana was paying them generously, feeding them, and keeping the booze flowing, but because it was a damn good time.

The neighbor was continually red-faced and on the verge of blowing like Krakatoa every time he set foot outside. He'd thought of a dozen different reasons to call the cops on us over the course of the week, but we weren't breaking any laws. The music was kept down to make sure we weren't violating the noise ordinance, and even though showing an actual dick in public was verboten, phallic objects were A-OK.

When Zachary arrived, the fucking bronco was being ridden slowly and suggestively by two go-go boys who happened to be a couple. They were making out and putting on quite a show for the neighbor (and for the tourists who kept stopping by to take pictures). Five dancers were shaking their booties around the yard, and the rest were taking a break and flirting with each other while they cooled down with some dick-shaped popsicles. Nana had wholeheartedly embraced the theme, right down to the refreshments.

"It's like your own personal gay Club Med," Zachary said, smiling shyly when one of the dancers beamed at him.

"It is. The weather's even cooperating." It had been sunny and in the high sixties all week, augmented by outdoor heaters, which were dotted around the yard.

"How long are you planning to keep this up?"

"It's kind of open-ended. Nana said she'd keep Cockstock going until the neighbor apologized for tampering with her property, but I doubt he ever will."

"She's doing all this over some penis balloons?"

"Nah, the feud with this neighbor goes way back. When Nana hung a gay pride flag on her house, he complained to her about it. Big mistake. That put him at the top of her shit list. Then when the flag went missing, she blamed him. That was when she painted the big rainbow on the front of the house. She doesn't have any evidence he actually took it, but he'd been acting smug right after it disappeared, so I bet he's guilty. We did confirm he took the balloons, so given that, I'd say the chances he also nicked the flag are pretty high."

"Never mess with Nana," my friend said, raising a toast to her before taking a long draw from the straw jutting out of the water bottle.

"Truth."

"So, have you gotten any phone numbers?" Zachary tipped his head toward a blond guy across the yard with a perfect body, who kept checking me out. I had no idea why I was drawing his attention, given how drop-dead gorgeous the other dancers were.

"Not interested."

My friend raised an eyebrow at that. "Why not?"

"Because I can't stop thinking about Trigger," I admitted.

"That must have been quite a one-night stand."

"It was a little more involved than that." I told him about the next day's blowjob, followed by my misunderstanding at the art center and our argument when he showed up at my house. "I've been thinking about what he said all week. I had this negative opinion of him, and maybe it colored my perception. I was so sure I was right, especially about the crash. But the harder I look at it, the more I realize I really don't know what happened. It was over in a split second. What if I actually crashed into him?"

"What did the people watching the race say?"

"That it was Trigger's fault, but again, it was over so fast: the tire blew, our cars collided, and mine rolled. Right after it happened, one of the guys on the sidelines said Trigger swerved at my car and it looked deliberate, and everyone else picked up on that, me included. I became convinced I saw him coming at me. But who says that first witness was right? He hated Trigger because he always lost to him, so maybe he was quick to point the finger, just like I was. It wasn't like there was an impartial judge on the scene, or an instant replay. What if all of that was just mob mentality turning an unpopular driver into a scapegoat?"

"If that's true," Zachary said, "I feel bad for Trigger."

"Same here."

"So, what are you planning to do about all of this?"

"For starters, I'm going to apologize to him at the races tonight."

"Do you know he'll be there?"

"He should be. My friend told me Trigger hasn't missed a Saturday in the last year," I said. "I'm also planning to ask him out after I apologize, but I don't know why he'd say yes. He was absolutely right that I always assumed the worst of him. He must think I'm such a jerk."

"But hopefully he'll see he's wrong about you, just like you were probably wrong about him."

"I don't deserve another chance after all the accusations I made, but I hope he gives me one anyway."

"Good luck."

"Thanks." I took a drink from my cock bottle, then asked, "Want to come along tonight? Six will probably be there."

"That's a good reason to stay home."

"Why do you say that? He likes you, and I think it's mutual. I know he's young, but don't you want to see what happens?"

Zachary shook his head. "There's no point. A guy that age wouldn't be interested in a relationship."

"Is that what you want?"

He considered the question, and finally said, "I'm not sure, but I do know I don't just want casual sex."

"I wish you'd change your mind and come tonight, but it's your call."

The red-faced neighbor backed out of his garage just then. He glared at everyone in the yard as a vein bulged in his forehead and his Mercedes slowly rolled past. All the dancers smiled and waved pleasantly, including the two who were very nearly dry-humping on top of the cock-shaped mechanical bull. "Score one for Cockstock," Zachary said.

I grinned with satisfaction, then turned to face him and asked, "So, what's going on with you? What have you been doing this week?"

"I got a job."

"That's great! Why didn't you tell me sooner?"

"It's not that newsworthy. Finn's cousin Jamie hired me to work at his restaurant, I'll be a waiter on the lunch shift. I started training yesterday and it won't be hard to pick it up, since I waited tables in high school. Chance is still working at the restaurant too, and Colt and Elijah hang out there a lot, so it's basically an extension of home. I feel like a barnacle that's attached itself to Chance and Finn's life."

"I'm sure they don't see it that way."

"Maybe not, but I still feel like that." He took a long drink from his bottle, then added, "By the way, I spoke to Chance for you and he doesn't want to put his photos in the new artists show. He's convinced it's a pity thing and that Christopher Robin would never be interested if they weren't family."

I sighed and said, "He's such a brilliant photographer. Why would it be pity?"

"Chance doesn't believe in himself, never has."

I thought about it for a while, then asked, "How mad would he be if I borrowed some of his photos and put them in the show without asking?"

"Really, really angry."

"You think so?"

"Yup."

"But this could launch Chance's photography career! It's going to be a huge event, especially since it's paired with a masquerade ball for charity. Nana told me it'll get a ton of media attention. A national art magazine's even covering it!"

"Still."

I chewed my lower lip for a moment, then said, "If I bought a few of Chance's photos, then just happened to hang them in the venue where the event's taking place, maybe that'd kind of be a loophole."

"He'd still be mad."

"But probably less so than if I just went all kleptomaniac with his portfolio."

"True."

"I'm going to do it," I said, nodding resolutely. "Chance may be furious with me after that, but if his photography career takes off as a result, it's totally worth it."

He thought about it for a while, then said, "Yeah, okay. He really does need an opportunity like this. I'll help if you want."

"You shouldn't be too involved. It's one thing if he gets mad at me, but you guys are best friends and you're living with him, so I don't want my crazy idea to cause problems between you two. There is one thing you can do, though. You're more familiar with his work than I am, so you can tell me which photos I should buy. He must have thousands."

"You can't go wrong with any of them, but a couple weeks ago, he took some absolutely amazing photos around the city. Chance's dad was visiting with his foster son, this teenager named Cory. The kid has an interest in photography, so he and Chance took pictures all over San Francisco. When they came home and printed some of them, I was floored by what I saw. Chance let himself have fun and get a little experimental since he and Cory were just goofing around, and the results were stunning."

"Then that's what I'll ask for. This is going to be great!"

He looked worried, though. "I hope so, but people can be assholes sometimes. What if the critics at the art show have negative things to say about his stuff?"

"It's not just our opinion that Chance's work is brilliant, everyone who sees his photos thinks so, too. The people at the new artists show have to be able to see that."

"They'd better," Zachary said. "It would devastate him if they tore his work apart. A while back, he had an instructor in a junior college photography class who was overly critical of his work, and that alone was almost enough to make Chance quit photography. I think that teacher was just jealous of his talent, but Chance took the criticism to heart. Hopefully critics and reviewers at a show for new artists will be less cruel and petty, but you never know."

"It's sad that there are a few jerks in the world who build themselves up by tearing others down, but the vast majority of people aren't like that, thank God, and they'll love his work. I believe in Chance, and I have to believe this'll be a positive experience."

Zachary chewed his lower lip for a few moments, and then he nodded. "You're right." He pulled out his phone and clicked on Instagram, then handed it to me. "Cory got Chance to open an account and post his photos from their day out, I think they're all on here. Let's pick some for the show." I slid my lounge chair closer to his and we got to work.

*****

Since I never did talk him into coming to the races with me, I dropped Zachary off at Chance's house that night before continuing to the South Bay. The races had moved, just like every week, this time to a place I was unfamiliar with. We used over a dozen makeshift tracks in the most obscure, forgotten corners of the Bay Area, and it was never the same location two weeks in a row, to make it less likely for the police to find us.

The relatively new location was in the foothills to the east of Morgan Hill, so it took over an hour to get there. It was worth it though, because the track was outstanding: long, straight, and perfectly level. It was also in the middle of nowhere. That was vital. Not only did it mean our chances of being discovered were really slim, it also meant there was no chance of the general public getting hurt. It was one thing to risk our own lives, but endangering innocent bystanders was absolutely not okay.

Several guys were walking the strip with flashlights to check for rocks and debris when I arrived. I parked beside the other colorful, highly modified cars, my pulse already quickening with excitement. I popped my hood, then got out and immediately started talking shop with the nearest racer as I admired the long, sparkling row of machinery. There was a lot of variation. Both foreign and domestic models were well-represented, and they encompassed at least four decades. Each was its owner's pride and joy and so immaculately maintained that they gleamed like jewels, both on the outside and under the hood.

It was customary to do a mini car show before the racing got underway. I propped my hood open and felt a sense of pride as another racer admired my engine. Guys like me loved getting to talk about our cars, especially with other racers who could appreciate the blood, sweat, tears, and small fortunes we put into them.

Six pulled up beside me a couple minutes later and popped the hood like the rest of us. His engine in particular was enviable. He must have put well over thirty grand under the hood of his fire engine red Acura. As I leaned in and admired the pristine turbocharged V-8, he said, "Pleasure to see you, again, Rocket. Is your cute goth friend going to be joining you tonight?"

I grinned at that and straightened up to take a look at the tall eighteen-year-old. "Zachary's not goth, he just tends to wear a lot of black. And no, he couldn't make it this week." The hopeful expression on the guy's face drained away. I felt kind of bad for him, so I added, "You know, racing's not really his thing, so he probably won't come to most of these. But I happen to know he's going to be at a masquerade ball for charity end of next month. If you want, I can text you the link to the website so you can buy a ticket and conveniently run into him there."

Six eagerly agreed to that, and as we pulled out our phones and exchanged numbers, he grinned and said, "Meeting at the ball sounds a bit like Cinderella, yeah? Think a bloke like me has any chance of being your friend's Prince Charming?"

"Well, you certainly look and sound the part, and I think Zachary likes you. I'll be honest though, he's concerned about the 5-year age gap. I think he assumes guys your age are only interested in sex. If that's all you want, do me a favor and leave him alone, okay? Zachary's one of the kindest, gentlest, most genuine people I know, and he deserves so much more than just being treated like a piece of meat."

"I appreciate your candor," he said. "If it's any consolation, I'm not even sort of your typical eighteen-year-old, and I'd never treat anyone like that, not in a million years."

I hit send on the text with the event's website and told him, "In that case, I wish you luck."

"Thank you. Now please tell me you'll go head-to-head with me in a race tonight. I think you'll give me a decent run for my money."

I returned the phone to my pocket and smiled at him. "Think so? I think I'll leave you and this nice, shiny money pit in my rearview mirror."

He laughed and sounded very American when he exclaimed, "Oh, it's on!"

Chapter Five

Racing Six was the highlight of my evening. He was the only person I didn't beat in any of my five heats, but I still loved it. The race was incredibly close, which was a huge adrenaline rush, and he barely inched me out right at the end. Afterwards, we joked around and made each other laugh, and he promised me a rematch the following week. He seemed like a good guy, and I found myself rooting for him and Zachary.

My only disappointment that night was the fact that Trigger was a no-show. Kenji and a couple other racers even commented on it, since he'd been turning up like clockwork every Saturday. It made me worry about him.

The races wound down around one a.m. On the way home, I decided to swing past Trigger's shop just in case he was working late again, both to make sure he was okay and to apologize. Sure enough, a light was on in the garage when I parked out front an hour later. Trigger was under the hood of his Impala, once again dressed in a black tank top and worn-out Levi's. When I knocked on the door, he didn't respond. I gave it a little push and it swung open, setting off the chimes. He still didn't turn around, and after a moment I noticed the cords from a pair of earbuds trailing down the sides of his neck.

I stepped inside and chewed my lip for a few moments, waiting for him to notice me. I even waved my arms around when he turned his head to the side. Still nothing.

Trigger started singing and shaking his hips to an old Bob Seger song, and it was so sexy that I could barely stand it. He had a great voice, but the way he moved his ass was what really riveted my attention. When he straightened up and started belting out the chorus to 'Katmandu', using a wrench as a microphone and putting his whole body into it, I really wanted to cross the garage and join in. I knew he'd stop singing though, the moment he spotted me.

Instead of interrupting him, I decided to come back the next day and turned to leave. I'd just put my hand on the door when Trigger exclaimed, "What the actual fuck!"

I turned toward him as he pulled out his earbuds, and I mumbled, "Sorry," because I didn't know what else to say.

"How long have you been there?"

"A minute, maybe. I tried knocking. Then I tried flagging you down. You should start locking your door, an axe murderer could wander in here."

Trigger's expression went from startled to slightly amused, and he asked, "Is that why you're here, to axe murder me?"

"Obviously. Can I borrow an axe?"

"I already loaned mine out to a guy in a hockey mask, but I think there's a plastic takeout knife by the sink."

"Not quite as good."

"What are you actually doing here?" He wiped his hands on a clean shop rag, even though they didn't look dirty.

"I came to apologize," I said as I took a couple steps toward him. He in turn stepped around the front of his car and took a couple steps backwards. "What are you doing?"

"Maintaining a safe distance between us."

"Why?"

"Because if you get within five feet of me, we'll probably start fucking."

I took two steps forward, and he took two more backwards. "You're going to hit the wall pretty soon. Then what?"

"I'll attempt to burrow my way out of here."

I kept advancing, slowly. When he reached the wall he started moving along it, away from me. "Good thing you abandoned the burrowing idea," I said.

"I just cut my nails. I never would have made it."

"Why weren't you at the races tonight?"

"Because I thought you might be there." We were still slowly circling each other, and finally came to a stop with the trunk of the Impala between us.

"And you're so pissed off at me that you couldn't stand the thought of seeing me?"

"I wasn't nearly pissed off enough. That was the problem," he said.

"What does that mean?"

"It means that if I'd gone to the races and seen you there, I might have ended up sleeping with you again, and it's really fucking stupid to keep doing that with someone who thinks so little of me."

"But I don't. In fact, I was looking for you tonight to apologize to you. I did a lot of thinking over the last week, and I realized I could have been wrong about everything, about all those things I accused you of. Like you said, I never gave you the benefit of the doubt, and I should have."

Trigger looked surprised. "You seem so stubborn. I never thought I'd hear you say any of that."

"I'm stubborn when I know I'm right about something. But I haven't been right about you, have I?"

"I swear to you I didn't hit your car on purpose," he said. "I was definitely fishtailing when your tire blew, but that's not what caused the accident."

"I believe you."

"Finally."

I slowly circled around the back of the car, and he stood his ground. "Apologizing to you was only half the reason I hoped you'd be at the races tonight."

"Did you want a rematch?"

"No, not really. I don't always have to be on top." I grinned a little when I said that.

"So, what was the other reason?"

I stopped right in front of Trigger and looked up at him. "I wanted to ask you out. Or, well, in. Will you come over next Friday night and let me cook you dinner?"

Now it was his turn to grin. "Can you cook?"

"Yeah, as long as you like Italian. The woman I work for has a cooking show on cable TV. Mostly, she just cusses a lot and accidentally makes things look like a dick. But I've been helping her out for a while now, and in the process I've actually learned my way around a kitchen."

He smiled at me. "So, you can make dick-shaped Italian food."

"Basically. It's a funny thing. She doesn't set out to do it, but maybe she always has dicks in the back of her mind or something and it comes out subconsciously."

Trigger watched me for a moment, then said, "As fun as that sounds, we shouldn't go out."

"Why not?"

He turned partly away from me. "Even though I'd intended to ask you out on Valentine's Day, I thought afterwards that it was probably a good thing we ended up arguing. This would be a mistake."

"What makes you say that?"

"The fact that it was so intense when we had sex. I think I'd have a really hard time keeping my distance from you."

"And that's the goal? Keeping your distance?" Trigger nodded, and I said, "So, you don't want to start anything with me because we have amazing chemistry."

He frowned and said, "It sounds stupid when you put it that way."

"Hey, you came up with it, not me."

"Asking you out was impulsive. I don't date, so I really don't know what I was thinking there."

"You don't?"

"You already know I'm a parent, and my daughter comes first," he said. "If I dated, that would mean bringing people into Izzy's life who she'd probably get attached to, and when they eventually broke up with me, they'd break her heart in the process."

That sounded an awful lot like he was finding excuses for not getting involved with anyone, but I didn't call him on it. Instead I said, "Sounds lonely."

Trigger sighed and looked over his shoulder at me for a long moment, then headed toward a door at the back of the shop. "I need another drink. Do you want one?"

"Another? Sure. What are we drinking?" I asked as I followed him.

"Whiskey now. I finished off the beer before you got here."

The back room was part office with a cluttered desk, cluttered shelves, and a rickety-looking swivel chair, part kitchen with a mini fridge and small counter with a coffee maker, and part bedroom with an unmade twin bed. Beyond it, another door revealed a small restroom. "Do you live here?" I asked as he pulled a bottle and two coffee mugs from the shelves.

"No, I just spend the night here a couple times a week, after my daughter goes to bed. I tend to work really late, obviously, and sometimes I'm too tired to drive home."

"Where's home?"

"The other side of Bernal Heights. Izzy and I live with my sister, mom, and grandmother."

"You and four women. That's a lot of estrogen."

He poured some whiskey into a mug and handed it to me with a crooked grin. "Now you understand why I need this man cave."

After he poured a drink for himself, I raised a toast and said, "Cheers," before slamming it down. I didn't love the taste, but it left a nice, warm sensation in my belly. He tossed his back too before refilling our mugs.

On the shelves to my right, amid stacks of manuals and papers, were several family photos in wooden frames, and I wandered over to take a look at them. Unlike the rest of the room, they'd been dusted recently. There were a few snapshots of Trigger as a kid with a man I assumed was his dad, and the rest were all pictures of Izzy, spanning her infancy to the present day. There were photos of her with Trigger, his sister, and a couple older women with dark hair and bright smiles, but there was someone notably absent, and I said, "What happened to Izzy's mom, if you don't mind me asking?"

"She left."

"Left? What do you mean?"

"I got Candice pregnant our senior year of high school, and let's just say having a kid didn't fit into her plans. She gave birth two weeks before she left for Princeton, gave me full custody and never looked back."

"She didn't keep in touch?" I asked.

"Izzy's mom hasn't seen her since the day she was born. I think Candice likes to pretend the pregnancy never happened. She didn't stay in touch with me either, but we have a mutual friend, and he told me Candice never mentions her daughter. She was always really focused and ambitious, and after she graduated from Princeton, she went on to medical school on the east coast. By now, I guess she's moved on to her residency."

"She sounds cold."

"She's not. It's basically the same as a woman giving her baby up for adoption, only in this case instead of giving her to strangers, she gave Izzy to me."

I was a bit surprised he'd defend her, and asked gently, "Were you in love with her?"

"She was my best friend, so I did love her, but not in the way you mean."

I sat down in the office chair and took a sip from my mug before saying, "Now I get why you're so concerned about Izzy getting attached to people who might take off on her."

"Exactly."

"Does she miss her mom?"

Trigger sat down on the narrow bed and said, "In a way. I mean, Candice is a complete stranger to her, so I guess what she misses is the idea of a mom. She sees her classmates with their mothers and wonders why she doesn't have that. Izzy knows Candice is out there somewhere, and that she's chosen not to be a part of her life. I've always been careful not to talk about her, but my daughter's overheard my family saying things. My mom hates Candice and doesn't try very hard to conceal it. All of that's confusing for a kindergartener."

"I can imagine."

Trigger and I finished our drinks and he poured us another. Since each was probably the equivalent of two shots, I was definitely starting to feel a nice buzz. "She's still talking about you," he said after a while. "I don't know what you said to my daughter at that open house, but you made a huge impression. In fact, thanks to you, Izzy agreed to let me sign her up for music lessons and is looking forward to going back to the art center."

"Kids love me. I think it's basically because I'm Peter Pan. I never grew up, so they accept me as one of their own," I said with a grin. "I'm glad to hear she's going back, it's a terrific place. A good friend of mine runs it."

"Christian George? I wasn't sure what to make of that guy. He looked like a wanna-be rock star and seemed really young to be running such a big nonprofit."

"Christian's one of the greatest people you'll ever meet, and he has a heart of gold. He's smart, too. He brought in a lot of terrific people, both to run the business end of things and to teach classes. I'm incredibly proud of him. How often do you get to watch someone so young accomplish so much?"

"I feel a bit better about sending Izzy there now, since you obviously have a high opinion of him."

I smiled at Trigger and said, "Sounds like you're pretty overprotective."

"Of course I am. It's my job to look out for my little girl."

I thought that was touching. After a moment, I said, "Tell me something, Trigger."

"What do you want to know?"

"Your name. I only know your racing moniker."

He said, "I'll trade you. My name for yours."

"You already know mine, you've seen my driver's license."

"I saw what you changed it to. I want to know your birth name."

"Why?"

"I'm curious."

I frowned at him and asked, "Do you own this shop?"

"Yeah. Why do you ask?"

I reached to my right and rested my hand on an unopened stack of mail. "All I have to do to find out your name is flip over this envelope. I have no incentive for telling you my original name."

"Please? I promise I won't make fun of it."

"You wouldn't be able to keep that promise, once you found out what it was."

"Oh, come on. How bad could it be?"

"Really incredibly horrible."

"Now I'm dying of curiosity."

I picked up the business-size envelope and placed it face-down on my lap with a teasing grin. "I'll miss you when you die."

"Damn it, my name was my only bargaining chip!" He put down his mug, got up and crossed the three feet between us before dropping to his knees in front of me. As he captured my wrists, he said, "Please? Just tell me. I'll never use it, and I'll never make fun of it, I swear."

He was so handsome, and as he looked up at me with those big, dark eyes I had a powerful urge to kiss him. I fought it though, and instead leaned forward and rested my forehead against his. After a moment, I murmured, "What were we talking about?"

"Names. Yours and mine."

"Oh. Right."

"I got you drunk, didn't I? Sorry, that wasn't intentional."

I sat up a bit and looked at him. "I'm not that drunk, just nicely buzzed. And you know you have to let go of me eventually. When you do, I can pick up almost any envelope or sheet of paper in here and read your name, so I have zero incentive for telling you mine."

"Tell me anyway."

"Go out with me and I will," I said with a smile.

He rubbed my wrists with his thumbs and said, "I'm going to. I shouldn't, because I really think this might turn into more than I bargained for, but I'm way too attracted to you to deny myself at least a little time with you." Trigger let go of me and picked up a small notepad and a pen from the desk. He handed them to me, took the envelope, and said as he looked in my eyes, "Trade your name for mine, not because you have to, but because you want to. Write it on a piece of paper and hand it to me when I give back the envelope."

"This is really important to you."

He nodded. "It's not just because I'm curious. You came here to tell me you were wrong about me. Show me you believe that. I've promised not to laugh or make fun of your name. I want to know you trust me."

I watched him for a long moment. Then I wrote three words, tore the sheet off the pad, and folded it in half. As I returned the pen and notepad to the desk, I said, "I was teased mercilessly for this name all throughout my childhood. My dad's a Baptist minister, so my brothers and sister and I were all given Biblical names, but I got the worst of the lot. I changed it as soon as I was out on my own. Funnily enough, there's also a Jesse in the Bible, but I didn't think of that when I renamed myself. I just liked the name, especially the way I chose to spell it. It feels right to me, like this is what I should have been called all along."

I handed him the slip of paper, and he handed me the envelope. I watched him closely as he unfolded it, and I expected him to burst out laughing. But instead he said gently, "That's a pretty shitty thing to do to a kid. I'm sorry you had to grow up with that. It was an absolute guarantee you'd get teased."

"That showed remarkable willpower. I can't believe you didn't crack up."

He handed the note back to me. "I'm a dad. It's absolutely heartbreaking when my child gets teased. I'd do anything to protect her from the cruelty of other children, but your parents pretty much set you up for it. No way am I going to add to all you must have endured by laughing at you."

That meant more to me than he could ever imagine. I looked at what I'd written in my tiny handwriting and said, "Those names remind me not only of being teased mercilessly, but of a family that doesn't want me anymore. I'm so glad I don't have to be Jehosaphat James Jorgensen ever again." I crumpled the paper and tossed it into a nearby trash can, and embraced Trigger as a lot of emotion welled up in me. "I'd gotten so used to being laughed at. That's literally the first time in my life that someone my age didn't instantly treat my name like a big joke."

He kissed the side of my head and hugged me. "I didn't realize how much was behind your name change. I'm sorry I pushed."

"It's okay."

After a few moments, he said, "Your turn."

I let go of him and turned over the envelope in my hand. Then I grinned and asked, "How do you pronounce your last name?"

"Kah-hall-lay."

"It says, 'To the parent or guardian of Isabella Kahale.' I think it's from Izzy's school."

"Oops." He grabbed a few more envelopes from the desk and quickly rifled through them, then handed me one.

I read out loud, "Malakai Kahale."

"I just go by Kai."

"That's a beautiful name. Is Kahale Hawaiian?" He nodded and I asked, "Have you ever been there?"

"I was born on the Big Island and spent the first part of my life in a small town outside Hilo. But when my dad died, my mom moved us to San Francisco to live with her mother. I was fifteen when we came here."

"I'm sorry about your dad."

"Thanks."

"That must have been some pretty extreme culture shock, moving here after growing up in a small town in Hawaii," I said as I put down the envelope.

"It was like moving to a different planet."

"Do you think you'll ever move back?"

"No. My family's here now and I want to stay close to them."

I looked around at the wood-paneled walls and asked, "How long have you had this garage?"

He sat back on his heels and said, "I bought it when I turned eighteen."

"Wow. How'd you manage that?"

"My dad left me some money. He was the person who taught me to work on cars, they were his passion and they became mine, too. The Mustang I race was his prize possession, by the way. He wanted it to be a part of my inheritance, so my mom paid a fortune to ship it to the mainland when we moved here, way more than the car was worth at the time, actually. Anyway, I turned eighteen and got the rest of my inheritance three months before Izzy was born. I thought about how I could support myself and my child and decided to buy a garage, because fixing cars is the only thing I'm good at. I'm a shitty businessman though, and I've had a hard time getting it to turn a profit. I've had some pressure to sell it, but I can't give up. It means way too much to me." He stopped talking and grinned self-consciously. "That was a long answer to a simple question. Sorry."

"Was the garage named Kit's when you bought it?"

He shook his head, and then he moved back to the bed, pushed off his sneakers, and stretched out on his side. "I named it after my dad. His real name was Keikilani, but everyone called him Kit. Don't ask me how his family got that from his name."

"Is Malakai a Hawaiian name?"

"No, my mom just liked it."

I said, "I'm glad I have something else to call you now besides Trigger. Did you name yourself after a horse on purpose?"

He chuckled at that. "That word has other contexts too, you know. Why does it have to refer to a horse that's been dead for fifty years?"

"Good point. How'd you pick your racing name, anyway?"

"The first time I raced go-karts as a kid, my dad said I took off so fast that it was like someone had pulled a trigger. He started the nickname, and it just felt right to use it for racing."

"It sounds like you and your dad were really close."

"We were," Kai said. "I could tell him anything."

"What happened to him?"

"He died of stomach cancer at forty-three, a month and a day after being diagnosed with it. He showed symptoms for more than a year, but he just wrote it off as indigestion. He was always popping those chalky antacid tablets. My mom kept bugging him to go to a doctor, but he was a hard worker and didn't want to take time off for something he thought would just go away on its own. By the time he finally went in, it was already in stage four."

"I'm so sorry, Kai."

"It was a long time ago." I could tell it took a lot of effort for him to keep his emotions in check as he said that.

After a pause, I said, "Thank you for opening up to me. I didn't expect that. You always struck me as the strong, silent type."

"You just never bothered to talk to me. I mean, I'm not blaming you. I didn't talk to you either. I tend to keep to myself at the races."

"I noticed."

"I will say, normally I'm not this chatty. I've had a lot to drink tonight."

I asked, "How much beer did you have before I got here?"

"A six-pack."

I crossed the room and sat on the edge of the bed. "I know this isn't how you usually spend your Saturday night. Will you be back at the races next weekend?"

"Will you be there?"

"Does that change your answer?"

"No. I was just curious."

I said, "I'm planning on going."

The whiskey was making me bold, so I reached out and lightly stroked his hair. He watched me for a while before asking, "Does the offer of dinner Friday still stand?"

I nodded and told him, "I would have asked you out for tomorrow night, but the kitchen will be in use. Nana always makes a big Sunday dinner for the family. Actually, you should join us if you want to, it's a lot of fun."

"Dinner with your family is probably more than we should be aiming for at this point. If we're going to start dating, I have to take this slow. I meant what I said about letting Izzy get attached to people who might not always be around."

"I'm fine with taking this slowly," I told him. "Just so you know though, I'm not related to Nana, so it's not exactly like I'm inviting you home to meet the folks. I love that the Dombrusos make me feel like I'm part of their family. But my real family disowned me when I came out, so getting to introduce you to my parents will never actually happen."

"I made a lot of assumptions about you when I saw where you live. I'm sorry I accused you of being a spoiled rich kid."

"What I actually am is a preacher's son from a hick town outside Fresno. I grew up sharing a bedroom with two brothers in a sagging, seventy-year-old farmhouse behind our church. Nana's world and mine couldn't be more different," I said. "But you don't need to apologize. I made worse assumptions about you." His eyelids were getting heavy, and I said softly, "I'm going to call a cab and head home, you should lock up behind me. I'll come back for my car in the morning, since I'm feeling that whiskey."

"Just sleep here. I can make room," he said, sliding over on the mattress until his back was against the wall.

"Really?"

"Spending the night together probably contradicts the whole taking it slow thing, but it's really late. And I am just talking about sleeping, not sex, since we're both kind of drunk."

"Okay. I'm going to go lock the door, I'll be right back. It totally freaks me out that you leave it unlocked when you're here alone."

He grinned at me and said, "What with the axe murderers and all."

"Aren't you worried about getting robbed?"

"Have you seen this place from the outside? Who would rob it?"

I returned to the garage, locked the side door, checked that the sliding doors at the front were secured, and turned off the lights before returning to the office. As I closed the connecting door behind me, I asked, "Do you have employees who are going to show up for work in the morning and find our sleeping arrangement odd?"

"No. I work alone."

Even after I turned off the overhead light, it wasn't very dark. There was one window in the room, high up on the wall beside the bed, and its blinds didn't fully block the glow of a nearby streetlamp. I took off my sneakers and hoodie and emptied my pockets before sliding under the covers with Kai. "Switch places with me," he said. "I don't want you to fall out of this tiny bed in the middle of the night."

I climbed over him and he put his arm around me as I settled in with my head on his chest. "Are you going to be okay sleeping like this?" I asked. "If not, I can go sleep in the Impala or something. Those things have huge backseats."

"Don't go anywhere," he murmured. "This feels so good. I've never spent the night with anyone before, and it's even better than I imagined."

"Never?"

He shook his head. "Candice and I were in high school when we dated. It wasn't like our parents would have let us have a sleepover. For good reason, obviously."

"What about the people you've dated since then?"

"What people? I told you I don't date."

"I thought you meant you don't get serious with anyone. What about dating casually?"

"I haven't been dating at all. Besides what I said before about bringing people into Izzy's life, I also have my hands full, between raising her as a single dad and trying to run a business. Dating hasn't been a priority."

"If you don't date, what do you do?"

"I occasionally hook up with random people I pick up in bars. That's about it."

I thought about that, then said, "Asking me out was kind of a big deal for you, wasn't it?"

He grinned a little. "You could say that."

"I'm sorry I messed it up so badly."

"We both messed it up."

I took his hand. "What made you ask me out in the first place?"

"After we slept together, I couldn't get you out of my mind. An attraction that strong doesn't exactly come along every day."

It really didn't. "I have to ask. If you're gay, how did Candice fit into the picture?"

"Back then, I didn't really know what I was. I mean, I knew I was attracted to guys, but I hadn't ruled out the possibility of being bisexual. Like I said, Candice was my best friend, but she wanted us to be more than that, so we gave it a shot. We only dated for two weeks and went to the winter formal together, which was when we both lost our virginity and Candice got pregnant. I won't say it was a mistake, because I wound up with my beautiful daughter and she's the best thing that ever happened to me. But trying to turn our friendship into a romance was just never going to work."

I mulled that over before asking, "If we get to the point where you want to introduce me to your family, how will they feel about you dating a guy?"

"They'll be fine with it. I've always been open about my sexuality, and they're totally supportive."

"You're lucky."

"I know." He ran his fingertips along my jaw and said, "I wish you'd gotten the same response from your family."

"Me too, but I always knew how it'd go over. I sat through many of my dad's sermons on the sins of homosexuality while I was growing up. That's why I waited to come out until I was nineteen. I even asked one of my friends if I could sleep on his couch and packed my stuff before I told them, and then my family completely lived up, or down, to my expectations."

Kai began to lightly rub my back, and after a while he asked, "Would it throw off this just-sleeping-together-platonically thing we're doing tonight if I kissed you?"

I grinned at him. "I can control myself if you can."

He brushed his lips to mine, and I cupped his face in my hands and deepened the kiss a little, but kept my libido in check. We kissed tenderly, taking our time, and I closed my eyes and let myself get lost in it. I couldn't remember the last time I'd kissed just for kissing's sake, and not as a prelude to or a component of sex. I'd really been missing out.

Chapter Six

I woke up alone in the little bed the next morning, but there was a note taped to the wall, which simply said: *Be right back.* I used the restroom, put on my shoes and jacket, and poured a cup of coffee before wandering out into the garage. The Impala was gone, and I checked out the second one, which he was using for parts. Then I slid under the open hood of his Mustang and studied his engine configuration, mostly for something to do.

A garage door opener whirred to life a couple minutes later, and after one of the rolling doors rattled open, the Impala pulled into its usual spot. "I'm being nosy, I hope you don't mind," I called when Kai got out of the car with a pink bakery box.

"I don't." He reached back into his car through the open window and hit a remote, and the door rattled shut again. His hair was damp, and he'd put on clean clothes.

"You've done some clever things here," I said, still studying the engine. "A lot of these parts look like they've been rebuilt or retrofitted, so I doubt you're sinking a ton of money into it, but you're getting a hell of a lot of power out of this thing."

"Spending a lot isn't an option. Most of my parts come from the salvage yard."

"In that case, you must be a genius of a mechanic."

"Nah, I just really understand this car. I've been working on her since I was old enough to hold a wrench. My dad was great about letting me learn by doing."

"You're being modest," I said. "This took a lot of ingenuity. So many street racers think it's just about spending a fortune on a car to make it go faster, but you're proving them wrong."

He came up behind me and looked over my shoulder. "Oh believe me, I'd love to have an extra few grand to spend on upgrades, but that's never going to happen. Whenever I win a race, a portion of the prize money goes back into the car, although most of my winnings go toward Izzy's and my living expenses."

"Is that why you race, because you make money at it?"

"That part's awesome, but no. Everything else I do is for my daughter, but this is the one thing in my life that's just for me. It's pretty much the only time I get to act my age and cut loose. I can't even tell you how much I need that outlet."

"I get it."

He grinned a little and said, "I just realized the advantage of dating a fellow racer. You probably do understand, in a way other people never will. My family gets so pissed off whenever they find out I've been racing. They love to lecture me about how dangerous it is, and they're always trying to get me to quit. They don't understand what it means to me."

"That must get annoying."

"They mean well, but yeah, it does." He changed the subject by holding up the box and saying, "I got us some breakfast. I didn't know what you like, so I got a few different things for you to choose from."

"Thank you. I'm not picky, I'll eat whatever's put in front of me."

"Good to know. There's a table out back, we can eat there if you want."

"I'll get us some coffee."

I filled a second mug and followed him out the side door, then through a gate in a chain link fence. The cement patio and the back of the building were covered in Izzy's colorful chalk drawings (and a few that were probably made by Kai to entertain his daughter, which put a smile on my face). It was furnished with a couple patio chairs and a red picnic table. The chain link surrounding the space had been completely engulfed by an attractive, flowering vine, which made the yard feel really private. "It's nice out here," I told him.

"Glad you like it."

I sat down beside him at the table and asked, "Am I keeping you from your family?"

"No, they're in Sacramento for a girls' weekend. My mom's best friend lives there, and they're staying with her so they can go to some big dollhouse show at Cal Expo. I sent along some money and told them I'd gladly build Izzy a dollhouse if she finds a kit she likes, but I just couldn't make myself spend an entire day oohing and aahing over tiny furniture and picking out sweaters for miniature people."

"Can't say I blame you."

He opened the bakery box and turned it to face me, and as I selected a blueberry muffin I asked, "So, what are your plans for today?"

"I'm going to work on a DIY project. With the whole family out of town, now's the perfect time for it."

"Want help?"

He grinned a little. "If you're there, I doubt I'll get much work done."

"Sure you will. I think last night proves we can be around each other without constantly fucking like bunnies."

"You seemed a bit drunk after all that whiskey, which is the only reason I didn't initiate anything," Kai told me. "I was fairly drunk myself, actually. Now that we're both sober, it's all I can do to keep myself from ripping your clothes off."

I returned the muffin to its box and got up from the table. "Come on, let's go to your house. There's no reason we can't do both. Fuck my brains out first, then let me help you with your project."

He stood up too and grinned at me as he ran a hand down my arm. "I'm all for the fucking part, but I'm sure you have better things to do with your Sunday besides refinishing a deck."

"Actually, I enjoy DIY, and I have today wide open. If you'd like some company, I'm good at home improvement. I'm good at some other stuff, too." I flashed him a flirtatious smile.

Kai pulled me to him and his lips found mine. We ramped up quickly, and I clutched his navy blue hoodie in my fists, returning the kiss, tasting him, breathing him in. He grabbed my ass and drove our hips together, his swollen cock rubbing mine through our jeans. "I don't want to wait until we get to your house," I told him as he licked and kissed my neck.

"Me neither."

He stripped me in a matter of seconds. I found a condom and a couple lube packets in my wallet, and as he prepped himself, I spread out my jeans on the bench and knelt on them as I worked some lube into me. I wiped my fingers on my briefs and tossed them aside, then bent over, offering myself to him as I rested my elbows on the tabletop.

"Oh God," he murmured, caressing my ass with both hands before lining up his cock with my opening. Kai slid into me with one long, slow thrust as I pushed back to open myself for him. He pulled almost all the way out before rocking forward again and seating himself in me fully.

I started jerking off as he began to move in me. He sped up quickly, and within a minute he was slamming his cock into my ass. "Harder," I rasped, driving myself onto him, and he did as I asked. His body slapped against mine as he absolutely pounded me, both of us moaning and gasping for breath. It was wild and intense and exactly what I needed.

When he pulled out of me abruptly, I cried out in protest. But then Kai flipped me around so my back was on the table, climbed up between my legs and pushed into me again. He paused to yank off his sweatshirt and t-shirt, threw them aside and put my ankles on his shoulders, and then he began to fuck me again.

Kai held my gaze and murmured, "You're absolutely gorgeous," as he slid almost all the way out of me and sank back in slowly. I pulled him to me with my hand on the back of his neck and we kissed for a long moment.

He raised himself up on his elbows and watched me as he continued those deep, slow thrusts, sending jolts of pleasure through me every time he dragged his cock over my prostate. I rocked my hips, pushing myself onto his cock, completely consumed by and in awe of him as he overwhelmed my senses. His clean scent surrounded me and he filled my field of vision. He was bathed in sunlight, which brought out caramel highlights in his ebony-brown hair, and his skin almost glowed under a light, sexy sheen of sweat. I reached up and touched his full lips, and he grinned before kissing my fingertips.

He sat up and brought me with him, holding me in his arms, and I straddled his lap and planted my feet on the table, picking up the pace, riding him hard and fast. I felt my orgasm approaching, and as the intensity built, I closed my eyes and moaned.

Kai's voice was low and insistent when he said, "Look at me, Jessie."

I did as he asked and locked eyes with him as my orgasm tore from me, our connection absolutely electric. I crushed him to me as I shot again and again onto both of us, grabbing at his body, trying to get as close to him as I possibly could. He came a moment later with a low moan, holding me tight and thrusting hard as my ass clenched his thick cock.

My emotions were all over the place and I was shaking as I came down from the intensity of that orgasm. Kai shifted around a bit so he was sitting instead of kneeling on the table and enveloped me in an embrace. He felt so warm and solid as I wrapped my arms and legs around him, and he kissed the side of my head and rubbed my back as I tried to get myself together.

After a few moments, I became aware of some whooping and cheering in the distance. I sat up a bit and looked around, and Kai burst out laughing and muttered, "Oh God."

The yard had seemed pretty private, but apparently it wasn't at all if people happened to be on the roof of a tall building across the street. The five guys in our audience looked like they were in their twenties and were probably gay, given the fact that four of them were paired up with their arms around each other. When they held up pieces of cardboard with big numbers written on them, I started laughing too and eased off Kai's cock, then scrambled after my clothes.

"Two tens and a nine-point-five," he said, turning his back to the spectators. "I feel pretty good about that score." He was blushing vividly and clearly embarrassed, just like I was, but I loved the fact that he was laughing it off.

While I rushed to put on my jeans, Kai peeled off the condom and pulled up his pants, then wiped off his chest with his t-shirt. I used my briefs to do the same thing, since I'd doused both of us when I came. The group was still cheering, so after I scooped up the rest of our clothes and Kai grabbed the bakery box, I took a quick bow and we hurried from the yard.

"That was a new one," he said as we jogged along the side of the building, "sex with a live audience. I hope it doesn't end up on Tumblr."

"I didn't see any of them holding phones, so hopefully not."

Once inside, I stuck my briefs in my pocket and got dressed, and Kai threw the condom in a trash barrel and pulled on his sweatshirt. As soon as we were both reassembled, he said, "Come here a minute," and took my hand.

He led me to the office and curled up with me on the mattress. "We weren't done cuddling yet," he said as he held me securely and I put my head on his chest.

"You're so nice," I said softly as I wrapped an arm around him. "I was utterly wrong about you."

"You didn't have much to go by. It's not like I let most people see this side of me."

"Still."

He began to stroke my hair, and after a while Kai asked, "Are you okay? You seemed kind of rattled when we finished."

"I'm fine. That was just really intense. I guess I'm not used to that."

"Oh God, you're not inexperienced, are you? If so, I should be going so much slower."

I glanced at him and shook my head, then looked away as I admitted, "I've dated a hell of a lot of guys. It sometimes feels like my entire life has just been an endless string of short-term relationships."

He thought about that for a moment before saying, "I'm curious about where I fit into that. Are you still just looking for something short-term?"

"I was never looking for something short-term, and that was the problem. I'd get emotionally invested way too soon, and I'd scare men away. What guy wants to go from 'hi, nice to meet you' to 'let's move in together' over the course of dinner? And yes, I'm exaggerating, but not by much."

"I can see why that might be problematic."

After a pause, I said quietly, "Now that you know I'm both clingy and have slept with half the city, I won't blame you one bit if you change your mind about going out with me."

He shifted us around so we were face-to-face and asked, "You don't seriously think what you just told me makes the slightest difference, do you?"

"Doesn't it?"

"Hell no. I don't expect you to be perfect."

"But you probably didn't expect me to be quite that defective, either," I said.

"You're too hard on yourself."

"I'm not. I've just watched myself mess up *a lot*. But I want you to know I heard you when you said you need to take this slow, and I'm totally on board with that." God, I hoped I'd be able to pull that off. Given my track record, it seemed unlikely that I could avoid rushing things and sending him running, but I was going to hope for a miracle. "Come on," I said, swinging out of bed and changing the subject before I made things even more awkward. "That deck's not going to paint itself. Wait, did you say yes to me coming over and helping you?"

Kai got up too and told me, "I'd love the help, and the company." Well, that was a relief. He took my hand as we headed for the door.

Chapter Seven

The pink, two-story home Kai shared with his family was an oddity by San Francisco standards, because it was actually free-standing, instead of being sandwiched between other buildings like the majority of houses in the city. It wasn't fancy, but it would have been worth a fortune in the current real estate market, especially given its great location right across the street from the wide open expanse of Bernal Heights Park. Kai told me his grandparents had bought it in the nineteen-sixties, back when the city was still relatively affordable. They'd totally scored.

After we ate our preempted breakfast in the sunny kitchen, Kai went to change into some work clothes and I waited for him in the living room. The almost rural view through the picture window and the comfortable family home felt surprisingly nostalgic. I squatted down and ran my hand over a braided area rug, and flashed to a memory of my brother Jed and me playing with toy cars on a rug just like that when we were kids. I wasn't expecting the flood of emotions which accompanied that memory and blinked repeatedly against the prickling at the back of my eyes as I straightened up and took a breath.

When Kai came back downstairs a few minutes later in sexy ripped jeans and a tight t-shirt, he said, "You really don't have to do this if you don't want to. I feel like an asshole for putting you to work the first time you're at my house."

"This is fun for me. I hardly ever get to do DIY."

He looked skeptical. "Okay, but feel free to bail out at any time."

The back deck wasn't huge, and we worked for maybe an hour sanding the rough spots and the chipping paint. A beat-up radio was tuned to a classic rock station, and I kept catching Kai silently mouthing song lyrics, which I thought was very cute. Whenever he'd notice me watching him, he'd get embarrassed and stop. I finally said, "Just sing! I'm not going to judge. In fact, I'll join in on the songs I know. Come on, I already know you have a good voice."

"Based on what?"

"I walked in on your one-man concert last night, remember?"

"Oh hell. I'd forgotten about that."

"Come on, don't be shy. I'll go first, even though I can't carry a tune in a bucket, just to prove you have nothing to be embarrassed about." Under Pressure by Queen and David Bowie started playing, which I happened to love, and I exclaimed, "Oh my God, perfect!" I got to my feet and used the sanding block in my hand as a microphone as I belted out the lyrics.

Kai chuckled and got up too, brushing his hands off on his dusty jeans before picking up his own sanding block microphone and joining in. He ended up taking Freddie Mercury's lines and I took Bowie's, and we circled around each other on the deck and really got into it. When the song ended, I cheered and applauded, and Kai grinned at me. Then he said, "I think I just found our musical common ground. Classic rock's not really your thing, right?"

"It's not usually my go-to, but I do like it."

"I think I know what you'll enjoy more than this radio station." Kai jogged into the house and returned a few moments later with a stack of tapes. "These used to be my dad's, in case you're wondering about the cassettes."

He popped a tape into the player, and Bowie's Space Oddity enveloped me. "God I love this song," I said, closing my eyes and swaying a bit as I let myself get lost in the music.

Kai came up behind me, slipped his arms around my waist and moved with me. After a minute, he began to sing along, and I smiled and leaned against him. He took my hand and spun me slowly, then pulled me into his arms and danced with me as he continued the serenade.

When the song ended, I admitted, "I cried when Bowie died."

"I teared up, too. My dad was always playing his music, it was a part of my childhood. So it kind of felt like losing another piece of my father when Bowie died."

"The tattoos of the ravens on your back represent you and your dad, don't they?"

He nodded. "Not the most subtle symbolism, but I came up with the idea and got those tattoos when I was fifteen. My mom took me on a road trip to Boise to get them, because she knew how important it was to me."

"Why Boise?"

"You have to be eighteen to get a tattoo here, but you only have to be fourteen in Idaho if your parent signs a consent form."

"You have the most supportive mom ever."

"She really is. I think she would have done just about anything to help me cope with the loss of my dad."

"What does the tattoo on your ribs say?"

He grinned at me. "I'll explain it next time you get me naked."

I grinned at that too and pulled him down to my height and kissed him. But then I stepped back and said, "This is me distracting you, just like you said I would."

"No you're not, it's break time. Let's lie down for a few minutes, my back's knotted up after all that sanding."

He took my hand and led me down the stairs to the little yard. A faded floral quilt was draped over an Adirondack chair, and he unfurled it and let it drift onto the tidy lawn. We both stretched out and held hands as we watched the clouds drift across an impossibly blue sky. "What a perfect day," he murmured. I had to agree, and it had nothing to do with the weather.

After a moment, I said, "Teddy bear."

"Love muffin." There was a sparkle in his dark eyes when he turned his head to look at me. "Are we coming up with terrible nicknames for each other?"

I chuckled at that and said, "I was naming a shape I saw in the clouds." I pointed to the east with my free hand.

Kai smiled and looked at the sky, and while he did that, I studied his handsome profile. "That looks nothing like a teddy bear. That, however, looks exactly like a Star Destroyer." He pointed to the west.

I looked up and asked, "You mean that slice of pie?"

"You see pie, I see cool ships from Star Wars."

We kept playing the cloud game for another twenty minutes or so as Bowie sang in the background. Finally I stood up and held a hand out to him as I said, "Come on, let's get back to work. I really am distracting you, and I don't want your project to go unfinished because of me."

He took my hand, but didn't really use it to hoist himself up, since that would have pulled me right over. Kai kissed the tip of my nose when he got to his feet and said, "The worst part's almost over, sanding is a chore. Painting's fun though, and it'll probably go pretty quickly with the two of us."

"Let's do this thing," I said and returned to work with a bounce in my step.

*****

He was right. After the surface was sanded and cleaned thoroughly, we took a lunch break, then tackled phase two. The white deck paint went on easily. When we finished, we both stood on the lawn and admired our accomplishment. "That's why I enjoy painting. It's such instant gratification," he said.

"It looks great."

"Hopefully it'll be completely dry by the time my daughter gets home. She'll definitely want to run around on it."

"What time are they getting home tonight?" I asked.

"Actually, it won't be until midafternoon tomorrow, so the paint can cure for twenty-four hours. Izzy has Monday off from school for Presidents' Day and my sister and mom are off work, so my family's taking full advantage of the three-day weekend."

"In that case, you should change your mind and have dinner at Nana's tonight. It's always a good time, especially if she decides to film an episode of her cooking show while she's preparing the meal."

"She films from home?"

"Yup. The show's totally low-budget and somewhat less than professional. It airs once a week, late at night on a cable TV network. She always has at least a dozen episodes in the can, so she films randomly, whenever the mood strikes her."

"In the can?"

"Slang for done and ready to be broadcast."

"Ah."

"So, do you want to come over?"

Kai grinned and said, "Sure. Sounds like fun."

"It will be, I promise."

He pulled me into his arms and said, "Thank you for helping today. I'm sorry my power sander was on the fritz and that all ended up being way more labor-intensive than it should have been."

"I had a great time." He raised an eyebrow, and I said, "Seriously. I wasn't kidding when I said I enjoy doing DIY projects."

"Well, I really appreciate your help. I would have hours of work left today, but you cut the time in half. You were great company, too."

"So were you."

He kissed me tenderly, then said, "Come on, let's get cleaned up." We started walking hand-in-hand to the side gate, but he stopped abruptly and said, "Shit, I screwed up."

"How?"

"I didn't put my house keys in my pocket when I switched to this pair of jeans. We won't be able to get in the front door, and the back door's inaccessible with the wet paint."

"You never lock doors. Are you sure we can't get in the front?"

"I always lock up the house automatically, to keep my family safe. We can go check, but I'm sure we'll find the front door's locked."

Kai was right. After we went around to the front and jiggled the handle, we circled the house looking for open windows. When we returned to the front yard, I said, "That looks like the only way in." I pointed to an open window directly below the peak of the pitched roof. "Is that the attic?"

"Yeah. It's also my room. I'm too big to fit through that window, though."

"But I'm not. Wait here, I'll let you in."

"Be careful."

I climbed onto the roof of the front porch, and when I stood on the highest point in the center and stretched up, I was just able to reach the windowsill. I grabbed onto it with both hands and hung there for a moment, and Kai called, "Please don't fall."

"I won't."

"Do you want me to come up there and give you a boost?"

"I'm not sure the porch roof would hold you, it doesn't seem very sturdy. Just give me a minute." My arms were tired from all that sanding and painting, but I managed to pull myself up with some effort. After I shimmied through the window and landed on a desk, I sat there for a moment and shook out my hands.

From down below, Kai called, "You okay?" I stuck my hand out the window and gave him a thumbs-up.

The attic had pale blue walls, which were covered with posters of American muscle cars and slanted sharply with the pitch of the roof. The only place to stand up straight was a four-foot section right down the middle. A twin bed was centered under a bigger window at the opposite end of the attic, and a dresser, a few storage chests, and a rowing machine were tucked under the eaves. I slid off the desk and paused to look at the framed photos clustered on top of his dresser. Just like in the shop, there were a lot of snapshots of Kai and his dad, and several photos of Izzy.

I climbed down a retractable wooden ladder and emerged in the hallway on the second floor. There were four small, decidedly feminine bedrooms and a very pink bathroom off the hallway. I jogged downstairs and opened the front door for Kai, and he thanked me.

"The more I see of your house, the more I understand your man cave at the shop," I told him. "Do you get ready every morning in that pink bathroom?"

"I have no choice, since there's only a half-bath on the first floor. I don't mind the color scheme so much, but it's kind of a pain when everyone's trying to get ready at the same time. Beggars can't be choosers though, and I'm damn lucky Izzy and I get to live here. This city's way too expensive for me to afford a place of our own."

"You own the garage though, right?"

"Well, the bank does and I'll be paying it off for the next twenty years, but basically."

"Have you ever thought about building an apartment on top of it? The roof's flat, so it seems fairly straightforward."

"I think about that all the time. Like most things in life though, it comes down to money."

"We just need to figure out how to get the garage to turn a profit," I told him.

"We?"

I grinned and said, "Sorry, I know that sounded presumptuous. I like helping my friends in any way I can, that's all I meant by that."

He grinned, too. "It's nice that you think of me as a friend."

"Of course I do." My phone buzzed, and I pulled it from my pocket and read the text. Then I told him, "The cooking show's a go for tonight, and Nana asked if I can be there in an hour to help her out. I'm her on-air assistant."

"I didn't realize you appear on TV with her. Where can I find episodes of this show?"

"You sound impressed, but you shouldn't be," I said as I shot a text back to Nana. "The show is…well, you'll see. Mostly what you'll find are outtakes on the internet. I can't even call them blooper reels. They're more like disaster footage."

He said, "I look forward to seeing them. Now let's get cleaned up and get going so you're not late."

I flashed him a big smile and said, "We should probably shower together to save time." Kai smiled too, and we almost ran to the pink bathroom.

Chapter Eight

Not surprisingly, showering together ended up taking a lot longer than showering separately. We ended up making out and jerking each other off, so I was running a bit late when I finally pulled into Nana's driveway. Kai parked down the street, and I chatted with a couple go-go boys while I waited for him. When he walked up to the house and took in the spectacle of Cockstock, he said, "Your household takes being out to a whole new level."

"Feud with a neighbor. Kind of a long story." I introduced the dancers to Kai, then asked them, "Are you guys hungry? If so, come on in and I'll make you some snacks."

"Thanks," a blond, buff dancer named Will said, "but Nana's been stuffing us all day." He patted his flat belly. "I'll need to step up my gym time to twice a day at this rate."

Once I was sure the dancers didn't need anything, we went inside and I found Zachary hovering in the doorway of the kitchen. "Hey, you're early," I said, giving him a hug.

"Nana asked Chance to come at five and bring his camera, and he was my ride. I guess she wants him to take some photos for a cookbook she's had on the back burner for a while now," my friend said. He then noticed Kai behind me, and his dark eyes went wide.

"Zachary Paleki, Kai Kahale. I need to run upstairs and change. Do you guys want to come with me or stay down here?"

"Come with you," they both said simultaneously.

When we got to my room, I shut the door behind us and tossed the plastic bag with my soiled clothes in the laundry hamper. As I took off the big t-shirt Kai had lent me, Zachary moved my bear to the desk and sat on the one chair in the room. I asked him, "How did today go at the restaurant?"

"It was alright. Like I told you, I waited tables before, so I know how to play that role. You smile for the customers, you pretend you're outgoing, and you try not to mess up their orders. That's pretty much all there is to it," he said quietly. He stole a glance at Kai from beneath his lashes and frowned almost imperceptibly. Almost.

I told Kai as I pulled a yellow polo shirt over my head, "Zachary just got hired at Nolan's in the Richmond District. It's an Irish pub and sports bar."

"I love that place," Kai said. He was sitting on the foot of my bed and looking around curiously.

"In that case, you should come have lunch with me when I visit Zachary at work." I glanced at my friend, who frowned again, and hoped he'd be able to gain a fresh perspective on Kai, like I had. I changed the subject by asking what was on Nana's menu that evening.

"Seafood. I don't know what exactly," Zachary said, studying the floor.

"That could be problematic." I flashed back to a cooking show episode with Nana, me, and a geoduck clam, which had ended up far more phallic than intended. It still made our friends chuckle whenever anyone brought it up.

I pulled on a pair of briefs and a decent pair of jeans, and as I tucked my shirt in, I asked Kai, "How do you feel about seafood?"

"Like you, I'm not picky. I'll eat most anything," he said.

After I put on shoes and socks and ran a brush through my hair, I asked, "Okay, are we ready to face the madness?"

"I'm both terrified and looking forward to seeing what happens," Zachary said with a little half-smile. "I was a bit disappointed last time I was here, when everything actually went according to plan and Nana just cooked a nice pasta dish. Although it was delicious."

When we went back downstairs, we found Nana perched on a barstool as Mr. Mario put up her white hair in an elaborate twist. Zachary took a seat at the kitchen table in the corner with Chance's brother Colt and Colt's boyfriend Elijah while I waved hello to everyone and led Kai over to Nana.

"Hi boys!" She grabbed her glasses off the counter and put them on so she could assess Kai, and exclaimed, "You're a handsome one! Are you a gay homosexual?"

"A, um…what now?"

"That's Nanaspeak for gay. She has her own unique spin on how to be politically correct," I explained, then introduced Kai to Nana, Ollie, Mr. Mario, and the dogs. "The big one's Tom Selleck, and the little one's Diego Rivera. Tommy used to have a crush on me, but I'm pretty sure he and Diego are now in a committed relationship."

Kai grinned at that, and I pointed across the room and introduced the teenagers at the table with Zachary. Then I said, "The brunet behind the camera is Trevor. He's married to Vincent, the tall guy with glasses right beside him. Vincent is one of Nana's grandsons." They all exchanged greetings, and I asked the couple, "Where's your son?"

"Josh and his friend Emma are out back, along with a few other people. They wanted to see how Skye's sculpture is coming," Trevor said as he adjusted the tripod.

"Do you have everything you need to begin filming, Nana?" I asked as I surveyed the ingredients lined up on the kitchen island. A large Styrofoam cooler was at one end, which I assumed contained the seafood.

Mr. Mario finished what he was doing, and Nana hopped off the barstool and adjusted the jacket of her pale yellow suit. We matched. She said, "We're all set. Vinnie, will you call in everyone from the backyard? This is going to be our best episode yet, I can feel it!"

While her grandson did as she asked, I turned on the stage lights that had been installed over the kitchen island, preheated the oven and put a big pot of water on the stove to boil. I knew from experience that it was good to be as prepared as possible before the cameras started rolling.

"Can I help with anything?" Kai asked.

Nana told him, "Absolutely. You stay right up here with Jessie and me and give us a hand. We've got a lot of recipes to get through."

"Oh. Okay." Kai seemed nervous all of a sudden and re-tucked his black, long-sleeved T-shirt into his jeans before smoothing his hair.

"You look great," I told him.

He said, "I've never been on TV before. What if I mess something up?"

"You have nothing to worry about. It's pretty much the norm for things to go wrong on this show, so there's absolutely no pressure. The show airs late at night on cable TV, and a lot of viewers turn it into a drinking game and do a shot whenever Nana drops the F-bomb. Since she does that a lot, the audience will probably be way too wasted to notice if you make a mistake." He gave me a nervous smile and I squeezed his hand.

As everyone filtered in from the backyard, Chance came over to say hello, and I introduced him to Kai. My friend snapped a couple pictures of the ingredients on the counter with the big camera around his neck, and I asked, "Did Zachary tell you I want to buy some of the photos you posted on the internet the other day?"

"Yeah, but I'll just give them to you," Chance said. "I'll email you a link so you can download high resolution copies of whatever you want."

"But I want to buy them. You're an amazing photographer, Chance, and you should be making money from it."

"I appreciate the compliment, but I'm not going to charge you for some snapshots."

"They're not snapshots, and step one to becoming a professional photographer is actually accepting money for your photographs." Chance looked like he wanted to argue, and I said, "I want to pick out ten photos, and I'll pay you fifty dollars apiece for them."

"Oh come on. That's five hundred bucks!"

"That's a fraction of what they're worth. I wish I could afford to pay more."

"No way," Chance said. "Even five bucks apiece is too much."

"How about if I give the money to your brother on your behalf?"

"You don't have to."

"But I want to," I insisted.

"You're very stubborn."

"So are you!"

Chance sighed, and after a moment he grinned at me. "Fine, I'll agree to five dollars each, and you can give the money to Colt. He's been saving up for a game console, so he'll be thrilled."

I grabbed my wallet and pulled out fifty dollars, which I handed to Chance as I told him, "Speaking of Colt, it looks like he's trying to flag you down."

"Thanks. Be right back."

When Chance crossed the room and gave the money to his ecstatic-looking brother, Kai asked, "What was that about?"

I lowered my voice and said, "I want to help my friend launch his photography career, but as you can probably tell from that conversation, he totally undervalues himself and his work. There's a huge art show coming up that would be wonderful exposure, but he keeps making excuses for why he can't be a part of it. I'm operating under the logic that if I buy some of his photos, then they're my property and I can do whatever I want with them, including putting them in the show. I'm doing this behind his back, so he'll probably be pretty mad at me. But if it ends up launching his career, I'll gladly take the heat."

Kai said, "You weren't kidding when you told me you try to help your friends in any way you can."

"I'd do anything for the people I care about."

"He's probably going to be pissed off that you're doing this without his permission, but your heart's in the right place and I hope he forgives you."

"I hope so, too."

Kai gently brushed my hair from my eyes, and as I looked up at him under the bright stage lights I took in every detail, from his long, black lashes, to the way his hair curled slightly at the ends, to the tiny scar above his left eyebrow. His dark eyes crinkled at the corners when he smiled at me, and I traced the curve of his upper lip with my fingertip. I forgot anyone else was in the room until Nana appeared beside us wearing a big chef's hat and exclaimed,

"You two are adorable together! I'm so happy you found yourself a fox, Jessie! You were single way too long. I was starting to think I needed to put up an ad for you on one of those dating sites. What's that one called? Grind me?"

Kai and I stepped back from each other and I colored slightly as I tried to redirect Nana to the task at hand. She climbed up on her stepstool behind the kitchen island, and Mr. Mario picked up a camcorder while our audience settled in. I told Nana as I surveyed the bowls of ingredients, "I'm sorry I wasn't around earlier to help with the grocery shopping and set-up."

"Oh, that's fine," she said. "You were supposed to have today off, especially with all the extra time you put in this last week supervising Cockstock. I just called that new gourmet market over on Fillmore, and they delivered everything I needed. They even have a fresh seafood counter, so it was one-stop shopping."

From behind the main camera, Trevor called, "Hang on, this battery's low. I'm going to run out to my car and grab the second one."

As he jogged out of the kitchen, I asked Nana, "Speaking of Cockstock, how much longer do you think you're going to keep it up?"

"Good question. I think that fucker Humpington is getting used to it. He's not turning red anymore when he drives past the house, and I've given up on getting an apology for tampering with my shit. Maybe it's time for some kind of grand finale. We should do that tonight, I noticed he has company. If he's hosting a boring little dinner party, let's give him and his guests something to talk about."

"Want me to see if a few more of the dancers can come in tonight?"

"Good idea, Jessie." I pulled out my phone and sent a group text to every dancer who'd been working in shifts during Cockstock, and Nana said, "Send a message to my girlfriends, too. They'll want to be here if this turns into a big go-go boy dance party." I found the group entitled 'Nanettes' on my phone and sent them a text as well.

Nana yelled across the kitchen, "Mr. Mario, we're going to wrap up the dickfest tonight, and we want to go out with a bang. Will you see if your drag queen friends want to join us?"

He agreed enthusiastically, juggling the camcorder as he pulled out his phone. Mr. Mario speed-dialed a number, and when someone answered, I could hear pulsating dance music in the background, even from a few feet away. He had a quick conversation in Spanish, and when he hung up, he told Nana, "They are coming! We will, as you say, go out with the bang!"

"Mr. Mario," I said, "I just realized I don't know your drag name."

"I am Carmen Gettit," he said, "and the fellow I've been dating is Dixie Normous. You see why I asked him out."

I grinned at that and turned to Kai. "I hope you can stick around after dinner. There's every chance tonight's going to snowball into quite the party."

"Love to." His eyes sparkled with amusement as he said, "You live in Oz. You know that, right?"

"I do."

Trevor returned and switched out the battery, then asked, "You ready, Nana?"

"Let's do this thing," she said, rubbing her bony hands together.

Trevor clicked a button and called, "We're rolling," and the audience fell silent.

"We got a lot to do today," Nana said, looking at the camera. "That's why I got two assistants up here. You already know Jessie, and that sexy, dark haired boy next to him is Kai. I assume he and Jessie are ridin' the baloney pony these days, but nobody tells me anything, so I gotta reach my own conclusions." She turned to him and said, "Welcome to the show, Kai."

He'd gone a bit deer-in-headlights, probably thanks to Nana's sex euphemism, and stammered, "I, um…thanks."

She turned back to the camera and said, "I got two courses planned out here for a nice seafood dinner. We're gonna start with a beautiful crab cake appetizer, and then we're gonna make some linguini and clams. Now, I only got thirty minutes, because the fuckers at the cable TV network won't give me a whole hour, so we gotta get moving. Before we do any of that, though," Nana said, "we're gonna start with a cum shot. Help me out, Jessie."

Now it was my turn to stammer. "We…what?"

She picked up a couple bottles of booze and told me, "Grab that tray on the counter behind us, the one that's full of shot glasses. We're gonna start off with a quick, easy cocktail. Kai, take these bottles and fill each of the glasses with equal parts butterscotch schnapps and Irish cream. Then top each one with a dollop of whipped cream. There's one of those spray containers in the fridge. That's all you need to make a cum shot, easy peasy."

I brought over the glasses, and as Kai got to work I asked Nana, "Okay, what's next?"

"I gotta get these appetizers going. It's real simple to make crab cakes. Now look here." She started pointing to bowls on the counter. "I got some crackers that I ground up in the food processor, they're tastier than just using bread crumbs. I also got some eggs and mayo for binder, and a few veggies, nothing fancy, just a little finely chopped green onion and red bell pepper. Not everybody puts veggies in their crab cakes. If you don't like it, leave it out! What the fuck do I care? You're not gonna hurt my feelings if you don't put 'em in there. Jessie, start dumping everything into a big mixing bowl, will you? Oh, but first, slide that cooler down here."

"Is this the crab meat, Nana?" I asked as I picked up the surprisingly heavy Styrofoam cooler and brought it to her.

"Yeah, I thought we should keep it on ice," she said as I put the cooler down in front of her. "You can never be too careful when handling your meat."

"Safety first," I said with a grin.

She peeled off the packing tape holding the lid to the cooler as she explained, "I told the guy on the phone at the gourmet market to send enough crab to feed thirty people. This looks like an awful big cooler, but I'm guessing there's a lot of ice in here to keep the crab meat fresh. I got this bowl here," she said, sliding a large serving dish closer to her. "Let's just dump everything out real careful-like, instead of trying to fish through a bunch of ice."

Nana tossed the lid aside. The cooler was filled to the top with ice, and she and I tipped it over gingerly. At first, nothing but ice cubes fell into the bowl. "Fucker's heavy," she said. We tilted it just a little more, and all at once, a huge mass of live blue crabs fell onto the counter. A few landed on their backs, legs and claws waving in the air, and the rest started skittering in every direction. "Holy shit!" Nana yelled. "Look at all these fuckin' crabs!"

Everyone in the kitchen jumped up and started talking at once as several crabs fell off the counter. It didn't seem to harm the crustaceans in the slightest, and they darted off sideways across the floor. All the teens and Zachary climbed up on the kitchen table while Trevor and Vincent tried and failed to herd the crabs.

Meanwhile, Mr. Mario kept filming the whole spectacle like a reporter in a war zone, zooming in on Nana as she tried to keep a little crab with a cracked shell from falling off the counter. When it almost pinched her, she grabbed a thin knife with a wooden handle, held it by the blade and prodded the crab. "What are you doing, Nana?" I asked her, dancing around to avoid the crabs on the floor.

"I don't want to stab the fucker, that'd be inhumane," she said, poking it again with the handle. "I'm just trying to discourage it from jumpin' off the counter and joining its comrades. We gotta keep this shit contained!" She poked it once more, and the crab grabbed the handle with one of its claws. Nana let go of the knife and yelled, "Sweet baby Jesus, the fucker's armed!" The crab skittered sideways, waving the knife as it rushed across the kitchen island.

I turned to look at Kai. He held a crab in each hand and was right in the path of the armed crustacean. As soon as he and I made eye contact, we both burst out laughing. He hurried to the doorway and tried to keep the crabs in the kitchen by blocking them with his sneakers, but half a dozen or so were already dashing across the foyer.

Mr. Mario turned his attention to the crab with the knife, coming in for a tight shot with his camcorder. He climbed onto the island and leaned over to get a better angle, ignoring the other crabs around him. When one of them latched onto the front of his pants, Mr. Mario was up like a shot, yelling, "*Madre de Dios*, it's got me by the *cojones*!" For some reason, he decided to run from the crab that had attached itself to his family jewels, and Kai stepped out of the way as he bolted from the kitchen and out the front door.

Nana and Ollie's dogs dashed into the kitchen, alerted by all the commotion. They started barking excitedly, lunging at the crabs and jumping out of the way of their pinchers, and Ollie went into superhero mode. He dove into the fray and grabbed his Chihuahua with one hand, then plucked Nana off the stepstool in a fireman's carry as he bellowed, "Tom Selleck! Come!" Surprisingly, the big mutt actually listened and followed Ollie as he bustled out the back door.

Mr. Mario had left the front door open as he retreated, and ten go-go boys in colorful briefs ran into the house to see what was going on. I gingerly grabbed a couple crabs by their shells, pointing the claws away from me, and noticed Trevor's son Josh had taken over filming. He was standing on a chair and shaking with laughter as he panned the kitchen with his dad's video camera. This episode of the cooking show was going to go viral, no question.

In all the mayhem, the Styrofoam cooler had cracked in two when it got dropped and stepped on, so I didn't quite know what to do with the crabs I was holding. I tried putting them in the sink, but one climbed on top of the other and started to haul itself out. I picked them up again and thought for a moment, then told Kai, "Let's put them in the bathtub."

He and a long procession of go-go boys with crabs all rushed down the hall with me. I put the creatures in the big claw-foot tub in the mint green downstairs bathroom, plugged the drain and ran a shallow pool of cool water for them. The dancers added their crabs to the tub, and Vincent and Trevor followed. Trevor held one crab at arm's length, and his husband was reading from an invoice he must have found in the kitchen. "There are thirty crabs in all," Vincent said. "How many do we have here?"

Kai counted and said, "Nineteen."

"Oh man," Josh exclaimed from behind the video camera, "Ocean's Eleven are still on the lam." The kid pushed his thick, black-framed glasses up the bridge of his nose and grinned.

Josh's friend Emma, a pretty thirteen-year-old with glasses, appeared behind him with three crabs in an ice bucket and carefully slid them into the tub. "This is why I'm a vegetarian," Josh said, shuddering a bit as his friend gently tugged a reluctant crab out of the bucket by one of its legs.

"This is fun," Emma exclaimed, straightening up and swinging her long, brown hair behind her shoulder. "The crabs are finding all kinds of interesting hiding places, so it's like a big game of hide and seek. Let's go get Colt and Elijah off the table and find some more. Team Teen versus Team Go-Go Boy, whoever finds the most crabs wins!"

"Oh, it's on," a smiling, red-haired dancer named Patrick exclaimed, hiking up his tiny, neon-yellow briefs. He told his teammates, "Fan out, boys! Let's go catch some crabs!" The kids and dancers hurried out of the bathroom with excited woops and yells while I washed my hands, which smelled decidedly crabby.

Kai washed his hands too, and then we sat on the edge of the tub and looked at the teeming crustaceans. "They're kind of cute," I said.

"Kind of."

"I feel bad for them, all crammed in the cooler like that. They were in there a long time, too. I wonder if they're hungry. I also wonder what the hell blue crabs eat." I pulled out my phone and did a quick internet search, then said, "Oh, ew."

"What is it?"

"Well, they eat clams, mussels, oysters and dead fish, but they'll also eat smaller blue crabs." I jumped up and said, "I'm going to get them something to eat before they go all Donner party in there."

I hurried to the kitchen, grabbed a bag of clams I found in the refrigerator and a small knife, and hurried back to the bathroom. I held a clam with a wash cloth and forced the knife between the shell halves with some effort. As I slowly and awkwardly worked on prying it open, Kai said, "You know that's the rest of tonight's dinner, right?"

"I know, but I feel sorry for the crabs. They need these more than we do."

Kai watched me for a moment, then asked, "Do you have any more of those knives?"

"They're in the drawer beneath the microwave."

He left the bathroom, returned a few moments later with a second knife and a hand towel, and sat beside me again as we both concentrated on shucking the clams. Nana and Ollie appeared in the doorway a couple minutes later. "They're probably hungry," I told her when she asked what was going on. "Let's not eat them, okay? They've already had a rotten day."

"We won't eat 'em, Sweet Pea," Nana said, patting my shoulder. "We can always order pizza for dinner."

Ollie found a couple more knives and towels, then sat on the lid of the toilet while Nana perched daintily on a chair at the vanity, and they helped us shuck. I finally got one clam open and dropped it into the tub, and the crabs fought over it. "They're totally starving. Poor things," I said.

We put the opened clams in the sink as we worked so we wouldn't cause a feeding frenzy, and Ollie asked Kai as they both knit their brows and worked on prying the shells open, "How'd you boys meet?"

"We belong to the same street racing club," Kai said.

Ollie glanced up with a sparkle in his dark eyes. He might look like the little old man from the movie Up, but he had the enthusiasm and energy of a kid. "I used to love motorsports back in the day. Motorcycles were my thing. For a while, I even was part of a motorcycle stunt show while I worked my way through college. What do you race?"

"A '73 Mustang. It was my dad's. He raced it when he was my age," Kai said.

Ollie and Kai chatted about racing for a while, and when he finally got his clam open, Ollie yelled, "Ha!"

A moment later, I jabbed my palm. The towel protected me, but I still sharply drew in my breath. Kai dropped everything he was holding and grabbed my hand as he asked, "Are you okay?"

"I'm fine. It didn't break the skin." He pushed the towel aside and ran his thumb over my palm, and seemed relieved when he saw I was uninjured. It was pretty obvious sometimes that he was a parent, and I thought his concern was incredibly sweet.

"When are you going to start racing again, Jessie?" Nana asked. She was shucking clams like a pro, doing five for every one of mine.

"I actually did already, over Valentine's weekend," I admitted.

"Oh, that's where you went during the party. I thought maybe you met someone and snuck off to, you know, plow the back forty. Or get your back forty plowed. Either way." Nana smiled at me while I colored a little. It occurred to Kai and me at about the same time that we actually had slept together for the first time that night, and we glanced at each other, then quickly looked away. Nana noticed, of course, and said, "So there was some plowing after all!"

A short, African-American dancer named Levi saved us from further embarrassment by running into the bathroom, depositing a crab in the tub and asking, "How many are still out there?"

"Seven, I think, counting the one that rode out of here on Mr. Mario's lap," I said.

"Damn, those things have gone into stealth mode," Levi said.

I asked, "Did anyone disarm the one with a knife?"

"No, that tricky little bastard fell off the counter and made a break for it. We think it's still armed. I better get back, the losing team is buying ice cream for everyone." He smiled and ran from the room.

I looked into the tub and pulled out the new addition, then spread a towel on my lap and put a shucked clam in front of the crab. When Kai glanced at me, I said, "None of them are very big, but this one's even smaller than the rest. His shell's not even the size of my palm. I don't want him to end up on the cannibal crabs' menu." The little creature started picking at the clam and feeding himself with his claws. "I'm going to name him Virgil."

"Why?" Kai asked.

"Because he looks like a Virgil." I rubbed the crab's shell with a fingertip.

A moment later, Zachary and Elijah came in. Both of them were wielding long-handled tongs, and were holding one crab between them like it was made of uranium. They carefully deposited the crab in the tub, and I grinned and said, "Good job, guys."

Elijah looked happy. He tucked a strand of blond hair behind his ear as he asked, "Who's winnin'?" Normally, Colt's boyfriend was painfully shy and really reserved, so it was nice to see him enjoying himself.

"It's tied, one apiece. I only started counting after the official start of the competition to keep it fair. If you find the crab holding a knife, he counts double." I turned to Zachary, who also looked like he was having fun, and asked, "Are you on Team Teen?"

"I've been declared an honorary teenager for this contest, since the go-go dancers outnumber the kids," he said. "Vincent and Trevor are honorary teens, too. Skye, Dare, and Haley have declared themselves neutral, claimed the kitchen table for Switzerland, and are sitting on it out of crab range, having cocktails."

Emma ran in with the ice bucket and a spatula and slid two crabs into the tub. She'd tied a sash around her forehead and was in full warrior woman mode. "The teens are winning," I said.

"Yes!" She did a fist-pump and headed for the door. "Come on, guys, let's go search the front yard. The door was left open, and some of the convicts might have gone over the wall!" Zachary and Elijah hurried after her.

"There we go," Nana announced, standing and picking up her towel by the corners. It held at least two dozen shucked clams. "We're all done here. Let's feed those little fellas, call in a pizza order, and relocate to Switzerland while the crab wranglers do their thing."

We quickly distributed all the clams around the tub, and the crabs really went for them. As we took turns washing our hands, I asked, "What are we going to do with them?"

"We're gonna keep 'em. Poor little things, being stuffed in a cooler like that! It's a wonder they're still alive. This tub's no kind of habitat for them either though, so we gotta figure out something better." She pulled her phone from her bra as she said, "I'm gonna call Dante, he's real smart. He's a good problem-solver too, so he'll know what to do."

Nana punched some numbers, and when her oldest grandson answered, she yelled into the phone, "I know you and Charlie are planning to come for dinner, but you need to drop whatever you're doing and get here as soon as possible Dante, because I got crabs! There are so many of them, it's like a swarm! I figure you've got a lot of experience with stuff like this, so hurry up and get over here!" She disconnected without waiting for a response, and I bit my lip to keep from laughing. I would have given anything to see Dante's face during that call.

"Why do you think he has experience with crabs, Nana?" I asked.

"Well, because he and his husband own that nice restaurant, and they serve a few seafood dishes. I'm thinking they might order crabs occasionally and know what to do to keep them alive." Nana took Ollie's hand and they headed out of the bathroom as she called, "Come join us for cocktails. Bring Virgil too, if you want."

I made a nest for the tiny crab out of a clean hand towel, and he seemed pretty content as he peeked out of the folds. Kai held him for me as I rummaged through a few Christmas decorations in one of the storage closets in the hall. Finally I announced, "Just what I was looking for," and pulled a stuffed snowman from one of the shelves. I plucked off its little red and white mittens and gingerly slipped them over Virgil's claws as I explained, "Now he can't pinch us. Funnily enough, they're a perfect fit. Not too tight, I don't want him to be uncomfortable." On a whim, I took the snowman's red and white knit hat with a red pompom on top and centered it on Virgil's shell. A bit of double-stick tape on its underside held it in place. I held up the crab to admire his outfit and said, "It looks like we just found Waldo."

"That's adorable. So are you." Kai kissed me and said with a smile, "Thank you for inviting me over tonight. I don't know when I've ever had this much fun." I didn't either.

*****

An impromptu block party in the front yard followed the cocktails, pizza, and lots of ice cream (courtesy of the dancers, who were gracious about losing the crab roundup to the kids). Colorful drag queens, a couple dozen go-go boys, neighbors from up and down the street, and several of Nana's little senior girlfriends danced, laughed and mingled with some of her dark-suited family members, who looked like they hadn't left their mafia roots far behind. All in all, Cockstock went out with style, and Humpington and his stodgy dinner guests seemed sufficiently horrified, so Nana counted it as a win.

Kai and I lingered on the sidewalk in the early morning hours, long after the last guest had gone home. He brushed his lips to mine and ran his fingers into my hair. We kissed each other tenderly for a long time, and when we finally broke apart, he rested his forehead against mine and said softly, "You keep surprising me, over and over, in the best possible way."

We made idle small talk, trying to postpone the inevitable. But finally, he kissed me once more and told me, "I'm already looking forward to Friday," before getting in his car.

After he drove off, I remained rooted to the sidewalk and wrapped my arms around myself. I could still taste him on my lips, and instantly missed the warmth of his body against mine. His clean scent lingered on my jacket, and I closed my eyes and breathed him in.

The entire day, and Kai, had been so wonderfully unexpected, and it felt like whatever was happening between us had the potential to grow into something beautiful and amazing. But I couldn't do what I always did and try to turn it into an instant relationship. That never worked out, and I already knew he wanted to take it slow, for both his sake and his daughter's. I had to keep some distance between us, because if I tried to rush it, I'd ruin everything. I turned my face to the heavens and whispered, "Please don't let me screw this up."

Chapter Nine

Zachary dropped into the booth across from me and muttered, "Kill me now." It was Friday afternoon, and I'd come to visit my friend at work just as the lunch rush ended. "I'm so tired, and I wish I could take off my aching feet and throw them away. I think I need to take all the money I earned this week and buy a better pair of shoes. That'll leave me with zero net gain, but at least I'll have a chance of surviving my next shift."

"That's probably a good idea. Do you have any more tables?"

"Just you. For the love of God, don't order anything."

I grinned at that and said, "If I do, I'll go to the kitchen and put the order in myself. I'm friends with the two guys who own this place, they won't care."

"You're right, they won't. Jamie and Dmitri are incredibly nice. It makes me feel guilty for hating this job so much. In their defense, it's not Nolan's I hate, it's waiting tables in general."

Cole came up to us and put glasses of water in front of Zachary and me, and after we thanked him I said, "I didn't know you were working here again."

"It's just for the time being. My friend Miranda tends bar here and told me they've been short-handed at lunch, so I'm picking up a few shifts while I figure some things out."

I studied River's boyfriend as he took off his wire-framed glasses and wiped them with the short, black apron he wore with his jeans and green Nolan's t-shirt. He was half African-American and half Jewish, and that lineage had bestowed him with a lot of tightly spiraled caramel-colored curls, which he'd been growing out into a wild cascade. Cole was about my age, but he looked older, especially that day. There was weariness in his dark eyes, and they were underscored with shadows.

Instead of immediately hitting him with a million questions about how he and River were doing, I pulled something from the pocket of my t-shirt and said, "I'm glad you're here, it saves me a trip to your apartment. I was at Christopher Robin's art gallery earlier today and bought a stack of tickets for his upcoming new artists show and masquerade ball." I handed a colorful ticket to Zachary and gave another one to Cole. Its background was a landscape painting by Ignacio Mondelvano, one of the show's featured artists.

"Wow, thanks," Cole said.

"You're welcome. I'm doing my part to make sure this event sells out, not only because it's raising money for a great cause, but because Skye and Chance are both featured in the show, and I want a lot of their friends to be there to support them. Chance doesn't know his photographs are going to be on display though, so keep it under your hat."

Cole slipped the ticket in his pocket and asked, "Do I have to dress up?"

"Yes and no. It doesn't have to be elaborate. A mask and whatever you'd normally wear for a party will totally get the job done. Of course, if you want to get really dressed up, there will be people who do that, too. Just go with whatever makes you comfortable."

Zachary thanked me, but like the true introvert he was, he seemed a little concerned about the dressing up part. I told him, "I've already worked out costumes for you and me, so all you have to do is show up and sparkle." That only increased his concern.

"I assume River will be there, since his brother Skye is part of the show," Cole said.

"I guess. The place holds close to a thousand people though, so it's not like you'll be forced to get up close and personal or anything."

Cole put his glasses back on and raised an eyebrow as he asked, "Did you give me this ticket because you're hoping River and I will see each other across the crowded room, all our troubles will magically disappear, and we'll reconcile on the spot?"

Yes. Totally. "No, of course not," I said. "I just want you and all our friends there. I'm going to feel really bad for everyone involved if that huge venue is half-empty." I pulled ten more tickets from my shirt pocket, fanned them out, and showed them to Cole. "This is how I'm doing my part to help Christopher, Skye, Chance, Ignacio and the other artists, all at the same time." If it also ended up benefitting Cole and River like I hoped it would, that would be a huge bonus.

"You're a good friend, Jessie," Cole said.

"Thanks. I try."

Cole changed the subject by asking, "Do you want me to put in an order for you? Zachary, you should eat too, you never took a lunch break."

"I was too behind to take a break," Zachary said, "and you don't have to wait on me."

"It's no big deal," Cole told him.

"I'll take two orders of Nana's pasta with marinara," I said. "I happen to know Zachary likes that."

"You got it." Cole headed to the kitchen.

"Do you know why one of Nana's Italian dishes is sold at an Irish restaurant?" Zachary asked before downing most of his glass of water.

"Her grandson Dante put it on the menu when he won the pub from its original owner in a poker game. Later on, Dmitri won it from him, and he gave it to his husband Jamie as a wedding present. That's when the name changed to Nolan's. I wonder if Dante and Dmitri still participate in those poker games. They sounded epic."

"No kidding. I love poker, but I can't imagine playing for stakes this high," Zachary said, waving his hand to indicate the attractive restaurant with its dark wood booths.

"Me neither."

He changed the subject by asking, "Do you really have our costumes picked out for the masquerade ball?"

"I do, but they're a surprise. All I'll say is, don't change your hair color, because it's perfect right now with what you'll be wearing."

Zachary looked worried. "Please don't do anything too elaborate. I don't want to stand out."

"I won't, I promise."

"Shouldn't you be planning a couples costume with Kai? I assume you'll want to ask him to be your date."

"I'm saving a ticket for him, and I'll ask him to come with us when it gets closer. Right now though, it's too far off," I said. "I don't want him to think I'm making assumptions about us being together a month from now."

"Why not?"

"I refuse to make the same mistakes with Kai that I've made with so many guys before him. I really like him, and I want to give us a fighting chance. That means taking it slow and not putting any pressure on him."

"Sounds reasonable. When are you seeing him again?"

I said, "Tonight. Nana and Ollie are going to a charity gala, so I'll have the house to myself and I'm cooking him dinner."

"Did you see him this week?"

"God I wanted to. I thought about him all the time, but like I said, I can't rush this."

One of the restaurant's owners brought out our meal a few minutes later. Jamie said, "Hi Jessie! This is on the house. Thanks for getting Zachary to sit down and actually eat something. He worked so hard during the lunch rush that I was worried he was going to keel over."

"Thanks. I have something for you and Dmitri, too." I handed him two tickets to the masquerade ball. "I hope you and your husband can find a sitter for your little girl and turn it into a date night. I've heard through the grapevine that you're overdue for one." He thanked me and seemed excited about it, and when he went to find his husband to tell him about the event, I said, "This is fun. I feel like I get to be a fairy godmother and send everyone to the ball."

As we ate, Zachary asked, "Did Christopher give you some input on Chance's photos while you were at the gallery today?"

"He did. I helped him paint these big, portable display walls for the event, and then he and I finalized what'll be included in the show. He even offered to print them onto canvas for me. He's excited about this. He said he'll share the blame if Chance is mad we're doing this without asking him, but I told him I'd take the blame. Chance's husband and Christopher's are cousins, so I don't want to cause problems among family."

Cole came over to refill our water glasses, and I said, "Since this place has emptied out, why don't you sit down for a few minutes?" I slid over to make room for him in the booth, and he put the pitcher on the tabletop and sat beside me. "You know I have to ask what's going on with you and River," I told him. "I'm worried about you guys. This separation is just temporary, right?"

Cole sighed and said, "I don't know."

"What happened? I thought everything was going great between you two."

"It started out so good. We totally clicked when we met, right from the start. But over time, it just started unraveling. Conversations that should have happened didn't. Little resentments got pushed down instead of being aired. Feelings got hurt. A hundred little things kept building and building, until I couldn't take it anymore." Cole looked like he wanted to cry, but he didn't give in to it.

"I can tell you still love him," I said gently.

"Of course I do. I always will. But we were making each other crazy. I know a lot of it was my fault. This is only my second real relationship, and the first one ended horribly. I was trying not to make the same mistakes with River, but instead, I made all new ones. I think you know I used to date Hunter, the former porn star," Cole said. "He and I used to fight like cats and dogs. Every little thing would turn into a yelling match. I vowed I wouldn't do that again, so River and I never fought at all. I was too afraid of ruining our relationship the way I ruined the last one. If something he said or did bothered me, I just kept my feelings bottled up. You can only do that for so long though, before you reach your breaking point."

"You seem to have a really good grasp of what went wrong," I told him.

"I should. I've been in therapy for a long time," Cole said quietly. "I started a year after my first relationship ended, when I realized I couldn't move past it on my own. But the thing is, even though I understand what happened with River and I can clearly see my role in it, I can't seem to let go of all this anger and hurt."

"Have you told River any of this?" Zachary asked. He'd stopped eating and was fully focused on his coworker.

"I tried, but it just ended up sounding like I was blaming him for all those little things that had been building up. I really wasn't, but I guess it came across that way. He started to get defensive, and I got upset, and that made me withdraw from him again. It's like there's this disconnect when we try to communicate. I'm saying 'apples', he's hearing 'oranges', and we both just end up frustrated and angry. Since I don't see that changing, I don't know how this could ever work out."

"But you love him, and I know he loves you," I said.

Cole slid from the booth and said, "If only that was all it took to be in a relationship. But if you can't talk things out, you're kind of doomed from the start. Anyway, sorry if all of that was TMI. I just wanted you to know what happened, and that it wasn't River's fault. I know you're friends with him, Jessie, so I hope you'll be there for him. I know he has to be hurting right now."

"It sounds like you both are."

He nodded, trying to keep his voice steady as he said, "I wanted to be with River forever, but we can't keep making each other miserable. We just can't." Cole took a step back from the table and gestured at Zachary's plate. "I'm sorry to interrupt your lunch with all of that. Please keep eating. I'm going to go change, I'll talk to you both later." He turned and fled the dining room.

Zachary watched Cole leave. His voice was almost a whisper as he said, "I don't get it. If I ever found someone I loved, who loved me in return, I'd fight for that person with everything I had. But it seems like he's just giving up."

"There's a context, though. His relationship with Hunter completely devastated him. Maybe he's afraid of getting hurt that bad again, and it's making him pull away from River. I mean, I'm just guessing, but that makes sense to me," I said. "But it sounds like they still love each other, so maybe there's a chance they'll find their way back together."

"I hope so. I don't know them very well, but I hate to see any couple struggling like that."

We decided we were done eating and packed up the remainder of our lunch in to-go boxes. I then helped Zachary wipe down his tables and restock his station, then asked, "Do you want a ride home?"

"I'd love one, but I don't want to go home yet. Chance and Finn are spending the day together before working late shifts this evening, and I don't want to intrude on their couple time, so could you drop me off at the LGBT community center instead?"

"Not a problem."

We said goodbye to his bosses and coworkers and headed to my car. After the quiet calm (at least after the lunch rush) of the restaurant, San Francisco's Richmond District felt frenetic. The sidewalk was crowded with people, who all seemed to be in a hurry. A massive double-length bus, jointed in the center with what looked like a huge accordion, cut through the ever-present traffic. It pulled up right in front of us with a loud hiss of hydraulics, and the door swung open and even more people began spilling out.

I fed off the city's energy, but I watched Zachary recoil as all that noise and activity battered him. He put on his sunglasses and hunched his shoulders against the throng, almost shrinking into himself. My heart went out to him, and I linked my arm with his. "On second thought, come to Nana's house with me," I told him. "I have plenty of time before my date, and we can hang out." I wanted to give him an oasis, at least for a little while, since he didn't want to go home. He really needed that. He gave me a grateful smile.

Chapter Ten

Kai was right on time. When he rang the bell at six p.m., I looked down at myself and unfastened an extra button on my shirt. Then I decided it made me look like I was trying too hard and buttoned it again. I was wearing my version of a sexy outfit: a fitted, bright blue, button-down shirt that I'd been told brought out my blue eyes, and a pair of dark indigo jeans that made my butt look good. That was about all I could manage, as far as sexy went. I adjusted the rolled-back cuff of my shirt and headed for the front door.

Kai was trying to smooth down his thick, unruly hair with his palm, but stopped as soon as I swung the door open. "Hey. You look great," he said, juggling a couple items under his arm.

"So do you." He was wearing a tight Henley, jeans, cowboy boots, and a motorcycle jacket, all in black. Now *that* was how to do sexy.

I stepped back and held the door for him, and when he came in, he handed me a brown paper shopping bag and a bouquet of white daisies. "I brought wine, but I have no idea if you like it, so I also brought beer." He was nervous, which struck me as incredibly cute.

"Thank you." I stretched up to kiss his cheek.

We went into the kitchen together, and as I looked for a vase I said, "I don't remember if I thanked you the first time you brought me flowers. I probably didn't since it all went wrong that night, and I'm so sorry about that. They meant a lot to me, and so do these."

"I'm glad you like them. I probably shouldn't have brought daisies again, but there's not much else blooming in my yard right now."

"You grew them? Now it's doubly sweet."

I filled a blue glass vase with water, and as I carefully arranged the flowers, he said, "I wanted to tell you about something funny that happened this week. Remember the guys on the roof, the ones who caught us in the act when we were messing around on the picnic table?" When I nodded, he said, "Well, one of them brought his car to me this week. He said he'd never realized it was a gay-owned business until he saw you and me…you know. He also said he wasn't sure if the garage was open, since it looks abandoned from the outside. I need to do something about that."

"If you decide you want to paint it, I'll be happy to help. A little color would do wonders."

"Thanks. I'm rebuilding this guy's transmission, so I'll have some money coming in soon. Maybe I can use some of it on paint and supplies."

I grinned and said, "Who'd have thought an act of public indecency would lead to a job?"

"It's weird, I know, but I'm glad to get the business. It might even be more than just a one-time thing. This guy Ash is a DJ and knows a lot of people, and he said he's going to tell his friends about me. I guess some other garages can kind of feel like hetero boys' clubs, which makes him uncomfortable. That's not going to happen at my place."

"It sounds like you two hit it off."

"We did, even though he's the exact opposite of me, really talkative and social. Actually, he reminds me of you."

"You think you and I are opposites?"

"In some ways. You know how I am, we've been in the same racing club a long time. We have our love of cars in common, but you're colorful, and upbeat, and you have a million friends. I have one, his name's Sawyer. I'm not counting my twin, because that's dorky."

"I'm sure you have more than one friend."

"Not really, but that's all I need. It did get a little lonely when Sawyer joined the Army and got shipped overseas, but Malia's still here."

"I hope I get to meet your friend sometime," I said.

"You will."

I opened two of the beers he'd brought, and as I handed him one of the bottles, I said, "You're so different with me than you are with the other guys in the racing club. Why don't you let them see this side of you?"

"Why should I?"

"So they know they're wrong about you, just like I was."

"I really don't care what they think of me. They decided I was an asshole a long time ago, just because I tend to keep to myself. If they want to believe that, let 'em."

I thought about that for a moment, then said, "We really are different. I try so hard to get people to like me. Too hard. It's kind of pathetic. One guy I dated compared me to a needy little puppy, always jumping around trying to please everyone. It obviously wasn't a compliment. It wasn't even a very good analogy. It still hurt, though."

"That guy was a dick. It's sweet, the way you love your friends so much and try to take care of them. That doesn't make you needy, it makes you one of the kindest people I've ever met."

"He *was* a dick." I took another sip of beer, then changed the subject. "Are you hungry?" He nodded and I said, "Let's grab a couple more beers and head to the third floor. I thought it'd be fun to eat upstairs in the grand ballroom."

He picked up the remainder of the six-pack and the bottle opener. "Is there anything else I can carry?"

"No, everything's already up there." I took the flowers along, and as we climbed the stairs side by side, I asked, "What's Izzy doing tonight?"

"She and my sister are going to make popcorn and have a princess movie film festival. I'm lucky to have three in-house babysitters."

"Aw, but you're missing the princess movies," I teased.

"Oh believe me, I have them all committed to memory. Izzy watches those things over and over. I guess we all need an escape from reality sometimes, and those movies are her happy place."

"She struck me as a pretty serious little kid when I met her."

Kai said, "I'd describe her as cautious. She's so afraid of making mistakes. I really don't know where she gets that. I make mistakes all the time and try to show her it's no big deal. But she holds herself to these impossible standards, and she's only in kindergarten. I worry about how that's going to play out later in life."

"I think, with a parent as loving and supportive as you in her corner, she's going to be just fine."

We reached the open double doors to the grand ballroom, and he stopped in his tracks and murmured, "Holy shit."

I said nervously, "I hope it's not too over the top." I'd suspended cording from a panel in the high ceiling, which held up several patterned and striped sheets. They formed a tent over a low table and a bunch of colorful pillows. Because it was kind of dark inside, I'd lined the tent with multiple strands of white Christmas lights, so the whole thing glowed like a paper lantern. I told him as we walked up to the tent, "This is my favorite room in the house, because of that mural of the snowy birch forest on the walls. It was painted by my friend Christopher Robin for a winter wedding a few years back."

"Is the blanket fort usually in here?"

I grinned and said, "I think of it more as a dining pavilion, and no. I rigged that for tonight. The room's so big, and I wanted to give us a more intimate place to have dinner."

"You went to so much trouble."

"It was no trouble at all," I said as I slid my shoes off. He pulled off his jacket and cowboy boots, and we both climbed into the tent and settled onto the pillows.

"Sure it was. My God, look at all this." He seemed a bit stunned as he gestured at the elaborately set table. The china and silverware sparkled in the soft light.

I made room for the daisies amid several low vases of wildflowers, and fidgeted by smoothing the yellow tablecloth. "Well, you told me you haven't dated since high school, so I wanted to do something special for you. I tend to get a bit carried away, sorry if I overdid it."

Kai crawled around to my side of the table and pulled me into an embrace. "Don't apologize. This is the nicest thing anyone's ever done for me. I just feel kind of bad, because I'll never be able to top it."

"Who says you have to?"

"Okay, wrong choice of words. It's not like I'm going to try to out-do you," he said, leaning back to look at me. "But I want to try to reciprocate. If I just take you to Nolan's next weekend like I was planning, it's going to seem like I'm not even trying."

"I'd love to go to Nolan's with you. Or anyplace at all," I said softly.

He touched my cheek and kissed me tenderly, then said as he held me to him, "Thank you for doing all of this for me."

"It was my pleasure." I wrapped my arms around him and buried my face in his shoulder. He smelled so good, like soap and cotton and Kai. "I missed you," I whispered.

"I missed you, too. I thought about you all the damn time."

Kai sat back a bit and ran his hands down my upper arms. I felt shy all of a sudden, and said, "Make yourself comfortable while I bring us the first course."

He arranged the pillows while I got up and retrieved the soup I'd made. Zachary had given it a big thumbs-up when I fed him a bowl before he went home, but I still worried about whether Kai would like it and the rest of the meal. I'd set up several chafing dishes on a table beside the wall of windows and checked them quickly to make sure they were keeping dinner warm. One of the great things about entertaining at Nana's house, besides the beautiful setting, was that she owned enough housewares to fully stock a major department store.

I served the soup and a basket of sliced Italian bread, then took a seat across from Kai. "It's minestrone. I hope you like it. The bread turned out a little dense, but it's not terrible if you dip it in the soup."

"You baked bread for me?"

"I tried to. Nana showed me how to make it once, but I clearly need another lesson."

I watched him from beneath my lashes as he tried the soup. When he said, "That's so good," I let out the breath I'd been holding.

As we ate, Kai asked, "What did you do this week?"

"I spent a lot of time in dress shops. I drove Nana and her girlfriends to nine different boutiques over four days, so we could try on wedding gowns."

"We?"

"Nana likes to see several gowns at once, but on people, not on hangers. So everyone joins in, me included."

"That's incredibly nice of you."

"I'm happy to help. Nana's getting married in June, which isn't all that far away, and she was nervous about finding the perfect dress. She never did find one after all of that, so she finally decided to let one of Mr. Mario's friends make something for her. He's a professional clothing designer, and he's also a drag queen with quite a flair for the dramatic, so it'll be interesting to see what he comes up with."

"Are you in the wedding party?"

"Yeah. There are a couple dozen groomsmen and almost as many bridesmaids. Her grandson Dante is best man, and he's walking Nana down the aisle."

"How many people are coming to the wedding?"

"About seven hundred. That's Nana's idea of keeping it small."

"I can't even imagine a wedding that big. Where's she getting married?"

"She rented out an entire boutique hotel in Nob Hill for the ceremony and the reception. That's also where she and Ollie are putting up their out-of-town guests. The banquet room is really pretty, it has panoramic city views and great art deco details from the 1920s."

"Sounds nice."

"It is. I hope it all goes off without a hitch. It'd break my heart if Nana didn't get her dream wedding."

"You really care about her."

"I love Nana. It meant so much to me when she made me feel like I was one of the family and invited me into her beautiful home. I'm going to miss living here and being a part of all this."

"You've moving out?"

I nodded. "Nana doesn't need me like she used to, now that she has Ollie. I'll still be her driver when she wants to go somewhere in the limo and I'll help out whenever I'm needed, but it's already not full-time anymore, and after the wedding I'll be needed even less. It's time to find my own apartment."

Kai asked, "What kind of place are you looking for?"

"Anything that's affordable, which will probably include several roommates. Nana's been paying me an overly generous salary, which actually needs to change now that I'm working fewer hours. I managed to build up my savings since I've been living rent-free, but I'll burn through my money way too fast if I get a place on my own."

"The cost of living is insane. If my grandparents hadn't bought that house in the sixties, there's no way in hell my family could afford to live in this city."

"What happened to your granddad?"

"He died of heart disease before I was born."

"I'm sorry you didn't get a chance to know him. My grandpa and I were pretty close. Before…well, you know."

"Fuck," Kai murmured, and I looked up from my soup. "I hate it so much that your family did that to you."

I tried to smooth out a wrinkle in the pale yellow tablecloth as I looked down again and said, "When I was a kid and realized I liked boys, I spent a lot of time wondering why God hated me so much. I'd been taught that being gay was a sin, and I was also told that God made us, so I couldn't figure out why he'd make me that way and condemn me to burn in hell. I used to go into our church when it was empty and kneel in front of the altar and pray to Him to change me, to make me like everyone else so I could go to heaven with the rest of my family." I pulled up a smile and added, "Obviously I was a clueless little kid, and in my teens I finally learned I'd been misled all my life." I was startled when two big tears spilled from my eyes, and I wiped them away quickly. "Shit, I'm sorry," I said. "I didn't mean to do this."

He reached across the table and took my hand. "Don't apologize."

"I don't know what's wrong with me. I mean, they disowned me years ago. I should be able to put this behind me, and I sure as hell shouldn't still be crying about it."

Kai's voice was so gentle when he said, "Mourning doesn't come with an expiration date. Believe me, I know. My dad's been gone a decade, and I still miss him every damn day. You lost more than that, you lost your entire family. If you need to cry, or scream, or yell, or do whatever it takes to make yourself feel better, you go right ahead and do that."

"I can't. The pain of losing my family almost swallowed me whole at first, I thought I'd never find my way out. But I realized after a while that it's kind of like driving through mud, you know? If you don't slow down and keep moving forward, you won't get stuck. The second you stop moving though, you're done for. That's what all of life feels like to me. I keep busy, I don't dwell on what happened to me, and I try so hard to stay positive, because if I don't, I'll drown in all that mud."

"That sounds exhausting."

I let go of his hand and got up, and as I cleared away the soup bowls I said, "That's just life."

He followed me out of the tent and touched my arm. "You don't have to pretend you're okay with me, Jessie. If you're hurting, I want you to talk about it. You need to let this stuff out."

I felt tears cueing up, but I held them back. "I don't want to break down in front of you and make you think I'm this pathetic little thing. You have enough on your plate without also feeling like you have to take care of me."

His voice was so soft when he said, "What if I want to take care of you?"

I shook my head and said, "I'm a full-grown man. I know I barely look it, but I need to take care of myself."

Kai stepped forward and touched my cheek. "What if I want you to take care of me, too?"

"How does any of this conversation fit with taking it slow?" I asked, retreating again by backing up to the table by the window. "This is our first real date. We should be talking about cars, or current events, you know, stuff like that! Light topics! I have no idea how we even got on the subject of my family."

Those intelligent dark eyes watched me for a moment, and then Kai said, "You're right. Light topics." He turned to the covered chafing dishes and said, "Whatever's in there smells terrific."

It was a clunky attempt at changing the subject, but I appreciated it. "I made lasagna. It's Nana's recipe, which means it made enough to feed twenty people. I hope you like it, and if you do, you can take some leftovers home with you."

He ended up polishing off two huge slabs of lasagna while we did, in fact, talk about cars. After he cleaned his plate for the second time, he said, "That was delicious, thank you. I'm so full now. I shouldn't have eaten that second piece, but I couldn't help myself."

"There's dessert too, but we can hold off on that for a while if you want."

"That's probably a good idea. Do you mind if we move the table out of here and just relax for a bit?"

"Sure, or we could go down to the living room."

"I like it inside the blanket fort."

"Dining pavilion," I corrected with a smile.

"Call it what you want. It's still a blanket fort, and I think it's awesome."

He helped me lift the coffee table carefully, and we moved it out of the tent and put it beside the serving table. I took a moment to extinguish the candles beneath the chafing dishes, and while I did that, he made a nest with the pillows and stretched out on his back. When I ducked inside the canopy, Kai held his arms out to me and I curled up beside him with my head on his bicep.

"Izzy would love this," he said, looking up at the twinkle lights, which bathed him in a golden glow. "I'm going to make her a blanket fort this weekend and include some Christmas lights."

"Make sure they're LEDs like these, they don't get as hot as traditional bulbs," I said. "I wouldn't want it to be a fire hazard."

He grinned at that. "Thank you for the blanket fort tip."

"Any time. Oh hey, speaking of Izzy, did she end up bringing a doll house home from the show in Sacramento?"

"She did. It's a kit, and it's in about a million tiny pieces. I've been working on that thing like a second job all week, and I've barely put a dent in it. Once it's together, I'll have to paint it, and then I'll need to start building furniture for it, because of course it didn't come with any."

"You're such a good dad. I feel guilty for taking you away from your daughter tonight."

"Don't feel guilty. She goes to bed at eight, and she'll have a great time hanging out with her Aunt Mal for a couple hours before that. They're really close, and they love spending time together."

"What's your sister like?"

"God, how do I describe Mal?" He thought for a minute, and finally said, "She's rough around the edges, but she has a heart of gold. And she's funny. No joke is too dirty as far as she's concerned. She's also a tomboy and spends absolutely no time worrying about her hair, clothes or makeup. Actually, my mom and grandma are like that, too, they'll wear anything as long as it's comfortable, sometimes with horrifying results. Meanwhile, here's my six-year-old, carrying a handbag and making sure her jacket matches her outfit. I'm not sure how Izzy ended up as such a girly girl, given her role models."

"What does Malia do?"

"She works at a fancy B and B where she does a little of everything, from cooking breakfast to cleaning the rooms. The second part of that isn't her idea of a good time, but this job's not forever. Malia and her boyfriend have been trying to buy a food truck. He's a line cook, and they're both tired of working for other people. He has some savings, and she still has some of the money she inherited from our dad, but I guess those trucks are way more expensive than you'd think. They're looking for a second-hand one, and I'll get it running if the engine needs work."

"It's nice of you to help out."

"Malia and I always have each other's back. I'm happy to do whatever I can for her and Adam." I rolled onto my side and draped an arm over Kai's chest, and he said, "She's dying to meet you, by the way. *Dying*. It just kills her that you were both at the Valentine's Day open house, but she didn't know to check you out."

I grinned and said, "You told her about me?"

"Of course. We don't keep secrets from each other. I did try to tell her you and I are just starting out and she needs to chill a bit, but she's incredibly curious."

"Given your dating history, or lack thereof, I can see why she would be."

"Exactly."

"Well, I look forward to meeting her."

Kai smiled at me. "Be forewarned, she's going to ask lots of embarrassing questions. Don't feel you have to answer them. I refuse to tell her anything about our sex life, apart from the fact that you and I have one."

"Yeah, I really won't feel the need to elaborate."

Kai rolled onto his side and kissed me gently. After a while, he said, "I want you to know how much I appreciate all you did tonight."

"I'm glad you liked it."

He grinned and looked embarrassed. "It made me feel special. I know I sound like an idiot saying that, but it's true."

"Well, good. Then it was totally worth the effort."

I kissed him again, and he slipped his hand around my waist and pulled me against him as he deepened the kiss. I draped my leg over his thigh and ran my fingers into his thick hair as my eyes slid shut. I let myself get totally immersed in him, in his taste, his scent, the way his warm body felt in my arms, the sound of his breath in my ear when he licked my lobe.

I was startled when Kai jerked his head up and asked, "Are the dogs home?"

"No. Ollie's friend Ignacio Mondelvano is dog-sitting tonight while Nana and Ollie are at a fundraising gala. Why do you ask?"

"I thought I saw the Chihuahua just now."

I sat up and said, "I think I would have heard Iggy if he brought them back early. What did you see?"

He pointed out the back of the tent, past the serving table. "I spotted movement out of the corner of my eye. It was back in that dark corner, by those stacked chairs and…are those stripper poles?"

"Yup. Nana got them ostensibly to change up her exercise routine, but really it's because she and her girlfriends like to watch Skye's sexy husband pole dance."

"I met him at Sunday dinner last weekend. I thought he was a ballet dancer," Kai said as he got to his feet.

I got up too and told him, "He's been both to pay the bills."

I turned on all the lights in the room while Kai went to the dark corner and leaned over the chairs to get a look behind them. While he did that, I tilted my head and enjoyed the view of his ass in those tight, black jeans. When he jumped back suddenly and exclaimed, "Holy shit," I jumped, too.

"What's in there?" I asked.

"I'm not sure, but it's pretty big. Bigger than a mouse."

"Oh God, is it a rat?"

"I don't know."

Kai yanked the chairs from the wall, and we both swore in surprise when a crab came scuttling out sideways. "It's one of the last two escapees! How the hell did she get to the third floor?" I exclaimed. "There's no way she climbed the stairs."

"Maybe she hitched a ride in a laundry basket or something."

"Maybe. The poor thing must be so stressed, it's been days." I ran after her and scooped her up gingerly while she tried her damnedest to pinch me. I turned to Kai and said, "I'm going to take her down to the backyard, want to come along?"

"Sure. How do you know it's a she?"

"The claw tips are red, which indicates a female. I've learned a hell of a lot about blue crabs in the last week." I slipped my shoes on, holding the crab at arm's length to avoid her pinchers, and Kai pulled on his boots. I asked him to grab the dish with the lasagna before we headed downstairs, and he put it in the refrigerator for me as we cut through the kitchen.

I was surprised to find Skye, Dare and their dog Benny in the yard. Skye was prying a jagged metal panel off the sculpture with a crowbar when we stepped out the back door. "Hey," I called, "you're working late."

"Hi! We were at Haley's apartment when inspiration struck, so I talked Dare into stopping by for a few minutes on the way home," Skye explained.

"That was over an hour ago," his husband said with a smile from a nearby patio chair, stretching his legs out in front of him and tucking his hands in the kangaroo pocket of his hoodie.

Skye told us, "Nana gave us a key to the back gate, so we let ourselves in. We didn't think anyone was home. I hope we're not disturbing you."

"Not at all," I said. "We didn't even know you were here. Do you want to come in and warm up a bit? I could make you some coffee."

"Or I could," Kai said with a little grin. Benny wandered over to investigate, and Kai scratched him behind the ears. "I seem to recall you and the espresso maker have a strained relationship."

"He has a point," I said.

"Are you sure we're not intruding? You two look like you're on a date," Dare said.

I turned to Kai, and he said, "It's fine. You guys must be freezing out here."

"Awesome, thanks. I'd love some coffee," Skye said.

"Just let me drop this girl off in the crab condo. Kai just found one of the last two missing crabs. She was up on the third floor, go figure."

Kai followed me to a prefabricated greenhouse in a far corner of the yard. The ground beneath it had been excavated a bit that week, and Nana's grandson Vincent had installed a nice saltwater pond with a pump and filter, and a little, sandy beach with a few edible plants around the edges. "Holy shit," Kai muttered as I opened the door, leaned over the baby gate, and turned the crab loose to join her friends. "You built them a resort."

"The greenhouse was my idea. I didn't want seagulls and raccoons to carry them off. We're concerned that it's still a bit too crowded for them though, so Nana's been trying to get some of the crabs adopted out, by people who aren't just going to throw them in a pot of boiling water." Kai grinned at me, and I told him, "What can I say? We bonded with them."

"Is Nigel in there?" he asked.

"Virgil, and no. He lives in a punchbowl in my room."

Kai's grin got wider. "Of course he does."

"Good night, kids. No fighting," I told the crabs before closing the door to the greenhouse.

Skye, Dare and Benny followed us inside, and while Kai worked his magic with the giant espresso machine, Dare asked, "You don't really have raccoons here, do you?"

"Sure we do. Haven't you ever seen them running down the sidewalk at night? They hide in the storm drains. They're big, hearty critters, too. Life in the city agrees with them," I said as I found a box of cookies in the cupboard and put some on a plate.

"I hope one never gets in the house," Kai said as he steamed some milk. "You'll probably adopt it as a pet, too."

I exclaimed, "Oh man, I'd love a pet raccoon! They're so cute with those little hands. I'd name him Laurence, and I'd make him a little red vest."

Kai chuckled at that. "Why?"

"Because raccoons look adorable in little red vests," I said, and gave him a playful smile.

He beamed at me as he handed lattes to Skye and Dare. Both drinks had a perfect crab drawn in foam on their milky surface. "I was going to make you a crab, too," Kai told me, "but hang on, let me see if I can pull off a raccoon."

As he turned back to the machine, Skye exclaimed, "Holy shit, you're seriously good at latte art!"

"I worked at a coffee house when I was in high school," Kai explained. "The assistant manager was the best barista I've ever seen in my life. He was an artist too, and showed me how to do this. Whenever it was slow, which was often after a Starbucks opened up right across the street, we'd practice. He actually went on to win a few regional barista competitions."

Kai turned to me and put a white ceramic cup in my hand. A three-dimensional face of a raccoon peered out at me, and little foam hands gripped the edge of the cup. "Oh my God," I murmured. "It's way too cute to drink." I put it on the counter and felt my pockets for my phone, then spotted it on the kitchen island.

As I grabbed the phone and snapped a few photos of Kai's creation, I asked, "Whatever happened to that assistant manager? I hope he went on to open his own coffee house."

"That was his dream. He wanted it so bad, but he knew he could never afford it. When he graduated from college, he followed in his dad's footsteps instead and enlisted in the Army."

I asked, "You don't mean your friend Sawyer, do you?"

"Yup. It's funny, you'd never guess he could do something like these delicate little foam drawings. He's this huge guy, almost six and a half feet tall, and he looks like he can bench-press a Buick. But this was his art. It's a shame he doesn't do it anymore, but I still try to practice what he taught me whenever I can," Kai said. "I guess it's my way of keeping his dream alive, even if he didn't."

Skye took a sip from his cup and said, "This is a damn fine cup of coffee. He taught you well."

"Thanks," Kai said. He'd left his latte plain, and blew on its surface before taking a sip.

"Which coffee house do you work at now?" Dare asked him. "We'll be sure to come by."

"I don't anymore. I own a garage in Bernal Heights."

"I know Jessie's a total gearhead, so is that how you guys met? Through the garage?" Skye asked.

"We're in the same street racing club, actually," I said as I sat on the counter and snapped a picture of Kai.

"How'd you two meet?" Kai asked my friends.

Skye smiled at his husband and said, "We both briefly moonlighted as pole dancers. I was a rank amateur, but Dare was something to behold."

"I noticed the poles upstairs. This'll sound stupid, and feel free to say no, but could you show me a couple moves sometime? I know that's totally random, but I've always wanted to try it," Kai said, coloring slightly.

I tilted my head and asked, "You have?"

He nodded. "It seems incredibly athletic. I always wondered if I could do it."

Skye was already heading for the stairs, coffee in hand. "No time like the present! I haven't done it in ages. I wonder if I remember how."

"I teach classes in pole dancing," Dare told Kai as we followed his husband, "so I get asked this all the time. Don't be embarrassed. It's fun, and a lot of people do it as a way to change up their exercise routine."

When we got to the ballroom, Skye gestured at the tent and exclaimed, "Oh shit, we *are* totally interrupting your date! This is adorable!"

"It's fine," I said. "I'm looking forward to this. Who knew Kai had this secret desire?" He chuckled and colored slightly as I flashed him a smile.

There were four poles, conveniently, and they were on round, heavy bases. We tilted them at an angle and rolled them out to an open part of the room while the dog climbed inside the tent and made himself a nest amid the pillows. As Dare tossed his jacket aside and did some stretches, Skye came up to us and said, "Wait 'til you see this." His blue eyes were sparkling. "I started to fall in love with Dare when I first saw him perform."

"No you didn't," Dare said, bending over at the waist and pressing his palms to the floor. "You totally hated me when we first started working together."

"You hated me too," Skye said. "I got over it quicker."

"I hated everybody, not just you," Dare said with a smile as he stretched out his arms. "Okay, let me see if I've still got this."

"He does," his husband said. Dare ran at the pole and grabbed it high up, then lifted his body gracefully into the air. As he spun around, Skye murmured, "Damn. Why don't we have one of these in our apartment? That's so hot."

Dare did a few stunningly graceful moves that seemed to defy the rules of gravity and human capability, and when he jumped down, he picked up Skye's hand, slapped his palm, and said, "Tag, your turn. You didn't warm up though, so take it slow."

"I'll be fine. I'd been dismantling metal for the past hour, I think that counts as warming up my muscles." Skye walked up to the pole and pulled himself up effortlessly. He wrapped a leg around the pole and extended his arms over his head, then did a couple athletic spins before jumping down and exclaiming, "Damn, I'm out of shape. I can't believe I used to do that for hours at a time." He pushed his blue hair out of his eyes and tried again.

Kai took off his cowboy boots, and while Dare showed him a couple basics, I took a run at one of the poles and tried to swing myself around it. "Oh hell no," I said as I landed on my feet.

"These pants are way too tight. I'll be right back." Kai shot me a smile as I hurried from the room.

When I returned a few minutes later, I was barefoot and dressed in red athletic shorts and a pink t-shirt with a cartoon of a guy dressed like a unicorn straddling a rainbow. The caption read: 'I am that gay.' Kai burst out laughing and almost fell off the pole. "Nice shirt. I've never seen a cartoon of someone having sex with a rainbow before," he said.

"He's not having sex with it, he's just straddling it," I said as I did a few stretches.

"Oh no, he's having sex with it," Skye chimed in cheerfully. "If you want, I can go get a marker and draw in a couple motion lines for you. Then you'll see the humpage."

I laughed at 'humpage' and said, "You just have dirty minds. The shirt's perfectly innocent."

"Except for the rainbow humping," Dare said. He was hanging upside down from one of the poles and flashed me a big smile.

"Perverts, the whole lot of you," I said as I went over to the unused pole and pulled myself up.

"Hey, you're the one wearing a shirt with a guy fornicating with a rainbow," Dare told me as he swung around the pole, then held on with just one leg.

For the next hour or so, the four of us laughed and joked and kind of learned some pole dancing. Kai made a real effort, even though he almost immediately pronounced it much harder than it looked. I gave up after about twenty minutes, got comfortable on the floor, and cheered him on. "Come back," he said. "If I can do this, you can."

"Oh no. I have the upper body strength of a baby bunny. I'm just going to leave the feats of strength to y'all," I said as I adjusted my pillow and tucked my hands under my head. Benny the dog swung his head around and rested it on my thigh.

"Come on," Dare cajoled. "If Nana and her girlfriends can pole dance, so can you."

"They really only do it so they can ogle your muscles," I told him.

"I know. But they end up learning stuff, too."

"I'm fine right here. The view is awesome." Kai looked at me over his shoulder and grinned when he saw me checking out his ass. I added, "I'm surprised you can get your pole dance on in those jeans, Captain Tight Pants."

"Oh my God, you just made a Firefly reference," he exclaimed with a huge smile.

I beamed at him and said, "And you just *got* a Firefly reference! I think I love you!"

He chuckled at that and said, "Be sure to tell me when you know for sure."

"Awww, they're having a nerd moment," Skye joked. He jumped off the pole and shook out his arms. "I think we should let you two get back to your date and the upcoming Joss Whedon love fest that's probably about to ensue."

We thanked our friends for the pole dancing lesson, and they invited us to dinner at their apartment the following week. After Skye, Dare and their dog left, Kai said, "Let me see if I can impress you with my totally graceless flailing about before my arms snap off at the shoulder." He pulled himself up, did several spins, then turned upside down and flipped himself over, landing on his feet. "That's all I got," he said with a shy smile, and I whistled and applauded. "I'm going to go die in the blanket fort now. I figured that'd be strenuous, but holy shit."

We went back to the tent and curled up together on the pillows. Kai said, "I hurt all over. I thought I was in shape, but I discovered some brand new muscles this evening, ones that apparently have never, ever been used before."

I told him, "I'm both surprised and impressed that you wanted to try that."

"Life is short. I know that all too well. Whenever the universe presents you with the opportunity to try something new, you have to go for it. Who knows when you'll ever have the chance again? I felt like an idiot asking your friends to show me how to pole dance, and I really didn't intend for that to happen *tonight*, but Skye and Dare are really good guys. I liked them a lot when I met them last week, and I figured they wouldn't laugh in my face when I asked them to show me some stuff."

"You're right, they're terrific. They obviously like you, too."

I leaned in for a kiss, and he told me, "I'm all gross and sweat-drenched."

"It's sexy." I kissed him gently, and he reached up and brushed my hair back as I told him, "You know, if you keep being social like this, you're going to have to revise your previous statement about only having one friend."

"I already had to revise it. My friend count doubled when you and I spent time together last weekend."

I smiled at that. "And now it's doubled again with the addition of Skye and Dare. It's multiplying exponentially! Pretty impressive for the guy who never says a word to anyone in our racing club."

"I'm an outsider there, and I always will be. The guys we race with made up their minds about me a long time ago, and I really have no interest in trying to invest my time or energy into convincing them they're wrong," he said. "They're not what's important anyway. You are. You bring me out of my shell. I wouldn't risk total humiliation by learning to pole dance for anyone else."

"I'm glad you decided to push yourself out of your comfort zone."

"I have to. The last thing I want is for you to get bored with me, so I need to show you I'm willing to make an effort."

"You don't really think I would, do you?"

He shrugged and changed the subject by getting to his feet and saying, "Wasn't there talk of dessert at some point?"

I got up too and followed him to the table by the window. "I made cannoli. Not the most imaginative dessert, given my Italian theme, but I've seen Nana make it so many times that I was pretty sure I'd get it right."

"Sounds good."

I fished a plastic bag out of a bowl of ice water and removed the pastry bag inside it, then retrieved a couple cylindrical shells from a storage container. As I got ready to fill the cannoli, I said, "I hope you don't actually think I could get bored with you. There's just no way."

He didn't look at me as he said, "I know how I am. I'm just this quiet guy, living a simple life. But you, you're like a garden in full bloom, beautiful and colorful and so full of life and energy. If I'm going to have a shot in hell at holding your attention, I need to be more. Otherwise, you're going to get tired of me so damn fast."

"That's an amazing compliment, but you have nothing to worry about. Seriously." I stretched up and kissed him, and said gently, "You have my full attention."

"Glad to hear it." He kissed me again, then asked, "What can I do to help with dessert?"

"Why don't you fill the cannoli while I get the plates ready?"

I handed him the pastry bag and one of the shells, and he said, "Is there a trick to this?"

"Just keep the end of the bag twisted so the filling doesn't fall out. Then just insert the tip into the cookie shell and squeeze gently. Do one end, then the other."

I found the dessert plates and piled a few fresh raspberries on them while Kai tried to follow my instructions, but after a moment he said, "I think it's jammed up or something. Nothing's coming out."

He held the bag tip-side up and squeezed it a bit, and I leaned over to take a look. Just then, whatever had been blocking it was forced through, and I was sprayed with ricotta filling. "Shit, I'm really sorry," he exclaimed. He looked horrified, but then I burst out laughing and he did, too. "I swear that wasn't on purpose."

"I know. Don't worry about it, I can just go wash up." I pinched a strand of hair and slid it between my fingers to remove a clump of filling.

Kai startled me by leaning in and giving my cheek a big lick, and I started laughing all over again. "You taste great," he said. "Even sweeter than usual."

He licked me again and I batted at him and exclaimed, "Oh my God, it's like dating a puppy!"

"You taste so good, though!" Kai pulled me into his arms and licked my lower lip, and my tongue darted out to meet his.

Things accelerated quickly from there, and soon we were making out wildly. He lifted me off my feet and I wrapped myself around him, my cock pressed to his as lust shot through me. I said between kisses, "I need to be inside you, Kai. I know we haven't talked about this, but I really want to fuck you. Would you be willing?"

"God yes." He pulled my collar aside and kissed my shoulder, then rubbed his cheek to mine as he said, "I was going to bring that up tonight. I even prepped myself ahead of time."

I shuddered with pleasure, and when he put me down we rushed hand-in-hand to my bedroom on the second floor. After we stripped each other, I spent a long time fingering him and kissing him. I got the impression he hadn't bottomed very often, but he was so trusting, and it was such a turn on to watch him relaxing under my caresses and moaning as I massaged his prostate. He kissed me deeply as I pushed two fingers deep inside him, and his voice was rough when he whispered against my lips, "Fuck me, Jessie." The words made my cock swell.

I got myself ready with lube and a condom and worked even more lube into him before I wiped my hands and knelt between his legs. He was the sexiest thing I'd ever seen. His strong body glistened with sweat as he spread his long legs as he offered himself to me.

When I lined up the tip of my cock with his opening, he looked nervous, but he followed my instructions and pushed back as I pushed in. For a moment, I met with resistance, but then he opened just enough to let me in. I took my time, sinking into him in slow motion, giving his body time to adjust. His ass felt so damn good, warm and tight around my cock, and I took a deep breath and kept reminding myself not to rush it. It didn't matter that I was shaking with need and desperate to thrust into him. It was pretty clear that he was inexperienced, based on his reactions, and no way on earth was I going to make it a bad experience for him.

I slid in and out of him slowly as he tried to adjust. There was still worry in his eyes, and I held his gaze and whispered, "You doing okay, Kai?" He nodded and I asked, "Do you want to keep going?"

"God yes! Please don't stop."

It took several minutes of fucking him slowly before I saw a change come over him. Pleasure edged out pain as I slid my cock over his prostate again and again, and he opened up as he relaxed underneath me. When he grabbed my ass with both hands and pulled me into him, I knew he was ready to ramp it up. I pushed myself into him harder, deeper. Soon we were both moaning. I fell forward and kissed him, sliding my tongue into his mouth as I pumped in and out of his tight hole, and he grasped my body, holding me to him as he returned the kiss.

When I was about to cum, I raised myself up on my elbows so I could look at him. He was moaning through parted lips, his half-lidded eyes so dilated they were black. As my orgasm shook me, he held my gaze, right there in the moment with me. It was so intense, so perfect. *He* was perfect. I pushed into him again and again until my body had nothing left to give.

It wasn't over yet, though. I slid from him carefully and threw the condom in the trash, and then I stroked his hard cock as I said, "Fuck me, Kai."

We both tumbled off the bed as we scrambled to switch positions. Lube and a condom happened quickly. I knelt on the bed and he stood behind me, grasping my hip with one hand as he fingered me open. When I was ready, he slid into me until his body was pressed to my ass, and murmured, "Oh fuck." He pulled almost all the way out of me before sinking in again.

Kai sped up quickly, slamming into me as I knelt on the mattress, bent over, ass in the air for him. I cried out as he took me and pleasure and sensation radiated through every part of my body. He lifted me to his chest and held me tightly, and I braced my feet on the mattress, trying to drive myself onto his cock as he pounded into me again and again.

By the time he came a few minutes later, I was in some other place, far from rational thought, a place with just sex and pleasure and Kai. I was hard again but too far gone to do anything about it. Little gasps and moans slid from me, and he grunted as he came, shoving his cock into me, clutching my body. When he reached around and started jerking me off, I was sure I had nothing left to give.

I was wrong. I arched my back as my body emptied itself of every last drop of cum and his thick cock stretched and impaled me. I parted my lips in a silent yell, almost convulsing. By the time the orgasm ebbed, I was barely lucid. I let my head fall back onto Kai's shoulder as I concentrated on nothing more than filling my lungs with air and listened to my heart pounding in my ears.

I was only vaguely aware of what was happening. Kai slid his cock from me, and I whimpered a little because I suddenly felt so empty. He picked me up, carried me to the bathroom and turned on the taps. I dozed off on his lap while the tub was filling, but revived slightly as Kai lowered us into a bath. His big, solid body felt so good beneath me. He washed me gently, tipping me back to wet my hair, shampooing it, and tipping me back again to rinse. I grinned at him groggily and mumbled, "You're so nice." He grinned too and ran his soapy hands over my bare skin. My eyes slid shut as I let him take care of me.

I was barely awake when he lifted me from the tub and dried me off. A brush slid through my wet hair, and Kai gently kissed my forehead. The last thing I remembered was getting wrapped up in soft, warm blankets, and in Kai.

*****

My room was dark when I awoke with a start sometime later. When I raised my head and looked around, trying to get my bearings, Kai stirred beneath me, opening his eyes just a little and murmuring, "Hey."

"I passed out on you. Literally on you," I said, rubbing his bare chest.

"Well, you did have two massive orgasms, barely twenty minutes apart," he said. "I think passing out was mandatory after something like that."

"Apparently." I looked up at him in the darkness. The curtains weren't closed, so I could see his handsome features just a little, illuminated by the constant glow of the city outside my windows. "Are you okay?"

"I'm so damn good," he said with a goofy grin. "I'd wanted to try that forever. I'm glad you were willing."

"Wait, are you saying that was your first time bottoming?" When he nodded, I sat up a bit and said. "I had no idea. I just thought it was something you didn't do very often. Maybe we should have waited."

"I didn't want to wait. I'd been looking forward to trying that with you. Like I said, I even prepped myself ahead of time."

"But doesn't that kind of go against our taking it slow policy?"

"Nah. Given the way you and I started out, the whole taking it slow thing clearly doesn't apply to sex. It just has to do with barreling into a relationship."

Yeah, that was definitely the hard part. "Why had you never done that before?"

"Well, you know. I already told you I didn't date, and that most of my sexual experience was with guys I met in bars. The idea of getting penetrated was kind of intimidating, and it's also something that would have sucked with a hurried, indifferent partner, so I didn't want my first time bottoming to be with an anonymous stranger."

"Thank you for trusting me enough to do that."

"I knew you'd see I was nervous and you'd be careful, even without me explaining all of this to you beforehand." He kissed my forehead as I settled back on his chest and said, "I'm glad you're versatile. Apparently I am, too."

"I'd been wanting to fuck you all night, from the moment I opened the door and saw you standing there looking so damn sexy in your leather jacket and tight jeans."

He grinned embarrassedly. "The reason they were tight is because I put on weight. I wasn't trying to be all seductive or anything."

"Like you have to try." I traced his bare shoulder, and after a while I asked, "Do you have to get home?"

"If it's okay with you, I'd like to stay here tonight. I set the alarm on my phone for seven a.m., which will give me plenty of time to get home before Izzy wakes up. She almost always sleeps in on the weekends, thank God."

"I'd love it if you stayed."

Kai shifted a bit and pulled me closer. He was quiet for a minute before saying quietly, "Tonight was amazing, and I don't just mean the mind-blowing sex. Thank you again for the great company, for cooking, for building the tent, all of it. I'm not used to the royal treatment, and I want you to know I appreciated it so damn much."

"You're more than welcome." After a moment, I sat up and said, "I almost forgot something."

I reached over him and found a small reading lamp in the drawer of my nightstand, then pulled the covers back and directed the light at Kai's midsection, being careful not to shine it in his eyes. He chuckled and asked, "What are you doing?"

"I was going to check out your other tattoo the next time I got you naked, remember?"

"Oh, that's right."

I panned the beam over the rows of text on his ribcage, then knit my brows. "It's all in Hawaiian. What does it say?"

"It's a bedtime story my dad used to tell me, about a family of birds who lived on an island. One day, one of the birds decided to spread his wings, and he flew to another island across the sea. He was sad at first, because he missed the other birds. But eventually he realized he was never really that far from the ones he loved, because he carried them with him always, in his heart. It was meant to be an allegory about me growing up and moving out someday, but it took on a whole new meaning after my dad's death."

I asked if he'd read it to me, and Kai closed his eyes and began reciting softly. The language was soft and melodic. I followed along with the words written on his body, and when he reached the end, I said, "I've never heard anyone speak Hawaiian before. It's a beautiful language."

"I think so, too. My dad made sure my sister and I both learned it. The language was starting to fade out in our culture, since everyone speaks English on the islands now. In the last couple decades though, there's been a push to teach it in schools in Hawaii as a second language. My dad would have been happy to see its resurgence. Of course, it's not offered in schools here on the mainland, so I'm trying to teach Izzy myself."

"It's great you're doing that."

"It's a part of who she is, so I think it's important. My dad was proud of his Native Hawaiian heritage, and he made a point of teaching us about our culture and history. The language is a big part of that. I'm trying to do for her what he did for my sister and me."

"Is your mom Native Hawaiian, too?"

"She is, but her side of the family didn't embrace our culture the way my dad did."

I put the light away and wrapped myself around Kai. "Thanks for reading it to me."

"Thanks for asking." When I tilted my head to look up at him again, he kissed me gently. After a while, he said, "This has been the best night ever. I don't want it to end." I didn't either.

Chapter Eleven

Five Weeks Later

"I miss you."

"I miss you, too," I told Kai, rolling over in bed and switching the phone to my other ear.

"Friday feels like it's so far away."

"It does, although technically it's Wednesday now since it's midnight. Friday's getting closer."

"Not close enough," he said.

For the past month, I'd tried so hard to take it slow, even though I wanted to be with Kai all the time. He and I had a standing date every Friday night, and after the Saturday races we'd always go back to his garage and tear each other's clothes off. We spent the rest of each week apart, and the nightly phone calls after his daughter went to bed had become a tradition. Since I was letting him set the pace, Kai was always the one to call, and he did so without fail.

We kept the conversation light and mostly just talked about our day. I'd tell him about the ever-present craziness at Nana's house and what I was doing to help with her wedding planning, and he'd talk about what Izzy was up to and what he was working on at the garage. He'd gotten a couple more jobs from Ash, the DJ, who'd referred his friends as promised, and a few walk-ins after Kai and I repainted his garage a cheerful red and put up a flyer at the LGBT community center. The garage looked worlds better, even though the newly painted bay doors were tagged by some kid in the neighborhood at least a couple times a week, and Kai was forever painting over the graffiti.

After chatting for a few more minutes, Kai said, "I guess I should let you go. It's late."

We said goodnight and disconnected, and I got up and wandered around my room a bit, since I was wide awake. Eventually, I ended up at the window and perched on the narrow sill. I had a view of the backyard and studied Skye's sculpture for a while. It was beautiful, and slowly coming along. He had an interesting approach, very much one step forward, two steps back as he pried off almost every piece he welded into place and kept making adjustments until it felt exactly right to him.

Even though it was only partially completed, the sculpture stirred up a lot of emotions in me. There was so much longing and anticipation in those two faces and the way they were poised with their lips not quite touching. There was an underlying sadness too, at least to me. For all eternity, those two metal men would never be able to close that distance between them. They were frozen there, separated by just a few inches, but that was enough to keep them from what they both clearly wanted.

That longing in particular resonated with me. I wanted to be in Kai's arms more than anything. I'd done well for the past month. I hadn't rushed him or pressured him into making whatever was happening between us into too much too fast. But God, I missed him like crazy when we were apart. He was all I could think about. Every week just became something to get through as I counted down the hours to Friday night.

After a while, I stuck my bare feet into my sneakers, threw on a hoodie over my pajamas, and grabbed my keys. I tried to tell myself I was just going for a drive to clear my head. It was a lie. I drove straight to Kai's neighborhood, like I was caught in a tractor beam.

The pink house was dark, except for a light in the attic. I found a parking spot halfway down the block, and after a heated inner debate, I got out of the car and pocketed my keys. Damn it. This was the exact opposite of playing it cool, taking it slow, and all the other goals I was constantly working on. I knew I should get back in the car and drive away. I didn't.

I stood out on the lawn for a couple minutes, feeling like a stalker. If I hadn't forgotten my phone, I would have texted him, probably something stupid like, *Hey, so, I was in the neighborhood….* Instead, I decided to go old school and found a few pebbles in the flowerbed.

I stood back and tried to toss a pebble at the window on the third floor, not too hard, because breaking the glass would be ridiculous. I missed entirely. In my defense, it wasn't a big target, it was high up, and the porch was in the way. After a couple more of my attempts bounced off the wood siding, I sighed, found a few more pebbles and climbed onto the roof of the porch, like I had the day we'd painted the deck.

My target was far more accessible now, and I bounced a pebble off the glass on my first try (or my fourth, depending on how I looked at it). I had to duck out of the way when it rained back down on me. Nothing happened, so I tossed another pebble, and then one more. I was gearing up to toss my final pebble when the window slid open.

I couldn't see Kai from my angle, and he was probably looking out at the street and couldn't see me, either. I felt like an idiot as I called in a loud whisper, "Um, hi. I was going to claim I was just in the neighborhood and decided to drop by, but that's total bullshit."

I was shocked when Malia stuck her head out the window and smiled at me. "You must be Jessie."

I felt my face turning crimson as I stage-whispered, "Yeah, hi. Sorry about this. I was just looking for Kai."

"Can you get in here from there?" she asked, and when I nodded she said, "Come on up."

She ducked back inside, and I put the last pebble in my pocket and brushed my hands together to clean them off. I then jumped up, grabbed the windowsill, and pulled myself up. It was a lot of effort again. The first time, I'd tried to attribute it to the fact that I'd spent the day sanding and painting, but this time I just had to admit my upper body strength left a lot to be desired.

When I finally climbed in the open window, I had to catch my breath for a moment and sat on Kai's desk. His sister flashed me a big smile. She looked a bit like her brother with her thick, dark hair and clear olive skin, but only a bit. "Do you guys do this often?" she asked. "It's very Romeo and Juliet."

I shook my head. "I climbed in through that window once when we were painting the deck and couldn't get to the back door, but aside from that I've never come over."

She sat on the desk chair and said, "Yeah, that part I noticed! I've been begging Kai to let us meet you for weeks. Why haven't you come to dinner? Don't you want to meet the family?"

"I do, but Kai's worried about introducing Izzy to people who aren't going to be around long."

Malia leaned back and crossed her ankle over her knee as she studied me. She was wearing black yoga pants and a tank top under a black Ramones t-shirt. She'd cut the neck out of the tee, which I thought was cute and very eighties-retro. "Why won't you be around long?"

I looked down and realized I was wearing red pajamas with cartoon cats in tiaras all over them. Lord. I told her, "I want to be, but Kai might get tired of me."

"He might get tired of you? What about you getting tired of him?"

"That's impossible," I admitted quietly. "I'm crazy about your brother. But he and I are supposed to be taking it slow, and that's why he hasn't introduced me to the family yet."

"He's crazy about you too, so I don't get it. You guys have been seeing each other for weeks! When was he going to let us meet you, after six months? A year? I mean, getting Izzy involved is one thing. I know he worries about people breaking her heart the way the asshole who gave birth to her did. But it makes no sense that you, me, and Kai haven't met for coffee or something!"

"I'm not sure what his reasoning is, but I wasn't going to push."

"Maybe you should, though. My brother's clueless when it comes to relationships. An occasional push might be just what he needs."

I asked, "Um, is Kai downstairs?"

"No, he's staying at the garage tonight because he wanted to work late on an engine overhaul. I came up here to borrow his rowing machine, since I couldn't sleep and wanted to tire myself out."

"I messed up. I was talking to him half an hour ago and just assumed he was home."

She reached over to the dresser, picked up a phone, and fired off a quick text. "I just let him know you're here."

"Thank you. Do you want me to wait outside for him?"

"God no, I'm thrilled that I finally have a chance to talk to you! I've been looking for you whenever I take Izzy to her 'intro to instruments' class at the art center."

"That class is on Mondays and I volunteer on Thursdays. I'm sorry we didn't have a chance to meet when we were both there on Valentine's Day."

Malia's phone beeped, and she glanced at the screen and grinned. "Kai's on his way home. He told me not to embarrass him. I wonder what he thinks I'm going to tell you."

I grinned, too. "If anyone knows his secrets, it's you."

"Such as they are. His love life was nonexistent before he met you, he's totally boring when he's drunk so there are no good stories there, and his idea of a big night is futzing with the engine on that old Mustang. If I want to embarrass him, I have to go way back into the archives. For example, I could tell you about the summer when we were six and he wanted to be a superhero, so he wore a bath towel cape and his underwear on the outside of his pants for literally the entire month of August."

I laughed at that and said, "Please tell me there are pictures."

"Oh yeah, I made sure to hang on to those bad boys. I could also tell you about the five or six weeks when we were ten that he spoke with the *worst* British accent. He sounded like a cockney New Yorker with a lisp. It was truly awful."

I grinned at that and asked, "Why did he want to be British?"

"Because he saw the first Harry Potter movie and became obsessed with it."

"That's so cute! Did he like the books, too?"

She looked surprised. "No, reading was almost impossible for him at that point with his learning disability."

"What learning disability?"

Malia knit her brows. "Kai's severely dyslexic. He didn't tell you?" I shook my head. "That's why it takes him so long to answer a text. Both reading and writing take a lot of concentration, and he usually still mixes up letters."

"He's never texted me. He just calls. I thought it was because he's kind of old-school."

She looked concerned. "Maybe I wasn't supposed to tell you this, although I have no idea why he'd keep it a secret."

"Neither do I. It's not like I'd judge him for it."

"Yeah, you hardly seem the type. I mean, I know he's self-conscious about it, because some people are assholes and assume he's stupid when they see his writing, or when they see him struggling with reading. But Kai's incredibly smart. His brain just processes written language differently than yours or mine."

"I actually think he's a genius, literally, given what I've seen him do with his engines. It takes a brilliant mind to come up with the stuff he does."

His sister looked like she was trying not to get emotional, but her voice was a little rough when she said, "I always hoped Kai would find someone who could appreciate him for who he is. It sounds like you really do, and I can't tell you how happy that makes me. You even managed to break through that shell of his! He's so closed off with strangers that I used to worry he'd never find someone."

"Your brother is an amazing person. He probably told you that we had a lot of conflicts when we first met, and I'm so grateful we got past them."

Malia nodded. "He tells me pretty much everything. At least, I thought he did. It's news to me that he kept his dyslexia from you, though."

"Why wouldn't he trust me with something like that? He had to know I wouldn't think any less of him," I said.

Malia sighed. "Now I get why he didn't introduce us. I told you he was dyslexic within a few minutes of meeting you. It didn't even occur to me that he'd keep it a secret. He used to be so embarrassed about it when we were kids, and he got teased mercilessly. I guess he's still self-conscious about it, and that makes me sad."

"I got teased when I was a kid, too. He was so compassionate when I told him about it. I wish he would have let me return the favor."

I heard the throaty purr of the Impala's big engine as it pulled into the driveway, and a moment after it cut out, a door downstairs opened and closed. "Damn, he hauled ass getting here," Malia said. "He really didn't want to leave us unsupervised for longer than he had to."

"I hope he's not too mad at me for dropping by like this." I slid off the desk, and when Kai appeared at the top of the wooden ladder a few seconds later, I said, "Hey."

As he climbed into the room, Malia said, "Don't be mad at your honey. He was being all romantic and doing a Romeo and Juliet thing. He tossed pebbles at your window and climbed up on the roof of the porch, but then he found me instead of you. I was up here borrowing your rowing machine."

His expression was unreadable as he stared at me. "We've been quiet," I said. "I don't think anyone else knows I'm here."

As if to totally contradict me, Izzy's little voice called, "Daddy?" from the second floor.

Kai shot us a look and climbed back down the ladder, and I whispered, "Shit, I totally screwed up. I'd better go."

I started to climb out the window, and Malia jumped up and whispered, "Izzy heard his engine, that's why she called to him. She's really attuned to that sound."

"I bet I woke her, though. She wouldn't have heard it if she was fast asleep. Please tell Kai I'm so sorry."

I dropped onto the porch roof as lightly as I could, and Malia stuck her head out the window and said in a loud whisper, "Don't just run off. Wait and talk to my brother."

"That's not a good idea. I messed up by coming here, and I'm going to go before I make it even worse. Take care, Malia. I'm glad I got to meet you, although I wish it had been on Kai's terms."

I lowered myself to the lawn and ran to my car, cursing myself the whole way. Coming to his house had been an incredibly stupid idea. It could just as easily have been Izzy who'd discovered me, and I knew Kai didn't want to introduce us yet. What had I been thinking?

*****

I was still angry with myself as I sat up in bed, cocooned in my blanket maybe an hour later. The moment I deviated from the plan, I'd messed everything up. Showing up unannounced in the middle of the night at someone's house, especially someone with a family, was most definitely not playing it cool, or taking it slow. It threw a spotlight on my neediness, on that lonely part of me that was so desperate to be in a relationship.

That longing for commitment was something I was used to, a part of me I disliked, but that I understood. I'd always hated being alone, and that had been turned up to deafening levels after I lost my entire family with the words, "I'm gay." I totally got why I was driven to replace all I'd lost with someone of my own, someone who'd be there for me and love me and care about me, someone who wouldn't turn his back on me the way everyone I loved had.

But while I was used to wanting a relationship, the feelings behind whatever was happening between Kai and me were brand new. It wasn't that I needed just any random relationship, it was that I needed *him*. I needed to hear the sound of his voice, and to feel his hands on my body. I needed to talk to him for hours, and listen to everything he had to say. Malakai Kahale was unlike anyone I'd ever met. He was kind and loving, and smart and interesting. He was so sexy that I wanted to tear his clothes off, pretty much all the time. He fascinated me, and in turn, acted like I was fascinating, too. He'd become my best friend, and so very much more.

And if I'd just blown it with him, I was never going to forgive myself.

A faint sound caught my attention. I sat up a bit and pulled the blanket off my head. The sound came again after a moment, a little tap. I wasn't sure what I was hearing, but I tossed the comforter aside and got out of bed, then went and looked out in the hall. Nothing.

Another little tap drew my attention to the window, and I crossed the room and pulled my curtains aside. Kai was in the backyard, bathed in moonlight. My heart leapt and I dashed from my room. I took the stairs two at a time, ran through the foyer and kitchen, and out the back door.

Before he could say a word, I grabbed him in an embrace and said, "I'm so sorry. I know I shouldn't have dropped by like that. I won't do it again, I promise."

He picked me up and said as I wrapped my legs around his hips, "It's okay, Jessie."

I pulled back to look at him. "It is?"

"I was a little thrown off at first, but I'm not mad. Mal has a big mouth, so I'd always dreaded what she'd say when you two finally met. She told me about your conversation."

"I really am sorry. The fact that you have dyslexia is none of my business, and I wish she hadn't said anything."

"Oh, I don't care about that."

"You don't?"

He shook his head. "It's the stories about my childhood I could have done without. God, talk about embarrassing! I'm not ashamed that I have dyslexia, far from it. I hadn't told you about it yet because it doesn't define me. Yeah, while I was growing up, other kids were assholes to me because of it, and to this day people sometimes assume I'm illiterate or incompetent when they see me trying to read or write, but I know they're wrong. My challenges don't have a thing to do with my intelligence or how capable I am."

"I'm so glad you don't let them get to you."

"It took me a long time to get to this point. I used to be so self-conscious about reading or writing in front of other people and letting them see me struggling," Kai told me as he sat down on a bench with me on his lap. "But remember what I told you once about truly not giving a shit about what others think of me? That goes for my dyslexia, too. In fact, it's what made me learn not to let others' opinions get to me."

"You're so strong. I admire that."

"I'm not a hundred percent there yet. It still hurts sometimes when people are cruel and judgmental. But I've made a lot of progress."

I shivered a bit, since I was barefoot and in just my cat pajamas, and Kai said, "You should go back in, I don't want you to catch a chill."

"Will you come with me?" He nodded and carried me to the back door to keep my bare feet off the cold walkway. When we were in the kitchen and he'd put me down, I said, "I'm going to make some hot chocolate to warm up, would you like some?"

"Sure."

He sat on one of the barstools at the kitchen island and pulled off his leather jacket while I warmed some milk in a pot. I asked, "Was it hard to get Izzy back to sleep? I'm really sorry I woke her."

"It did take some time to get her to go to sleep again, but don't worry, I don't think you woke her. She'd been having a bad dream. It's good I came home when I did, actually. Not that her gran, great-gran or auntie couldn't have handled it, but I'm glad I was there for her."

"Does she have bad dreams a lot?"

"Fortunately no. She sleeps like a rock. That's why it usually doesn't matter if I spend the night at the garage."

I prepared a couple mugs with cocoa mix, then turned to Kai and offered him a little smile. "I was so happy to see you that I forgot to ask why you're here."

"Mal said you seemed worried when you left, and that you thought I'd be mad at you. I wanted to make sure you didn't think that was the case. I was going to call, but then I decided to take a chance and see if you were still up." He grinned at me and added, "Plus, I was sorry I missed out on seeing you."

"I'm glad you're here, and I'm so relieved you're not angry."

"I thought it was romantic, showing up in the middle of the night and tossing pebbles at my window. I wish I'd been there to enjoy it."

"I'm not supposed to do stuff like that, though. You didn't want me to meet your family yet, so I shouldn't have come to your house."

"The only reason I'm still keeping you and the adults in my family apart is because they're such loud-mouths. They can't keep quiet to save their lives! As soon as you meet my mom and gran, they're going to start gabbing about you all the freaking time, and Izzy will hear I'm dating someone and she'll get curious. I probably should have introduced you to Mal by now, but good lord, you two talked for less than ten minutes, and look how much humiliation she managed to pack into that short conversation! My twin has no filter."

"She's nice, though."

"I'm glad you think so. She can rub people the wrong way sometimes. I was dreading what would happen when you two met."

"Well, we've gotten that over with now, and it was only a minor catastrophe. On my part, not hers. She was great, and I was the weirdo climbing up onto your porch after midnight."

Kai pulled me to him, and as I draped my arms over his shoulders, he said, "This only-on-the-weekend thing is killing me. We have to find opportunities during the week to be together, even if it's just an hour or two so we can do this." He kissed me gently and I sank into it.

When the hot chocolate was ready, we took it upstairs to my room and curled up on top of the covers. We chatted for a while as we sipped our drinks, and then I said, "So, I have something I want to talk to you about. There's a masquerade ball next Saturday. It's also a new artists show, and it's raising money for an LGBT art scholarship. I mentioned it to you when we were talking about Chance and his photos a few weeks back."

"I remember."

"Originally, I was going to ask you to be my date. But then, I realized this would be an amazing experience for Izzy and thought you might want to take her. I have a couple tickets for the two of you if you want them. She'd get to dress up like a princess and go to the ball. Just so you know, it's all ages and a few other kids will be there, but it'll mostly be adults. I think she'd still enjoy it, though."

"I know she would."

I downed the last sip of cocoa and said as I looked into my empty mug, "The only thing that might be kind of awkward is the fact that I'll be there too, and I know you don't want to tell her we're dating. But we don't have to. We could just say hello and leave it at that. I mean, I'd love to share a dance with you, but if you don't want to for Izzy's sake, that's fine."

Kai said gently, "I'd love to dance with you at the ball."

I looked up at him. "I'm glad. I wasn't sure how you'd feel about any of this."

"There's no reason we can't both be there, and Izzy will be thrilled to see you. She hasn't forgotten about Valentine's Day." He kissed my forehead and said, "She's going to be so excited. Now I'll just have to figure out what we'll wear."

"I know this guy who owns a costume shop just outside Chinatown, he'll hook you both up. I bought a couple costumes from him and sent a bunch of my friends there, so he gave me a voucher for a free costume to say thank you. It's with your tickets. I hope you can find Izzy something pretty."

Kai put our empty mugs on the nightstand and drew me into a hug. "She's going to have the time of her life. Thank you for all of that, Jessie, and especially for wanting to do something nice for my daughter. I can't even tell you what it means to me."

"I'm so relieved. I'd been putting off asking you about this for a while now. I didn't know how you'd feel about me inviting Izzy to an event I'd also be attending. I didn't want you to think I was trying to worm my way into her life or something."

"I don't think that at all." He rubbed my back as he said, "You worry a lot, but you really don't need to."

Kai ended up spending the night. Long after he drifted off, I stayed awake with my head on his chest, holding on to him. His steady breathing and his heartbeat under my palm were incredibly soothing.

I felt fragile that night. My grandpa used to call it feeling puny. I knew I had to get it together. But just for that night, I let myself take comfort in Kai, in the feeling of his arms around me, in his warmth, in just being near him. He felt so good. So reassuring.

It was almost scary, how hard I was falling for Malakai Kahale.

Chapter Twelve

Zachary grinned at me and asked, "So, what are we, good and evil?"

"I think of it as fire and ice."

"Why are you ice?"

"It fits with my coloring. Just go with it."

It was the following weekend, and my friend and I were dressed for the costume ball in the outfits I'd gotten us. He was checking out his reflection in the full-length mirror on the inside of my closet door and trying to decide if he felt too stupid to go out in public. I thought he looked great.

He and I were both dressed like princes. Zachary's costume was black with a few red accents, and mine was white with ice blue embellishments at the neck, cuffs, and in my jacket's silky lining. Both outfits were fairly understated and comprised of dress pants, fitted collarless jackets, and crowns (mine silver, his black metal). The part he was having a hard time with was the sparkle. The pants were matte wool, but the jackets were covered in a fabric I didn't have a name for, which looked like it was sprinkled all over with fine, tone-on-tone glitter.

"You look amazing," I told him. "It fits like it was made for you." I was standing behind him and put my hands on his narrow waist, which was accentuated perfectly with the cut of the jacket.

"Do I have to wear the sash? I feel like a runner up in the Miss Preteen beauty contest."

"I won't make you wear the sash. Or the sword."

"Oh now, the sword's cool. That I'll wear."

I grinned and said, "Perfect. Then we can duel if the masquerade ball gets dull."

He tried on the elegant black mask I'd gotten to go with his costume and said, "And now I look like Gay Zorro. It would have just been Standard Zorro, but since you raided a really flamboyant figure skater's wardrobe for these jackets, it's gay all the way."

"Oh believe me, these outfits are mild compared to what I could have gotten us. We could be standing here in puff sleeves, satin capes, and tights."

Zachary turned to me and smiled as he said, "No, we really couldn't."

Someone knocked on the door, and when I called, "Come in," Ollie stuck his head into the room. He was wearing a white, powdered wig, a hot pink velvet overcoat with all kinds of fringe and trimmings, and white breeches and stockings. The outfit was very period-accurate, aside from the hot pink Converse hightops (which I'd lent him when the pointy dress shoes he'd gotten proved too uncomfortable to actually wear). "You look great," I told him.

"Thanks kiddo, so do you. I'm supposed to be Louis the sixteenth, on account of he was Marie Antoinette's hubby and that's more or less what Stana's going for with our costumes. She sent me to see if you boys are ready to go."

I glanced at Zachary, and he said, "Yeah, okay. I can sparkle for one night."

I grabbed a pair of belts with scabbards and swords, and as we headed downstairs, I said, "I'm glad you kept your hair black with a red streak, Zachary. It goes perfectly with your outfit. That's actually what inspired me to select these costumes."

He said, "Thank you, Jessie. I'm sorry if I seem ungrateful. It was nice of you to think of me and to buy us buddy costumes."

"Thank you for playing along. I hope you have fun tonight."

On the ground floor, Nana had struck a pose in the foyer. She wore an enormous, heavily embellished pink dress with a rainbow petticoat peeking out underneath, and a towering rainbow wig that swirled like a soft-serve cone. "You look beautiful Nana," I told her, and she beamed at me from beneath the ornate pink and white mask that framed her eyes.

"I love getting dressed up," she said, relaxing her pose and fluffing the layered silk skirt. "You boys are cute as can be, too." As we headed out the door, she bounced a bit and told us, "I can't wait to get to the masquerade ball! Christopher Robin's expecting a sold-out crowd. I hope this night's a huge success for him and for all the artists in the show."

I drove us to the venue in the rainbow limo, stopping to pick up Dante and Charlie on the way. They were both dressed in impeccable black tuxedos, and had donned coordinating Venetian masks in black and gold. "You guys look great," Zachary said.

"Yeah, but they don't have swords, so we win," I told him, and grinned at Dante and his husband in the rearview mirror.

Excitement was in the air when we pulled up to the venue. The ball was being held in an old warehouse that took up one of the piers along the Embarcadero. Both sides of the long structure were mostly glass, and warm, golden light spilled out and was reflected on the tranquil bay. A starry sky on a rich, indigo background and a nighttime cityscape had been painted onto the front of the warehouse just for that evening, transforming the usually utilitarian structure into something magical. I dropped off my passengers at the door, then headed to the VIP parking lot across the street, were Christopher had designated a spot for Nana.

I took in the spectacle as I walked back to the building. The valets were busy, but just as many people were arriving by public transit. A stop for the quaint, historic streetcars that ran up and down the Embarcadero was just a few yards away, and it seemed as if all the passengers were in costume when the little yellow streetcar came to a stop and everyone emptied out.

In true San Francisco style, the attendees had been pretty creative. While about half the crowd had opted for gowns, tuxedos or suits, and other finery, the other half had gone with straight-up cosplay. Superheroes, gladiators, giant stuffed animals, characters from books, movies and video games, and so much more converged on the warehouse. I loved the city so damn much at times like this.

I gave my ticket to one of the people manning the door in exchange for a hand stamp. Then I pulled my white silk mask over my eyes, stepped through the gauzy indigo drapes over the open doorway and muttered, "Damn."

Five giant chandeliers had been brought in for the event and sparkled from the thirty-foot ceiling, a gorgeous contrast to the industrial interior. At the far end, a big, eclectic band played, elevated on a high stage. It included a full horn section, electric guitars, drums, violins, and a male lead singer, and at the moment they were performing a slowed down version of a Britney Spears song. Oddly, it sounded terrific.

Four of Skye's sculptures dominated the big space. They rose above the vibrant crowd, like giants wading in a sea of humanity. I'd seen three of them before. He'd completed the sculptures of a male dancer leaping gracefully (inspired by his husband) when he was enrolled in art school.

The fourth was new, and it was astonishing. It was a slightly abstract male angel, knee deep in the crowd that was gathered around him, his face tilted up and his body arched back. He was almost twenty feet tall, wings and arms outstretched. The angel was comprised of an open framework of rusted metal, and the delicate-looking feathers of his wings were charred and mostly black. His wingspan was easily fifty feet across and the whole thing must have weighed a ton, so I had to wonder how they'd gotten it here. But it wasn't the scale that was so striking. Raw agony was conveyed perfectly and eloquently in his facial features and the position of his body and wings. A white light radiated from inside his chest and gave the impression his soul was being torn from him. Skye always seemed so happy and upbeat, but that sculpture made me think he must have gone through a dark period in his life. The pain was too genuine to come from anyplace but the heart.

Zachary found me in the crowd. He'd put his black and red mask on, and his hair spilled forward to cover even more of his face. He called over the din, "I think half of San Francisco is here." That wasn't a good thing from an introvert's perspective. I took his hand and held it tightly.

"Have you seen Chance or his photos?"

"Not yet. I haven't ventured far from the door, because I was waiting for you."

Seven artists were featured in the show, including Skye. The work of the four painters and two photographers was displayed on freestanding curved walls, spaced at regular intervals down the length of the warehouse, three to a side. The walls were all curved a bit differently, creating a kind of fluidity as we moved along the left side of the space. We came to Ignacio Mondelvano's bold, bright oil paintings first, and halfway down the warehouse, we found Chance's photos.

Christopher Robin had done them justice. He'd blown up the black and white photos into huge four foot by six foot canvases and framed them with minimalistic black frames. Each was highlighted by a carefully positioned spotlight, which hung from an industrial framework ten or twelve feet overhead. "They're so beautiful," I murmured as I approached the display. Modern black lettering spelled out 'Chance Matthews' on the top, center of the wall, above a horizontal photograph of a partially demolished building. Part of a mural remained on its crumbling brick façade, hands reaching out of the rubble.

We did a lap around the wall, admiring the photos on both sides. I felt we'd chosen well, and judging by the buzz all around us, people liked what they saw. We returned to our spot in front of Chance's name, and as I took it all in, a voice behind me said, "I should be so mad at you."

I turned to look at Chance. He looked handsome in a dark blue suit, and a simple black mask had been pushed to the top of his head. When I saw tears in his eyes, my heart sank. I was surprised when he pulled me into his arms, and I blurted, "I'm so sorry. I know I should have asked. But I believe in you so much, Chance! Your photos are gorgeous and brilliant, and I wanted to share them with the world."

He pulled back to look at me, and when he smiled and I realized they were happy tears, relief flooded me. "Christopher gave me a heads-up this morning and let me come look at what you guys had done before this place filled with people. It was terrifying at first, but I spent all day thinking about it, and I know this is actually a good thing. I always wanted to get up the courage to show my work, and now, well, it's a done deal. I wish you'd asked, but then again I would have just said no because I was so afraid of failing at this."

"You can't fail. Your work is too good."

Chance grinned a little. "Christopher says he now insists on selling my work in his gallery and won't take no for an answer. He's had more than a dozen people approach him about buying my photos. One of those people is the arts editor for a national magazine."

"I'm so glad something good came out of me being a total asshole and going behind your back."

He kissed my cheek and said, "You're not an asshole. Never do that again, okay? But this one time, it's kind of awesome. Thank you for believing in me enough to go through all this trouble."

We chatted a while longer, and when he went off to join his family, I exhaled slowly and told Zachary, "Thank God he's still speaking to me."

"You just launched his career. Look at that." Zachary gestured to a cameraman for a local news station, who was filming Chance's photographs. "He'll end up with a ton of exposure from tonight, and the ripple effect is going to go way beyond finally selling his work at Christopher's gallery."

"That goes for all the artists in the show, including Ignacio and Skye. Christopher Robin has done an amazing thing here."

My friend and I continued to make our way down the long warehouse, stopping to enjoy some colorful mixed-media canvases by an artist who went only by Carina before reaching the edge of the dance floor. It was crowded with couples, both gay and straight, families with kids, seniors, and everyone in between. The band was playing a rollicking big band number, and some people were swing dancing, while others just did their own thing to the music. It all just made me happy.

I turned to Zachary and asked, "Do you want to dance?"

Even behind the mask and the cascade of hair, I could tell he was giving me a look. "Have you met me?" he said with a self-conscious grin.

"Come on," I cajoled, stepping onto the dance floor, flinging my arms over my head and busting out some wild, exaggerated dance moves. "Dance with me, Zachary! Don't leave me hanging!"

He burst out laughing and turned red as he exclaimed, "Oh my God, stop!"

I twerked wildly and called, "Only if you dance with me!"

Just then, Nana and Ollie found me in the crowd, and they both started twerking right along with me. For some reason, that was her favorite dance and she never let an opportunity to twerk pass her by. Nana's big, twisted hairdo was starting to unravel, so she looked a bit like a troll doll with her fluffy, rainbow hair sticking straight up. She was having the time of her life though, and hiked up her dress to reveal her skinny little legs in rainbow-striped stockings as she shook everything she had.

Zachary was trying to back away slowly, but I pulled him onto the dance floor. I put an arm around him and held his hand in mine, and started dancing a waltz (more or less). He laughed and let me lead him for a while, and I was so happy to see him enjoying himself.

When the song ended and a slow one began, we stepped off the dance floor. Nana and Ollie went off to find the refreshments, and I glanced over Zachary's shoulder and grinned as I said, "Incoming."

Six was making his way through the crowd, his attention totally focused on Zachary. The tall blond was dressed like he'd just traveled through time from the eighteenth century. He wore a knee-length, royal blue velvet coat, heavily embroidered with silver thread down the front, over a black waistcoat, white ruffled shirt, and black breeches with period-appropriate stockings and shoes. The clothes played up his aristocratic features and seemed surprisingly natural on him. He'd seemed like the heir to the throne just in street clothes, but in that outfit he was the ruler of the kingdom.

Zachary glanced over his shoulder to see what I was talking about and murmured, "Oh wow."

When he reached us, Six greeted us both, then bowed gracefully, perfectly in character. He asked Zachary as he extended his hand to him, "Will you do me the honor of this dance?" His posh British accent just brought it all together.

I was more than a little surprised when Zachary put his hand in Six's and let the eighteen-year-old lead him to the center of the dance floor. The two didn't talk. They just held each other and swayed to the music, and my friend put his head on his taller partner's shoulder. There was a tenderness in the way they interacted, as if each was being so careful with the other. I really hoped something grew between them. I'd gotten to know Six a bit over the past couple months at the races and thought he'd be good for my friend, if Zachary just gave him a chance.

While the two of them danced, I was joined by Skye and Dare, Haley, and a handsome Japanese-American tattoo artist named Yoshi, who was best friends with one of Nana's grandsons. The first three were wearing street clothes and cute, cartoonish animal masks. Yoshi had gone all out, though. He was dressed in black leather pants and motorcycle boots, and had decorated his muscular arms and bare upper body with a temporary, black ink line drawing. An exotic, leafy vine wrapped around him and snaked up his neck, forming an elegant, swirling mask around his dark eyes. "You look amazing," I told him.

Yoshi grinned and said, "Thanks. I like your costume."

"Compared to how creative you were, I feel like I'm dressed to go trick-or-treating."

His perfect smile got wider. "This is what happens when you forget to plan a costume ahead of time, but have a pen sitting on your desk at work." Well sure, as long as you were also a creative genius and gifted artist.

We chatted for a while about our mutual friend, Nana's grandson Gianni, who was sailing around the world with his boyfriend. Then Yoshi said, "Don't look now, but I think you have an admirer."

I followed the tilt of his head and spotted Izzy a few feet away, watching me with wide-eyed anticipation. She was wearing a pretty, iridescent white dress with pastel butterfly wings and a butterfly-shaped mask, and she was carrying a wand with a fabric butterfly on top. I exclaimed, "Izzy!" then turned to Yoshi and excused myself.

He said, "Have fun, Jess," and went off to get a drink while I hurried over to the child. I knelt down in front of her so we'd be eye to eye and pulled off my mask. "Hi Izzy. You look so pretty in your princess dress! Do you remember me?"

She nodded shyly and said, "You're Jessie. I didn't know if you'd remember me."

"Of course I remember! I could never forget my Valentine!" She smiled at that, and I asked, "Where's your daddy?"

Kai's voice came from directly behind me. "I'm right here. We're experiencing a malfunction with the butterfly princess's crown. I went to see if the bartenders had a twist tie or something so I could try to put it back together, but they didn't."

"It fell off and I stepped on it," Izzy said disappointedly.

"Can I see?" I turned toward Kai and a huge smile spread across my face. "Wow, look at you."

"The costume was Izzy's idea," he said, coloring a bit. He was dressed like a medieval prince, or maybe a king, with a dark blue velvet tunic embroidered with a crest over a gray shirt. Black pants and boots, black leather gauntlets covering his arms from wrist to elbow, and a gold crown completed the outfit. He wore it well.

He handed me his daughter's little plastic and rhinestone tiara, which had snapped in two, and I turned it over in my hands as Izzy's big, brown eyes brimmed with tears and she said, "It was so pretty. I didn't mean to step on it."

"This is totally fixable," I said. I sat down cross-legged right in the middle of the floor, pulled out my phone, and sent a text to one of my friends. I then turned my attention back to Izzy and said, "I've called for help. While we're waiting, tell me, are you having fun at the party?"

"It was a lot of fun before I broke my crown," she said. "You can't be a princess without one."

I distracted the little girl for a few minutes by talking about all the costumes around us, and then Christopher Robin and his husband Kieran rushed up to us. Apparently they'd followed my instructions, since they were carrying a silver ice bucket and a cloth napkin. I stood up and introduced everyone as they handed me the bucket and I glanced inside it.

"Christopher organized this entire masquerade ball," I told Izzy. "He brought a lot of magic here tonight, and some of it's left over and in this special silver chalice." I held up the ice bucket and said, "With this, we can turn the crown over to all the fairy godmothers who came here tonight, and they'll completely rebuild it for us, just like when they made Cinderella's coach out of a pumpkin. This only works once every hundred years, on a night like this, at a magical ball with a beautiful princess like you." I waved the broken crown in a circle above my head and placed it in the bucket, then covered the opening with the white napkin and said, "All we have to do to summon the fairy godmothers is to believe with all our hearts that magic is real and miracles do happen. Do you believe, Izzy?" The little girl's eyes were big as saucers behind her butterfly mask, and she nodded her head solemnly. I turned to my friends and asked, "Do you believe, too?"

Christopher put his arm around his husband. "I absolutely believe," he said.

"Me too," Kieran agreed, and kissed Christopher's forehead.

"So do I," Kai said with a little half-smile.

I waved my hand over the bucket, pressed my eyes shut and said, "I believe," then quickly pulled away the cloth. I peered into the bucket and loudly exclaimed, "Oh my gosh! It worked!"

I carefully lifted an ornate rhinestone tiara out of the bucket, then stuffed the napkin over the broken pieces of the other crown and handed the whole thing to Kieran, who quickly hurried away with it. "Princess Isabella Kahale, on behalf of the fairy godmothers, I present you with your new crown." I bowed deeply and put it in her hands as she stood there with her mouth hanging open. I then straightened up, pulled Christopher into a hug, and whispered, "I owe you one. Was it hard to find a tiara?"

"At a masquerade ball in San Francisco?" he whispered back. "Hell no. I traded one of my friends a stack of drink coupons for it. He felt he came out ahead."

"You're the best." When I let go of him, I said, "You did an amazing job with this event, by the way. You really can work miracles."

"I had a lot of wonderful people helping me, including you and Nana," he said modestly, tucking a stray blond curl behind his ears. His phone beeped and he pulled it out of the pocket of his elegant tuxedo. When he glanced at the screen, he said, "I need to address a potential vodka crisis at the bar. I also need to figure out where I left my mask. Have fun, guys!" He bowed to Izzy and said, "Thank you for being here tonight, Princess Isabella. A ball just isn't a ball without a royal princess."

As he hurried off, Izzy looked at me and said, "Your friend thought I was a real princess."

"Of course he did, and that's because you are. Do you want me to help you put on the crown?" When she nodded, I picked it up and carefully guided its built-in combs into her thick hair, which had been twisted up into an approximation of a bun. The new tiara was made of metal, so it had a better chance of survival than the last one.

She asked solemnly, "Is my new crown going to turn back into a broken one at midnight, the way Cinderella's coach turned back into a pumpkin?"

"No, it'll stay like this. That changing back at midnight thing was old fairy godmother technology. But it's a whole different century now than when Cinderella went to the ball, and they've learned a few new tricks."

"Okay, good," she said.

I turned to her father and said, "King Malakai, may I request a dance with your daughter, the lovely Princess Isabella?"

He grinned and said, "Only if you hug me first." I was a bit surprised he'd do that in front of Izzy, since we weren't going to tell her we were dating yet. When he pulled me into his arms, he whispered, "Thank you so damn much. You're my hero. Izzy's, too." I gave him a big smile when I let go of him, then took Izzy's hand and led her to the dance floor.

We got the band to play her favorite song from the movie 'Frozen', surprisingly not the overplayed theme song, but one called 'Love is an Open Door.' For the next few minutes, Izzy and I laughed and danced and spun all around, and Skye and Dare joined in. I introduced them when the song ended, and when I told her Skye had made the sculptures, she exclaimed, "You made the sad angel!"

She was fascinated and wanted to hear all about it, so we all went over to the big sculpture. While Skye was telling her about all the weird objects he'd torn apart and recycled into the angel, Kai picked up my hand and gave it a squeeze. "Izzy might see," I whispered, even though her back was to us.

He kept holding my hand as he whispered, "I want you to know I think you're amazing. Watching Izzy laughing like that on the dance floor made me so happy. You really have a way with kids."

"The trick is to truly not care what anybody thinks. If you want to do a crazy dance, go right ahead. If you feel like standing on a tabletop and crowing, go for it. Kids are taught to feel embarrassed, they don't start out that way. You have to be willing to act like you did before society tried to make you 'behave'. If you can do that, kids accept you as one of their own."

Kai grinned at that. "You obviously have it all figured out. Izzy is mesmerized by you."

"She's such a great little girl."

He kissed my forehead, then whispered, "I meant to tell you earlier that you look gorgeous tonight. I mean, you always do, but I also like your costume." Kai ducked his head embarrassedly. "I suck at giving compliments."

"No you don't."

Izzy turned to us abruptly and I dropped his hand and stepped back from Kai. She said, "I love this song," which made me smile. The band was doing a stepped-up rendition of a classic rock song, which she'd probably heard her dad playing. "Can we dance again, Jessie? Maybe my daddy and your friends can come, too."

We all returned to the dance floor. Kai was self-conscious and shuffled from foot to foot, so Skye and I tried to loosen him up by dancing on either side of him like total lunatics. That made Izzy double over with laughter, and it worked to some extent as Kai smiled and swayed a bit more to the music. I could tell he was making an effort, like he had the night he'd tried pole dancing.

When the song ended and a slow one started playing, Kai said, "Please dance with me, Princess Isabella." She beamed at him delightedly. He held her hands and she stood on his shoes, and father and daughter circled around the dance floor. "Aw, how sweet is that?" Skye said. I watched the two of them looking at each other with so much love and was overcome with happiness.

Later on, Kai went to get his daughter a drink, and Izzy sat on a tabletop with her white patent leather Mary Janes beside her. She wiggled her toes in her pink tights and said, "You and my daddy like each other, don't you?"

I wasn't sure what to tell her, so I stalled with, "What makes you say that?"

She was very serious when she said, "You have stars in your eyes when you look at each other. It's just like in the movies when the princess sees her true love. Only this time, it's two princes." To my left, Skye and Dare both grinned at that, and Skye nodded.

That made me smile, and I said, "Your daddy is a really special person."

Izzy nodded. "I know."

Kai returned and handed her an apple juice with a straw, then gently brushed a few escaped tendrils from his daughter's face as he told me, "She's getting tired, we'd better go soon."

"Did you drive?" I asked.

"No, Mal dropped us off. I figured parking would be impossible. I'm supposed to call her when we're ready to go and she'll come back for us."

"Hang on a sec," I said, and stood up and scanned the crowd. It was pretty easy to spot Nana on the dance floor with her rainbow troll doll hair, and I jogged over to her and asked her how much longer she was planning to stay, even though I knew the answer (until the party shut down and they kicked her out). I asked her one more question, then fired off a text to Zachary, who I hadn't seen in an hour, and jogged back to my little group. I told Kai, "If you want, I can drive you home in Nana's limo."

"You sure?"

"Yeah, Nana's all for it. I think Izzy will enjoy it, too."

"She'll love it. Thank you."

I told Skye and Dare I'd be back soon, and Dare said, "You two can't leave yet. You forgot something important."

I turned to him and raised an eyebrow. "We did?"

He smiled at me. "You and Kai haven't slow-danced. We can stay here with Izzy while you do that."

I glanced at Kai, and Izzy chimed in, "Go dance! Have fun, Daddy."

He took my hand and led me to the dance floor. A slow song was playing, and he slipped his arm around me and held my left hand in his right. I rested my head on his shoulder and relaxed in his arms. The evening had been full of wonderful moments, but that was the absolute pinnacle.

"I can't even thank you enough for tonight," he said softly. "Seeing Izzy so happy meant the world to me, and I'm so glad you and I got to share this."

The song ended all too soon, and Kai and I stepped back from each other with self-conscious smiles, since we had an audience. When we returned to the table, I said, "I'm going to pull the limo around. I'll have to circle the block because of where I'm parked, so it'll take me a couple minutes."

"We'll meet you out front," Kai said. He picked up one of her little shoes and slid it on Izzy's foot carefully while she drank her juice. It was such a tiny thing, but seeing that tenderness warmed my heart.

I told Skye and Dare I'd be back later (not only because I'd be driving Nana and Ollie home, but because it was barely ten p.m.) then headed for the door. My phone beeped, and I frowned as I read the text from Zachary telling me he was back home. I dialed his number, and when he answered, I asked, "Are you okay?"

"I'm fine. Sorry, I know I should have told you I was leaving. But you looked like you were having so much fun on the dance floor, and I didn't want to be a buzzkill."

"Why'd you bail out?'

"It all got to be a bit too much, the noise, the crowd, Six."

"Did he do something wrong?" I paused on the sidewalk in front of the building.

"No, not at all. He's great. Maybe that was the problem, actually. I can't get involved with an eighteen-year-old, but I was sorely tempted when we were dancing."

I said gently, "Do you think you might be using his age as an excuse? You guys seem really good together."

"I don't know. It doesn't matter. Nothing will come of it."

"I'm sorry," I said. "I encouraged him to come here, and I guess I shouldn't have. I didn't mean to make you uncomfortable or drive you away."

"You didn't at all. Neither did he. I had fun, but after an hour I was just done and wanted to come home. It's nice and quiet here, since Chance and his family are all at the dance."

As I crossed the Embarcadero, I told him, "If you change your mind and want to come back, I'll pick you up. I'm about to run Kai and his daughter home so I'll already be out for the next hour or so."

"I won't change my mind, but thanks."

We talked for another minute. After we disconnected, I returned the phone to my pocket and sighed quietly. I should have known a big, crowded event wasn't within Zachary's comfort zone, and that probably helped set up the not-so-chance-encounter with Six for failure.

When I reached the limo, I pulled my mask from my pocket and tossed it on the seat beside me. I'd given up on it pretty quickly, after realizing it was giving me tunnel vision. I glanced in the rearview mirror and fixed my hair, then straightened my silver crown. That I liked.

I pulled up in front of the warehouse a short time later. Kai and Izzy weren't outside, so I double-parked and went around to the passenger door. When they appeared after a minute, I held the door for them. Kai was carrying Izzy. She wore a puffy pink ski jacket over her dress and he clutched her wand and mask in one hand. The little girl's mouth fell open at the sight of the rainbow limo. "It's better than a carriage," she said. Kai gave me the sweetest smile over the top of her head before climbing in the back with his daughter.

She was sound asleep by the time we pulled up in front of the pink house in Bernal Heights. I double-parked and cut the engine, then hurried to open the door. Kai got out with Izzy in his arms, then leaned in and kissed me tenderly. "I've been wanting to do that all night," he whispered, resting his forehead against mine.

"Me too."

He said softly, "So, why don't you come on in for a couple minutes? I mean, unless you have to get right back...."

"But what about your family?"

"That's why I'm asking you to come in. We've been going out for two months, Jessie. It's time you met them."

I was nervous all of a sudden and stepped back a little, searching his face as I stammered, "Are you sure? What about Izzy? You were worried she'd get hurt."

He grinned a little and shifted his sleeping daughter in his arms. "I already know this thing between us isn't a short-term fling. I had my reasons for wanting to wait before bringing you two together, but Izzy's missing out. You're so great with her! You make her happy, in a way no one else does. You're fun, and positive, and upbeat, and it's kind of amazing to watch her respond to that. She's a different kid when she's with you, and seeing her laugh and enjoy herself means everything to me. You have the same effect on me, by the way." I smiled shyly and ducked my head, and Kai said, "I know meeting the rest of my family is a big deal, and if you're not comfortable doing it tonight, we can wait. But I'd love it if we took this next step."

I looked up at him and said softly, "What if your mom and grandma don't like me?"

"That's absolutely impossible."

I didn't share his confidence, but I took a deep breath and said, "Okay. Let's do this."

We went up to the house together and I started to help him unlock the front door since his hands were full, but Malia flung it open and said in a loud whisper, "We were wondering when you two were going to get your asses in here! Let me take Iz upstairs. Mom and Gran are in the living room, and they're ready to burst at the seams. If you hadn't brought Jessie inside, I think they would have chased the limo down the block! Nice ride, by the way."

"It belongs to my employer," I explained as she gingerly lifted the sleeping girl from her brother's arms.

Malia headed upstairs with Izzy and Kai put his daughter's mask and wand on a side table. He picked up my hand, and as I took a couple deep breaths, a voice from the other room called, "Would you come on already? I'm gettin' old over here!"

"That would be Gran," he said with a grin, and led me into the living room.

Kai's mom and grandmother looked a lot alike. They were both around five-five with thick, black hair to their elbows, shot through with grey. Both were also full-figured, dressed in pajamas, and grinning ear-to-ear. "It's about damn time," Kai's mom said as she hurried over and grabbed me in a bear hug. "We knew Kai was dating someone, but he's so hush hush! He tried to pretend nothing was going on. Like we don't have eyes! I can pinpoint right when you two started going out, because it was like a cloud was lifted from that boy." She took my face in her hands. "Holy Moses, look how cute you are! Please tell me you're over eighteen."

A startled bark of laughter slipped from me, and Kai exclaimed, "Oh my God, Mom, he's twenty-four!"

"Quit hogging the boy, Ginnie," his grandmother exclaimed, hip-checking her daughter a bit to push her out of the way. "Let me get a look at him!" She reminded me a lot of Nana when she squinted at me, then put on a pair of big glasses. "Oh my! You're just beautiful! Normally, I wouldn't use that word for a boy, but it fits in this case. Doesn't it, Kai?"

"Please don't embarrass him," he begged.

"They're not," I told him. To his Gran I said, "Thank you for the compliment. I think you're beautiful, too."

"You lie, but I don't mind," Kai's grandmother said with a gummy smile.

"Oh geez, Gran, where did you put your teeth?" Kai asked, looking around in a near-panic.

"Don't get your shorts in a bunch, Kai-Kai," she said. "I don't think your honey cares if I'm wearing my dentures. And I would have gotten dolled up a bit for this momentous occasion, but nobody bothered to tell us ahead of time that we'd be meeting your sweetie tonight!" She had a point there.

"I'm so glad I got to meet both of you, but I'd better go," I said. "I'm double-parked and my employer is expecting me back at the dance. I hope to see you again soon."

His mom said, "Now that Kai's done with the worst-kept secret ever, I want you to come for dinner, Jessie. How about tomorrow night?"

"I'd love to come to dinner, but I'm not sure about tomorrow. My employer usually makes a big Sunday dinner, and I help out, especially when she records it for her cable TV show."

Gran clapped her hands together and exclaimed, "Oh my God, Cooking with Nana! Am I right? That's why you look familiar, you're *that* Jessie!"

It was rare that I got recognized. I grinned and said, "That's me. Kai was supposed to be in an episode of the show, but we ended up with almost no useable footage after a crab crisis."

"I didn't know you watch that show, Gran," Kai said.

"Sure I do, I'm a big fan! Nana's my kind of woman," she said with a huge, toothless smile.

"In that case, why don't all of you come to dinner tomorrow night? Nana loves having company. I mean, if it's alright with

Kai," I said. He was all for it, so I shot Nana a text. She wrote back: *Hell yes, the more the merrier!*

We made a few plans for the next night, and then Kai told me, "I'll walk you out. I hope you haven't gotten a ticket."

"What do you mean, walk him out?" his mother said. "It's still early! You know Izzy's going to sleep like a rock after all the excitement tonight, so there's no need to stick around. Go back to the party and have fun!"

Kai glanced at me and said, "It's up to you. I don't want to make assumptions, since I know you were meeting friends at the dance."

I took his hand. "Please come back with me. We only got one slow dance in, that wasn't nearly enough."

He smiled at me, and we said goodnight to his mom and grandmother before heading out the door. When we reached the limo, he pulled me into his arms and kissed me, and then he said, "Thank you."

"For what?"

"Everything. Tonight meant so much to Izzy, and to me."

I kissed him again and told him, "It meant a lot to me too, and the night's not over yet."

When we returned to the Embarcadero, I hopped out of the limo full of energy and optimism, but then I murmured, "Oh no."

"What's wrong?" Kai asked, coming around to my side of the vehicle.

"That looks like my friend Cole over in the far corner of the parking lot. By the way his shoulders are shaking, I think he's crying. That means I messed up."

"How?"

"I gave him a ticket to the masquerade ball, knowing his boyfriend River would be here. I was hoping they'd reconcile, but it doesn't look like things went according to plan." I locked the limo door as I said, "I'm oh-for-two. I tried to fix up Zachary and Six tonight too, and that also backfired. I suck as a matchmaker."

"It's sweet that you tried, though."

"I'll meet you inside in a minute, okay? I'm going to go see if he's alright." Kai kissed my forehead before heading to the warehouse.

Cole's back was to me, and he wasn't just crying, he was sobbing. "Hey," I said softly as I walked up to him. He jumped a bit at the sound of my voice and spun around, then quickly wiped his face with the sleeve of his black dress shirt. "I guess it didn't go well. I'm so sorry for setting this up."

He took a couple shaky breaths as he pulled off his glasses and ran a hand over his swollen eyes. His voice was raspy when he said, "Don't apologize. I knew he'd be here since his brother's sculptures are in the show, and I came anyway. I guess I needed to know if it really was over, and I sure as hell have my answer now."

"Did you talk to him?"

"I tried, and it just turned into a huge fight. I'm so embarrassed. The last thing I wanted was to start screaming at him in front of a crowd. But see, that's why we never brought up anything serious the whole time we were together, because we both knew it'd turn into a yelling match."

He took a couple more ragged, deep breaths, and I said, "Why don't you come back to the warehouse and get a drink of water?"

But he shook his head. "River's still inside with his brother and a lot of their friends. I'm just going to go home to Miranda's apartment. Shit. I really need to find my own place."

Jamie and Dmitri came up to us just then, and Jamie asked, "Are you alright, Cole?"

"Oh great, so that also happened in front of my employers." Cole put a hand over his face. "I didn't know you guys were in there."

"Hey, shit happens," Jamie said. "You have no reason to be embarrassed."

"I really do," Cole muttered.

"We're heading home because my sister's babysitting and can't stay late," Dmitri said. "Why don't you come with us and crash at our apartment tonight? I'll drive your car for you if you want, since you seem pretty shaken up."

"You don't have to take care of me," Cole mumbled as his hands dropped to his sides.

"You're our friend, Cole, and we want to help. Come with us," Jamie said. "As an added incentive, the bar is right downstairs. That might be a really good thing tonight." Cole had to agree. He put his glasses back on and gave Dmitri his keys.

After the two of them drove off, I walked Jamie to his car as he said, "Thank you again for the tickets, Jessie. Dmitri and I had a great time. You were right that we'd been way overdue for a night out."

"At least I did one thing right tonight. Getting Cole to come here was obviously a mistake, though. Was the fight bad?"

"It was intense. Dmitri and I were ready to step in, we were afraid they were going to start punching each other."

"Holy crap," I muttered. "How does that happen? How can two people who loved each other end up that far from where they started?"

We reached his white SUV, and as Jamie pulled off his navy suit jacket and loosened his pale blue tie, he said, "You know I used to go out with Charlie, back in the day. When he broke up with me, I really thought I hated him for a while. I guess when emotions run that deep, there's a tendency to replace one extreme with the other, love with hate. He's one of my best friends now, but that took some time. Maybe River and Cole will get to that place eventually. I hope so, anyway."

"Do you think there's any chance they'll get back together?"

"I doubt it. That fight seemed like a bridge-burner, if you know what I mean. Things were said that nobody can take back."

"That sucks," I said. "They seemed so good together."

"I know, but couples don't always show their real face to the world. I hope they both go on to find people who truly make them happy."

"I hope so, too."

Jamie tossed his jacket into the SUV and gave me a hug. "Go have fun with your handsome prince. I'll talk to you soon."

After he left, I walked slowly back to the warehouse. Kai was waiting outside the door and drew me into an embrace when I reached him and kissed the top of my head. "River and Cole will both be okay in the long run," he said. "I know you must be upset because you care so much about everyone who's lucky enough to call you a friend, but sooner or later they'll find people who fit them perfectly."

"That's what Jamie said, too."

"He's right."

For most of the partygoers, the fight had been just a momentary distraction, and the atmosphere was festive when we went back inside. My friends were the exception. They sat in a corner by the bar, their expressions grave. River was well on his way to getting very drunk, and Skye sat right beside his brother with his head on River's shoulder. Ignacio and Dare were handing out shot glasses, and Haley and Yoshi leaned against the wall with solemn expressions.

Dare came up to us and gave us both a shot of amber liquid as he said quietly, "You guys missed all the excitement."

"We heard. How's River?"

"Drunk and stoic. We're going to take him home with us tonight, but he refuses to leave yet because he wants Skye to enjoy his evening in the spotlight."

River overheard us and surged to his feet. "That's right, tonight is about my baby brother." Skye got up too, and River grabbed him in a bear hug. "I love you, bro. You're so fucking talented! I mean, holy shit! Look at what you can do." He kept an arm around his brother's shoulders and pivoted a bit so he could wave his hand at the angel sculpture. "We all need to stop acting like we're at a damn funeral and start celebrating! My brother is going to be a famous artist after tonight. So are you, Iggy," he said, pointing at Ignacio. "I'm sorry that my personal drama had to gush out all over the place tonight, but it's over and done now. No more scenes, no more fighting. Just a whole lot of whatever this is," he said, scooping up a shot glass from the table and tossing it back.

River almost fell over after that, and Haley stepped forward and held him up with an arm around his waist. "He's right that you should stay, Skye. You promised an interview to that art blogger. I'll take your brother back to your apartment."

Yoshi stepped forward and put his arm around River's shoulders as he said, "I'll help." He'd put on a black t-shirt over his body art, but was still sporting the hand-drawn mask.

River nodded, and that was almost enough to tip him over again. "This is good. Skye can stay and get famous. We can go drink all his tequila."

"I still feel like I should go with him," Skye said, pushing his blue bangs out of his eyes.

"He just needs to sleep it off, there's nothing you can do for him tonight," Yoshi told Skye. "We promise to stay with him until you get home, right Haley?"

"Exactly," Haley said. "Alright, we're out of here. All y'all stay and have fun, that's an order." The trio swung around and headed for the door.

As soon as they were gone, Ignacio sighed and tossed back a drink. The tall Spaniard looked a bit like a pirate that night, with his tousled shoulder-length hair, tattoos, and a white shirt that really could only be described as swashbuckling. He spoke with a heavy accent, and said, "This is why I am single. No offense to you married fellows, I wish you all the luck in the world, believe you me. But it's like they say in Barcelona." He rattled off a long saying in his native language and explained, "Loosely translated, it says 'love will kick your ass.' It sounds better in Catalan." He gave a salute and wandered off into the crowd.

Dare put his arm around his husband and said, "Come dance with me, Skye. River's in good hands, you have nothing to worry about." After a bit of cajoling, Skye finally followed his husband to the dance floor. A slow song was playing, and they held each other tight as they swayed to the music.

I looked around and said, "I wonder where Nana is."

"Probably stirring up trouble. Come dance with me, Jessie." Kai took my hand and we followed Skye and Dare's lead.

*****

We ended up closing out the party, as did Nana and Ollie. I suspected they'd snuck out for some nookie at one point, because they returned looking rumpled and grinning ear-to-ear. We finally said goodnight to our friends around two a.m., after making sure Christopher Robin and his husband didn't need any help closing up.

We dropped off Nana and Ollie at her house, and then I got behind the wheel of my Honda to drive Kai home. He turned to me and picked up my hand. "Not quite yet, okay? If you're not too tired, let's go for a drive."

I didn't want the night to end either, so I eagerly agreed and headed north, out of the city. I looked down at our hands, which were joined and resting on my thigh, and was struck by the absolute perfection of that moment, of being behind the wheel with my boyfriend by my side. *My boyfriend.* I loved those words. He'd brought me home to meet his family, and that made it feel official somehow.

We crossed the Golden Gate Bridge and I drove him to the parking lot with a great view, the one where I'd spent part of Valentine's Day alone. It was so late that the lot was deserted, and we got out and sat on the hood of my car, resting against each other. Both of us were still in full costume, right down to the crowns, and while I should have felt silly, somehow it just added to the magic of the evening.

Across the bay, San Francisco shone in all its wondrous glory. From Coit Tower off by itself on a hilltop to the iconic skyline dominated by the Transamerica Pyramid, it was a view that commanded attention. And yet, I was far more captivated by the beautiful man beside me.

We both leaned in for a kiss at the same time, and Kai's fingertips brushed my cheek as I ran my hand around the back of his neck. We kissed for a long time, revving up in increments. After a while, I climbed on top of him, kissing and licking his neck and ear as I pulled at his clothes. I finally got my hand around his thick erection and began stroking him, and he unzipped my pants and grasped my cock. He then shifted us a bit, pressing our cocks together and wrapping his big hand around both of them. I moaned as he jerked us off, rocking on my knees as I straddled his lap. When I knew he was getting close, I slid down and sucked him, sliding my lips to the base of his cock and pulling back up slowly before picking up my pace. Within minutes, he was crying out and cumming down my throat, and I swallowed all he had to give.

The moment I straightened up, Kai leapt to his feet and glanced around quickly. "What are you looking for?" I asked.

"Teams of gay men with score cards," he said, and flashed me a big smile as he zipped his pants. "If I spot any, I'm going to give them a flyer for my garage. The last time we messed around in public, it was good for business."

I laughed at that and started to pull up my pants, but Kai came up behind me and lifted me off my feet with his arms around my waist. That made me laugh even more, and I exclaimed as he rushed over to the drop-off at the edge of the parking lot, "What are you doing?"

"You haven't finished yet. We need to do something about that."

He stood me on a rock and kept one arm around me as he started to jerk me off, and I asked, "Why here?"

"It's kind of tacky to shoot all over a parking lot frequented by tourists. So, we're going to be classy and help you shoot all over the breakwater down below."

I couldn't argue with that. Actually, I couldn't say much of anything, because he tightened his grip on my cock and started stroking me hard and fast. I leaned against him and moaned with pleasure, and before long I was doing just what he'd intended and shooting my load out over the rocks below us. It was oddly thrilling to orgasm like that, totally exposed, and I came so hard that by the time I finished, I was shaking, gasping for breath, and leaning heavily against Kai. He tucked me in and zipped me up, then tossed me over his shoulder like a caveman and carried me back to the car while I chuckled and said, "What are you doing, Fred Flintstone? Put me down."

"Can't. You're all rubbery, so you might tip over and hurt yourself. I need to take care of you."

He deposited me in the driver's seat, then went around and sat beside me. We leaned over the stick shift and rested on each other, and I murmured, "Epic day."

"It really was."

We ended up talking until just before dawn. As the sky turned pink, I drove us back over the Golden Gate, my fingers once again intertwined with Kai's and our hands on my leg. I'd never even suspected it was possible to feel that good.

Chapter Thirteen

The Kahale family had dressed up for dinner at Nana's, more or less. Izzy was once again wearing her princess dress and tiara, but had forgone the mask and wings. The rest of the family had also made an effort. Malia and Kai were in jeans and long-sleeved shirts, but Kai explained they were his 'good' jeans. His mom wore a light blue nylon jumpsuit with elastic around the ankles. Kai said she'd had it since the eighties, and that she insisted good taste never went out of style.

But the real star of the show was his grandmother Kiki. She was wearing a forest green satin dress with huge puff sleeves and a lace panel which could only be described as a bib, and she'd paired the frock with sneakers. Kiki had capped off the look by twisting her long, mostly grey hair into a couple Princess Leia buns on the sides of her head.

"You can tell we don't get out much," Kai said as I led them to the kitchen.

Nana and Ollie stopped what they were doing to greet their guests. When Kiki was introduced, she grabbed Nana in a hug. "I'm such a fan, Mrs. Dombruso," she gushed. "I never miss your show. I record it, because it's on kind of late, and I watch it when I'm on the crapper."

I fought back a laugh, and Kai whispered, "Kill me now."

Nana was absolutely thrilled, though. "Now look, you call me Stana and make yourself right at home. It's nice to meet a fan of the show. I got some appetizers over here, you like drunken wieners?"

"Hell yes, there's nothing better than a drunken wiener," Kiki exclaimed. I had to chuckle at that. Even though she was probably ten years her junior, Kai's Gran was definitely cut from the same cloth as Nana.

As the two little old ladies bustled over to the crock pot, Kai asked, "Is that really a thing?"

"It is! I think it's those weird little canned Vienna sausages in some kind of sauce with a lot of booze. Nana's going old-school tonight."

"Well, then my family will fit right in," he said.

Izzy was awestruck by Nana's rainbow mansion and took in the lavish surroundings and all the hubbub solemnly. She finally cracked a smile when I introduced her to the dogs. The little girl was particularly taken by the Chihuahua in his red sweater, especially when Ollie showed her where the dog treats were, and that the little dog would dance around on his hind legs when he thought he was about to get a biscuit.

Nana's grandson Mikey arrived a few minutes later with his three young sons and his girlfriend Marie. The kids bonded instantly, in a way that only kids could, and the boys took Izzy out back to see the treehouse. Malia wanted to see it too, so she tagged along, as did Marie, who seemed glad to have another woman around her age in the house.

Dante and Charlie arrived next with their cousin Nico and his boyfriend Luca. I yelled, "Oh my God, you're back," and rushed across the kitchen to give Nico a hug. He'd been my housemate at Casa Nana for a while, before falling in love and moving in with Luca. For the past couple months, they'd been in Italy, because Luca's grandfather had passed and they'd needed to settle his estate, clean out his house, and put it on the market. I introduced Kai and his family, then asked Nico, "Did you hear about medical school yet?"

He grinned shyly and said, "By some miracle, I got accepted to my first choice, which means we get to stay in San Francisco." Nana yelled and fist-pumped before kissing her grandson's cheeks and giving him a big hug.

As Dante and Ollie got busy finding champagne and glasses to drink a toast to Nico, I pulled Kai into my arms and said, "Hi."

"Hi." He smiled and kissed me, then said, "Everyone seems to be getting along well."

"I knew they would." I kissed him again and asked, "Did you get any sleep last night?"

"Maybe an hour before Izzy got up. What about you?"

"I got to sleep in a bit. You must be exhausted."

He said, "Totally with it."

I kissed him again, and we got pretty caught up in it until his mother said, "Would you take this champagne already? My arms are about to fall off!" I hadn't even noticed her standing beside us holding up two glasses, and I felt myself blushing as we took the drinks and thanked her.

Chance and his family came into the kitchen as we were toasting Nico. I asked him how his photos had been received at the event the night before, and Chance embarrassedly admitted they'd gotten rave reviews. More cheering, champagne, and toasting followed.

A little later, Chance pulled me aside and asked, "Have you heard from Zachary today?"

"No. Why?"

"He seemed a bit off this morning and said he was going out to look at apartments. I texted him an hour ago asking if we should wait for him so we could give him a ride to Nana's, and he told me he was going away for a couple days and that I shouldn't worry."

"Going away where?"

"He wouldn't say. That's why I'm concerned. I don't know why that would be a secret."

I frowned and asked, "Does he do that a lot?"

Chance lowered his voice. "He used to do it all the time, back when we were both sex workers. I always assumed he was on multi-day jobs with clients, not that he'd ever tell me what was actually going on. He hadn't taken off like this since he'd been living with my family and me, though."

"You don't think he went back to prostitution, do you?"

"I hope not. I know first-hand what that job does to your self-esteem and I was so happy when he left it behind."

"I was, too."

Chance sighed and said, "I'm probably overreacting. There's no reason to assume that's what he's doing. Maybe he just needed some time away and took a little vacation. I don't know why he wouldn't just tell me, though, if that was the case."

"He was saving every penny for an apartment," I told him. "I'd be surprised if he decided to spend money on something like that."

"You're right."

I asked, "Does he have any other friends he might stay with?"

"As far as I know, you and I and my family are pretty much it."

"Let me know if you hear from him, okay?" He promised he would, and asked me to do the same.

Meanwhile, Ignacio Mondelvano arrived with a case of Spanish wine, and Ollie clapped his hands together delightedly, then turned to Nana and exclaimed, "You gotta try this, hot stuff! I think we should serve it at our reception."

Nana started grabbing wine glasses from the cupboard as she told Kiki, "You and your family need to come to the wedding! Ollie and I are getting married in June. Make sure you leave your address with me so I can send you an invitation."

Kiki beamed at her. "That's so nice of you, especially considering you just met us."

"I like you," Nana said, "you've got style, and I know you and I are going to be great friends. Plus, our kids are crazy about each other, and hopefully they'll get married and unite our families."

"Oh, I didn't realize Jessie was your grandson," Kiki said as she helped line up wine glasses on the counter. "I thought you were just his employer."

Nana said, "Jessie may have started out as my driver, but he's so much more than that now. He's a part of my family."

I felt a surge of emotion when I heard that. I loved being a part of Nana's family, but I knew from experience that family didn't always mean forever. I was getting ready to move out, and I really had to wonder how my relationship with the Dombrusos was going to change when I did.

I tried to snap myself out of my melancholy mood as we sampled the wine, and a few minutes later Trevor, Vincent, and their son Josh came into the kitchen. Trevor was carrying his tripod, and I said, "I didn't realize we were filming tonight." I circled the kitchen island and took a look at the ingredients Nana had arranged on the counter.

"I wasn't planning to at first," Nana said, "but we got an honest-to-God fan here, so I thought Kiki should see how we make the magic happen."

"Mr. Mario won't be here tonight, so who's going to work the hand-held camera?" I asked.

"That would be me," Josh said with a grin. He hopped up on the counter and started adjusting the settings on Nana's compact video camera. "I got inspired by Crabmageddon a few weeks back and have started to play around with filmmaking. We probably won't luck out with that same level of action footage this time, but I'm keeping my fingers crossed. Hey, that reminds me, did you end up finding all those little bastards?"

I shook my head. "We recovered twenty-nine of them, but the one with the knife hasn't turned up. He has a distinct crack in his shell, so we've been looking for a crab with that marking. We keep leaving shucked clams around the house, places a crab could get to but the dogs can't, and sometimes they're gone in the morning. Either the Chihuahua is sneakier than we think, or Scarface is still around here somewhere."

Josh raised an eyebrow at me and pushed his black-framed glasses up the bridge of his nose. "But they can't live that long out of water, can they?"

"There are stories on the internet about crabs escaping after they're caught, then being found alive on the fishing boat weeks later. Just to help him along a bit, we've also put shallow pans of water around the house. I keep expecting to find him in one of them, but so far, that crab is a master of stealth mode."

"That's all just weird," Josh said. I had to agree.

I turned my attention to Nana, who was quickly and efficiently forming little potato gnocchi and lining them up on a sheet tray, and asked, "What can I help with?"

"Could you find my deep-fryer and fill it with oil? I think it's in the cabinet below the espresso machine. Kiki pointed out the fact that we don't do much frying on the show."

Kai frowned at his grandmother. "You know you're not supposed to eat fried stuff. Doctor's orders."

Kiki put her hands on her hips and said, "Bah! I'm not going to keel over if I indulge for one night! That doctor is just sizeist anyway. He thinks everyone should be a skinny Minnie. I mean, it looks good on you, Stana, but women come in all body types, know what I'm saying? Why can't I enjoy fried food every once in a while, just because I'm naturally curvy?"

"Right on, sister," Nana exclaimed. "Me, I wish I had hips and curves. I've always been built like a stick, but that's not from some starvation diet, it's just my body type."

"Like I said, we're all built different," Kiki said.

"Exactly! I don't believe in depriving myself. I say, if it tastes good, put it in your mouth." Nana gave Ollie a roguish wink and added, "That's also true in the bedroom." Kai nearly choked on his wine, but managed to stop short of a spit-take.

I tried to get the conversation back on track by asking as I plugged in the deep fryer, "When do you want to start rolling, Nana?"

"Now's as good a time as any," she said, and Trevor and Josh both turned on their cameras.

I filled the machine with vegetable oil while she introduced her guest and talked about the recipe for the gnocchi she'd made.

Then she said, "I'm going to try something different today, since my new friend Kiki likes fried food. I wasn't gonna film this meal at first, because if you've seen gnocchi made once, you've seen it a thousand times. But then, I got to thinking. Gnocchi are made of potatoes, so why not cook them up just like a French fry?"

"Brilliant," Kiki said.

"I've had deep-fried ravioli before, and they're damn tasty, so I think I'm inventing a whole new thing here with deep-fried gnocchi." Nana looked pretty proud of herself. "I already got my marinara simmering on the stove, it's been going a couple hours. I figure it can become a dipping sauce and these gnocchi can turn into an appetizer. After that, we'll go nuts and fry up all kinds of stuff. I was in a Mexican restaurant once, and they had deep-fried ice cream! You know we gotta give that a try!"

Nana showed Kiki and me how to finish the potato dumplings by running the tines of a fork over them and giving them grooves, and when we'd done that to all of them, she loaded up the basket that went with the fryer and said, "It looks like the oil's at temperature. That's important when you're deep-frying. If it's too cold, your food just steeps in it and sucks up too much oil, and then it ends up greasy. That's no good."

She climbed up on her stepstool and lowered the basket into the hot oil, and I asked, "How long should they cook, Nana?"

"Hell, I don't know. They're pretty small, so I'm thinking they'll go fast. We'll just check them at the three minute mark and see if they're golden brown. Meanwhile, we can talk about what else we want to fry. I'm makin' a salad, and deep-fried zucchini is a thing, so maybe we can fry up some other veggies, too. What do you think about the idea of fried cucumber?"

"Um, I'm not sure about that idea, Nana," I told her.

"Yeah, maybe not," she said. All of a sudden, something sailed across the kitchen with a loud popping sound, and Nana yelled, "Sweet baby Jesus on a Pride parade float, what the hell was that?"

"I have no idea," I said. Josh panned all around the kitchen with the video camera, and I asked the group on the other side of the kitchen island, "Anybody see what that was?" They all shook their heads. A moment later, three more pops came in quick succession, and a couple tiny UFOs sailed around the room.

I leaned over and peered into the deep fryer, which was bubbling away, and said, "Oh shit, I think it's the—"

I didn't get to finish my sentence though, because all of a sudden, gnocchi started exploding like fireworks and shooting all over the room, and I had to duck and cover. "Son of a whore," Nana yelled, bobbing quickly to avoid a flying gnocchi. "What are those little fuckers doing?"

I pulled Nana and Kiki back to a safe distance, then grabbed a pot lid to use as a shield. Kai jumped in to help, and I handed him a second lid. After I thought about it a moment, I also handed him a pair of oven mitts, then pulled open a junk drawer and looked for eye protection. All I found were several pairs of Nana's huge, round sunglasses, but they were better than nothing. I handed a pair to Kai, shoved another pair onto my face, and stuck my hands into some big oven mitts before he and I moved in on the fryer.

Everyone was talking at once and running around the kitchen as the gnocchi kept popping loudly and zinging around us. Fortunately, the little kids were still outside, so they were safe from both the potato projectiles and the very long, very colorful list of expletives Nana came up with to express her frustration with the exploding edibles. Meanwhile, Josh, the thirteen-year-old, hid under a black umbrella and grinned delightedly as he calmly filmed the spectacle.

As Nana yelled, "It's like a meteor shower, and we're the dinosaurs," I pulled the plug on the fryer, and Kai lifted the basket out of the oil. The dumplings still had a grand finale in store for us though, and several popped at once, flying off in every direction. He put the basket in the sink and jumped back, and everyone waited and held their breath.

Just when we started to relax, another gnocchi went off. After another moment, we relaxed again. And then, *pop!* It went on like that for a while. When we were finally sure nothing else was going to explode, Kiki started clapping and yelled, "Now *that* is Cooking with Nana!"

The crowd chuckled appreciatively and applauded, and Kai and I looked at each other. He was wearing huge, round, bright yellow sunglasses worthy of Elton John, and lobster claw oven mitts that someone had given Nana as a gift. We both started laughing at the same moment. Kai doubled over, then fell onto the kitchen floor. I landed on top of him, and we held on to each other as we howled with laughter. Every time we looked at each other, we'd just start up again. It was a couple minutes before we finally calmed down, dabbing our tears beneath the giant eyewear.

"You're both silly," a little voice said.

I rolled onto my back, looked up at Izzy, and smiled at her. "Thank you."

"What are you doing on the floor?" she asked.

"Having a great, big giggle fit. You need one, too." I plucked her off her feet and deposited her between Kai and me, and when her father dotted kisses all over her face, she shrieked and started laughing, too.

Josh snapped a picture with his phone and said, "You guys are the cutest family ever. I'll text you this photo, Jess."

I looked at Kai as Josh's words sank in, then sat up quickly and pulled off my sunglasses. "Can I try them on?" Izzy asked, sitting up, too. I carefully slid them onto her face, and she smiled at me and said, "How do I look?"

"Like a glamorous movie star," I told her as I got to my feet. "Are you hungry? I think dinner's going to be a little late, but there are some chopped up veggies in the fridge. Want some with dip?" She nodded and I lifted her onto one of the stools at the kitchen island, then went and made a plate for her.

As several people got busy making more gnocchi for dinner (to be boiled, not fried), Nana said, "I wonder why they blew up like that."

"I think they produced steam inside when they were frying, and that made them explode," Kai said. "That's my theory, anyway."

I put together a big salad while the gnocchi assembly line did its thing, and Vincent appointed himself bartender. He made juice drinks for the kids and handed around a potent rum punch for the grown-ups. A few people buzzed around wiping down the cabinets and counters and gathering up dumpling shrapnel, and with everyone helping, the kitchen survived another cooking show episode and a great dinner came together.

We gathered in the dining room about an hour later. There were twenty-five people around the table. Izzy wanted to sit beside me, and she watched all that was going on around her with a little grin. The conversation was loud and food and laughter were plentiful. We went through several bottles of the Spanish wine, and when they ran out, I pushed back from the table and said, "I'll get some more."

In the quiet kitchen, I unpacked two more bottles of wine from the case and lined them up on the counter. I didn't go right back to the dining room, though. Instead, I took a moment and closed my eyes. My emotions were raw that evening, but I didn't know why.

I sensed Kai behind me even before he asked, "You okay?"

"Fine." I said it automatically.

"That comment Josh made earlier about you, me and Izzy looking like a family," he said softly, "that really freaked you out. I saw your face, Jessie. You understand I'm a package deal, right? If you're getting cold feet about this, I really need to know."

I was quiet for a long moment before whispering, "Have you ever wanted something so bad that it scared the hell out of you?" I turned to look at him and stretched my arm out, spanning most of the distance between us. "Everything I've ever wanted is almost within my grasp. This perfect life: the most sensational guy, the cutest, sweetest kid, a family of my own. It's *right there*. And shit, Kai, it's going to crush me when this falls apart."

He grabbed my hand. "That's what's worrying you? I totally misinterpreted what happened back there." Kai stepped forward and pressed my palm to his chest. "Jessie, I'm yours for the asking. In case you haven't figured it out yet, I'm crazy about you, and I'm not going anywhere."

I slipped my hand from his and let it fall to my side. "Not today. Maybe not tomorrow either. But it's so damn hard to believe in forever, after my entire family proved to me there's no such thing."

"I get that you're scared, Jessie. I really do. And you know what? So am I. Who wouldn't be? Opening up your heart to someone means taking a huge risk and making yourself incredibly vulnerable, but consider the potential payoff!"

I said softly, "But right along with that is the potential for total devastation. I mean, God, look at Cole and River. It sure seemed like their love was going to last a lifetime, but in the end, all they got was a couple years and a pair of broken hearts."

"We're not them, Jessie."

"I know."

Kai said gently, "So what are you going to do? Close yourself off from the world? From me? Are you never going to take a chance on love, because you might possibly get hurt? You know, I tried that for quite a while after my best friend left me and our daughter without so much as a backward glance, and let me tell you, it was pretty goddamn lonely."

"I don't want to do that." My voice sounded so small.

"Then trust me, Jessie! Believe me when I say I'm not going anywhere."

My first impulse was to argue. I wanted to tell Kai trusting not just him, but anyone, was nearly impossible after what my family had done to me. I wanted to point out that being abandoned by everyone who'd loved me had left me damaged, maybe beyond repair. It was so easy to say 'trust me' but incredibly difficult to put aside a lifetime of hurt.

But as I looked up at him and he held my gaze unwaveringly, I realized something. I *did* trust him. It hadn't been a conscious decision. It had just happened, all on its own, even though I didn't believe I was capable of it anymore. I trusted Malakai Kahale with my heart, my soul, with all of me. He was a good man. He was kind, and decent, and genuine. I knew that for a fact, and I knew he was worthy of my trust.

He looked surprised when I said, so quietly, "Okay." Kai closed the distance between us and grabbed my shoulders, pulling me against him as his lips claimed mine. I sank into it.

When we finally broke apart, Kai touched my face gently, and watched me for a long moment. Then he picked up one of the bottles of wine. "Come on," he said, trying to lighten the mood. "Let's get back. Nana was mentioning the fact that she owns a karaoke machine when I left the table. We need to head off that potential catastrophe." I grinned at him and picked up the other bottle, and we returned to the dining room hand in hand.

*****

Later that night, after a lot of food, wine, and truly awful karaoke, I snuggled against Kai in my little bed and kissed his bare shoulder. Izzy had fallen asleep an hour before, and his family had driven her home. "See how much my family likes you? They absolutely insisted that I stay behind and spend a little more time with you," he said, draping his arm over my waist.

"They're great," I said. "Nana and Gran bonded big-time. I thought they were going to run off and get matching tattoos after their hour-long Tina Turner medley."

"Oh man, don't give them any ideas." Kai idly ran his fingertips down my upper arm.

"I'm disappointed though that you didn't sing any karaoke. You were literally the only person in that room who could carry a tune, but you kept finding excuses not to join in!"

"I hate singing in front of people."

"Will you sing me something now?"

Kai glanced at me and asked, "Seriously?"

"Please? I love the sound of your voice."

"Oh man. It's crazy, the things I'm willing to do for you." He paused for a moment, then started to sing 'Can't Find my Way Home' by Blind Faith. His voice was much deeper and his *a Capella* version a lot slower than the original, which gave the song a haunted, almost sorrowful quality. It was one of the most beautiful things I'd ever heard.

When he finished, I picked up his hand and ran it over my forearm. "I literally have goosebumps," I told him. He tried to laugh it off, but I could tell he was pleased.

After a while he said, "I've been wanting to ask you something. Before I do, I want to tell you it's completely fine to say no. It's also fine to take as long as you need to think about it."

"Okay."

"What do you think about coming to work with me part-time at the garage? Business has been picking up, ever since I advertised at the community center. I just got a major restoration project on a '68 Mustang Fastback, and that's going to take a hell of a lot of time over the next few months. I have other work coming in on top of that, and I hate to turn people away, especially when I'm trying to build a customer base. Since you said your job's not really full-time anymore, I was thinking you might want to split your time between the garage and Nana, around her schedule, of course."

I sat up and asked, "Wouldn't it make things weird between us if I worked for you?"

He sat up too and gently brushed my hair back. "Not *for* me, with me. I want you to be my coworker, not my employee."

"Why me? Why not just hire someone?"

"Because you're the best mechanic I know, and because working with you would make me incredibly happy. I hate the thought of working with some random stranger, who I may or may not get along with. But working side-by-side with my boyfriend every day sounds like bliss." It actually really did, but there were so many ways it could backfire. Kai continued, "There are other reasons, too. You have an in-depth understanding of newer imports, and my thing has always been older American cars. While you and I can obviously both work on anything, those different areas of expertise would complement each other perfectly."

"You've given this a lot of thought."

Kai nodded. "I never do anything without thinking it through first." He grinned and added, "Well, except for the first couple times we slept together, and thank God I didn't overthink that."

I knew I needed to find another job, especially since I'd barely worked ten hours over the last week. Ollie had been driving Nana everywhere in his convertible, and most of the wedding planning had been taken care of, so I was feeling pretty obsolete. I'd even approached her about cutting my salary, because in no way was I working enough to justify what she paid me. She'd completely shut me down, but I was going to have to get her to listen to me.

Changes were definitely ahead, and what he was proposing excited me, but I had a lot of concerns, too. I said, "What if it ends up affecting our relationship? I have to wonder if Cole and River would still be a couple if they hadn't worked together."

"You told me once that the catering business was River's passion, but it didn't sound like it was Cole's. Maybe that left him feeling unfulfilled, or like he was living someone else's dream and not his own. I don't know, I'm just speculating. But none of that would be the case here. You love working on cars, and I think you'd be happy at the garage."

"But if you're signing my paycheck...I don't know. It seems like we're just setting ourselves up for conflict down the road."

"Or maybe it would go great."

I flailed around, trying to put into words all that was worrying me, but finally just ended up with, "Are you sure you want to bring someone on and give up part of your income? The money you'd be paying me could make a difference to you and your family."

"But with the two of us working at the garage, we'll have a lot more money coming in than if it's just me. I want to grow my business, but I'm not going to start working fourteen-hour days and taking time away from my daughter to keep up with the work load."

I chewed my lower lip for a moment before saying, "This sounds so great. I'd love to work at the garage, and to see you every day. But what if it's the wrong choice? What if working together is too much pressure and ends up costing us our relationship?"

"It won't."

"How do you know?"

"Because we won't let it."

I thought about it for a while before saying, "Maybe we can do this on a trial basis. We could give it a month and then see where we are. You concentrate on that restoration project and I'll pick up the small jobs that come in. If there's any sign that our work arrangement is having a negative impact on us, I'll resign from the shop at the end of thirty days. I'll even help you hire someone in my place if you want. I know a lot of mechanics."

Kai hugged me and said, "I'm so glad you're willing to give this a shot."

"Thank you for thinking of me."

He sat back a bit and looked at me. "There's something else I've been wanting to tell you. I've decided to quit racing."

"Are you serious?"

He nodded. "There comes a time, you know? I've been racing since I was sixteen and I already stuck with it longer than I should have. I think it's best to walk away at this point and not keep tempting fate. I don't need the money like I used to, and I guess I really don't need anything else from it, either. Not anymore."

"Don't you? It was such an important outlet for you."

"How can I put this?" Kai paused for a moment, then said, "Racing used to be an absolute necessity, because it was the one thing I had that was just mine, and that didn't have a thing to do with being a parent. It was the only time I could act my age. It made me happy, and made me feel fulfilled." He touched my face and said softly, "I don't need racing to feel happy and fulfilled now, Jessie. I have something so much better for that." I grinned and pulled him into a kiss.

Chapter Fourteen

Izzy held out a little bouquet of dandelions and said shyly, "These are for you."

I pulled off my work gloves and crouched down so we were eye-to-eye. "Thank you so much," I said as I took the flowers from her. "This was really nice of you." She smiled and looked at her little pink sneakers, which matched her tiny, pink handbag, her pink shorts, and her pink sweatshirt with a silhouette of Tinkerbell on the front.

"Sorry if we're interrupting," Malia said as she gestured at the silver Corolla I'd been working on.

"You're not. This customer's picking up her car at six, and it's already done. I was just fine-tuning the engine to increase its fuel efficiency."

I'd been working at the garage for two weeks, and so far it had been a huge success. I loved the job. It was deeply satisfying to roll up my sleeves and spend each day fixing things. The fact that I got to see Kai all the time was the best part though, and not just for the hugs and kisses we snuck in throughout the day. He was incredibly easy to work with. I appreciated the fact that he let me work independently and never gave unsolicited advice. We'd consult with each other whenever one of us wanted a second opinion, but there was no sense of him looking over my shoulder or acting like he was my boss. He respected me and treated me like an equal, and I loved that it felt like a partnership.

I asked Izzy, "Want to come with me to find a vase for these?" She nodded and slipped her hand in mine, and the three of us went back to the office. I found an old glass bottle, filled it with water and the dandelions, and put them on the photo shelf. Then I asked Izzy and Malia if they wanted a drink, and when they said yes, I handed them both an apple juice from the mini-fridge.

As Izzy sat on the blue quilt I'd found for the daybed, sipping her juice and swinging her feet, Malia said, "I like what you've done with the place."

"I didn't do much. Mostly, I just cleaned," I said, indicating the tidy shelves and desk. "The curtains and new bedding did freshen it up a bit, though." Kai and I spent the night in the office two or three times a week. We'd go to his house around five, spend every afternoon and evening with his family and tuck Izzy in before returning to the garage and working until midnight. Of course, whenever Nana called, I'd drop everything and go help her, but those calls were few and far between.

Malia said, "It's a huge improvement. My brother doesn't usually give much thought to his surroundings. Where is he, anyway?"

"He said he had a meeting and took off maybe forty minutes ago."

"What kind of meeting?"

"No clue. I expect him back soon though, since he said he'd only be gone an hour."

"I just assumed he'd be here. Mom and Gran are both out, and I'm supposed to pick up my boyfriend and drive to Redwood City to look at a second-hand food truck. I can take Iz along, but I think she'll be bored out of her mind."

"You can leave Izzy with me if you want. We'll go out to the patio and draw pictures, right Princess Isabella?" The little girl gave me a bashful grin and nodded.

Malia thanked me and apologized before heading to the door, but there was no need to. I loved spending time with Izzy, and she and I had really bonded over the past few weeks. I gathered up the pads of drawing paper and the Mason jar full of colored pencils I'd bought for her visits to the shop, along with a tiny, pink gift bag. Then I closed and locked the garage and headed to the patio with my cute companion.

The mid-May weather was absolutely perfect. Izzy sat beside me on the bench at the red picnic table, and when I put the three-by-three-inch gift bag in front of her, Izzy's eyes went wide and she said, "It's not my birthday."

"I know. I just saw something pretty at the store and thought of you." She carefully pulled out the tuft of pale pink tissue paper and when she peered into the bag, her face erupted into a huge smile. As she carefully pulled the pair of rhinestone butterfly-shaped barrettes from the bag, I explained, "On days you can't wear your tiara, you can wear these and still be the butterfly princess."

She scrambled up onto the bench and grabbed me in a hug, strangling me a bit, but it was totally worth it. "They're the most beautiful things in the whole world! Thank you so much, Jessie," she exclaimed. It was a far bigger reaction than I'd expected from a three-dollar set of hair clips.

I hugged her gently and said, "You're welcome, Princess Isabella."

When she let go of me, she asked, "Will you help me put them in my hair?"

"Love to." She opened her little fabric handbag and pulled out a tiny brush. Its handle was clear plastic with hot pink glitter throughout it. Izzy handed me the brush and sat with her back to me, and as I carefully untangled the ponytail holder from her thick, dark hair, I asked, "Do you want me to French braid it for you?"

She looked at me over her shoulder. "Do you know how?"

I nodded. "My sister Ruthie taught me so I could do her hair. She only had brothers, and our mom was usually too busy with something or another to fuss with things like that. I'm out of practice, but I haven't forgotten how it's done." Izzy seemed impressed.

As I ran the brush through her hair, she asked, "Do you think you and my daddy will get married?"

That caught me off guard, and I stammered, "I, um, I don't know."

"I hope you do," she said. "I like how happy Daddy is now that you're his boyfriend. I used to want him to find a mommy for me because I don't have one, but I've been thinking. I kind of already have three mommies, between Auntie Mal and Gran and Great-Gran. But I only have one Daddy. Our family could use one more, even though we'll still have way more girls than boys." I had to grin at that logic.

When the braid was completed and the hair clips were in place on either side of her head, I snapped pictures with my phone so Izzy could see the results. She was absolutely delighted, and said, "You and Daddy need to start spending the night at our house instead of here. That way, you can braid my hair before school. I know you guys do sleepovers a lot, because he's so happy and smiley in the morning."

It was nice to hear I had a visible effect on him. "Doesn't anyone in your family do this?"

She turned to me and shook her head solemnly. "Auntie Mal goes to work really early, and when Gran or Great-Gran try to braid my hair it turns out all lumpy. You made it perfect. Why don't you spend the night tonight so my hair can be pretty for school tomorrow?"

"I'll have to ask your dad," I said.

"He'll say yes."

I turned our attention to the three spiral bound drawing pads and handed Izzy hers. The other two were labeled 'Jessie' and 'Kai'. He mostly drew cars whenever we roped him into doodling with us (he thought he was terrible at it, so it usually took some cajoling), and I was basically the stick figure king, but I enjoyed it.

Izzy concentrated on her drawing, her brows knit as she gripped a yellow colored pencil. The tip of her tongue peeked out from between her lips, and when she saw me grinning and watching her, she hooked her arm around the drawing and admonished, "Don't peek!"

I assured her I wasn't and went back to my stick figures. A few minutes later, Izzy carefully tore the sheet from her drawing pad and handed it to me. "I made you a present. I drew a frame around it, so you can put it on the picture shelf in the office. You need to be up there, too."

A lump formed in my throat as I looked at the carefully rendered portrait. Izzy had drawn herself holding hands with me on her left and Kai on her right. We were all smiling and surrounded by hearts. She'd drawn a golden frame around the edge of the paper, and misspelled 'famly' at the top of the paper in her adorable, chunky block print. It meant more to me than she could possibly realize. I pulled the little girl into another hug and whispered, "Thank you."

"Do you like it?"

"It's the most wonderful present anyone's ever given me in my entire life." I really meant that.

She seemed pleased, and when I let go of her, she started drawing flowers on a fresh sheet of paper as she hummed to herself. I took another look at the picture before tucking it carefully between a couple clean pages of my drawing pad. Her ability to open her heart like that, to decide I was family after just a few short weeks, was both touching and humbling. It was so genuine, completely without ulterior motives or the need for explanation. It just *was*.

I realized something all of a sudden. Nana had proclaimed me family in exactly the same way, just weeks after I went to work for her. With Nana, just as with Izzy, you could take them at their word. If they said I was family, then as far as either one of them was concerned, I absolutely was. They wouldn't tell me what I wanted to hear. Instead, they spoke from the heart, always.

I couldn't remember if I'd ever told Nana I loved her, and if I hadn't, that was a huge oversight. I picked up the phone and texted: *I love you, Nana. Thank you for letting me be a part of your family.*

She texted back: *I love you too, Sweet Pea, and you'll always be a part of my family. Are you at the garage? I have something for you.* I told her I was, then went back to drawing.

Fifteen minutes later, Nana and Kai's Gran bustled into the yard. They were both wearing velour track suits and had styled their hair in matching Princess Leia buns. "Oh, Izzy's here, too," Kiki exclaimed. "I have something in the car for her."

She started to turn back the way she came, but Izzy called, "Great-Gran, wait! You have to look at my hair. Jessie did it! He gave me a present, too. Are they sparkly?" She gingerly touched the butterfly clips with her stubby fingers.

"Oh my heavens, they're just as sparkly as can be! They look like diamonds. That Jessie is one heck of a braider, too, I tell you what," Kiki said. "You look beautiful, Iz. Now just wait until you see what Nana Stana and I got you today!" She hurried from the yard.

"Where's Ollie?" I asked as Nana sat across from us and put a tall, pink, bakery box on the table.

"He's with Ignacio. They're talking business with Christopher Robin, so Kiki and I decided to go out and make some bachelorette party plans. We found one of those 'adult bakeries' and got you and Kai some treats for later. Kiki also got some G-rated stuff for dessert tonight, so Princess Isabella can enjoy, too. Just not what's in this box. That'll result in years of therapy." Nana moved the box to the bench beside her and smiled cheerfully.

Kiki returned a minute later with a tiny garment bag, which she unzipped with a flourish. Inside was a gorgeous pink dress with a tulle rainbow petticoat. Izzy gasped, and Nana said, "I need a flower girl for my wedding, and I can't think of a prettier, smarter, more perfect little girl in all the world. Will you be in my wedding, Princess Isabella?" Izzy nodded, staring at the dress in absolute wonder.

Finally the little girl managed, "Can I wear my new butterfly barrettes in the wedding?" That made me feel good.

"Of course you can!" Nana told her. "They'll be perfect with this dress. We'll go out and get you some pretty new shoes, too. Those you have to try on. You gotta have comfortable shoes, that's important in life. Do you want to try on the dress to make sure it fits?"

Izzy nodded, and Kiki said, "Come on, Iz, I'll take you to the office to change."

I handed her the key to the side door, and when the two of them went off hand-in-hand, I slid the little girl's drawing from my notebook and showed Nana. Her brown eyes crinkled in the corners as she smiled and said, "I know how much family means to you, Jessie, and I'm so happy you're getting one of your own."

"I've never felt like this about anyone. He's everything I could want, and so much more. And Izzy, God, what a great kid. His whole family has been amazing."

"Kai's crazy about you. It's so obvious when I see the two of you together. And good gravy, just wait until you see what he's doing for you right now! It shows true devotion, if you ask me."

"What do you mean? Where is he?"

"He's with Dante, and they're hatching a surprise for you. That's all I'll say. I shouldn't have even said that much." Nana pantomimed locking her lips and throwing away the key. Her eyes sparkled mischievously.

"I didn't realize Kai and Dante had become friends at some point."

Nana mimed unlocking her mouth, then said, "Kai needed help with this surprise and figured Dante was a good resource for what he needed. He was right, of course. My grandson is one smart cookie. Don't tell him I said that, I don't want him to get a big head. Now quit talking about what he and your honey are putting together for you before I accidentally let something slip!"

Izzy returned a couple minutes later, looking radiant in her new dress. It fit perfectly, and she held her head high. "Oh my gosh," I exclaimed. "It's just as pretty as your butterfly princess dress!"

She hoisted up the mid-calf-length skirt a few inches and admired the cloud of rainbow tulle underneath, then looked up at the adults around her and asked, "Is this real? So much good stuff has been happening and I'm scared that I'm dreaming."

I swung off the bench and crouched down to her level. "You know what? I've been feeling like that a lot lately, too. But it turns out, we're not dreaming. We just have awesome families who do incredibly nice things for us. We're pretty lucky, you and me." She nodded solemnly.

My phone buzzed and I looked at the screen, then told her, "Your Daddy is going to be here in fifteen minutes. Do you want to show him your new dress, or keep it as a surprise?"

She considered the question carefully, then said, "Is it okay if I show him? I want him to see it with my nice hair and the sparkly butterflies."

"Absolutely."

"Will you make my hair nice for Nana's wedding, Jessie?"

"Sure. We'll do whatever you want, a braid, or curls, or a fancy up-do. We can even practice beforehand and then you can pick the style you like best for the wedding."

She was completely delighted. I'd never realized it before, but kids were incredibly easy to please. All they wanted was your attention. When you gave them that, all was right in their world.

About ten minutes later, Dante came into the yard. As usual, he was dressed in a perfectly tailored black suit, along with a black dress shirt that was open at the collar. "Looks like a party," he said.

"Hey, Dante. What sort of scheme are you and Kai hatching?" I asked him with a smile.

He shot Nana a look, and she exclaimed, "I barely said anything! Where's Kai? Is he bringing you-know-who?"

Dante sighed dramatically, then said, "Why don't you come with me, Jess? Kai's right behind me, and you may want a little privacy with your guest." Kiki winked at me and tossed me my keys. Apparently everyone was in on whatever was happening but me.

As I fell into step with Dante and we headed to the side door of the garage, I asked, "Is this a good surprise? You're not ambushing me with a fashion intervention, are you? I swear, if that TV show with the abrasive host telling me my wardrobe is crap shows up, I'm bolting. No way am I letting go of my flannel pajamas and sexual innuendo t-shirts. Looking like you stepped off the pages of Funeral Director Monthly is working for you, but I've spent years cultivating my own personal style."

Dante chuckled as I unlocked the side door. "No need to go on the defensive there, Sparky. Your flannel pajama collection is, in fact, a complete train wreck, but that's not what this is about. Gives me some ideas for next time, though."

When we went into the garage, I hit the buttons to get both bay doors to slide up and out of the way, and peered up and down the street. Kai's Impala was nowhere to be seen. "Sorry about dissing your grim wardrobe choices," I said. "The Man in Black look works for you. It does." I turned to look at him as he leaned against the fender of Kai's Mustang, and said, "This is a total subject change, but I just thought of something. You handle Nana's finances, right?" He gave a single nod. "Will you please stop paying me? Nana won't do it, even though she barely needs me anymore. Whenever she wants to go somewhere in the limo, I'll gladly drive her, free of charge. She was incredibly generous with my salary and the free room and board, but now I can't keep taking her money. It's not right."

"Nana would kill me if I cut you off."

I frowned at that. "Do it anyway. Please? I feel like a total mooch."

He considered it for a moment, then said, "I'll see what I can do."

"Thanks, Dante." I hopped up on a tool bench, then asked, "How've you been? I haven't seen much of you lately."

"I've been alright. Just…you know. I've had some stuff to deal with."

"Stuff like Jerry?"

"Don't repeat this to Nana, obviously, but I found out my cousin's gone to work for the Messina family. I was surprised they took him into the fold, since their family and ours has a long history of tension and I couldn't see why they'd trust him. But then, I got to thinking. In order to earn their trust, he must have given them information on our family. We're not involved in much that's illegal these days, but let's just say Jerry knows where all the bodies are buried." Dante shot me a look and added, "Figuratively speaking."

"What does that mean for the family?"

"That's hard to say. If Jerry's end game was a power play to get himself back in charge of the Dombruso organization, he'd have to go through a lot of layers, not just Vincent and me, but everyone who's loyal to us. I can't see how he'd hope to pull that off. So maybe it's just revenge, plain and simple. Maybe he's looking to hurt us financially, or maybe he wants real pain and suffering, since as far as he's concerned we turned on him. Who knows? I will say, it's ironic as hell, him going over to a family we've long considered our enemy," Dante said, straightening the cuff of his suit. "That's exactly what started this. He was so pissed off at our cousin Nico for fraternizing with someone from a warring family that he took a hit out on him, and that led directly to me removing Jerry as the head of our organization. But now here he is, cozying up with the Messinas! I can only wonder how he somehow justifies his actions."

"I think that last sentence applies to every dick in history, Jerry included."

Dante grinned at that, then pushed himself upright and said, "There's Kai. I really hope this surprise ends up being a good one. If not, just remember that your boyfriend meant well."

As Kai eased the Impala into its usual parking space, his passenger turned to look at me and I stopped breathing. When the car came to a stop, the guy got out of the car and said, "J.J.?" He'd grown from a teenager to a man, but my kid brother's voice was exactly like I remembered it.

"Oh my God, Jedidiah." It came out as a whisper.

"It's really you!" He ran to me and grabbed me in a hug. "I thought I'd never see you again! I looked for you for such a long time!"

"You did? But…I don't understand. You never wrote back. I left a letter for you and Ruthie with our friend Samuel, telling you where I was going, but I never heard from either of you."

Jed pulled back to look at me, his blue eyes wide behind his glasses. "Oh God. Samuel never gave us a letter, J.J., and he said a lot of awful things about you after you took off."

"He did? I thought we were friends. I wrote to him after I moved to San Francisco, and when he didn't write back, I assumed his family had moved like they'd been talking about and that my letters weren't reaching him."

A tear snaked down my brother's cheek, and he grabbed me in another hug. "I wish you'd told me ahead of time when you were planning to come out. I would have helped you."

"You were only seventeen, and sis was even younger. I didn't want either of you to get in trouble, since you had to go on living under his roof, and Dad would have made your lives hell if you'd sided with me," I said. "That's why I told Samuel to wait until I was gone before he gave you the letter. It's also why I came out when you and Ruthie were at Bible study, to make sure you didn't get caught up in all that hatefulness."

"But you shouldn't have gone through that alone, J.J."

"It's Jessie now. I legally changed it." I took a long look at my brother, and touched his upper arm as if to prove to myself he was really there. The kid I'd last seen at seventeen was taller than me by a good couple inches, and his short, golden blond hair was a few shades darker. He'd filled out a lot, too, and probably had thirty pounds of muscle on me. Behind his glasses his blue eyes were exactly the same though, and they crinkled at the corners as he smiled at me.

"You always liked the name Jessie. Remember when we were little and we'd pretend we were spies and hide clues in the barn? Sometimes, you used Jessie as your code name. You insisted on spelling it with an i-e, even though I told you it was a girl's name that way."

"Oh my God, I'd totally forgotten about that, and you know what? I ended up spelling it that way." I tried to laugh, but it came out as a sob. My brother pulled me into another hug and I stammered, "I thought I'd never see you again, Jed. I thought you hated me."

"I could never hate you, J.J. I mean, Jessie. You're my brother."

"How did Kai and Dante find you?" I raised my head from my brother's shoulder and looked around, and only then did I realize my friend and boyfriend had cleared out to give us some privacy.

"I'm not sure. Dante ended up approaching me on the S.F. State campus between classes." He grinned and added, "I thought I was in trouble at first. He's a pretty intimidating guy."

"Wait. You go to college here? In San Francisco?"

Jed nodded. "Ruthie's at U.C. San Diego. She started crying when I called her and told her I might be seeing you. I didn't know what to expect, though. Kai swore you'd be happy to see me, but I thought maybe you'd cut ties with the whole family on purpose."

I wiped my eyes with the hem of my light blue t-shirt and said, "I thought everyone sided with Mom and Dad."

"Jacob did. No surprise there, right?"

"None at all." My older brother had always been every bit as bigoted as our father.

"Our grandparents, and our aunts and uncles sided with them, too. Pretty much everyone in the older generation was ranting about how you'd chosen the path to damnation when you 'chose' to be gay. They held a big prayer meeting for you, which from what I hear turned into a three hour sermon on the sins of homosexuality. Most of the congregation joined in. Ruthie and I and our cousin Bethany all pretended we had the stomach flu. We weren't going to participate in everyone damning you."

"I thought I lost everyone when I didn't hear from you. I thought I was all alone," I said softly. "I had no idea. And here you were, living in the same city!"

"I know! It's wild. We have so much to catch up on," he said.

"We really do. But first, come with me to the patio out back. I need to thank Kai and Dante, and I'll introduce you to some more of my family."

"Is Kai your boyfriend?" I nodded as I headed to the side door and hit the buttons to lower the garage doors. "He's gorgeous. Does he have a brother?"

I turned to Jed and grinned. "Oh my God, are you gay?"

"Imagine Mom and Dad's delight. Two gay kids out of four. Potentially three, I've always suspected Jacob is deep in the closet. I think anyone who yells that loudly about the sins of homosexuality probably has a lot they're trying to hide."

"I've always thought that, too. And no, Kai doesn't have a brother, just a twin sister."

"Dang."

"So you're single?"

"Very."

"Where do you live?"

"In a cramped apartment in the Western Addition with five roommates."

"Five, good lord," I said as I locked up and led him to the patio.

"I'm on a work-study program at school, and money's tight. I wish I'd studied harder in high school like Ruthie. She landed a full scholarship to UCSD, but then she always had the brains in the family. It's cool though, most of my roommates are really nice. There are two women and three gay guys. Well, four if you count me."

"I can't believe you turned out to be gay. There were never any signs."

"Well, no. I always hid it, just like you did. It's not surprising, given the way we were raised. I was closer to you than to anyone else, and I still didn't tell you."

"What happened when you came out to our parents?"

"I took the coward's way out and told them in a letter. According to Bethany, there was a lot of screaming and yelling and more prayer meetings. I guess Mom really milked it for sympathy. Poor her, punished so unfairly with two gay kids." Jed rolled his eyes.

We reached the yard, and I went up to Kai, pulled him down to my height, and kissed him passionately before whispering, "Thank you."

He grinned at me. "Good surprise, then. I was worried."

"*Great* surprise."

Dante called from across the patio, "Don't I get a kiss? I helped too, you know."

I chuckled at that, crossed the yard and pulled Dante down too so I could plant a big kiss on his forehead. "Ew, that felt moist. I'm sorry I asked," he joked.

"Don't make me lick your face, Dombruso. I'll do it," I threatened. He pretended to be horrified and playfully pushed me away.

I introduced my brother to everyone in the yard, and Nana spun on Jed and asked, "By any chance, are you a gay homosexual?" When he said he was, she clapped her hands, then said, "Don't get me wrong, I wouldn't hold it against you if you were straight. But somehow, when I find out a boy likes boys, it just feels like he was meant to be a part of my family." Jed blushed at that and fidgeted with the collar of his dark blue polo shirt, but he also smiled shyly and looked more than a little pleased.

*****

That night, I draped my arms around Kai as we reclined on the mattress in his little attic bedroom. It was late and the house was still. The only light was the one that radiated from the dollhouse on the desk across the room. It was almost done and had turned out beautifully. That night, I'd helped him finish painting it, and in the morning we were going to carry it downstairs for Izzy.

We'd been kissing ever since we finished painting. After a while, I said as I put my head on his shoulder, "I can't thank you enough for finding my brother."

"I had to believe at least one member of your family would prove to be a good person. If it hadn't been Jed, I would have kept looking."

"If he'd said he wanted nothing to do with me when you found him, would you have told me?"

"Eventually. It's not like I wanted to sneak around and keep things from you. But I would have found one supportive relative first. Anyone, I didn't care who: a second cousin twice removed, a great-great aunt, the family dog, whatever." I grinned at that, and he said, "I'm thrilled that we ended up with a three-fer, your brother, sister, and a cousin." Jed had come over for dinner that night, and we'd called Ruthie and my cousin Bethany on a video chat. There'd been a lot of happy tears and promises of get-togethers in the very near future.

"I love you so much, Kai," I said quietly as I looked into his dark eyes. "I've been afraid to say that out loud. I don't know why."

"I love you, too, Jessie. I didn't know when or how to tell you that. It kind of felt like it needed fireworks, or a parade, or skywriting or something, so you'd know how much is behind those words."

"I already know. You show me you love me all the time, in a million ways."

He turned his head away from me as he admitted quietly, "I was always worried about being enough for you. You're like this exotic tropical bird, bright and colorful and beautiful, and by comparison, I felt like a plain old crow that somehow found its way into your amazing, vibrant world."

"You don't still feel that way, do you?"

Kai turned toward me again and brushed my hair from my eyes. "I'll always wonder how you fell for someone like me, especially given how closed off and defensive I was when you met me. But I don't question that it's real. I knew you loved me too, long before you said it. It's always there, in every look you give me, and in the way you say my name, and the way you reach for me when you start to wake up at night." He smiled at me and said, "I sound completely corny, but oh well. I just needed to say all of that to you, and now I have, so I'm going to shut up."

We both shifted around and stretched out on the little bed. As I curled up against his right side with his arm around me, he said, "Just watch. Someday, when we have our own place and buy a king-size bed, we'll still only use this much of it." He held his hands a couple feet apart, encompassing the two of us. He was right. I'd always want to sleep just like that, wrapped up in the warmth and comfort of him.

I put my head on his bare chest and he kissed my hair. A few feet away, the drawing Izzy had made of the three of us sat among the family photos on Kai's dresser. He'd found a nice frame for it and treated it like the treasure it was. My heart felt like it was filled to overflowing.

Chapter Fifteen

One month later

"If Ollie's straight, explain his bachelor party to me," Jed yelled over the pulsating techno music. He leaned in close, holding his coke aloft and trying not to spill it on his plaid button-down shirt as people crowded around us.

We were in a gay nightclub on the outer edges of the Mission District, two nights before Nana and Ollie's wedding. Dante had booked the small club in its entirety for the private party. Some of the guests had gone home, given the late hour, but maybe seventy-five Dombrusos and friends of the family planned to party until dawn. Meanwhile, across town, Nana and sixty of her closest girlfriends and relatives were probably getting arrested at a gay strip club.

"Ollie just wanted someplace we could go and get drunk," I told my brother. "He has no interest in ogling women, and a lot of Nana's family members are gay, so he figured, why not a gay bar?"

"And he's actually cool with all the half-naked go-go boys?"

"Of course. They're all friends of the family," I said, gesturing at the dozen buff, bronzed guys who'd stripped down to colorful briefs and were shaking it on the bar, tabletops, and on the tiny dance floor. "You missed Cockstock, when all those guys were working at Nana and Ollie's house around the clock. I'll tell you about it sometime when I don't have to yell."

"This is such a different world from the way you and I grew up. Ollie's the same age as Grandpa Howard, but could you imagine Grandpa or any of the other church elders in a place like this, acting like it's all as normal as breathing?"

I looked over at Ollie and smiled. He was wearing an old-fashioned 3-piece suit and a captain's hat that one of the dancers had given him, and was on the dance floor teaching three go-go boys the right way to do the twist. When I turned back to Jed, he looked wistful, and I asked, "Do you miss Grandpa and the rest of the family?"

"Yeah. I mean, I try not to dwell on it too much, you know? Classes and my job on campus keep me really busy, and I've been applying to graduate school. Between all that, there's not much time to mope. There's not much time for anything at all, actually," he said as he turned to watch Will, one of the Cockstock dancers, cross the room in a pair of tight, red briefs.

"Want me to introduce you to that guy? He's so nice."

"Oh man, no way. He's totally out of my league."

"He is not," I insisted.

"Sure he is. I mean, what would I even talk about with a guy like that?"

I smiled at my brother and said, "Who says you have to talk at all?" By the way Jed colored at that, I got the impression my nerdy kid brother was pretty inexperienced.

Zachary appeared at my side and kissed my cheek, then said, "I'm out of here. Thanks for inviting me, this was surreal."

My friend had only shown up half an hour earlier. I was surprised he'd come at all. He was still living with Chance and working at the restaurant part-time, but he'd been disappearing for days at a time, then insisting everything was fine and refusing to talk about where he'd been when he resurfaced. I still wondered if he'd gone back to prostitution, but he'd always spoken openly to me about that, so I didn't know why he'd suddenly start keeping it a secret. "I'm so glad you stopped by, Zachary. I've missed you. I'll come by the restaurant one day this week if you want, so we can catch up."

"Sounds good." He turned to my brother and took his hand, as if he was going to shake it, but he just held it instead. "I'm glad I got to meet you, Jedidiah. I hope I see you again sometime."

"I hope so, too." My brother hugged him awkwardly, and when he let go, Zachary gave him a shy smile before turning and disappearing into the crowd.

Jed watched him go, and I did too, for different reasons. Something was obviously wrong, and it killed me that I didn't know what to do about it. When I told Jed I was worried about my friend, he said, "You can't help people who don't want to be helped, Jessie. All you can do is be his friend and make sure he knows he can always talk to you."

"You're right."

Jed grinned at me and lowered his voice when a slower song started playing. "You've always been a caretaker, Jessie. That's why being a second daddy to Kai's little girl comes so naturally to you. It's just like when we were kids, if Ruthie or I scraped our knee or needed help with something, we'd come to you, even though you weren't much older than us. We always knew you'd fix it." He sighed and said, "Shoot, I mean Rue. That's going to take some getting used to. Maybe I should change my name too, it seems to be all the rage." Our sister had visited us the weekend before and insisted that at twenty, she was far too old to be called Ruthie anymore.

"Well hey, I adopted my spy name, maybe you can start using yours too, Steele Skywalker."

Jed chuckled and said, "Oh my God, never call me that again! Talk about embarrassing."

"What is?" Skye asked as he came up to us with Dare, Haley, and Kai.

"My brother's thinking about changing his name, since all the cool kids are doing it. He wants to be called Steele Skywalker." I winked at Jed.

He grinned and turned red as he said, "I hate you so bad."

Haley grabbed his hand. "Come on, Steele, dance with us. We're going to go tell the DJ to pick it up a bit."

"Oh no, I don't dance," my brother insisted, his blush deepening.

"Of course you do," Skye said as he helped Dare and Haley herd him away. My brother looked to me for help, and when I smiled and waved, he shook his head and went with his new friends.

"Alone at last," Kai said, which was kind of funny since we were surrounded by people we knew. He kissed me, then handed me a soda and the keys to his Impala. "I've had too much beer. Can you drive us home later?"

"Absolutely."

"You're the best," he said, and draped his arms around my shoulders.

We were kissing deeply sometime later, when someone came up beside us and said, "Sorry to interrupt, but we wanted to say goodnight."

I turned to Chance and Finn and exclaimed, "You're leaving already? The night is young!"

Chance said, "It's two a.m., party animal."

"Exactly! It's only two! We booked this place until five."

"You'll just have to carry on without us, and just so you know, it's your fault we have to leave. I have a nine a.m. interview with a bigtime photography blogger to talk about my show at Christopher's gallery, and I want to sound at least somewhat coherent. You just *had* to push me into my dream job." He grinned and gathered me into a hug. "I love you, Jessie. Don't forget that you, Kai and Izzy are coming for dinner next week."

"Looking forward to it."

We said goodbye to our friends, and Kai put his arms around me again after they took off and asked, "Where were we?"

"Right here."

I kissed him deeply and he said, "Dance with me, Jessie."

An up-tempo song was playing as we found a spot in the center of the dance floor. My brother was trying his best to rock out with Skye and company, and everyone was dancing with abandon all around us. But Kai and I put our arms around each other and slow-danced as if the most romantic song in the world was playing. After a few moments, we were joined by Trevor and Vincent, who grinned at us and started doing the same thing we were.

Kai and I kissed and slow-danced our way through three songs, and finally he whispered in my ear, "Would it be totally low class to sneak out to the back alley for a few minutes? I really need to give you a blowjob."

I smiled at him as my cock twitched at the suggestion. "Well, if you insist."

We joined hands and wove through the crowd, greeting people along the way. Dante and Ollie were doing a shot contest at a little table by the bar as a bunch of family and friends gathered around. Dante looked a bit tipsy, but Ollie was steady as a rock as Charlie leaned in and refilled their glasses. "Ollie's totally got this," I told Kai on the way past, then flashed Dante a big smile.

Kai and I ducked through a swinging door and cut through a disused industrial kitchen, a leftover from one of the many lives the old warehouse had lived. Apparently the kitchen was mostly used as a store room, since cardboard boxes were piled to the ceiling in the left half of the space. There was one door at the back of the kitchen, a service entrance leading to an alley used for deliveries, and I jiggled the handle before saying, "It's locked."

"There's plenty of privacy back here, though," Kai said as he led me into the dark kitchen.

I chuckled and said, "This looks exactly like the set of a horror movie. The two dumb kids sneak off to have sex in the creepy, abandoned kitchen, and then blammo! Ice pick to the cranium."

Kai laughed at that as he picked me up and sat me on a stainless steel counter. "You should write romance novels," he told me. "You're so good at setting the mood. Make sure to watch over my shoulder while I'm sucking you to make sure nobody ice picks me."

I grinned at him and said, "I'll always keep you safe, Kai. I even finally got you to lock up your shop when you're working at night, which I consider a major personal safety victory."

Kai kissed me, then corrected, "*Our* shop."

"What? No. Kit's is your baby."

"You've brought in so much business, even before you started working with me."

"By sleeping with you outside and attracting the attention of Ash and his friends?" I gave him a teasing smile.

"I meant when you gave up a whole weekend to paint the building, then told me about the bulletin board at the community center and designed a flyer to put up. You've been a part of this business since we first got together, and the fact that it's actually profitable for once is totally due to you."

"You give me too much credit. I'm glad it's turning a profit, though."

"It is, and I really believe it's just going to keep improving. It's the snowball effect, we gain a new customer and do a good job for them, and in turn they refer a couple friends. At this rate, I think we can start construction on that upstairs apartment we've been talking about next month, assuming we can get some blueprints drawn up and obtain all the permits."

"It'd be great if that could happen."

"It really would. Just think, a bedroom where I can walk from wall to wall without hitting my head, what a luxury! And Izzy's bedroom can be twice as big as the one she has now, so she can build an entire stuffed animal empire," he said. "You and I will have room for a king-size bed, but I hope we only ever use two feet of it." Even in the faint, blue light of the exit sign, I could tell his eyes were sparkling.

"You and I...."

"I'll be building this as a home for all three of us, Jessie, you and me and Iz."

"Living together is a big step. You sure we're ready?"

"When was the last time you and I slept apart? I can't even remember. The whole living together thing already happened automatically, no discussion required. You probably have as much stuff at Gran's house as you do at Nana's right now, don't you?" I nodded, and he said, "We're ready, Jessie."

I thought about it for a few moments, and then I said, "Okay."

"Really?"

"I want this too. God I want this. But if I'm moving in, then I plan to help pay for the construction of that second-story apartment."

He pulled me close and kissed me, then said, "This is awesome. You and I can plan it out together. But we'll do that later. For now, less talking, more sucking." I chuckled and kissed him deeply as he massaged the bulge in my jeans.

After a moment, a faint rustling sound to my left caught my attention, and a few seconds after that I heard the door connecting the kitchen to the club swing on its hinges. "Okay, that's creepy," I said, turning my head to peer into the darkness. "I don't think we were alone back here."

"Figures. Some of the go-go dancers were getting pretty friendly with each other out on the dance floor. A couple of them probably snuck off to do exactly what we're doing." Kai kissed my neck, but then an odd, crackling sound made both of us pause. After a moment, as we both listened intently, he asked, "What do you suppose that was?"

"It almost sounded electrical."

"It did, didn't it?"

We stayed still for another moment, and I said, "Is it my imagination, or do you smell smoke?"

"Oh shit, I think you're right." I slid off the counter and Kai took my hand. "It's faint, but I definitely smell it. We'd better get everyone outside."

We hurried into the club and found that Nana and forty of her friends had arrived. She was sitting on Ollie's lap, and waved when she saw us and called, "Hi boys! We've crashed the stag party! Did you two sneak out for a little nookie?"

I jogged to her and yelled over the music, "Come with me, Nana. You too, Ollie. Dante, start directing everyone to the door. Get Vincent to help. There's smoke in the kitchen. It's faint, but everyone needs to get outside."

I took Nana's hand and hurried to the exit with her, just to make sure she got out safely. But when I grabbed the door handle, it wouldn't budge. I shook it, hard, then stepped aside and let Kai try to open it. "It's locked," he said after giving it his all for a minute. The smoke smell was more noticeable, and a murmur went through the crowd.

"We need the key." I ran over to the bar and looked around as I asked, "Where did the bartender go?"

One of the waiters, a young, red-haired guy, was behind the bar and told me, "He left about five minutes ago and told me to cover for him. He said he needed a cigarette break. The only keys I know of are on his key chain and on the club owner's, and the owner hasn't been in all night."

"Look behind the bar," I said. "Look everywhere for a spare set, including in the register. Does the club owner have an office? Maybe he keeps an extra set of keys in there."

"Not on site." The red-haired guy grabbed another waiter by the arm and the two of them searched for a key.

"What about the back door?" Dante asked.

"We were just there, it's locked too."

Everyone was starting to get nervous, and a buzz went around the room. The smell of smoke was still subtle but more pronounced, and I could see worry on many people's faces. Across the room, Vincent ran to the DJ booth and cut the music, then grabbed the mic and said, "Everyone, stay calm. We have a bit of a situation, but we're handling it."

Dante and I ran back to the door and he tried kicking it a few times, but it was solid metal and didn't budge. As he bent to examine the lock, Kai held up his phone and said, "I've called nine-one-one. The fire department is on the way."

Another buzz went through the crowd, and Nana exclaimed, "Everyone just keep calm! My boys are going to get us out of here!"

"There are no keys," the redhead yelled.

I shouted, "Keep searching," and looked around, trying to think. The crowd was getting louder and louder. I could hear panic in their voices.

The club had no windows, and only the two doors. I looked up at the high ceiling. It was painted black, just like the walls and every other surface in the club. Someone had brought up the lights, and I noticed a black, framed rectangle above the doorway that was slicker than the textured walls. I grabbed Kai's arm and said, "I think that might be a transom. If it is, I can try to squeeze through. Do you have a crowbar in your trunk? If so, I can try to pry the door open from the outside."

"There are a few tools in there, but I have no idea if there's a crowbar. It's worth a look, though."

He laced his fingers together to boost me up, and I stepped onto his hand. The painted surface above the door felt like glass when I ran my palm over it. The transom was nearly the width of the doorway but less than a foot high. I shoved on the frame and felt it give, just a little.

With a loud 'whoosh', an orange sheet of flames suddenly shot up the far wall behind the DJ booth, then rolled across the ceiling like a burning tide. My heart leapt as fear jolted me, and someone screamed. An oppressive wall of heat radiated down from above and I cowered, even though there were eight feet between me and the fire.

Below me, people were screaming and trying to rush away from the burning wall. There were way too many people in that small space, and some of them started pushing and shoving as panic took control. In the center of it all, Dante had one arm around his husband Charlie and one around Nana, trying to shield them both from the crushing throng. Ollie embraced her too, and Nana clung to him. Several more layers of loved ones formed rings of protection around their beloved Nana in a desperate attempt to keep her safe. It wouldn't be enough at the rate the fire was spreading.

My heart pounded in my ears as fear made the hair on my arms stand on end. I was terrified, more than I'd ever been in my life. I looked down at Kai. There was fear in his eyes, but he was trying not to let it show.

He couldn't die here. He just couldn't. I had to get him out of here, and Jed and Nana and all of these people, all of my family.

I straightened up and put my fist through the glass. Pain shot through my hand, but that didn't matter. I used the hole I'd made to grasp the edge of the window frame with both hands, and blood ran between my fingers as I sliced my palms on the rim of broken glass. Kai clutched me with his arms around my legs, trying to steady me as I threw everything I had into wrenching that frame. The heat of the fire was bearing down on me, and I was coughing from the smoke, which had begun to fill the room. Below me, Vincent was telling everyone to get low, down to the fresher air near the floor. I yelled as I tore at the frame.

Finally, it swung open from the top as countless layers of paint gave way, but I needed more room to get through. Somehow, I found the strength to wrench it off its rusty hinges and threw it out into the street. I slipped my head and shoulders through the narrow opening and looked around. The industrial neighborhood was deserted, there was no one I could ask for help.

I pushed my torso through, my body bruising and my skin and clothes tearing on the remains of the rusty hinges. It was an incredibly tight fit, and for a nightmarish moment, I was sure I was stuck. I cried out and grasped the opening, using my arms for leverage, pushing with all my strength as I tried to wriggle myself free. By sheer force of will, I somehow managed to force my butt and thighs through.

I tried to twist around as I fell so I wouldn't land head-first, and when I hit the sidewalk, excruciating pain shot up my leg. I pushed myself to my feet, gritting my teeth through the pain, and tried the door from the outside, shaking the handle. The screams of terror from inside the building were the most horrible thing I'd ever heard. I pulled at the handle with all my strength. Inside, I could hear someone trying to bust through it, probably kicking it. That door was never going to give.

I bent down to look at the handle, trying to figure out what was wrong. A twisted piece of metal was broken off inside the lock, jamming it. A fresh shock of fear, cold and terrible, ran through me as some pieces fell into place. There had been no fire alarm. The sprinkler system hadn't gone off.

This had been intentional.

I turned and limp-ran down the middle of the street. Pain radiated up my right leg with each step. I ignored it.

When I finally reached the Impala, half a block away, I unlocked the trunk and searched it frantically. There was no crowbar, nothing I could use to get the door open. Oh God. I looked around me, trying to think, trying not to panic, as my heart felt like it was going to burst through my chest.

Suddenly, I had an idea. I grabbed my phone and speed-dialed Kai, and when he answered I yelled, "I need you to get everyone away from the front of the building. Hurry, Kai. I'm coming to save you, but I need everyone away from the wall beside the door because I'm about to come through it!"

"Oh God. Okay, Jessie." He had his phone on speaker, and he yelled over the noise, "Vincent and Trevor, help me! You too, Jed and Skye. We need to get everyone away from this wall. Make a line, join hands and push everyone back!" He erupted into a coughing fit.

"I love you so much, Kai," I told him as I got the door unlocked and dove behind the wheel of the Impala. I didn't think he'd heard me over the yelling. I dropped the phone and fumbled with his keys.

I finally heard sirens in the distance. What the fuck was taking them so long? My hands were bleeding and shaking, but somehow I got the key in the ignition and took a deep breath as the big engine roared to life. I fastened my seatbelt, threw the car in gear and floored it. Thank God that the front of the club was a fire lane, and for once, people had actually obeyed the red zone and left the opening I needed.

An odd calm settled over me, and time seemed to slow down in the few seconds it took me to reach the building. I became focused, trying to judge my speed and the weight of the Impala in relation to the brick wall I was about to smash into. If I overshot, I'd run people down. Not enough force and the wall wouldn't give. It might also knock out the engine, so I potentially only had one shot at this.

I flung the wheel to the left and gunned the engine as the big car hopped the curb. Immediately, I hit the brakes and braced myself as the front fender smashed into the wall. The impact was jarring, even worse than I'd expected. I slammed against the seatbelt and my head bounced off the steering wheel. It took me a moment to recover. When I looked up, I was overcome with relief, because there was a huge hole in the wall.

I threw the car into reverse and backed it out of the opening. Immediately, people began running from the building. I kept backing down the street to get out of the way and ended up swinging the car back into its original parking space at an odd angle.

When I tried to get out of the car, I cried out and collapsed onto the pavement. My right leg wouldn't hold me up, and the pain was unbearable. I leaned against the door for a moment, catching my breath, and patted the Impala as I whispered, "Good girl. You did great."

I had to know if my family was safe, so after a moment I began crawling down the street toward the burning building. Flames shot from the roof, lighting up the night. People were running. I saw Dante carrying Nana. Ollie and Jed were right beside them. There was one person I didn't see though, and I called out, "Kai?" My voice sounded weak.

Finally, a big fire truck and an ambulance pulled onto the street, lights flashing and sirens shrieking. Rescue workers spilled from the vehicles and went to work immediately. As they pulled hoses from the truck and flung open the bay doors of the ambulance, I almost cried with relief. They'd help my family. It was out of my hands.

Jed spotted me crawling down the roadway and ran to me. When he reached me, my brother scooped me up in his arms and I asked, "Where's Kai? Is he okay?"

"I think so," he stammered. "Oh God, Jessie, you're covered in blood."

"Did I hit anyone with the car? Did I kill anyone?" I kept blinking and couldn't figure out why I couldn't make my left eye focus.

"No, Jessie, no one got hurt. We got everyone back from the wall, just like you said. Then we all ran to safety."

"Where's Kai?" I asked again. My voice sounded hollow and it was hard to keep my eyes open. An odd prickling sensation ran through my body.

"I'm right here, sweetheart." I felt Kai pick me up and tried to grasp his shirt. I couldn't move my arm.

"I love you, Kai," I murmured. "I didn't know if you heard me."

"I love you, too, Jessie. You need to stay with me, baby. Can you hear me?"

I forced my eyes open and tried to nod. I wasn't sure if my head actually moved. It felt like we were running. Everything was swirling around me. It got harder and harder to make sense of what was happening, so I let my eyes slide shut again.

"This man needs medical attention!"

Kai was yelling that. He put me down and I wanted to protest. I missed the warmth of his body. It was so incredibly cold without his arms around me.

I felt pressure on my forehead. I forced my eyes open and dropped my head to the right. Nana was on a stretcher beside me. She looked so little and pale. There was an oxygen mask on her face, and she wasn't moving. Oh God.

I tried to call to her. I wasn't sure if I made a sound. I felt a tear spill down my cheek.

Blackness closed in on me from all sides, narrowing my field of vision further and further until there was nothing left. *Please God, please help Nana. Don't let her die.* I sent that prayer into the universe.

I realized I wasn't cold anymore.

I wasn't anything at all.

Chapter Sixteen

I felt like I was swimming up through cloudy water. I didn't know where I was, but it was bright. Too bright. My eyelids fluttered, but I didn't want to open them.

"Jessie?" I heard Nana right beside me and felt her hand on my cheek.

"Shit," I murmured. "Are we both dead? I love you, Nana. I didn't want you to die."

"I tell you what, that's no way to go. When I eventually get to heaven, I plan to slide in sideways on the back of a motorcycle. What I don't plan to do is keel over like one of those fainting goats and then wake up at the pearly gates. Have you ever seen those things? You say 'boo' to them and over they go, legs stiff and sticking straight up in the air."

I grinned a little. "I'm sorry you're dead, but I'm glad I'm not alone in heaven. I think it'd probably be really boring without you."

She chuckled at that. "Oh honey, you're not dead. You're just on a shitload of narcotic pain killers. You probably won't even remember this conversation when you sober up a bit."

"I'm going to miss Kai," I slurred. "And Izzy. I love them so much. I finally got my own family. He was so pretty, too. Wasn't Kai pretty, Nana?"

"He's very pretty, Jessie."

"I didn't just love him because he was so pretty. He was such a good guy. The best. He was just the best guy. He was so kind and considerate. And sexy. Gawd, those tight jeans he wore would drive me nuts. I'd take one look at him and get an instaboner. Should I be saying instaboner in heaven? Am I going to get kicked out for that?"

"Well shit, if they hold bad language against you, I'm fucked," Nana said.

"Kai was so sexy, but he was more than that," I went on. I had an important point to make, I just had to find it. "He made me feel loved. He was such a great dad, too. Oh God, him and Izzy together, it was just the sweetest thing. And he found my brother and sister and cousin Bet-Bet! Who does that? Who tries so hard to make things good? Mal'kai Kahale, that's who."

"Jessie, baby, you should try to rest." That voice was Kai's.

My eyes flew open and I flailed around as I exclaimed, "No, Kai! You can't be dead, too! Izzy needs you! Get the fuck away from the light!"

He chuckled gently and said, "Poor guy. He's completely wasted." I felt him rest his hand on my arm, and I closed my eyes because keeping them open was way too much work.

"Don't be dead, Kai," I whispered as I felt myself sinking back under that cloudy water.

"I'm not, baby. None of us are."

"Think they'd let me try some of what he's on?" Nana asked. "Maybe not quite so much. But, you know, just a little hit?"

"Heaven's super fuckin' weird," I muttered before the light went away again.

*****

The next time I woke up, Nana was sitting at my bedside, trying to knit. Ollie had been teaching her. She wasn't a sit-still kind of person though, and after a minute she tossed the yarn and needles into a trashcan and told them, "You just stay in there, you uncooperative fuckers. This is why they have stores, so we don't have to make our own clothes like some damn sheep farming craft bitch."

I shifted position a bit and winced, and Nana exclaimed, "You're awake! How do you feel, Sweet Pea?"

"I hurt all over."

"Let me call the nurse for you. I guess your pain meds have worn off." She picked up a white cylinder on a cord and pushed the button at the end of it. "Do you remember what happened?"

"I'm not sure."

"Well, let me refresh your memory. You saved more than a hundred of our friends and family members. In the process, you broke your ankle, gave yourself a concussion and cut your head, probably when you hit the steering wheel. You were gushing blood from a head wound, it looked like something out of a horror movie! You did some other damage to yourself, too. You sliced up your hands and back real good when you climbed through that transom. Fortunately, your jeans protected your lower half from getting cut up, but you also bruised almost every inch of yourself. Now for the good news: all of that is fixable, and you're going to be fine. So are all the people you saved. Aside from a few people getting treated for smoke inhalation, everyone's A-OK, thanks to you. You're a hero, Jessie."

"No I'm not. I was just the only one skinny enough to fit through the transom."

"Bullshit. You kept your head and thought of a solution. We all would be dead if you hadn't used that big, heavy car to knock down a wall," she said.

"The fire department arrived, they would have pried the door open."

"Eventually. But it was bad inside that building. It had filled with smoke, and people were panicking. I'm surprised no one got trampled. Now just admit you're a hero and stop arguing with an old lady!"

I grinned at her and said, "I don't see any old ladies here."

"That's my boy." She leaned in and kissed my cheek.

"Are you okay? I saw you on a stretcher. I was so scared."

"I passed out. It was all just too much excitement, especially on the heels of about a gallon of margaritas at the strip club. Everyone freaked out and thought I had another heart attack. I had a minor one a couple years ago, key word *minor*. Dante made me go to the hospital to get checked out. He's such a worrier."

A nurse stuck her head in the door, and Nana exclaimed, "About damn time! This boy's in pain, so you need to get him some drugs, stat!"

The nurse frowned a bit and said, "I'll get the doctor," before disappearing again.

I asked, "Where's Kai?"

"He's right there." Nana gestured to my left, and with some difficulty I rolled over a bit and saw him curled up on a gurney against the wall, fast asleep. "He maintained a constant bedside vigil from the moment you first arrived at the hospital. It was the sweetest thing. Finally though, after two days I told him he had to get some sleep or he was going to go loopy. They wheeled in that bed for him because he refused to leave your side. That boy's madly in love with you, Jessie."

"It's mutual." I grinned at his sleeping form and turned back to Nana.

"Your brother and sister have been here, too. They sat up with you all last night, and just left a couple hours ago to get some sleep at Jed's apartment. They'll be back this evening."

"Ruthie's here?"

She nodded. "Your sister drove up from San Diego as soon as Jed called her. They're both such sweet kids."

I replayed the last few minutes of our conversation. Something Nana had said seemed to raise a red flag, and as my groggy brain tried to work out what it was, I asked, "What day is it?"

"Monday, and it's about two p.m."

"Why was I asleep so long?"

"You weren't sleeping the whole time. They've kept you hopped up on pain killers, which did knock you out for a lot of it, but you'd wake up periodically and have a lot to say. You're incredibly foul-mouthed when you're on drugs. I'm not complaining! It gave me a good chuckle," Nana said. "Do you remember any of our conversations?"

"I think I remember one. Did we talk about fainting goats and instaboners at some point, or did I dream that?"

"That was the first time you woke up. You were drugged off your gourd and were convinced you, me and your sweetie were all lined up at the pearly gates. But that's just silly. You ought to know by now I'm way too ornery to die."

"Oh man," I mumbled. "I hate to think about what else I said."

"Since then, they've been gradually dialing back your pain meds. You seem a lot more with-it this time."

"I feel like I'm forgetting something really important, but my head's in a fog...." All of a sudden, it hit me and I exclaimed, "Monday! Oh no, I slept through your wedding! How was it? Please tell me it was perfect!"

Nana waved her hand. "You didn't sleep through anything. Ollie and I are postponing it until you're better. You really think we'd go out and party while you're alone in the hospital, battered and bruised from saving us and dozens of our friends and family? Come on. I'd have to be a real tool to do something like that."

I grinned a little. "I've never heard you use the word tool."

"I just learned it from my great-grandson Joshie. It's a good word. I've been trying to work it into more conversations. I think it fit pretty good there."

I grew serious and said, "I didn't want you to miss your wedding, Nana. You had it all planned! You'll never get the same hotel, it was booked through next year. Plus the food, the flowers, the cake, none of that will be refundable. And you and Ollie had people flying in from all over!"

"So they'll fly in again when you're well enough to be right there beside us. As for all the rest of it, what does that stuff matter, really? I'll admit, I got a bit caught up in all the hype and this crazy idea of the 'perfect' wedding. But a perfect wedding isn't one with the prettiest dress and the fanciest venue and the most stunning flowers. It's just me marrying my sweetie with the people we love most in the world around us to share our happiness. That absolutely has to include you, Sweet Pea, and it did even before you turned into Superman and saved us. I've been telling you forever that I love you and you're a part of my family. Maybe now you'll believe me."

"I did actually figure that out, even before you postponed your wedding for me."

"About damn time." I grinned at that, and Nana threw her hands up and exclaimed, "Oh, I didn't tell you what happened! My ex-husband showed up yesterday morning. He'd heard about the wedding and probably figured he'd make a scene, because he lives for shit like that. He came to the house, and as soon as my fiancé found out who he was, Ollie punched him in the nose! He doesn't look it, but my man's a tiger. Ollie told him that was for leaving his wife for some young hussy. Then Ollie said, 'Thank you for being a fucking moron. If you'd been smart enough to stay with Stana, I would have missed out on the most spectacular woman in the world.' Then Ollie slammed the door in his face." Nana looked delighted.

I smiled and said, "That's awesome."

She got up and said, "Now you rest for a minute while I go find that doctor and drag him in here by his hairy ball sack!" She pulled down the jacket of her purple velour tracksuit by its hem and bustled from the room while I chuckled to myself.

*****

That evening when Dante came to visit, he found Kai curled up in my hospital bed with me. My boyfriend was holding me gently and my head was on his chest. "Hey," I said as Dante sat beside us. "You just missed Nana, she left about ten minutes ago. Ollie insisted on taking her home for some dinner and a good night's sleep."

"I spoke to them in the parking lot. Sorry to immediately intrude on the first moment you two have probably had to yourselves."

"It's okay."

Dante grinned and said, "You know, I was in this same private hospital a couple years ago, and Charlie climbed into bed with me just like that. The nurses tried to pitch a fit. I think Nana finally threatened to buy the hospital and fire them all."

"She threatened them again today, so they're being nice to us," Kai said.

"Nana told me no one got hurt Friday night. She wasn't just saying that because she doesn't want to upset me, right?" I asked.

Dante said, "A couple dozen people got treated for smoke inhalation, and I'm sure a few people are going to have nightmares for a good, long time, but nobody got hurt, thanks to you."

I lowered my voice and said, "Someone broke off a key or something in the lock, Dante, and they must have disabled the sprinklers and alarms. Did you see the way that fire spread? None of it was an accident."

"I know. I've been talking to the SFPD, and it was definitely arson. The whole place was rigged to go up. There were two ignition points, one in the kitchen, one behind the DJ booth, and the walls and ceiling had been sprayed with a chemical accelerant. The electric starter in the kitchen misfired, which is a break for the arson investigator. He's a good guy, by the way, his name's Cameron Doyle. He sent the device to the lab, they should be able to gather forensic evidence from it. And then, when the SFPD finds the arsonist, he's going to tell me who hired him to try to take out my family." His voice was quiet, but something dark and dangerous flashed in his eyes. Whoever had crossed Dante Dombruso was going to pay, I knew that with absolute certainty.

"You already have some theories about who's behind it, don't you?" I asked.

"I assume it was the Messinas. If Jerry gave them information on our organization and they decided we were ripe for a hostile take-over, what a perfect opportunity to strike us down. Every adult male in my family was at the club that night. Nana and my female relatives weren't supposed to be there. My cousins Carla and Rachel hold key spots within the family structure, but an old-school Sicilian like Mick Messina would only think to target the men. It has classic mob hit written all over it."

"Jesus," Kai murmured.

Dante said, "Don't worry, I'm not going after them without solid evidence. Right now, we're trying to find the club owner and the bartender, because we think someone may have paid them off. And hopefully the arsonist can be identified. Any of those three will lead us to whoever was behind that fire."

"This conversation's kind of surreal," Kai said.

"I know how this must sound to someone on the outside," Dante said, "but my family's ties to organized crime go back centuries. From the time I was seven and my parents and sister were murdered, this has been my life. You saw first-hand Friday night why I need to protect my family."

Kai said quietly, "If anyone tried to hurt my family the way someone tried to hurt yours...let's just say I get it."

A look of understanding passed between the two men. Dante turned to me and said, "Besides wanting to check on you and make sure you're okay, I also wanted to give you a heads up that Doyle, the arson investigator, is planning to speak to you sometime this week, Jessie. I hadn't planned on telling him about our feud with the Messinas, because right now we don't know they had anything to do with this. But Doyle's family goes way back in organized crime in Dublin, so he immediately recognized the signs of a mob hit. He was also a detective before switching over to arson, so he knows the Dombruso name, not that we've ever been convicted of anything. Anyway, don't worry about letting anything slip when you speak to him, because he's already put most of the pieces together."

"Did you tell him about Jerry?"

"There's nothing to tell, I have no idea if he was involved. My cousin made some terrible mistakes in the past, but I want to believe he isn't capable of trying to annihilate his entire family and that the Messinas, or whoever, acted on their own. Without solid, undeniable evidence, I'm not going to assume the worst about Jerry." Dante's voice dropped as he said, "But if I find evidence he was involved, God help him."

We visited for another half-hour or so before Dante pushed himself to his feet. "I have to go, Charlie's expecting me." He surprised me by leaning down and kissing my bandaged forehead. He then straightened up and said, "I'm indebted to you forever, Jessie. My husband, my grandmother, my brothers, so many people I love could have died Friday night. I can't even begin to tell you how grateful I am for what you did."

I said embarrassedly, "It was just the one time it paid to be the scrawniest guy in the room. If you could have fit through that transom, you'd have been the one to save your family."

Dante grinned at me. "Nana said you're modest about it, but damn. Jessie, you're a hero, plain and simple. I love you, my brother, and I'll always have your back, just like you have mine. Now try to get some rest, I'll see you tomorrow."

After Dante left, Kai said, "My boyfriend is under the protection of the mafia. That's the basic message I took away from that. It's kind of like finding yourself in the middle of The Godfather."

"I've always known the mafia thing is a part of who the Dombrusos are, but Friday was the first time the full reality of what that means really hit home. The thing is, now that I know, it doesn't make me want to run from them. Just the opposite. It makes me want to pick up a shield and stand beside Dante to try to protect them, because they're my family, and that's what families do, the good ones, anyway. They stick up for each other."

I looked up at Kai as I added, "This is probably freaking you out, isn't it? If it helps, the Dombrusos aren't criminals. At least, not anymore. They've gone legit and they're such good people, but old feuds surface sometimes. I hope you don't judge them by their enemies, and I hope you aren't having second thoughts about me, now that you know who I'm involved with."

"You don't seriously think I could have second thoughts, do you? In case you haven't figured this out yet, I adore you, and I'm not going anywhere. If you vouch for the Dombrusos, that's good enough for me. And if you decide to pick up a shield and stand beside Dante to defend your adopted family, guess what? I'm going to pick up a shield too, and I'm going to stand with you. Because that's what you do for the people you love, Jessie, you protect them, no matter how terrifying the dragon is that they're going up against."

I stretched up to kiss him and winced a little when I settled back in his arms. Kai asked, "Do you want me to call the nurse for some more pain meds?"

"No thanks. I'd rather ache a little and remain lucid than float back over to Cloud Cuckoo Land."

Kai grinned at me. "Did you just reference the Lego Movie?"

"Maybe. Don't judge me." I grinned and nuzzled his neck.

We were quiet for a while, and Kai gingerly traced the outline of a huge bruise on my left arm. Then he whispered, "I wish I could bear all this hurt for you. It just kills me that you're in pain, and I can't do anything to make it better."

"I'll heal. It's not a big deal."

"I know it embarrasses you to talk about it, so I'm just going to say this once and then I'll shut up about it. I already knew you were an amazing human being. You have a huge heart, and you love unconditionally. You put your family and friends' well-being ahead of your own. I've never met anyone so selfless, so genuinely kind, so loving, and I'm absolutely in awe of you. I see you blushing right now, and I know how hard it is for you to take a compliment, but I need you to hear this, just once. I consider myself the luckiest man on this whole damn planet, Jessie, because I get to love you and be loved by you, and my daughter and I get to share our lives with you. I don't know what I ever did to deserve such an extraordinary gift, but I'm going to spend every day of my life trying to be worthy of it."

"I—"

He gently touched my lips. "I know that was a lot. It was long, and flowery, and all about you, and you never want to be in the spotlight. That's why you try to brush it off when people call you a hero. I won't keep talking about this and embarrassing you. I just want you to know I *see you*, deep down. I see the huge, pure heart behind the pretty face, and my God Jessie, you're glorious."

I fought back tears, and for once I simply said, "Thank you."

Chapter Seventeen

It was the last Sunday in June, which meant it was Pride weekend in San Francisco. A huge crowd had gathered that early morning on a side street in the Castro, which was blocked off by police cars at both intersections. I glanced at the officer leaning against the car to my left, who happened to be Finn Nolan, and he smiled and gave me a little salute.

"Hey there, Rocket and Trigger," a familiar voice said, and Kai and I both turned to look at Six. The tall blond was holding a paper coffee cup and peering at us over an expensive pair of sunglasses. He asked me, "You alright, mate? You look a bit banged up."

I was on crutches, my ankle was still in a cast, and both my hands were bandaged because I had stitches in my palms (which made using the crutches a bit awkward). "I'm fine, and it's just Jessie and Kai now, since we've both retired from racing," I told him.

"Alastair," he said with a grin. "A bit uptight, I know. I've missed you at the races. Why'd you retire?"

I shrugged and said, "We both just get our kicks elsewhere these days." The answer was a lot more complex than that, of course, but I didn't really want to go into all the soul-searching that had gone into my decision, and how I'd ultimately decided the thrill of racing wasn't worth risking my life, not when I had so incredibly much to live for.

Six gestured at the crowd with his cup. "What's going on? Is there a celebrity in that building?"

Funnily enough, there actually were two major celebrities in the audience, both disguised with baseball caps and sunglasses and doing their best to blend in. Normally Zan Tillane, a pop star who was dating Nana's grandson Gianni, would be the biggest celebrity in any crowd. But in San Francisco's gay neighborhood, ex-porn star (and friend of the family) Hunter Storm might possibly give him a run for his money in terms of overall fan frenzy. "No," I said, "we're all here for a wedding. My grandmother's about to get married. But Nana is a rock star as far as I'm concerned."

"She's getting married at a sex shop?"

We were clustered around an establishment owned by one of Mr. Mario's friends, which did in fact sell all manner of adult entertainment. Its tidy, matte black storefront was completely festooned for Pride. Rows of briefs arranged by color formed rainbows in the huge display windows on either side of the entryway, and at least forty rainbow flags spanned the front of the building and jutted from the black awning over the door. Hot pink neon in the window on the left spelled out 'The Whack Shack'.

"Yes and no," Kai said. "Her procession will be coming out of the shop, and then she's getting married right here, in the middle of the street."

"You should stick around," I said. "It's going to be fun."

"I wish I could, but my bestie Rebecca is expecting me for breakfast three blocks over and she gets cross with me when I'm late. Don't be a stranger, both of you. Maybe we can go for coffee sometime and you can bring your friend Zachary."

After he took off, Jed and Ruthie found us in the crowd, and my sister said as she tucked her long, blonde hair behind her ear, "Do you want me to find you a chair? I don't think you should be doing this much standing." She'd come up to visit and check on me every weekend that month.

"I'm fine, Rue. Don't worry. It's going to be a quick ceremony, since Nana and Ollie don't want to jam up the neighborhood for too long, especially during Pride."

"The neighborhood's barely awake yet," Jed pointed out. "I happen to know it was partying hard last night, and I doubt tying up half a block is going to ruin anyone's day."

"Does that mean you were out at the clubs?" I asked him.

"He was, but don't get too excited," Ruthie said. "I was with him. He had two cokes, hid in the corner, and wouldn't ask anyone to dance. He's going to die a virgin."

"Oh my God, Ruthie, shut up!" My brother turned deep red.

Zachary came up to us and asked, "Who's going to die a virgin?" I did a double-take when I turned to look at him. His hair was shorter and dark brown, and he was wearing a pastel polo shirt and khakis. When I'd first met him, he would change his look about once a month, but I'd started to think the black-and-red hair and black clothes were here to stay.

"Nobody," Jed said quickly.

"Hey," I said, moving my crutches to one hand so I could give my friend a hug. "I'm glad you made it. You just missed Six, by the way, he was headed to breakfast. He asked about you and said we should all go out for coffee." I couldn't help but notice the way my brother paid close attention to Zachary's noncommittal response.

Just then, Kai's grandmother came bustling out of the sex shop in a red taffeta bridesmaid's dress. "We're ready to get started," she yelled. "Make a rainbow circle, people, just like we practiced!"

The crowd shifted around a bit, forming a big circle in the middle of the street. Nana and Ollie's groomsmen formed the inner ring, and we all took off our jackets, revealing rainbow tie-dyed t-shirts. We'd originally been fitted for tuxes, but Wedding 2.0 had gone far more casual. Jed took Kai's jacket and mine, and a lump formed in my throat as I looked around the circle at our family.

Directly across from Kai and me were Gianni and his boyfriend Zan, holding hands. Gianni's best friend Yoshi was right behind him, and to Zan's right, Gianni's brothers Mike and Vincent and their brother-in-law Charlie were joking and laughing. Vincent's husband Trevor and their son Josh also made up the circle, along with Nico, their cousin, and his boyfriend Luca, and a few more cousins.

Nana's adopted boys completed the circle. Skye and Dare stood with Haley and River, who looked happy. I didn't see Cole, but he could have been somewhere in the crowd. Christopher and Kieran lined up with Hunter and Brian, and Christian and Shea squeezed in with Chance and Finn (who had a rainbow flag sticking out of the pocket of his police uniform). Chance's brother Colt and Elijah were right behind them, along with Jamie and Dmitri, who were all smiles. Their toddler sat on Dmitri's shoulders, delightedly waving a little rainbow flag.

Ollie stepped through the crowd and took his place beside the wedding official, immediately to my right. He'd opted to stick with his white tux and tails, which he wore with a white top hat, pink shirt and rainbow bow tie. He was smiling ear to ear and his eyes were bright with tears of happiness.

Josh's best friend Emma was also in a tie-dyed shirt because she'd chosen to be a groomsman with her bestie instead of a bridesmaid. She was on the sidewalk in front of the shop with Izzy and with Mike's three little boys, and when she received a signal from inside the storefront, she leaned down and whispered to the little girl. Izzy held her head up proudly, clutched the white basket in her gloved hand, and took her place at the front of the procession. She looked adorable in her pink dress with her French braid and butterfly clips, and when she spotted Kai and me, she smiled and waved. She'd lost her front teeth in the last week, but that just made her cuter.

Kai's arm was around me, helping to support me as I balanced on one foot, and I leaned close and whispered, "You ready?"

"I think I'm going to pass out," he whispered back. "Why didn't Nana ask Zan to do this?"

"Both because he's incognito, and because Nana wanted to make you a part of the ceremony. You've totally got this."

He cleared his throat nervously, and when Kiki poked her head out of the shop and nodded, he began to sing Your Song by Elton John, one of Nana's favorites. He sang the first verse by himself, his voice strong and clear, as Izzy walked across the street dropping flower petals. The ring bearer followed, and behind him, his two older brothers walked Tommy and Diego, Nana and Ollie's dogs, on rhinestone-studded leashes. The dogs wore matching rainbow-striped sweaters, meticulously knit by Ollie. When the kids reached the groom, Izzy peeled off to the right and joined Kai and me, and the boys led the dogs to the left and joined their dad Mike.

The crowd joined in on the second verse and sang with Kai as a rainbow of nearly two dozen women followed the children. The bridesmaids carried bright, mixed flowers and wore solid-colored tea-length dresses. Kiki led the procession, dressed in red, with Mike's girlfriend Marie right behind her in reddish-orange. More family members and Nana's senior girlfriends followed, orange dresses giving way to yellow and so on down the rainbow. Mr. Mario was last, in full drag and wearing a deep violet dress. He looked beautiful.

The bridesmaids walked swiftly, looping around and arranging themselves in an arc on the sidewalk behind Ollie and the wedding official. Then, as a few hundred voices sang the final chorus of her favorite song, Nana appeared in the doorway with Dante on her arm. She'd shortened her gown to knee-length for Wedding 2.0, and wore it with its matching long-sleeved coat of the same length. She'd paired the outfit with white go-go boots, which were pure Nana. The dress and coat both had a fitted bodice and flared out at the waist, and were completely covered in sequins, which looked pink overall. But when she stepped out from under the awning and her dress caught the morning light, a million tiny prisms in the sequins lit her up like a rainbow.

She walked across the street, carrying a colorful, casual bouquet of mixed flowers as tears of joy streamed down her face. When she reached Ollie, Dante kissed her cheek and put her hand in her fiancé's. Dante tried to remain composed as he took his place to the couple's left and grasped his husband's hand.

The last verse ended, and the wedding official stepped forward. She was a beautiful, full-figured African-American woman of about seventy with salt-and-pepper dreadlocks to her waist. She welcomed the audience and said, "Stana and Olivio want to begin by saying a few words."

Ollie went first. "Stana, you're a dream come true. At my age, I didn't think I had too many dreams left. But then you came along, and I remembered how to dream again. You make me happier than I've ever been, and I love you with all my heart. Thank God for your grandson Nico and my dear friend Luca, who brought us together. If I'd missed out on you, I would have missed out on the very best part of my life. Every single day, I'm going to cherish you and laugh with you and make sure you know that you're adored. Thank you for saying yes when I asked you to marry me. You're my best friend, my love, and one hot mama, and I'm the luckiest man in the world to get to be your husband."

Nana dabbed at her tears with the back of her hand and smiled at Ollie. She said, "I always believed in true love and happily ever after. I wanted that for all my boys, and it's made me so happy to watch so many of them find love. Somehow though, I never thought it'd happen for me. I figured I had my shot at marriage and it didn't work out. It did get me my beautiful sons and a bunch of gorgeous grandkids and great-grandkids, which is pretty damn good, and I was gonna be content with that. But then I met you, and all of a sudden I realized what I'd been missing. I'm so lucky that we get to spend every single day that we've got left together. I love the hell out of you, Olivio Caravetti, and I'm glad you had the good sense to ask me to marry you. Otherwise, I was going to have to ask you myself." She looked at the wedding official and said, "Now hurry up and marry us, Greta! We gotta party with our family and friends and then we got a honeymoon to get to." Nana turned to Ollie and wiggled her eyebrows. "I did some shopping in that store before I marched down the aisle. I don't know what half the stuff I bought is for, but you and I are gonna have a damn good time figuring it out!"

Kai grinned and pulled me close and I hugged him as the official took them through their vows. After they were pronounced husband and wife and kissed passionately, the crowd went wild.

The couple then turned to us and raised their joined hands in a victory gesture. I'd never seen either of them look so happy.

Nana and Ollie led the procession, and as everyone headed to the rows of waiting tour buses on the next block, Kai picked up Izzy and put her on his shoulders. I carefully positioned my crutches so I could put my weight on the pads of my fingers and avoid my stitches, but before I could take a step, Skye scooped me up and yelled, "Piggy back ride!" Dare took my crutches while I burst out laughing. I held on tight while my friend jogged through the crowd with me, and then deposited me at Nana's rainbow limo.

Kai, Izzy and I rode in the back with Nana and Ollie. I'd really wanted to drive them, but I couldn't with my broken ankle, so they'd hired a replacement chauffeur for the day, then insisted I ride with them to make sure I was properly cared for. I'd been pampered a lot since the fire, and I'd stopped fighting it.

As we rolled out of the Castro, Izzy looked out the window and bounced in her car seat, and across from us, Nana and Ollie kissed each other tenderly. "Great wedding," I said as I rested my head on Kai's shoulder.

"Perfect." He tipped my chin up so he could kiss me gently, and then Kai smiled and whispered, "I can't wait until it's our turn."

Chapter Eighteen

Eight weeks later

The construction on the apartment above the garage was going remarkably quickly, thanks to Nana. When she and Ollie returned from their week-long honeymoon in Maui, it had immediately become her new pet project. She knew a hell of a lot of people, and within days of her return, an architect (the granddaughter of one of the Nanettes), had helped us design the perfect apartment, we'd sailed through the permit process (so easily that I had to wonder if someone had owed the Dombrusos a favor) and a construction crew had gone to work, beginning with reinforcing and earthquake retrofitting the ground floor garage. Their prices were far below the going rate, so I suspected Nana was secretly footing part of the bill, even though she swore she wasn't.

Since I hated being idle, I took an online course in bookkeeping while my hands were healing, so I could help Kai organize the garage's financial records. That was pretty dry though, and it felt great to get back to working on engines when my stitches came out. We had to vacate the garage for four weeks during the retrofit, but Dante let us work out of an empty warehouse just a few blocks away, one of a long list of investment properties he owned around the city, so it was pretty much business as usual. Soon enough, we were back in our own garage, while a beautiful, airy, two bedroom apartment went in overhead.

I was tuning up a Jetta one Friday afternoon, when Kai pulled the Impala into the space beside me. I stopped what I was doing and took off my gloves before patting the big Chevy's fender and saying, "Welcome home, girl."

I'd dented her up pretty good when I'd smashed her into that brick wall, but a friend of mine who owned a body shop had fixed her up and just finished with her that day. He'd even given her a new head-to-toe paint job, and the midnight black shone like lacquer. "She's good as new," Kai said, running a hand over the hood. He'd picked up my habit of referring to our cars as females, which made me grin. "Your friend's doing an excellent job on his part of the Fastback's restoration too, I'm glad you recommended him. It's great to have a boyfriend who's so well-connected." He grinned at me and kissed my forehead. He was always slipping in subtle jokes about me being in the mafia, since I was an honorary Dombruso.

I pulled him into a real kiss, and when we broke apart I asked, "Have you been home yet?"

"No, but I'm headed there now. When I come back, I'll find a parking space on the street. It's getting crowded in here."

"Don't you dare. She and your dad's Mustang both hold a place of honor in this garage. We can work around them."

Kai looked happy when I said that, and he kissed me again before saying, "I'll be back soon. Did I mention I'm ridiculously excited for this weekend?"

"So am I." Nana was taking Izzy, Kiki, Malia, and Kai's mom to a spa in Marin for a girls' weekend of pampering and beauty treatments, while Ollie travelled to L.A. with Ignacio Mondelvano. Iggy was meeting with a collector who was interested in his work, and since he was pretty new to the business end of the art world, Ollie was acting as his agent. All of that meant Kai and I were going to have a very rare weekend all to ourselves.

"Make sure they stop off here before they head to Marin," I told him. "I want to say goodbye."

"No freaking way would Izzy let them leave without stopping off to give you a hug," he said.

After he drove off, I glanced at my left hand and flexed my fingers. I'd damaged some nerves when I sliced up my hands, but thankfully it hadn't affected my motor skills to the point where I couldn't work on engines. It did make them ache a bit, but that was a small price to pay. I pulled a pair of work gloves back on and shook out my hands before turning back to the Jetta.

I was totally engrossed in the job when Dante appeared in the doorway and said, "Earth to Jessie."

He was with his husband Charlie and Cameron Doyle, the arson investigator. Surprisingly, Dante and Cameron had become close friends over the last few weeks. I glanced from one man to the other. Dante was impeccable as ever in his dark, expensive Italian suit, while Cameron looked like he'd slept in his clothes. The investigator reminded me of an Irish version of the character Castiel from the TV show Supernatural. Whenever I saw him, he was in a rumpled suit and white shirt with his tie askew, and was almost always wearing a trench coat. In that respect, he went well with the Impala, and if I ever decided to organize a full-scale Supernatural cosplay, I was well on my way.

"Hey," I said, pivoting on my stool as I was facing them. "Are you slumming? I'm sorry to tell you this, but Dante won't be able to find a twenty-dollar martini on this block. Try a few streets north, maybe on Cortland."

"Twenty dollar martinis are a crime against humanity." Doyle had left Dublin as a child, but still retained a faint brogue. He brushed his windblown dark-auburn hair back from his blue eyes and said, "The gentrification around this city has gotten completely out of hand if you ask me."

"We were having a late lunch at that taqueria on the next block," Charlie said as he pulled up a stool and sat beside me. He was the only one of the three who wasn't overdressed, and he looked good in a pair of khakis and a fitted black polo shirt that showed off his ex-football player physique.

I asked, "There are no tacos to be found in the Marina District?"

"It's the chimichangas that keep bringing me back to this place," Dante said, peering into the Jetta's engine.

I asked, "The what now?"

"Chimichangas. You know, a deep-fried burrito with sauce?"

I chuckled and said, "I know what a chimichanga is, I just wanted to hear you say it again."

Dante tried to scowl, but it got lost in a grin. "Why?"

"Because it's hilarious. You don't say it right. Makes you sound like an elderly white person at Taco Bell for the first time." I put on a rough old-man voice and barked, "You kids got some of them chee-me-chaaaaaangas?"

Charlie and Cameron burst out laughing, and Charlie said, "I keep telling him he's saying it wrong."

Dante redoubled his efforts to scowl at me, but ended up laughing, too. "I shouldn't even give this to you now," he said, holding out a pair of keys on a leather fob. "You're evil and you should be punished, not rewarded."

"What's this?" I asked as I took them from him.

"Nana mentioned you and Kai have a rare weekend to yourselves, so I thought you might like a little getaway. Charlie and I bought a vacation home a couple hours down the coast, sometimes it's nice to get out of the city."

Charlie added, "Although we've only used it once in six months."

Dante stepped around the car and put his arms around his husband. "I'm sorry, angel. I swear I'll make it up to you. There's just so much going on right now."

Charlie wrapped his arms around his husband's waist and looked up at him, his green eyes full of emotion. "I know, and that's exactly why you need a break. I'm worried about you."

"We'll go soon, I promise." As Dante said that, he tenderly caressed his husband's cheek.

I turned to Cameron and said, "I assume I would have heard if you'd had any breaks in the arson case."

"Whoever set those two devices to go off was a pro. He left no fingerprints, and the materials were all so generic that they could have been purchased anywhere. The fact that one of them misfired was a total fluke. Unfortunately, that means the forensic evidence is a dead-end," Cameron said, leaning against a tool rack. "The SFPD has been putting extensive resources into trying to track down the club owner and the bartender. It's no coincidence they conveniently stepped away before the fire started. Plus, the devices and accelerant would have been put in place ahead of time, and that would mean the arsonist needed access. We assume they were paid off, by who is the question."

"How hard could it be to find a bartender and a club owner? They don't sound like master criminals," I said.

"In all likelihood, they left San Francisco. There's also a good chance they're both dead. Whoever set this fire might tie up those loose ends to make sure they don't lead back to him," Cameron told me. "It's been frustrating, to say the least." He looked weary and older than his thirty years as his shoulders slumped.

"You sound like you're giving up," I exclaimed, "but you can't! The people behind this need to be punished! They almost killed my family and friends, dozens of people! And who says they won't try again?"

"I'm not giving up, Jessie. I'll never give up on this case, neither will the department. That arsonist attempted mass murder on a scale this city's never seen before! The lack of solid leads right now is demoralizing, but that doesn't mean I'm quitting," Cameron told me.

"What about the person who was back in the kitchen that night, the one Kai and I heard right before the device went off?"

"There were no security cameras inside the club, and we've reviewed the footage from every traffic camera in the area," Doyle said. "That didn't give us anything to work with."

"I hate this. I hate that my family is in danger and there's not a damn thing we can do," I said.

Dante told me, "We're doing plenty, believe me. I have security teams watching our family members around the clock in case there's another attempt on our lives, and I have dozens of men and women out there shaking the trees, trying to find out anything they can about whoever was behind the fire."

"And of course, once you find out, you'll tell me," Cameron said, giving him a pointed look.

Dante kept an arm around Charlie's shoulders as he turned to Doyle. "If I was planning to become a vigilante, why would I be palling around with the lead arson investigator on this case?"

"Because my sparkling personality and keen fashion sense make me irresistible?" Cameron suggested with a little grin.

"That must be it," Dante said. "Come on, we should get back to work. Jessie, enjoy the beach house, and please don't worry. I'm handling this. Go spend some quality time with your boyfriend. Oh, and in case you're wondering, the house is off the map, so to speak. It's not registered under my name, or Charlie's, or that of any member of our family, for that matter. And Jerry never knew about it, so no one's going to show up looking for me."

"Thanks, Dante," I said as I pocketed the keys. "I really appreciate this."

He handed me a slip of paper. "That's the address and the codes for the security gate and alarm system. You really don't want to trigger that alarm. The monitoring company is…enthusiastic."

"Does that mean they'll shoot us on sight?"

"No, but they'd probably wrestle you to the ground and sit on you until they got ahold of me and I called them off."

I said, "Maybe this little weekend retreat is a bad idea."

"Nah, it'll be fine. You'll be perfectly secure there, and it's a gorgeous location. Enjoy it."

Dante and Cameron started to head to the car, and Charlie slid off the stool and told them, "I'll be there in a minute."

Once they left the garage, Charlie hugged me and said, "Thank you."

"You already thanked me a million times for getting everyone out of the club," I reminded him as I returned the hug.

"I know. This one's for making Dante laugh. He doesn't do that nearly enough these days, but you always manage to lighten the mood. I want you to know how much I appreciate it." He let go of me and smiled, but I could still see the worry in his eyes.

After Charlie said goodbye, I watched him cross the street to a large, black SUV. A huge guy with a dark suit, sunglasses and an earpiece held the door for him, then looked up and down the street before getting behind the wheel. Man. Dante was a six-four wall of muscle who could intimidate a grizzly bear if he wanted to. He'd be the last person I'd ever think would want a bodyguard.

*****

Izzy, Nana and the gang came by the garage a few minutes later to say goodbye before their girls' weekend. Dante had hired a big bodyguard to drive them in the limo, not that Nana would be a likely target. She and her friends weren't even supposed to be at the club the night of the fire. But Dante was covering all his bases anyway.

Nana stuck her head out of the sunroof and called, "Hi, Sweet Pea! Did Dante come by?" It was funny to me how she always knew everything that went on.

"Yeah, just a few minutes ago."

"You and Kai have fun on your romantic weekend! Do you need any supplies? I still have a big shopping bag in the trunk from the Whack Shack!"

I grinned and said, "We're good. Thanks, though."

Kiki popped up beside Nana. The two had become BFFs along the way, and were wearing matching pink t-shirts which said, 'I love my gay grandson.' A rainbow-striped heart stood in for the word 'love'. She waved and called, "Hi Jessie! Next time, you and Kai should come to the spa with us. You could both use some pampering."

Malia leaned out the open door and grinned at me. "I'd pay to see my brother in a mud mask with cucumbers on his eyes." Her mom chuckled at that and flashed a thumbs-up.

Izzy climbed out of the limo and came over to me. She was wearing a light blue princess dress over a pair of jeans. The little girl gave me a big hug and kissed my cheek, then said, "I'll miss you, Jessie."

"I'll miss you, too, Princess Isabella, but you're going to have loads of fun at the fancy spa this weekend."

"Nana said I get to have nail polish," Izzy said with a big grin. Her new front teeth were oversized compared to the rest of her baby teeth, which made her cuter than ever.

I kissed her forehead and said, "I'll see you real soon. Take good care of Nana and Gran and Great Gran."

"What about Auntie Mal?"

"I guess you should probably take care of her, too," I said with a smile. "Did you get to say goodbye to your dad?"

She nodded. "Daddy's at the house. He helped me pack. At first he said five princess dresses were too many for this weekend, but then he let me bring them."

"Have the best time," I said, brushing back a lock of her dark hair. She was wearing her butterfly barrettes, which always made me happy. "I'll see you Sunday."

"Bye, Jessie. I love you." She threw that out with no fanfare as she hurried back to the limo. To her, it was a simple statement of fact.

She didn't realize she'd just given me the most amazing gift. I kept my voice steady, despite all the emotions those precious words stirred up in me, and called after her, "I love you too, sweet Izzy."

I waved as I watched the limo pull away. It felt a little odd that someone else was behind the wheel. But I reminded myself I'd moved on, and that was a good thing. I wasn't the chauffeur anymore, and Nana wasn't my employer. I didn't need that job to play an important role in her life, because we were family.

After they took off, I finished the Jetta's tune-up and chatted with the owner for a while when she came to get it. I was cleaning up when Kai returned, I told him about Dante's visit and said, "It doesn't sound like they're close to catching whoever was behind the fire. It's so disheartening."

"A lot of good people are on the case. I know this has been eating away at you, but just for this weekend, let's try to relax. You haven't been sleeping well since the fire, and you really need some downtime." I mentioned the beach house, and he said, "Perfect. Let's go home, throw some things in a bag and get on the road. It looks like you're all done here."

After we set the new alarm (a gift from Dante, not that there was any reason to believe we'd be a target for the Dombrusos' enemies, but he was in full security mode) and locked up the garage, Kai got behind the wheel of the Impala. I fired off a quick text to Zachary to see how he was doing as we drove home, then held my phone for a couple minutes and watched for a reply. He either wrote back within a minute, or in about two days, depending on whether or not he was off on one of his mysterious outings. When I'd asked him point-blank where he kept going, he'd said, "I don't want to talk about it," and changed the subject. It was incredibly frustrating, but I knew I couldn't keep pushing. That'd just make him withdraw from me, and I didn't want that to happen.

Apparently we were in a two-day-reply window, so after a while I sighed quietly and returned the phone to my pocket. Kai glanced at me when we hit a stoplight and asked, "Is Zachary on another walkabout?"

"Yeah. I know I shouldn't worry about him. He's a grown man, and if he doesn't want anyone to know what he's up to, that's his business."

"But you're still concerned about him."

I nodded. "I just wish I knew what was behind his disappearances. Jamie says he calls in sick at least once a week, but at least he calls. That shows he's kind of holding it together, doesn't it?"

"Yeah, more than if he was just blowing off work entirely."

"He's definitely hurting," I said, "and I wish I could do something about that. It's like my brother said though, you can't help people who don't want to be helped. I've made sure Zachary knows I care, and that I'm always available to listen or lend a hand in any way I can. I don't know what else I can do."

"That's pretty much it."

When we got to the house, Kai said, "Why don't you make a couple sandwiches while I pack a few clothes and toiletries for both of us?"

"Good idea."

I put together a picnic while he went up to the attic. I'd moved the last of my stuff out of Nana's house, so the makeshift bedroom was pretty cramped. It was going to be nice when our apartment was done, although I'd enjoyed living with Kai's family and would kind of miss it. I knew we'd be over all the time though, just like we were over at Nana's house a few times a week since I'd moved out.

When I finished putting our meal together, I carried the vintage wicker picnic basket into the living room and paused to admire the dollhouse. Izzy had given it a place of honor on a table in front of the picture window, and spent countless hours playing with it. I remembered something all of a sudden and pulled a little paper bag from my pocket, then took out a tiny hairbrush and comb and added them to the dresser in the miniature child's bedroom. I loved leaving tiny trinkets without telling Izzy, then watching her face light up when she discovered them. I almost had her convinced it was the work of fairies, but she was a bit skeptical.

Kai jogged downstairs, deposited a couple bags on the living room floor and went into the kitchen as he called, "Almost ready. How many clams should we leave for Virgil and Scarface?" My pet crab lived in a large, second-hand aquarium in the kitchen, along with the little fugitive I finally apprehended at Nana's house (he'd been living inside a disused fireplace, knife close at hand).

We made sure the crustaceans were situated, then scooped up the bags and headed for the door. As Kai locked up behind us, I stood on the porch, took a deep breath and exhaled slowly. I'd almost forgotten how to relax, but that weekend I was determined to remember.

*****

The sun was setting over the Pacific as we wound our way down the coast. The Impala's engine purred, and her new paint job mirrored the golden sky. I laced my fingers with Kai's as he drove, and he rested our joined hands on his thigh. He'd brought along his dad's tapes, and Bowie's songs kept us company. They always reminded me of that day early on when I'd helped Kai paint the deck, and our fledgling relationship had begun to flourish. Back then, I'd thought it was so important to keep my distance. I didn't think that anymore. The perfect distance between Kai and me was absolutely none at all.

It took about two hours to reach the house, which was just outside a charming little town called Carmel-by-the-Sea. We glanced at each other when we pulled up to an imposing electrified gate. Kai punched in the code and it slid open, then shut again once we'd driven through it. We followed a private road through stands of Monterey cypress and manzanita, and when we rounded a bend and saw the house, we both relaxed a little. The fence might have seemed like it belonged at Folsom Prison, but the attractive, dark wood cottage on a cliff above the ocean was welcoming.

"This'll work," Kai said with a grin as he pulled up beside the house.

When we got out of the car, he said, "Before we go inside, there's something we need to do." He took a lighter and a large, flat paper rectangle from the trunk, and I followed him around the side of the house.

"What is that?" I asked when he stopped near the edge of the cliff and pulled on the sides of the paper object he'd been carrying. It unfolded into almost the shape of a chef's hat, a cylinder closed and rounded off at the top and slightly narrower at its open base.

"It's called a sky lantern, and we're going to spark it up and send it out over the ocean. Just so you know, the frame is bamboo and the paper's made to dissolve as soon as it hits the water, so no little Virgils or Scarfaces or their aquatic friends will eat it and get in trouble." I loved that he thought of that. "I found it in Chinatown, and I've been carrying it around for a week. I think this is the perfect time to use it."

"What's it for?"

He turned to me and said, "Some people call this a worry lantern. The idea is to transfer all our concerns onto it, then turn it over to the universe. I'm not crazy enough to think this will actually solve anything, but the symbolism is kind of great. You've had so much on your mind, and just for a little while, maybe we can both let go of that worry and live in the moment. What do you think? Should we do it?"

"There's a hell of a lot to heap onto this little lantern."

"I know."

"Let's do it."

"I'll go first." Kai put his palm on the lantern and said, "I worry about Jessie and his nightmares."

I put my hand on top of his and said, "I worry about someone hurting the people I love."

We kept going like that, back and forth, naming Zachary's well-being and Izzy's struggles with a mean kid at school and a list of other concerns. Finally, Kai used the lighter to ignite some kind of wax core inside the lantern, and the whole thing lit up with a soft, golden glow. "It's beautiful," I whispered.

He handed it to me and said, "You do the honors."

I held it up with both hands, over the edge of the cliff. As soon as I let go, the miniature hot air balloon drifted heavenward. We put our arms around each other and watched it for a long time. It grew smaller and smaller in the night sky as it continued to climb and head out over the Pacific.

When it finally disappeared from sight, I stretched up and kissed Kai, then said, "Thank you. Somehow, I really do feel a bit lighter after that."

"Good," he said gently. "Me too."

We took one last look at the vast, black expanse of sea and sky as the waves crashed steadily onto the shore far below. Then we walked hand-in-hand back around to the front of the house. We grabbed our things, used the keys and let ourselves in, and I entered the code on the keypad inside the door very carefully. I was glad when it powered down.

Kai murmured, "Wow," when we stepped into the main living space. The house was exactly what I'd hoped for. Instead of being grand and flashy, it was cozy. The colors were warm and subdued. Overstuffed furnishings dotted with pillows and blankets were clustered around a big fireplace, and thick drapes made it feel like a cocoon when I pulled them closed and shut out the darkness.

He got a fire going while I unpacked our picnic. After we ate a leisurely meal on the couch, we curled up under a soft, velvety blanket and talked for hours. Most of our conversation centered on our new home. The architect had included a rooftop patio, and we planned out the little container vegetable garden we were going to put in. We also discussed the indoor playhouse shaped like a castle, which we'd be building together in the next couple weeks. We wanted it to be ready and waiting for Izzy the first time she saw her new room.

Kai's head was on my chest, and as I stroked his hair I said softly, "I love this, talking about our home and planning it together. It feels so good."

"It really does."

"Thank you, Kai."

He tilted his head back so he could look at me. "For what?"

I grinned a little. "I don't know. Everything. I was just feeling so grateful for you, and I needed to say that."

"I'm incredibly grateful for you, too."

We kissed for a long time, and after a while Kai said, "We should move to the bedroom. I saw a huge bed in there when I passed by earlier. Let's go use two feet of it."

He was right, the bed was enormous and was made up with luxurious, deep blue linens. There was a second fireplace in the bedroom, and I got the fire going. The warmth and soft golden glow were an immediate comfort.

Kai and I got ready for bed, then climbed under the thick duvet. We snuggled together on the right side of the bed, and when he wrapped his arms around me, I felt so safe and warm. That night, for the first time in weeks, I slept deeply and didn't have any nightmares.

*****

The next morning, Kai brought me coffee in bed before drawing back the heavy curtains to reveal a sunny, breathtaking ocean view. "Damn," he said as he looked out over the Pacific. "I feel like I'm at a fancy resort. We owe Dante and Charlie a big thank you."

I admired the view, too, but not the one outside. Instead, I was looking at my gorgeous, shirtless boyfriend as he stood at the window. His cotton pajama pants rode a bit low, revealing a pair of perfect dimples just above his waistband and the tantalizing curve of his ass. "Come back to bed," I said as my cock took notice and I put my coffee cup on the nightstand.

Kai glanced at me over his shoulder, and a grin spread across his face. He turned to me and walked across the room slowly, the embodiment of strength and grace. He took my breath away, and when I told him that, his grin got wider.

He peeled back the covers and ran his gaze down my body. I'd gone to bed in nothing but a pair of turquoise briefs, and it was gratifying to watch his very physical reaction as he looked at me. I reached for the growing bulge in his pajama pants and massaged it as I asked, "Did you pack condoms?"

"No. I thought we'd agreed we didn't need them anymore."

"Oh. Right. It's just so automatic." We'd been going out for seven months, and at the six month mark we'd both gotten tested and received clean bills of health. We were monogamous and knew we were ready for that next step.

But we hadn't had sex in quite a while, not since just before the fire. My injuries needed time to heal, and after that, I'd felt kind of fragile, so we hadn't gone there. In the last couple weeks, as my libido returned, we'd added back oral sex and jerking each other off. But this would be the first time in over two months that we'd be doing more than that, and the first time for either of us without a condom.

"You sure you want to do this?" He asked that gently as he cupped my face in his palm. "I can just suck you if you don't feel like you're ready for anal. And if you changed your mind about the condoms, that's fine, too. I know it's a big step."

"I'm more than ready. I don't want you to treat me like some delicate little thing, either. I want you to fuck me hard, don't hold back."

He looked concerned. "That's kind of like going from second gear to fifth with nothing in between. And are you sure you want me to top you? We can do the opposite too, you know."

"I need this, Kai. I need you in me, and I need it to be rough and messy and wild, just the way it's always been for us. If we do this slow and gentle, then I'm going to be reminded of why you're being careful with me, and I don't want to think about the fire. I just want to live in the moment with you."

"I can do that." Kai climbed on top of me and kissed me passionately. He pulled my briefs from my body and threw them across the room, then licked and kissed his way down my chest and stomach. When he reached my swelling cock, he sucked me to the root, and I let out a low moan as I threw my head back. After a couple minutes of that, I pushed him onto the mattress and stripped off his pajama pants. Then I flipped around, took his cock between my lips and moaned again as we sucked each other and I savored the taste of him.

We sixty-nined for a long time, and then Kai rolled out of bed, rifled through his backpack, and quickly returned with lube and a new, clean shop rag (which made me chuckle, because it was so perfectly us). We kissed each other deeply and I stroked his cock as he fingered me. When I was ready, he slicked his cock and wiped his hand on the shop rag. As he pushed against my opening, I wrapped my legs around him and pushed back, opening myself for him, letting him in.

Kai did just as I asked. He fucked me hard and fast, pleasure radiating through me as he clutched my body and drove his cock into me. But it was so much more than just sex. I locked eyes with him and was overwhelmed by the love, the connection, the incredible feeling of *oneness* as we melted into each other. Right then, in that moment, life was absolutely, utterly, beautifully perfect.

*****

We spent the entire day naked in bed, alternately napping, talking, and having sex. I was surprised I could feel so good, so at peace, in the wake of all that had happened. But then I realized something.

It all came down to trust: trusting Dante and Vincent to keep the family safe; trusting Cameron and the SFPD to do all they could to catch the people who'd tried to harm my family; trusting

God and the universe to look out for Zachary and help him find his way. And most of all, trusting Kai to always be there.

As we traveled through life, the road was going to have potholes, some of them absolutely huge. But I knew it was all manageable, every mile of it. I could handle anything I came up against, as long as Malakai Kahale was right there at my side.

"Hey," Kai whispered. I raised my head from his chest and looked up at him. "What are you doing next weekend?"

"There's nothing planned. Why?"

"Let's get married."

A big smile spread across my face. "Really?"

"I mean, assuming you want to marry me."

"Of course I do!"

He smiled at me and said, "Okay, good. That was kind of out of the blue, I know, but here's the thing. I kept thinking both my proposal and our wedding needed fanfare, fireworks, you know, something grand. But then I thought about Nana and Ollie's wedding and how perfect it was, and I realized we don't need the fancy stuff. We just need each other." Exactly.

I kissed him tenderly, and then I said, "Let's get married in the yard at Gran's house, on the deck we painted back when this was brand new. Izzy can be maid of honor, and she can wear her butterfly princess gown. We'll call our family and friends and tell them to show up in jeans, and after the ceremony, we'll all dance on the lawn to Bowie songs until the sun comes up. It'll be perfect."

"That really does sound perfect. I love you so much, Jessie."

I smiled as I brushed his hair from his eyes. "I love you more than anything." A thought occurred to me, and I sat up and asked, "What do you think about me taking your last name after we're married?"

"That would mean the world to me." He grinned and added, "Plus, it's good because you don't actually have a last name right now, just a middle name standing in for one."

"You're right. How does Jessie Kahale sound?"

Kai pulled me into his arms and said, "It sounds like every one of my dreams just came true."

Mine, too.

The End

#####

Thank you for reading!

Zachary will take center stage in the next book in the Firsts and Forever Series, available in Summer, 2016. As always, old friends will make appearances, new characters will be introduced, and questions will be answered as we follow Zachary on his journey to happily ever after.

*For more by Alexa Land, please visit her
Amazon author page*

Find Alexa on Facebook

on Twitter @AlexaLandWrites

*And on her blog at
AlexaLandWrites.blogspot.com*

The Firsts & Forever Family Tree

Please note: this family tree contains a few spoilers if you haven't read all the books and don't know who ends up with who in the rest of the series

The Dombruso Family:

Sicilian-American family with roots in organized crime

Stana Dombruso (**Nana**) is the head of the Dombruso clan.

Nana raised her four grandsons after their parents were killed. The brothers in order from oldest to youngest are: **Dante, Vincent, Gianni and Mikey.**

Nana is married to Olivio Caravetti (**Ollie**)

Jessie was hired as Nana's limo driver, and as far as she's concerned, he's part of the family.

Dante is married to **Charlie** (their story can be found in All In)

Vincent is married to **Trevor** (their story can be found in Salvation).

Josh is their adopted son.

Gianni is currently sailing around the world with his boyfriend **Zan** (Belonging is their story)

Mikey is a widower with three sons, and is dating **Marie** (they met in Belonging)

Nico Dombruso is their cousin. His boyfriend is **Luca** (their story can be found in All I Believe)

Nico's brother is **Constantino** (Connie). Connie's boyfriend is **Andreo** (their story can be found in Hitman's Holiday)

Andreo is **Luca's** half-brother.

The Friends:

Skye is a friend of the family and is married to **Dare** (their story can be found in Skye Blue)

Skye's half-brother **River** was living with **Cole**

Skye went to art school with his best friend **Christian**

Christian is married to **Shea** Nolan (Against the Wall is their story)

Christian is **Zan's** son

Skye and **Christian** also went to art school with **Christopher Robin**

Christopher Robin is married to **Kieran** Nolan (In Pieces is their story)

Christopher is friends with **Hunter** Jacobs, AKA Hunter Storm

Hunter is married to **Brian** Nolan (Gathering Storm is their story)

Chance and **Christian** are friends

Chance's husband is **Finn** Nolan (their story is Coming Home)

Chance's kid brother is named **Colt**

Colt's boyfriend is **Elijah**

Zachary is friends with **Chance** and **Jessie**

Yoshi is **Gianni's** friend

Charlie is **Jamie** Nolan's friend and ex-boyfriend

The Nolans:

Irish-American family, many of whom are in law enforcement

Kieran and **Brian** Nolan are brothers

Shea and **Finn** Nolan are brothers (Kieran and Brian are their cousins)

Jamie Nolan is also their cousin

Jamie is married to **Dmitri Teplov** (their story is Way Off Plan)

The Series in Order, and the Couples:

1. **Way Off Plan**: Jamie Nolan and Dmitri Teplov

2. **All In**: Charlie Connolly and Dante Dombruso

3. **In Pieces**: Christopher Robin Andrews and Kieran Nolan

4. **Gathering Storm**: Hunter Jacobs/Storm and Brian Nolan

5. **Salvation**: Trevor Dean and Vincent Dombruso

6. **Skye Blue**: Skye Fleischmann and Dare Evans

7. **Against the Wall**: Christian George and Shea Nolan

8. **Belonging**: Gianni Dombruso and Zan Tillane

9. **Coming Home**: Chance Matthews and Finn Nolan

10. **All I Believe**: Nico Dombruso and Luca Caruso

10.5 **Hitman's Holiday**: Andreo and Connie (Constantino) Dombruso

11. **The Distance** is Jessie and Kai's story

12. Book 12 will be Zachary's story

The series will continue on from there!

Made in the USA
San Bernardino, CA
19 June 2016